Tracking the Skies for Lacy

Bret
you are a hero
to me!

Steve Gladish

S.

ISBN 978-1-64258-380-9 (paperback)
ISBN 978-1-64258-381-6 (digital)

Christian Faith Publishing, Inc.
832 Park Avenue
Meadville, PA 16335
www.christianfaithpublishing.com

This book is a work of fiction. Names, characters, places, and incidents are the product of the author's imagination or are used fictitiously. Any resemblance to actual events, locales, business establishments, events, or persons, living or dead, is coincidental.

Printed in the United States of America

Dedication

SIXTH WEATHER SQUADRON (MOBILE)
FOURTH WEATHER GROUP, USAF.

Willing and Able

SIGNIFICANCE: The American bald eagle symbolizes the strength, speed, and alertness of the United States and of Sixth Weather Squadron (Mobile). Our helium balloons capture all the upper atmosphere weather elements for early warnings. Tornado Alley and nuclear detonation projects supported by the squadron are symbolized by the tornado funnel and atomic nuclear symbol. The ground mobile tracking device portrays an important item of equipment. Severe weather warning is symbolized by the cloud and lightning.

DEDICATION: I dedicate *Tracking the Skies for Lacy* to the most forceful and dangerous weather elements, especially to Sixth Weather Squadron (Mobile), and to all brother Air Force Units dedicated to providing the most complete weather reporting and forecasting system in the world. Firstly, they are responsible for the safety and safe passage and successful missions of thousands of military planes taking off and landing every minute around the globe, twenty-four hours a day, seven days a week, three-hundred-sixty-five days a year. Without them, the American people would have no security, no surveillance, no preemptive striking forces, and the hordes of terrorists and rogue countries and evil leaders around the globe would have free rein to commit havoc in any way they could. In addition, every day, every year, military weather forecasting has saved countless civilian lives with early warnings of tornadoes, hurricanes, floods, and heavy rains.

There have been hundreds of members over the past sixty years in the decades when Sixth Weather ruled the upper atmosphere with its hourly weather information gathering on Tornado Alley, Thermonuclear Missile Detonations and Testing in Nevada (total of 1021 detonations) and the Central Pacific, Marshall Islands HQ (total of 254 detonations). Our Upper Atmosphere Rawinsonde Operators and Technicians notably served during *Operation Dominic I and II*, with total of eighty-two thermonuclear detonations. The list of projects totals hundreds of pages: for example, surveillances on Russia and its thermonuclear testing in particular, as well as United Kingdom thermonuclear testing and French thermonuclear nuclear testing in the Pacific. Ramping up our nuclear capabilities until the Nuclear Test Ban Treaty in 1962 put us on a par with Russia and kept us safe and peaceful until the USSR was no more in 1989. In addition, we provided optimum weather conditions for long-distance bombing missions in Vietnam, photo-mapping of continents, and a host of other military and scientific missions.

Today, in particular, I want to give special mention to those who took the time during the reunions to give me vivid personal stories on numerous projects. I thank Joe Kerwin, Dave Guenther, Ed Skowron, Buck Bucklin, Paul Laman, Don Nissan, John Baker, Marty Piel, Gerry Guay, Neil Prete, Bill King, Tom Kinney, Irv

Watson, Carle Clark, Gordon McCann, Barbara McCann, Shirley Eldringhof, Tom Grace, Ernie Workman, Ken Brown, Chuck Miller, Carl Bishop, Chuck Hewitt, Ted Lungwitz, John Lassiter, Elmo Reddick, John Webb, Don Garbutt, Fred LaPerriere, Tom Warner, Ken Zinke, Edward Herman, Mitch Turner, Dave Weiner, Robert Bongiovanni, Robert Orshoski, and Michael Seaver. An entire volume could be written on each one.

A more complete list will be found in the Appendices.

Acknowledgments

I give a lifetime of heartfelt thanks first to my wife, partner and fellowparent of fifty-two years, Betsy. She has demonstrated the greatest patience and kindest support in the last fifteen years as I wrote, rewrote, and recreated three stand-alone novels—of which this is one.

Thanks to my two sons, Major Stephen Gladish II, and Major David Gladish, who over the past decade have provided superior role models and multiple examples of excellence in our continuing family military history.

Thanks to Chuck Miller for his long and inspired leadership in the Sixth Weather Squadron Alumni Association, and for his kind recognition of me which led to this book. Thanks to Gerry Guay for his support of my efforts and for his decades of webmaster duties, keeping the website and Sixth Weather Squadron current and all of us in touch and up to date.

Thanks to Ben Gastellum, a brother-in-name, for decades of unconditional friendship, and for his goal setting, which inspired me to follow in his footsteps and sign a contract with Christian Faith Publishing. Thanks to Sasha Silverman, in her role as a New Christian Church author and editor, for her wisdom, unremitting encouragement, and her spontaneous belief in me. Without it, I wouldn't have dared taken the leap of faith.

Thanks to my fellow Sixth Weather Alumni, who gave permission to publish their most vivid memories and stories shared during our reunions, as best as I could record them by hand and in person. I ask forgiveness for any imperfect recollections.

Sammie Alijagic's acute artistic skills and lifetime experience created a book cover designed to delight and attract readers of all ages at all levels of our society. Elizabeth Ohm's professional and painstaking proofreading burnished the story's content and kept the author's characters, settings, and adventures clear and uncluttered. Robert Yehling's proven editorial and publicist skills brought the manuscript up to the highest industry standards. His Self-Publishing Mastery website (the independent writer's home) highlight his lifetime of awards and professional services to the country and now to the world.

Key Photos

First Tornado Captured By Radar and Storm Chasers

Thermonuclear Explosion on Nevada Test Site

Luke's Huey MedEvac

Luke's Huey Gunship

Luke Whitewater Rafting on the River of No Return

Book One
LIFTOFF

1

The town with the catchy title, Broken Arrow, lay pitched on the prairie twenty miles southeast of Tulsa, Oklahoma. Luke LaCrosse and his dad, Matt had just arrived from outside Chicago to spend a week with Grandma and Grandpa LaCrosse during Luke's spring break. This was to be a vacation, a quiet family gathering. Luke was fourteen and taking life in fast.

They arrived late in the afternoon. Throughout the day, plump cumulus clouds had popped into the sky like runaway weather balloons from a nearby Air Force base. Surface winds began to growl and poke around homes in the Tulsa suburbs. Something was coming. Before April could close down and escape, Nature had begun her roundhouse punch from over Northern Nevada. While sisters Jessica, Rachel, and Luke's mother were homebodies happy to wait until June for spring to come, Matt and Luke were fleeing from the cold wintry winds and freezing snow in Chicagoland. Down here, Tornado Alley awoke and lived up to its name when the forerunner of a tornado burst out of its cumulonimbus prison late in the afternoon. Jabbed by the jet-stream winds that looped out of the northwest, the forerunner slammed into the wall of a low-pressure cold front that swirled counterclockwise out of Colorado. A hundred miles later, it hit another wall of warm, moisture-laden clouds billowing up from the Gulf of Mexico. Whirling and screaming, it viciously, capriciously barreled across the Texas panhandle and skimmed over the northern border of Oklahoma.

Meanwhile, Matt and Luke enjoyed a pleasant dinner and evening out on the back patio. Grandma still cooked as easily and as well
as she always had. Of course, during dinner, dessert, and afterwards,
the grandparents bombarded Luke with questions about his life, his
sisters, his school, his friends, his activities. Matt was proud to show
off his son, often reminding Luke of some other event or subject
to share. Too soon for Matt—but not soon enough for Luke—the
evening passed. He got up and hugged his grandparents one at a
time, and gratefully went to bed upstairs, a first for him. A window
breathed softly at the foot of his bed. Luke opened it wide and looked
out on a peaceful scene. No wind was apparent, but unbeknownst to
Luke, this was a bad sign. He tumbled back onto his pillow and fell
asleep.

Luke thought he knew wind. Not in Oklahoma he didn't. Wind
was associated especially with fall, winter, and spring up in Chicago,
not a friendly element in Chicago's inclement weather. *If you don't
like the weather in Chicago, wait fifteen minutes.* But he never knew
winds to bring death and destruction. Only in his nightmares. Luke
had strained, twisted, and turned in his bed as he had seen the same
monster spinning toward him in his dreams. And sure enough, the
nightmares came again tonight.

He didn't expect to see that monster howling down on him in
real life. He knew when it came, it would arrive in anger, its giant
hand raised against him. It could be a windstorm out of the western
plains of Oklahoma. Or it could come like Fat Boy from a B-29, a
terrifying rerun of his uncle's account from a Japanese POW camp
in 1945: the B-29, a toy far up in the sky, the pause, sun glinting on
a metallic object swiftly falling through the air. Then the explosion
erupted, with a shock wave and a heat wave that leveled and inciner-
ated a whole city only twenty miles away.

Flashing, burning images surrounded the coming disaster. A
Nagasaki in his colorful midnight dreams. A brilliant white flash
burned through the middle-layer clouds and changed to a green ball
that expanded into the sky. Great white finger-like upper-level clouds
rose above the horizon in sweeping arcs. Concentric rings moved out
from the nuclear blast at tremendous initial velocity. The greenish

light turned to purple and began to fade at the blast point. A bright red glow developed on the horizon, expanding inward and upward. This condition, streaked with tremendous white rainbows, went on and on, feverish.

Luke's eyes popped open in terror; his pajamas dark with feverish sweat. A stroke of lightning flashed through his eyelids, shutting down those past images. Good. But thunder still crashed. He rolled over, scrambled from his bed, and pressed his forehead against the cool windowpane. That other nightmare, tired of skulking, rushed headlong toward him. He could feel something in the air. He smelled the tornado's oncoming breath. His legs jerked out in terror. Winds howled and bedroom doors slammed open and closed.

The tornado forerunner morphed into a thunderstorm. Nature's fist mushroomed into a huge boxing glove, and the glove's eerie whistle raced through Luke's ears as it drew back its right-cross punch. Luke faced the window helplessly. Thunder rumbled incessantly; the lightning flashes increased. The roll cloud and its rush of wind slammed into the window and ruffled his blonde hair. The hair on the back of his neck sprouted up like quills on a porcupine. Luke gasped, but felt some comfort from the red bricks stoutly framing his window.

The rain came quickly, sideways. Luke never flinched. He knew about the whirling updrafts and downdrafts of these storms he had experienced in the science lab, and in person. He knew, just as his uncle had warned him, a downdraft was like swirling water being sucked down the drain in his bathtub, just a whole lot bigger. From Boy Scouts, he learned that a tornado updraft grew bigger and bigger, like whirlpools on a whitewater river that could suck up a boy and his kayak to disappear forever. Tornadoes fascinated Luke. They were born and bred especially in Oklahoma. His science teacher and baseball coach told him, "Oklahoma is the Yankee Stadium of tornadoes."

Luke stayed at his window to see if a tornado was really coming. He imagined that the tornado would tilt eastward behind the thunderstorm, a giant vacuum cleaner lurching from the sky. In his science journal, Luke had written that the funnel cloud would "drag its feet on the ground and shriek and scream and roar like the noise of a thousand freight trains being pulled backwards."

Now that he was hearing that noise, fear struck him right between the eyes. He curled up on the end of his bed and put his trembling hands on the windowsill. Once again, the winds howled, doors slammed, and he fell out of bed.

His bedroom door banged open. A light switch slapped upwards. His father's dark face appeared out of the darkness. The ceiling light blinded him; the room was silent. Ominous. Wordless. Must be a nightmare.

No nightmare. His bed and the whole house were shaking.

The vacuum created by the whirling clouds threatened to burst his eardrums. He covered his ears to shut out the pain and wished he could pinch his nose as well. Vile smells of rotten eggs and turpentine rushed through the window screen. He brought both hands tightly together and clutched them to his chest. His eyes shut in prayer, Luke tried to gather his wits and bearings. He could hardly breathe. Terror froze his lungs and endangered his heart. Luke's hands were shaking. He could stay frozen in action. Or not.

He sprang to his feet and stood near the window next to his dad, blinking and adjusting his sight. He looked out and then looked up, not believing what he saw. His father's eyes were blanched white. The house rocked back and forth, the roar of the wind obliterating all other sounds.

Luke peered through the solid steel bars installed outside all the windows. Constant flashes of lightning blasted three neighboring houses on fire. The flashes and flames brought images of disaster—cars scattered across roads, some upside down. In the groves across the street, most of the trees had been toppled over and uprooted, trunks and limbs snapped off, leveled, or debarked. Glass flashed all over the ground.

Lightning of all kinds gyrated from cloud to cloud, deadly spears being hurled to the ground as though Zeus was throwing javelins through the greenish-black cloud banks. Through these flickering flashes, Luke saw buildings flattened, their cement slabs exposed in their bareness. Whole frame houses were splintered into giant piles of pickup sticks. Screams stuck in his throat, paralyzed. He was sure he was going to die. Just like his grandpa described it, he was in the middle of hell.

"Luke! Can you hear me? Son, I'm talking to you!"

Luke looked to the huge shadow standing over him. By the reddened cheeks and wide-open eyes, he could tell his dad had been yelling at him, but he never heard a word. He tried to respond. His voice was stuck in his throat. The second time he yelled, "What did you say, Dad?"

Luke was all too aware of his father's appearance: six feet two inches tall, a lean one hundred ninety pounds. His dad leaned down and said brusquely, "Get *away* from the window. We didn't hear the tornado siren. Your grandmother is down in the basement. Your grandfather is huddled with her. My mom and dad. They are older. They need you. You must go downstairs *right now.*"

Luke looked up and implored, "Where are you going, Dad? Can't you go with me? The winds are blowing inside and the stairs are shaking. I can't go down there by myself."

His dad shook his head. "Luke, I have to get out there and help."

The whole world screamed in dismay, the winds sucking, howling and raging around every obstacle. Luke's window began to buckle and emit a high-pitched whine, almost a scream. Like a man on a high-dive, he felt himself lean forward. Just as he began to explode through his window and slam into the metal bars, his dad grabbed his shoulder and pulled him back. "Luke! Come on! Let's get out!"

He pulled Luke into the hallway. Luke's eyes blurred and then refocused. His dad was uncharacteristically disheveled, with rumpled bedclothes and a bathrobe hastily half-tied.

"Okay, Dad, okay! Let me go."

Luke turned to reach into the hall closet to grab his clothes. He whirled back around. "Dad, I want to go with you."

His dad shook his head and shot a look across the room. They both gathered clothes. Then his dad grabbed Luke by the arm and practically dragged him down a flight of sixteen steep steps. When they reached the hallway he leaned down and yelled even louder than the tornado. "It's not bloody safe for you!"

Just then, the house rocked and creaked, and the roof cracked in a handful of places. With a hellishly loud tearing sound, the roof surrendered, and the wind swallowed it into the black night and fierce winds. Only the first floor ceiling protected them.

Timbers crashed down, blocking the way to the basement, the tornado shelter. Luke's dad grabbed him again. "Quick! The fireplace!"

They ran crab-like to the family room. They bent over to take shelter in the large colonial fireplace. They tossed out the logs and the steel holder, crashing out of the fireplace onto the rug. Three feet away, on the other side out of the fireplace, stood a unique pane of thick clear glass, designed to bring heat and light to the porch.

As they leaned forward to look through the window, they held onto the strong metal bars on each side of the fireplace. Hands shaking, they peered out, thankful that to the left, an elm tree's long trunk protected them. The roar and howling intensified. Objects looking strangely like people flew out of the house where windows and doors had been. Further away, Luke saw an old Ford and a newer Oldsmobile tumbling end over end down the road to Tulsa.

Luke couldn't help his yell of sadness and dismay. He had never faced imminent death before. He couldn't help it. "No, no, no!"

He turned for comfort and safety. His dad pushed him away. "I don't have time for this."

"Wait! Look, Dad!" Luke swung his head and peered at the trees near their neighbor's house. They were weirdly horizontal and unnatural, pinned on the ground by a dozen other fallen wooden poles. Luke tilted his head, thinking it was his line of sight.

Nope. He raised himself to his knees and pointed wordlessly. Both boy and man watched as blades of straw and grass were driven into the groaning elm tree's trunk next to the porch.

Luke froze. "How can that happen, Dad?"

"Don't ask any more questions!" His father admonished, shaking his finger as he always had.

Luke began to walk away, then stood behind his dad and peeked out the window, breathless, waiting for the banshees to stop breathing fire. They huddled close so they could talk, afraid to move or to try descending the basement stairs.

Minutes later, the deafening roar diminished and the deadly howling stopped. His dad stood up and began dressing. "I have got to get out there. People are injured or dying."

Luke rose to his feet, excited to go out. "Can I go out with you, Dad?"

"I won't have it, Luke. Do you hear me? I'm a Navy medic, always will be. I know how to tend to the wounded. I have to get out there!"

Luke shook his head. He did not want his dad to leave him.

Luke swallowed hard and nodded. "Okay, okay, Dad, I'll find a way through the boards and go down to the basement."

The front door banged insistently. His father strode to the door in the anteroom and yelled, "What do you want?"

"Matt! Matt! We need a Corpsman! And a doctor! It's me, Ralph! You can help. We need your help! People are injured and in danger of dying! Some might be dying. Conditions are terrible."

"I'm coming! I'm coming!"

Luke ducked back into the fireplace.

Five minutes later, the former Navy medic rumbled out of the downstairs bathroom, threw aside the boards blocking the basement door, and put his head through the door to the basement stairs. "Is everybody safe and sound down there?"

"We are okay," his dad called. "We are fine. We are safe. Matt, we have been down here before. See what you can do out there. Pronto!"

Matt responded, "Copy that! "I'll be back as soon as I can." He slammed the door shut.

Striding to the front door, he yelled, "Get down to the basement, Luke!"

Before Luke could answer, his dad banged through the front door, slamming it behind him.

Police cars from every township converged on the ravaged community. The multitude of sirens mimicked the screams of the tornado. Ambulances from the area hospitals screeched up, their rear doors opening, the white-clad attendants rushing with stretchers and gurneys to bring the injured back to their vehicles. Then the military search and rescue crews appeared, driving up as if they were in a war zone, sliding to stops on the slippery streets.

Luke recorded this terrible tornado battlefield with his eyes and ears. These images would repeatedly return and angle back to him like a boomerang.

Amidst the fallen trees and debris from broken houses, he spotted his dad as he ran from one casualty to the next and examined each injured person, often kneeling down. By the time Matt reached the third victim, Luke stood crouched down right behind him. Matt of course was used to the chaos, but not immune to it, from his World War II Navy days in the far Pacific. Luke was not used to it or immune to it, but he did whatever he could to help. He held medical instruments for his dad, and other times, he held the victim's hand or even her head. Sometimes, Matt signaled for an ambulance. At others, he shook his head and got up slowly, moving to the next victim. And he did more than just tolerate Luke; he spoke gently and said, "Thank you, Luke," impressed with his care-taking ability.

Later that night, Luke created a prayer. He gazed at a photo he had taken the year before, outside the window.

> *You love me, Lord, because at times when negative voices from outside me and within try to convince me that I am unlovable, your Holy Spirit challenges me to believe that you love me. You love me, Lord, because you want to know me and you want me to know you. You love me, Lord, because you want to meet with me daily, as any parent might. You love me, Lord, because meeting alone with me each day is a constant for you. You love me, Lord, because you send messengers and surround me with angels who care about and protect me from negative emotions and evil spirits.*

The following spring, Matt included Luke in his plan to visit his parents and see in person how they were doing. Both Matt and Luke were tired of Chicago winter and knew Oklahoma weather would prove far more temperate. But then they both changed their minds. After that Level 5 tornado, Matt could hardly think about going down there again. It was just too much like war. The tornado brought back all the stresses of his deployment, the delayed shock, the disbelief of all the wounded and dead. And there was no way Luke wished to return either. Personal nightmares were bad, but tornadoes in person were much worse.

2

In 1937, Luke's dad, Matt LaCrosse, met and fell in love with Maria during their senior year of high school. She was a classmate who had co-starred in a musical with him. Three months after graduation, they got married. Both families were ecstatic. Luke burst into their lives in 1939. Everybody loved the little baby. His personality blossomed by the time he turned one. He could repeat words, stand on his feet to throw a miniature football, and feed himself in the high chair while singing, talking, or making faces.

Jobs were easy to get and Matt was happy to be working as a plumber, tree surgeon or carpenter, along with many of his friends in the blue-collar community. The Chicago Bears were beginning to look like the Monsters of the Midway. It was a work hard, drink beer and cheer kind of life. Matt fit in with the typical Cubs or Bears fans.

World War II had fired up Europe in September of 1939. It exploded onto the U.S. peace-time stage on December 7, 1941. Luke turned two and Matt picked up the offensive gauntlet. Everybody in his home town had enlisted. Matt joined the Navy, barreled through basic training, kissed his little family goodbye at Great Lakes Naval Air Station, and disappeared from their lives, off to become a Navy Corpsman. When he finished his medical training, he came back to say good-bye at Glenview Naval Air Station. Then the Navy flew him and a planeful of others to Coronado Island outside San Diego, California.

Maria hugged him, clung to him, and saw him off amidst a crowd of other distraught wives. Matt didn't know what to say. Maria cried in the beginning and at the end but was silent and speechless in between. Luke remembered his dad holding him in his arms during the whole good-bye ceremony. He had no idea what good-bye meant. His mom was crying. Everybody was crying. Luke was happy being so close to his dad. It was something so new and he loved it. He had no idea it might be his last.

Matt got advanced and intensive training at Coronado Island before being shipped out. They needed him on the beaches, not on a ship, and he would care for the combat-wounded, nurse them back to health, and save lives. From one battleground island to another, his hospital ship followed and Matt went ashore. Or the Navy dropped him off by aircraft. Island names blurred for him. Days went by, weeks, months. The hospital ship was on the move from one battleground to another. Many seriously wounded men had to be flown to Hawaii for further life-saving treatment.

As a Navy medic in the far Pacific, Matt saw plenty of action with wounds and injuries and illnesses. So many grown men crying and shrieking in pain: legs amputated, eyes blinded, horrible stomach wounds so complex and so apt to be germ infested, facial wounds so bad the man could not be identified. Other medics were numb, getting sick themselves, exhausted. Everything went overtime. It was 24/7 duty. Malaria, dysentery, and other diseases common to the Pacific decimated the Marines and Naval personnel.

Matt began to sing to avoid the images and death, fear, and insanity. Surprised and encouraged by buddies, the wounded and other personnel, Matt started singing in GI entertainment. Up to his discharge in 1946 and afterwards, he got continual requests to sing wherever he went. The men loved the morale-boosting marching song from the British. Matt sang loud and pretended to march, instead of sitting in the back of a troop carrier. "I've got sixpence, jolly, jolly sixpence, I've got sixpence to last me all my life." What a laugh! All my life. What life? Life was plenty, plenty bad, just like their pay.

They always howled on the second verse: "I've got tu'ppence to spend, and tu'ppence to lend, and no pence to send home to my wife, poor wife." Who had time to worry about wives and girlfriends, when death and disease surrounded them?

And the chorus helped them stay in the land of make-believe. "No cares have I to grieve me, no pretty little girls to deceive me, I'm happy as a lark, bele-eive me, as we go rolling, rolling home." The exhausted troops laughed, the wounded troops laughed and cried at the same time.

When Christmas came, slowly, painfully, one year after the other, in the sweltering tropics, the troops begged Matt to sing Bing Crosby's hit, late in 1942, "I'm dreaming of a White Christmas." Everybody was sure he sang the song and made it a hit for all the soldiers and sailors, Army, and Marines overseas. He brought to them images of Christmas, family, gentle peaceful snow, church bells, and baby Jesus in a manger. Songs of innocence.

A Navy chaplain suggested Matt sing Christmas hymns, and once he began, Matt was always in demand for weeks before Christmas: "Merry Christmas Bells," "The First Noel," "Come All Ye Faithful," "We Three Kings," "So Sweet and Clear" (which he could never finish), "From the Eastern Mountains," "Hark the Herald Angels Sing," "Silent Night." Matt taught the chorus to the men— the ill, wounded, tired, and homesick. One of the Navy men, Victor, brought his guitar out from his ship locker and began to strum the right chords. He could sing backup, too. Before long, another crew-member, Owen, created a drum out of some kind of animal skin and joined the band. From childhood, he had always wanted to play drums, but the noise had proved too much for his parents.

The audience had favorite lines and requested them all the time. "Merry Christmas bells are ringing . . . Angel's voices sweetly singing . . . Happy voices catch the echo . . . Precious Christmas gifts are gladdening many a heart at home."

They identified with the shepherds out on a lonely hillside: "The first Noel, the angels did say was to certain poor shepherds in fields where they lay." They identified with the three wise men who traveled for years in far-away lands: "We Three Kings of Orient are, bearing gifts we traverse far, field and fountain, moor and mountain, following yonder star." They thought about home: "From the eastern mountains . . . onward through the darkness of the lonely light . . . guide them alien kindred, homeward from afar." And there were no lines from "Silent Night" that they did not treasure. A favorite: "Silent night, holy night, only for shepherds' sight, came blest visions of angel throngs, with their [sweet] hallelujah songs."

Finally, in the summer of 1944, hit favorites for loved ones back home became the men's favorite songs too. Of course, Matt had to sing them: Harry James's, "I'll Get By (As Long as I Have You)" and Bing Crosby's, "I'll be Seeing You (in All Our Old Familiar Places)."

Whenever he could, Matt went to the top of any mountain or hill, praying to keep up his own morale.

> *With outstretched hands I turn to you, O Lord, my supreme unchanging Friend. I request from the depths of my heart that I might see with the light of your wisdom to dispel darkness in my mind, and the secret side of my shadow self. Give me the goal of an enlightened mind so I may grasp a little of your infinity. Help me to heal my mental afflictions and escape from the prison of my war. Nourish me with Your Divine Goodness, so I can nourish all beings I meet.*

In the fall, it was the Mills Brothers, "You Always Hurt the One You Love, (the One You Love the Most of All)," and Dinah Shore's, "I'll Walk Alone." By December, Matt was singing Bing Crosby's, "Don't Fence Me In," and in the beginning of 1945, he sang the Andrews Sisters', "Rum and Coca-Cola," because the men were thinking of getting home. Doris Day and Les Brown in May of 1945 totally entranced all the men overseas with the song, "Going to Take a Sentimental Journey." Matt sang that all summer, until Japan surrendered in September, and all fall, when he expected to rotate back home.

Meanwhile, back home there was nothing sure about Matt's return or the war's ending. Luke felt more like an orphan. Taking walks with his mom and baby sister lying in the baby carriage did not increase his sense of being protected. Warplanes skimmed over his head as the pilots trained for combat. So often the Corsairs flew too low, roaring louder than any animal he had imagined, right above where his mother liked to walk in the church's "back forty," a small nursery and preserve. This is where she and Matt planned to build a house when he mustered out. But to Luke, the far corner of the neighborhood terrified him. He knew his mom was not able to protect him. He kept his eye on one crater after another, each empty hole in the ground showed where a tree's roots had been blown up and the tall tree removed. The pilots needed more airspace near the end of the runway. Luke jumped into a crater twice for safety, twisted in terror when he was sure all three of them would be killed. He still eyed each crater as his savior and protector, especially after a Corsair crash-landed close to the back forty.

Finally, like waking up from a crash-landing nightmare, Maria rushed into his room one morning. "Daddy's coming home! Daddy's coming home!"

Matt began the long trip home in late 1945. He was again full of hope. Such a sense of relief he felt standing on General McArthur's aircraft carrier while witnessing the signatures that ended the war. The battlefields on the beaches and battleship injuries he had tended to for over three years still held him in their grip. All those agonized faces and serious wounds still seared his mind.

But he was so relieved. Thank God, Maria had been hired part-time by the Navy. As a favor to her and to Matt's family, she worked in routine secretarial and financial assignments at the Glenview Naval Air Station. She and little Luke could still live in that small apartment near her mother. Matt's checks and pay came at such irregular intervals.

Striding down the gangplank from his troopship on Lake Michigan to the docks at Great Lakes Naval Air Station, Matt spotted Maria and Luke. He was the first one off the ship. And he ran, arms waving, yelling, "Maria! Maria! Maria!" She ran toward Matt crying and screaming. With his incredible good sense, Luke held back a little. For ten minutes, he stood right behind his mom. When Matt and Maria came up to breathe, they remembered their little boy and looked around for Luke. Matt picked him up and spun him around. Maria crowded in, hugging them both and crying. In the carriage, baby Jessica cooed and clapped her little hands.

For the first week at home, Luke stayed at his grandma's house every night. Matt and Maria were delirious, starving, and hungry for each other after three years of longing and loneliness. In the little town of Glenview, Illinois, everybody was on vacation. Work came sometime later.

3

What would he do when he came home? Just any job would not do anymore. He went back to work in the huge Nelson Nursery. Now he had a good-paying job as a supervisor. And he was grateful for the job they gave to him, he with little experience. His crews respected him. They knew his record in the Navy. They even knew some of the men Matt had saved, even though Matt would not take any credit.

Every day, Matt had dinner at home, played baseball with seven-year-old Luke out on the ball field, put him to bed, said prayers, kissed Maria goodbye, and often spent a few too many hours at the Crystal Lake Inn with his newfound veteran friends and a few old friends. They told war stories, described in detail the fun they had with Polynesian or Asian women, and the violence of the enemy they killed or captured. They sang old military favorites, American or not, and the new songs hot on the radio waves, especially after a few extra beers. Matt's reputation had preceded him, and he was called on almost every time to sing a song or two. Bing Crosby and the Les Brown Trio crooned, "It's Been a Long, Long Time." And Matt sang it in the shower and to Maria every day. Finally, after four beers lined up in front of him, at the request of the bartender, Stan, who served and was wounded in the Pacific, Matt sang it at the Glenview Inn.

Once he had walked up six steps onto a long concrete patio he could see in the big front windows. Inside was crowded. Besides the stools at the bar and the little stage Matt sang from, there were funny little square tables scattered pell-mell around the room. Each had four chairs stuffed around it. They looked more like cassocks or footstools, not comfortable, but the tables were close to one another, allowing for great camaraderie. Under the front windows were long, thin straight tables with booths behind them stretching from one end of the large room to the other. Matt took it all in as he walked up to the bar. He had been here as a patron, never as an entertainer.

He picked up the mike and began to sing, "It's Been a Long, Long Time." At first, he was nervous. To make the song work, he realized he had to sing the song to the women sitting around the room. And he had to have some eye contact. His audience was rapt, the song was unexpected, and he became an instant hit. Before he could finish the final note, two attractive women, Ginger and Patty, jumped up from their table, rushed over to Matt, and wrapped their arms around him. They took turns kissing him and he could no longer sing.

"Wait! I'm married!" he exclaimed.

"Where have *you* been?" Ginger demanded. "It's wartime. It's still wartime. Don't worry about your home front."

He was unaware he had been singing right in front of a sexy painting—and he never expected the painting to affect the female portion of the audience. For guys who had fought in the Pacific, the bar owner painted a six-foot-high scene on the wall with a gorgeous well-formed Polynesian woman kneeling sideways with a skimpy grass skirt, turning toward the customers in a red halter-top that threatened to burst any minute. She had a demure come-hither look on her face, red lips, white teeth, lovely dark eyebrows and eyelashes. Her neck was turned a bit to the left, her long dark hair spilled down below her shoulders, a red flower blossomed over her right ear, and sexy red lei circled her neck. She held a cocktail cupped in her right hand and a red cherry flew out of her left hand as she stretched her arm back.

Matt looked behind him and saw the Tahitian Island goddess on the wall. He saw the cherry coming right at him. He disengaged himself quickly and moved away from the two affectionate women who seemed to be affected by the allure of the painting. Matt realized she looked as if she were in love with him. Perhaps it encouraged other women as well. He didn't mean for that to happen. The audience clapped and cheered at his singing and his behavior. They yelled for more.

To help Matt out, some of the men called out, "Sing us a fighting song!" Matt got carried away and sang his favorite British marching song, "I've got six pence, jolly, jolly, six pence. I've got six pence to last me all my life . . . I've got six pence to spend and six pence to lend and six pence to send home to my wife, poor wife."

Everybody cheered and clapped. Matt plunged on, "No-oh cares have I to grieve me, no pretty little girl to de-cee-eve-me, as we go rolling, rolling home."

Men in the audience got up and started marching to its beat. Donny, the bartender, ran up. "Matt, why didn't you tell me you could sing like that? You will bring in more friends than you knew you had."

The crowd inspired Matt. He joked, "You ain't seen nothing yet, Donny." And he sang one song after another to an enthusiastic audience. Two hours later, he repeated his repertoire to a second audience, equally happy, and louder. The customers stayed and at the end of the night the bartender said, "Here's your pay."

Matt stared at the fistful of dollars. "Hey," Donny said. "Somebody put out a tip jar too." And he poured the coins and bills into Matt's hands. He floated home, happy. He woke up Maria. He couldn't wait to tell her. Maria blinked from the sudden light, listened, and then looked down at the money. "I'm so happy," she said. "I'm so happy for you. And for us."

The next week Matt sang at one of the bars in Wilmette, a few miles away. He noticed it seemed much more comfortable for its patrons. Big picture windows were on the front. Near the door, the closest window had an advertisement, "*Cocktail Ice*" in huge letters, with "*Sold Here,*" in italics below it.

Matt stood near the bar, to one side in the corner, and looked out on a roomful of huge red booths each with seating for eight, and sometimes, nine jammed in. Lighting came from lamps on side tables, and round globes hung low from the ceiling, very bright. The booths showed a glossy good style and more expensive manufacturing. But there were cheap and questionably small brown tables in the middle jammed with drinks and ashtrays. These tables were round and plain, not very accommodating. Matt guessed that some would be drinking their neighbor's cocktails or beer. Before he began, he looked around. The room was L-shaped so there was room for five booths, plus individual seating at the bar and along the wall. The ceilings were high, with fans for the hot nights. In a back room, there was a small restaurant. But most of the customers were here for the cocktails and the entertainment.

Matt knew he had to reach a majority of customers at each booth or the booth would not be paying attention. Facing each other and having a private audience, it would be hard to keep the war stories and the flirting out of the limelight. So his gig and the surroundings had more challenges. It took more gusto than the Glenview Inn, but the place was classier. There may have been more officers than enlisted men. And the audience by and large was well dressed, for a postwar era. When he introduced himself, he announced something new and something risky. "Good evening, folks! Raise your hand if you like any songs you hear on the radio?" They all cheered. Many had gone without radio for years.

Matt jumped up in boyish enthusiasm. "I do too! I get caught singing on the job, or singing in the shower." He adjusted his collar, then the microphone. "I love singing. Didn't even know I could do it until the wounded and the homesick men called out for songs in the Pacific Theatre. I am working on a routine, a list of songs, old songs and new. If *you guys* in each booth could talk among yourselves and come up with a few songs you want me to sing, bring them on up any time."

"Yes, yes, yes," a chorus of voices responded around the room.

"We'll keep you busy," a sailor with a butch haircut called from the side of the room at a table near the door. The guy could not stop smoking. After Matt looked over a few times, Donny came up and said, "I'll tell you more about Ray later. His fighter crashed, caught fire, and it took a while for them to hack him out of his flaming plane. Now he's addicted to fire."

Matt's popularity had preceded him. All the men were trying to catch up on romance. They wanted to get lucky tonight. So he sang Johnny Mercer's, "Personality," and Perry Como's, "Prisoner of Love," each request from a different booth. By the end of his first call, he had sung more than a dozen songs. He did the same thing with his later show. "Come back next week," his favorite fans would call.

Towards the end of 1946, at four or five of his favorite bars and restaurants, Matt had to sing Perry Como's, "Surrender" and Frank Sinatra's, "Five Minutes More." Then in 1947, as Matt became more and more popular, he was asked to sing, for fun, Count Basie's, "Open the Door, Richard" and Tex Williams' hilarious, "Smoke! Smoke! Smoke! (That Cigarette)." After WWII, everybody smoked, and although Matt hated the idea of smoking, he put up with all the secondhand smoke. His tip jar was always full. Plus, the bar and restaurant owners paid him his fee and extra cash under the table.

A week later, Donny took him aside. "Are you happy where you are working? Hard, outdoor work, colder weather coming?"

"Hell no," Matt said. "What can I do? I am not doing anything in the medical field, even though I have gotten offers."

Donny jumped a little in excitement. "I have a friend, Anthony, who has been limping through the war with his fading sales at the furniture store. Nobody has money for furniture, or anything else except food."

"What the heck?" Matt interrupted. "What in hell does that have to do with me?"

"Stick with me, buddy, I'll tell you. The war is over. Anthony is looking for a handsome young man who can sing, who can carry on a conversation, someone who can bring the customers in and bring the customers back. You could do it, Matt. You could sing at places near Anthony's store. You could even sing at his store, while you are unknowingly enticing the women into buying new furniture, new beds maybe, new high chairs." He winked.

"Come on, Donny," Matt objected. "I'm married. I have family."

"No, no," Donny protested. "You will be a real salesman. If you do well, you could find a career in furniture that would pay for a new house, another baby. Maria would love that. It's just a job, not a chance for romance."

"Tell that to Maria," Matt said, turning away.

"Come back tomorrow," Donny said. "Anthony will come in. I'll introduce you. You are a vet looking for a career, not a job. You sing a few songs and then come over to his table."

Tomorrow came. Cold and windy was the weather in the nursery where he labored.

The plants and trees have to stay alive, he thought. *Wait a minute! I have to stay alive.*

After an early dinner, Matt went back to the Crystal Lake Inn. He brought folders of old military songs and late forties hits.

Anthony arrived and sat at a table nearby. Donny waved Matt up to the bar.

Donny turned around to the crowd. "I discovered this new singer right here in my bar. Matt LaCrosse, back from war in the Pacific." The crowd cheered. Some even stood up and applauded. Anthony smiled. What a great start. "Okay folks. Give him a listen."

Matt stood tall. "Thank you, folks! He had his guitar and sang a few of his favorites, walking around in front of the bar, then stopped, bowed, and stepped back.

"This is from 1944," he told his listeners. "Remember Harry James? We all felt the same way, thinking about our girlfriends and wives at home. I swear sometimes as I sang this, there were grown men crying. No brag, just fact." Matt looked around and sang, "I'll get by, as long as I have you…" He sang to each listener just for a moment, and saw husbands and wives squeezing each other's hands, heads bowed down. The audience loved the song. When he finished, he saw eyes all over the room affected by the message. Matt softly said, "Many of us will never forget this song."

Marianne, sitting on the far right, raised her hand and called out, "Matt, will you sing Bing Crosby's song which came out the same time in 1944? Before my husband died of wounds out there, he was always hopeful, never told me what his wounds were. He would write and tell me to listen to Bing Crosby sing, 'I'll Be Seeing You in All the Old Familiar Places.' That's me singing to you." She cried. "And I can't see him in all our old familiar places."

When she opened her eyes and looked up, Matt was singing to her, just as her husband would have. Everybody loved it, cheering and clapping. She closed her eyes again and imagined it was her husband.

Shortly after, a muscular man took out his trusty brown pipe he was never seen without. He ran a machine shop in the middle of town, and kept all the farmers and mechanics supplied with parts they needed. People depended on him. Men from other tables leaned forward.

A rare thing, Matt thought. He leaned over. "Who is that?"

Donny said, "It's Tracker. He will get this place rocking."

Just then, Tracker frowned and bellowed out, "Matt, for godssakes, think of the men here too! We want some guy songs too, some adventure. No teardrops! Something that makes a man stand taller. Can you sing, 'Don't Fence Me In?'?"

Matt straightened up and went at it. As he sang, a roomful of men blended in with him, swinging and swaying, as if they were cowboys on horses. Western movies were popular in the late forties, featuring Roy Rogers, Gene Autry, and many others. The women looked around and laughed, shaken out of their momentary sorrow. "Let's hear it for the cowboys, and all the men who came back from the front," Matt called out. "I'm back in the saddle again, back where a friend is a friend." The audience got up and cheered, singing along.

Then Matt had to introduce the next song. He cleared his throat. "This is for those who didn't come back. He thought of those he couldn't save out on the islands or even on a ship. He paused, and took a deep breath. "Empty Saddles in the Old Corral." Tears came to his eyes as he sang it, and he almost couldn't finish. The room stayed still for almost a minute.

Matt just stood there. Donny came over to the mike. "There will be a short intermission," he announced.

"Thank you! Thank you bartender! We need more beer, more whiskey!" The men all crowded to the bar, while their wives waited for them at the tables, talking to each other quietly.

When they reconvened, a woman called out, "Will you sing something from Doris Day? Something romantic?"

"Okay!" Matt smiled. "I don't have Les Brown's Band of Reknown to accompany me. But I'll do my best. Here it is, 'Sentimental Journey.'" He took his time and enjoyed it, sang it with the same catchy rhythm as Doris Day, swaying gently, just as if he were going to travel. When he finished, the audience rose. They couldn't resist. They all sang, "Gonna take a sentimental journey . . . Why oh why-hi did I roam?"

Anthony came up to the bar and shook Matt's hand. "You have a natural talent," he said. "I can't believe nobody saw it before." He smiled. "Not even you."

Matt shrugged his shoulders. "I never even thought about it. My dad was tone deaf. He did not want anybody to prove him wrong. So I didn't sing."

Anthony said, "I sang before, just like you. The women loved it. The men put up with it. Then I grew older and nobody wanted to listen. What could I do?" He shrugged. "Now the young women and mothers want to hear and admire somebody young, dashing, handsome, with the charisma I once had."

He leaned forward. "Come work for me, Matt. You can be both an entertainer and a beginning junior salesman. I need you. I can pay you much more than you make at Nelson Nursery. And my place is always warm in the winter."

Matt frowned. "Donny told me I could make good money entertaining at the bars and clubs around here. I can play the piano, and a little guitar. I could make good money."

Anthony laughed. "You can do both. You work for me, you sing for fun. We both make good money. And if you work out as a salesman, you could end up a manager, a person who gets a share of the profits as well. I am not getting any younger."

Somehow, Matt convinced Maria, who really wanted a nice home, and a car, after all the poverty-like living she endured during the war. At the end of the year, his reputation as a singer and entertainer had boomed. Many women came to the store and then returned. Some dragged their husbands along. Business was booming, too. Matt already had money coming in as a singer, as a salesman, and now he had a share of the profits as well. In another year, he was the store manager. By then Luke had another baby sister, instead of the brother he hoped for. He and his mom watched their new home being built.

Both of Matt's uncles owned furniture stores nearby, and they were envious of Matt's business success. They had spent their lives building up their businesses, and they were visibly envious of Anthony's and Matt's success. It all started with Matt's singing, for godssakes. They had been distant to begin with. But they couldn't argue with success.

Right after Christmas of 1948, after a few years of Matt's new career, all three LaCrosses got together, enjoying holiday eggnog and making holiday talk. Then Anthony leaned over. "I have a New Year's Resolution. If Walter, Jeffrey, and I consolidate our three individual stores into one big Chicagoland Furniture Company, our future will have no limit." Jeffrey and Walter beamed and nodded, clinked glasses, and reached up to clink Anthony's.

Matt jumped up. "Perfect! We are all family. We can do this!"

Walter jumped up and yelled, "It's about time we got together!"

That night, Matt prayed in thanksgiving, with a photo his uncle had sent him.

> *May no one be separated from their happiness. May everyone have equanimity, freedom from hatred, attachment to wealth, ignorance, and affliction. The path begins with strong reliance on our kind Teacher. Source of All Good, fill me with this understanding to follow you with great devotion. With this firm knowledge, bless me to be cautious and mindful, always to avoid harmful words and actions, and to gather abundant virtue through the doing of kindness.*
>
> *May we all have companions with long lives. May those angels around me guide me on the good path. Bless me to pacify all outer and inner obsta-*

cles. Help me to use only skillful actions and practice good karma, so that I may learn to keep my mind and body free from discomfort and disease, wounds and injury. May my skillful actions provide health and happiness to others.

4

In 1948, Luke was nine and ready to sing. He and his dad had practiced at home every weekend. Matt got Luke to sing Kay Kiser's song, "Woody Wood-Pecker," and the audiences thought it was hilarious. Luke was a natural, just like his dad. Then in 1949, Luke was ten and Matt taught him to sing Spike Jones' song, "All I Want for Christmas (Is My Two Front Teeth)." The audiences loved Luke's voice and acting, but he could not go to some of the bars with Matt. Both of them sang Vaughn Monroe's hit, "Riders in the Sky, A Cowboy Legend," and they sang it like a couple of cowboys, dressed up in cowboy garb. When Frankie Lane came out with, "That Lucky Old Sun" and "Mule Train," Matt and Luke hammed it up. There were parts they sang solo and parts they sang together.

A year later, Luke had been chosen to sing at school concerts, church holidays, and even at a few birthday parties. The neighborhood kids loved him. He was so kind and fun to be around, making up songs just to make them laugh. He sang so many songs from the church liturgy, all taught to him at home by his grandma and at school by his curmudgeonly old music teacher. He loved playing the piano. The first time he sang, "The Lord is My Shepherd" at church, more than his family was moved. Matt had taught him the Christmas hymns, and he became a favorite at Christmas tableaux and concerts. When he sang, "This Is My Father's World", one verse always caused Luke's voice to quaver: "He shines in all that's fair. In rustling grass, I hear him pass, and His voice is everywhere." It reminded him of watching two fawns running across the long grass of Oaklawn Cemetery after his twelve-year-old friend's funeral.

His church taught him well; he sang in Latin, he sang in Greek, he sang a Dakota Sioux Indian song. For nonreligious concerts, he sang a great solo, "Ghost Riders in the Sky." The piano served him well. His dad sang at his side, so proud. So happy.

Matt's furniture company grew. The three owners worked to enlarge and remodel their outdated stores. In the early fifties, the economy climbed dramatically, acomplete contrast to the dismal thirties and war-torn forties. Matt had proven himself and became the new CEO, bringing in plans for new buildings and better locations. The three brothers knew Matt had proven himself worthy. Anthony considered him a son. Newly placed ads brought in even more customers. Matt had ceased singing in his favorite bars and clubs, except on holidays. He didn't need the money and he didn't have the time. His reputation was intact. Everybody knew him as an entertainer, and everybody respected him as an honest businessman. The times that he sang in the front of his biggest store still attracted the old customers, especially during the holidays, Thanksgiving, Christmas, the Fourth of July, and Veterans Day. The nearby Windy City lived up to its name, but at times, he still sang outside the store, and the local news picked it up.

Luke stood tall in the school. He played football, baseball, and soccer, though there were few real soccer games. He loved the Bears and Cubs, and followed them assiduously. Through delivering newspapers every morning, he kept up with the teams, especially the White Sox. He loved competition and discipline, learning both from Matt's Navy days and business ways. He learned it from how his dad developed a career in singing.

His dad was the success story of The Park and volunteered at both the church and the school. He raised money for both, on one committee or another. People dropped in to see him and he was always right there for them, just as he had been as a medic in the Navy. Luke loved being the big brother to his two little sisters, Jessica and Rachel. He organized hide-and-seek games in his neighborhood during the summer. They played baseball in his side yard. They cut bike trails through the woods.

The LaCrosse house was home base. At dusk and as night came on, the games got more and more exciting. So many kids came, both younger and older, and they all went home happy, as parents allowed the later curfew. If their sons or daughters suffered any trips, falls or scrapes, they knew Matt had copious training as a Navy medic during the war in the Pacific. If a summer party at "the lake" took hold, you can bet Matt and Maria were there with drinks and treats for the kids. Cold water gushed up to replenish the lake from a nearby well, but it continually drew kids to the short rock wall, where pure water gushed out as if Moses had struck it with his staff. The lake itself wasn't totally clear of seaweed, but the kids loved that pond every summer. Luke could swim out underwater over a hundred feet and still be over a hundred feet from the far shore near the tennis courts. Kids watched to see where he would pop up. Nobody dared go further. The south bank had weeds and turtles and duck poop that stopped them from climbing ashore. Nobody wanted to walk in that mess.

A log was tied twelve feet out from shore, and the moms made sure the little ones went no further. The lake was safe. But one Sunday afternoon, soon after church, after one weak call for help, Mr. Farrington shocked everybody when he jumped in the lake with his best church suit on and wallet in his pocket. Everybody was astonished to see how close to them Daniel had been struggling and they didn't notice it. Moms and kids felt reassured after that. The big seventh grader was about to drown, and Mr. Farrington was hero for life.

Life was good, peaceful, calm, trusting—doors were never locked. The milkman still delivered milk right to the back door. Every year, Luke had shiny report cards.

Luke wrote new prayers whenever he could, using his own photo collection enlarged by additional ones from his family.

I know you love me, Lord, because you lifted me out of the depths. O Lord my God, I called to you for help, and you healed me. You love me, Lord, because you turned your ear to me, and came quickly to my rescue. You are my rock and refuge, a strong fortress to save me. I know you love me, Lord, because you taught me that to fear you does not mean you will punish me, but rather, to trust and obey you as my Shepherd. You love me, Lord, because you promise, "whoever of you loves life and desires to see many good days, turn from evil and do good, seek peace and pursue it.'

Luke's family life was like the fruitful rural valley, protected by God's invisible promontories from the bustling cities and outside world rebuilding its disasters. He loved the old German Farmer Rance's long rows of cornfields, and large garden plots of fresh tomatoes, cucumbers, asparagus, spinach, and lettuce. The Rance Farm was just a quarter mile away, with his little roadside stand on Shermer Road in the summer and fall. And on the other side of the Navy Base, another farm grew the same produce, had a roadside stand, but raised hogs as well. Bornhof Dairy four miles up the road provided milk for the surrounding area with all its cows. Small pastures, huge barns.

Then in 1951, the Navy wanted land to extend its runways, population was exploding. Some builders made Farmer Rance a deal he could not refuse, not at his age. When he left to live with his son downstate, his heritage along with his culture disappeared. Housing for GI's spread out and covered the farmer's fields and little family gardens appeared in the backyards of Glenview. A construction company appeared and built a mansion on Farmer Rance's former fields. When completed months later, the mansion impressed everybody. Only a wealthy man could own such an estate, with copious grassy lawns surrounding the house, the trees and shrubs all trimmed and manicured, and flowers all around the home, especially the entrances.

The owner, Dr. Mossberg, had a thriving practice in Chicago's north suburbs, his wife had one of the first real estate licenses, and they wanted land that could not be surrounded by other homes. They had only two kids, Janet, a pretty blonde girl age fourteen, and a little brother, Samuel, age ten. The family kept to themselves and attended a Community Church less than a mile away. Luke still ran out to watch the fighters landing, and got to meet Janet one Saturday morning. When she told him about the movies at her church, she and Luke went to the Community Church for Saturday morning movies starring Roy Rogers or Hopalong Cassidy. Riding their bikes on the side streets down to the church was always fun.

But before the year was over the Glenview Naval Air Station had enlarged their North-South runway two thousand feet to handle the new breed of prop fighters, and jet fighters. The Mossberg mansion became a secondary landmark for the Navy carrier pilots. The air traffic doubled with the Korean War coming up, and more aircraft carriers preparing for war. The first landmark was the big Shermer Avenue water tank with its blinking red lights. Even at Glenview Naval Air Station, the Navy insisted pilots and carrier crew on the ground be trained to take the 180-degree aircraft carrier landing. They first flew north over the Mossberg mansion, and then over the Naval Air Station to get on target. They practiced the line-up on target; they assessed the winds, checked the immediate weather and precipitation, the condition of the aircraft and the runway, and then turned in a long, low half-circle to come back in for a landing. Once, at night and in a storm, a pilot almost rammed the water tower. Still, it was the best approach.

. Less than a half-mile later, the Mossberg mansion appeared on the flight path an eighth of a mile from the fence and close to the end of the runway. Luke had often sprinted out to stand next to and under the fence on Rance's tilled soil in the past. Then the Navy acquired a hundred foot right of way to give the fighters a better view of the fence. Luke could still sprint out there without trespassing. The F4U gull-winged Corsairs still came in too low, forcing the pilots to gun their engines to top the fence, with fierce roars and hot smoke trailing. None of his friends could handle the noise and landing gear growling overhead and still remain standing. They skittered left or right or dove onto the ground. The Mossbergs hated the incredible racket. Especially with the new jet fighters. They had come to get away from the noise of the city. The mansion went up for sale.

5

The De'Luca family moved in close to The Park Place Academy, not far from the LaCrosses. They were from a fellow church center in California, wealthy and stand-offish, but glad to be part of the Park Community. Mr. De'Luca wanted to attend Luke's Immanuel Church, to send his daughters to Park Academy, and perhaps even to become a leader in the society. They immediately came to church every Sunday and granted themselves third-row seats on the left side. No newcomers had ever done that before. The churchgoers were shocked. Luke was entranced.

Lacy's dad, Francesco De'Luca, had come from Italy in 1935 with his brother, Giovanni. They settled outside Palo Alto, on the San Francisco Bay peninsula north of San Jose. Francesco married Sophia Mancini in 1936, shortly after they first met. It took four years and long hours of work, but in 1940 he and his brother opened up a department store similar to what they owned in Italy, near San Marino, selling clothing, shoes, and handbags. Frank and John De'Luca had an exclusive on Italian shoes, the best on the market, with two in-store shoemakers. Then they capitalized on creating their own market for Levi's jeans, headquartered in San Francisco. The jeans had been on the market since 1890 and were worn by cowboys, ranchers, and regular workers. During World War II, the De'Luca Brothers made a fortune. Because of their hardiness, the jeans were sold almost exclusively to defense workers and especially to Californians. The jeans craze began after World War II. They became more fashionable to wear and sales boomed for the upper class as well.

Giovanni De'Luca stayed in the San Francisco area, and Francesco De'Luca relocated to the Chicago area where for a percentage of the ownership he helped Neiman Marcus double their sales by first introducing Italian shoes and the Levi's Jeans brands. By then the De'Lucas had two daughters, Courtney and Lacy. Luke was fifteen when his mom first introduced herself to Mrs. De'Luca, and then brought Lacy over to introduce her to Luke.

Mrs. De'Luca came up with Lacy and said, "Now that school begins in two weeks, I thought you two should meet first."

Lacy interrupted by stepping right up. "Hi, Luke. I'm Lacy."

Luke was speechless. Mrs. LaCrosse continued, "I told Mrs. De'Luca that you liked to sing, Luke, and she told me Lacy sang in her school concerts."

He couldn't help his first response. "I love that name. Lacy! It's so new to me. I've read about Lacy but I never met one."

It was Lacy's turn to be startled. She gave him a smile that she tried to hide. As if on cue Mr. De'Luca came up and took Lacy away.

"I love that name!" he exclaimed. "Everybody else here has the same common names."

Luke rushed home to his grandfather's scholarly dictionary. He looked up Lacy, with its English origin and French overtones. The definition "*lace-like*" intrigued him. Such a feminine sound. "Who wears lace around here?" he mumbled. "Only rich people."

He copied down everything he could find about lace. *Lace: to join, to unite, an intersecting adornment, detail, texture, embroidery, embellishes, to beautify.* All those words entranced him, and so did Lacy when he got to know her. Lacy arrived in early 1954 and found her place in ninth grade. She was fourteen but looked at least two years older. Luke was in tenth grade and smart enough to know Lacy was used to male attention.

The De'Lucas came from a wealthy city south of San Francisco near Palo Alto. The Park Academy pastor, Mr. Acton, called it "La Jolla" when he introduced the De'Luca family. In one of the few times the Reverend was corrected, someone called out in front of the whole church, it's 'La Hoi-ya.'" Some guessed it was Mr. De'Luca himself who spoke up, dressed in a fancy three-piece suit and tie, the likes of which nobody had seen. Luke knew it was Mr. De'Luca because his eyes were focused on Lacy, standing in front of her dad. Mrs. De'Luca stood in place behind her husband, elegantly dressed, a bit shy. She wore lace on a fancy collar, something Luke had never seen.

The first day of school he walked past Lacy in the hallway. Wow! She was strikingly beautiful. All Luke had to compare was Dorothy Gale in "The Wizard of Oz." Judy Garland had the most precious and beautiful face of a young teenager, and so did Lacy. They both had a precious cameo face, and for their age, beautiful lips—lower lip full, both sides of the upper lip curved down like a bow beneath perfectly shaped noses. The intensely personal effect of those big brown eyes sometimes showing a slight silver and black, always mesmerized viewers with their movie-star eyebrows, long eyelashes, a smaller forehead, and masses of long black hair. At times, Lacy put her hair in long pigtails with little ribbons that hung down in front. They both had pixie-like ears, cute and even more adorable. But Lacy was taller than Dorothy and more athletic, and more her own person.

Lacy was said to be age fourteen, but nobody believed it. Her older sister, Courtney, was in Luke's tenth grade while Lacy moved into ninth grade. Luke felt sorry for Courtney. Lacy truly had all the beauty in the family. She sat by the window in the catty-corner of her classroom, while Luke changed seating in an adjoining classroom, so he could see Lacy out of the corners of his eyes. She was all academic, paying strict attention to her teacher. She knew Park Place Academy was the gem, set in the middle of a large mainly forested tract of land called "The Park." Scores of homes lined the outer edges of the long circular drive with groves of trees. Everybody had a spacious front and back yard, some big enough for sports.

There was a large pond called, "The Lake," for skating and swimming, two large ball fields, and many beautiful paths leading through field and forest everywhere. Many headed especially toward the unique Immanuel Church with stained-glass windows and architecture reminiscent of Europe. The Church was adjoined to the

Academy, and everybody attended both. All around the "The Park" were thick and tall hedges of lilacs. Outsiders thought it looked like a country club for "the people behind the lilacs." Park Place Academy was exclusive, with classes from kindergarten to tenth grade, a feeder to many prestigious high schools. Most families lived around the outer edge of a half-mile road inside the lilacs, along with others who lived on adjoining streets, all part of one society. In the middle was the Park Academy L-shaped building with grades K–10, adjoined to the beautiful church with stained-glass windows.

Luke's father had trained him well in singing and even acting in plays and musicals, Gilbert and Sullivan for example. Lacy along with Luke became the star entertainers of the academy. She sang and performed the heroine role in two plays that year; she played soccer so well that Mr. Acton looked into more competition with other academies nearby. It was too late for Luke, but not too late for Lacy. Before she finished ninth grade, she was unbeatable. She even won oratorical contests. She earned straight A's in all her courses one marking period after another. As the year unfolded, Lacy's slimness became accentuated with hints of curves and fullness. She stood, talked, and moved with grace. She knew how to enunciate when she spoke and when she sang, indicating previous voice lessons and upper-class schools. After all, she was from California, the cutting edge. The pastor from California had been inspiring, and Lacy knew about the importance of women's roles in the Bible. She sang praises of Abigail Adams, the First Lady so long ago, who spoke up for women, and even for teaching black children.

At recess and after school, both classes played soccer in the adjoining field, used for sports and all activities. The kids held the field in their hearts, especially because of the Fourth of July summer celebration with games and food and fun, following the parade of veterans around Park Drive. Both adults and children competed in one activity or sport after another. Luke and his dad played on the same mixed team.

But during the school year, no matter where Luke ran on the field with the soccer ball, Lacy kept up with him and agilely attempted to get the ball away. She was the new kid in school, and nobody had seen a girl with such abilities and such self-acceptance. Whatever self-deprecating roles girls played back then, she knew nothing about them.

Where did she learn that? Luke would think to himself, and later even say to his friends, "Who is this girl? Who taught her she could do anything she wanted?" Lacy at times charged right at Luke. He had been taught to be careful with girls, to treat them with gentleness, never bump into them, never-ever knock them down, and for gosh sakes, and never kick the ball at them – especially near their faces. That did not work well with Lacy. She'd elbow him, snag the ball, and pass it to her teammate. What could he do? It didn't matter that Audrey was the fastest runner in the school. She was timid and never took advantage of her abilities. Not Lacy.

Dwight, known as Whitey, and Brian, the friends he played soccer and baseball and football with all the time, even in the winter with snow on the ground, began to banter. "Come on, Luke, you're being pushed around by a girl."

Even Jim and Chris, in grades behind him, began to whistle to each other when Luke was outsmarted. Luke took it silently, shaking his head. What could he do? Finally, one squalling fall day, Lacy had the ball and was going around Luke. He got up his courage and charged Lacy. Instead of kicking the ball away from her, in a fit of nervous apprehension he tripped her by mistake. He had been determined not to be caught off guard by a girl. She would not steal the ball away from him again.

Gasping in fear, he grabbed her by the waist, and they both twirled around with her momentum. Somehow, she did not fall. She was shocked and surprised. So was Luke. She forgot about the soccer ball, sure he was going to shove her away and catch her off balance, even toss her aside. He didn't. He even held her a little longer without thinking. Luke, as astonished as Lacy, drew in a sharp breath of shock and wrongdoing as they meshed for that split second. They instinctively grasped each other to keep from caroming off to the side and falling to the ground. Something electric, a tiny bolt of lightning, flashed through him from his sternum up to his brain and back. A new imagination and realization flashed through his consciousness—

the breath of puberty birthed throughout his whole being. A girl had caught his fancy. First time. And in more than one way.

Lacy looked at Luke for a second as if she knew him, recognized him. And as she felt his presence, a double-beat of her heart came all the way up to her ears. She blushed, and then she was gone. He didn't care if Mr. Acton shouted his name and took him out of the game. He had defended his honor. No more smart jibes from his friends. He didn't even know Lacy, didn't think about her feelings. He wanted his buddies to stop insulting him. Not just during recess, but any time of the day.

Recess finally ended. Luke hoped nobody noticed. After all, Lacy was a newcomer and younger than he, anathema for any boys in tenth grade, *the upper class*. But somehow, their lives would never be the same. From then on, Lacy and Luke found ways to see each other, call each other, go skating on the pond at the same time, star in the same school plays. One of their favorite songs for jitter-bugging together had the simplest message, but lively beat.

"Every time, I look at you, something is on my mind, If you do what I want you, baby, we'd be so fine, Sh-Boom, sha-Boom. Ya da da da da da, sha-Boom, sha-boom."

6

Lacy and Luke found ways to talk on the phone, not an easy thing to do back then. They made memories; they grew in their young love and friendship. They both read books and the Bible and other spiritual teachings, which none of their peers were mature enough to do. And then they talked about the books and the ideas and how they felt about them. They loved "Catcher in the Rye." They lived the hero's attitudes and actions vicariously. They took sides when they discussed, "Gone with the Wind." When he walked her home, he even volunteered to work in her yard as her parents might direct. He got to see her longer. And her parents were surprised at his willingness to work. Neither set of parents made anything big about it. "They're just kids." "It's puppy love." "She will get tired of him."

But Luke and Lacy were the bright stars over Lake Michigan's skies that last year together. They starred in the musical "South Pacific." They never tried to get away with things like holding hands too long and dancing too close. They sometimes stayed after class to ask the professor more questions. Especially Dr. King, the religion teacher. Luke's friends began asking him if he was headed toward a religious college and a theological degree.

"Are you kidding? The ministry?" Luke would protest. "I come from a military family. We have soldiers, sailors, marines sprinkled throughout the last two hundred years and at least six wars or conflicts. Country first. Country foremost. There is no way I'd be a preacher, not even a chaplain in the military. My uncles have told me so many real-life stories. The military—how to become a man."

That didn't work so after a while the boys tried something new. "Luke, man, you are with Lacy all the time. Have you even kissed her?" Luke shook his head and closed his eyes.

"Are you afraid of her father?" Luke shook his head and closed his eyes. The De'Luca family was a big deal in their small community. Mr. De'Luca owned a chain of department stores both in Chicago and in California. He was a self-made millionaire and made sure everybody knew it.

The boys kept at it. "How do you expect to win Lacy? She comes from a rich family. Her dad is going to want a son-in-law who can work for him or help him get richer. You couldn't handle that. Working for somebody who thinks he's better than you, and not good enough for his daughter. The military is the last thing on his wish list for Lacy."

They got him there for a few days. He talked to his dad over the weekend. His dad understood his dilemma. So that next Monday, he got them together after classes. "Just give me a few minutes," he said. They nodded and took their seats in the back of the classroom. It had been a long day and the halls were empty.

"Hey, my dad never even thought of himself as middle class. Maybe people thought of him as less than middle class. That never stopped him. As a Navy Medic he saved many lives. He never thought of himself as a hero, but everybody else did. He came home and tried something new, singing. And one person after another gave him a chance. Now he is a co-owner of three furniture stores here in the Chicago area. People think of him as upper class because of it. But anybody can talk to him. Nobody is less than him. Our family knows how to move up. Nobody's attitude is going to stop us."

Nobody argued or was a smart ass. Whitey, who never had an unkind word for anybody, took it to heart. "Hey, Luke, you're right. Maybe we all will have a chance to move up."

Luke's close relationship with Lacy continued. She was the pride of her family. Her dad took a special interest in her, encouraging her to be active in sports and extracurricular activities. Even though Mr.

De'Luca loved his wife, due to the unequal status in which he and society placed her, she could not provide an inspiring role model for Lacy. Her dad wanted Lacy to be more like him, someone he could influence, make him proud, and benefit him as well as she worked her way up in his company. He believed in competitiveness and watched her play soccer and tennis, shouting encouragement from the sidelines. Those were some of her favorite memories. Few other girls competed and nobody's father showed up. Later in life, she realized how well respected he was in the community. He was so handsome, so well dressed, a model of a successful Italian immigrant. Conservative, hard-working; wanting nothing from the government, he worked himself up from a man with no family to speak of, to the head of a blue-ribbon American family.

Lacy took an interest in the history of her ancestry and somehow followed her curiosity of other families' ancestry. The city library had articles on the Rance family, and she learned about the hard-working life Mr. Rance had brought from Germany. The Synnestvedt family owned a big nursery and lived the same life as they had in Norway. Lacy knew Luke had French and Native American blood in his heritage from the Minnesota and North Dakota areas, even stretching into Canada. And she never held it against him. She had the same compassion for everybody. Her love for people came from her Italian ancestors, not from her father. Lacy was much more concerned about the world community, in particular, elevating people out of poverty. At an early age, she looked beyond her family or town walls and at a much broader world—something that pleased Luke to no end. His heritage was not as yet much respected. French fur traders and American Indians—definitely in the lower class.

Mrs. De'Luca, on the other hand, felt trapped in a wealthy family, always providing social dinners and outings, which helped her husband's business and professional relationships. She felt she had no choice but to live in high society and associate with others in the same class, though it gave her little personal satisfaction.

Although she was very intelligent, she kept that to herself. She felt close to Lacy because of their perceived similarities. Mrs. De'Luca did not want Lacy to be trapped in the same way and was sympathetic to Lacy's relationship with Luke. She wanted to see more freedom for Lacy, with relationships based on natural and innocent attraction. She had affection for, not an aversion to, so-called puppy love.

Lacy and Luke grew up together, even though she came from a wealthy family and he was happy to be "in the middle class," as his father would say, just a little bit proudly. She didn't know yet how affected she would be by the money and status posture of her family, but she couldn't help herself. She and Luke played soccer, baseball; they ran around the park trails; they skated in the winter, even played hockey. They tied their sleds to the back of a friendly father's car, part of a long string of kids being pulled around the snowy and slippery Park Drive.

Luke worked hard on the next prayer. His dad helped him. He knew he would have to be somebody special to keep Lacy interested in him. And he found photos from his collections that said the same thing. Living in a forest of redwood trees, he was protected and comforted, with all the mighty trees around and above him, and not a single bad soul near him.

> *But you, O Lord, watch over me. You are the shade at my right hand; the sun will not harm me by day, nor the moon by night. But you, O Lord, watch over me, my coming and going, today, tomorrow, and forever.*

> *Blessed is the man you discipline, O Lord.*
> *Blessed is the man you teach with your law.*
> *Grant me relief from days of trouble.*
> *I will sing of your love and justice.*
> *I will be careful to lead a blameless life,*
> *And I will walk in my house with a blameless heart.*

7

Luke and Lacy created a relationship they handled strictly. None of their parents spent late nights worrying. Luke lived for self-respect, respect for Lacy, and respect for all the parents. Lacy had her own self-delineation. There were so many little meetings, innocent meetings, after school, walking her home, staying for ice cream.

Lacy brushed off Luke's attempts to find out more about her. She did not want him to notice the difference in their social status. Every chance she got, she asked him questions he had never thought of or prepared for.

One day, she looked over to him on the walk home. "What's bothering you today, Luke?"

"When Mr. Odhner finished his lesson with the Fourth Commandment admonition," Luke said, "Honor thy father and mother that thy days may be long." His voice dwindled off. He shook his head slowly with a sigh. "You and so many of my friends have such caring moms. They hug me, and give me extra ice cream and ask me questions as if they care. My mom is busy and ice cream is limited. Her new status as a rich person makes her focus on things. New houses and more clothes, more lunches away from home. They are all just *things*. I honor, love, and respect Mom, but it would be nice if it went both ways."

Lacy bumped him a little. "It doesn't go both ways. It goes up. You to your mom, your mom to her mom."

She nudged him. "Never mind moms. You are older now. You just need a girlfriend, Luke. That's like, *out and back*: You send love and honor out, and the girl sends it back. Or the other way around." She looked behind her. "By the way, who was your first girlfriend, Luke?"

Luke covered up a nervous cough. "The first girl I dared to see after school was younger. Before you came. She was shy, shy but sweet. I knew she liked me. I could see it in her eyes. We only had about twenty minutes after school before her dad came to pick her up. They lived farther away than you and your sister, maybe ten miles."

He stopped; unsure he wanted to go on. Lacy tugged his arm. "Okay," he said. "We tried to find places out of any student traffic. No luck really. After a while, my classmates ridiculed me for my choice. She was so young, too young to be a girlfriend. But Sophie was so sweet in any way you could imagine."

"Did you think of her as your girlfriend?"

He hesitated. "Yes."

"Were you too young to think about kissing her?"

Luke blinked.

Lacy smiled. "Your first kiss?"

"What do you mean?"

"You know," she nodded and smiled again, a little nervous.

"Yes," said Luke. "She was my first kiss…in my whole life."

"What was it like?"

"I felt butterflies were all around me and in my stomach too. I was in a whole new world. Like I had just jumped out of a plane and was drifting down in my parachute."

"How did it make you feel, Luke?"

"I was transported into a whole new world. I never thought a girl could do that to me. I was uplifted, and squeezed—like a butterfly out of my cocoon.

"Sophie wouldn't tell me what it was like for her. She had a little tear in her eye. I thought I had spoiled things. But later, she said the tear was from happiness, not sadness."

"So did you kiss her again?"

"I kissed every time I got up the nerve." Luke blushed and looked away. "I had no idea what I was missing. And then her father had a talk with me."

Lacy giggled. Luke said, "I should never have said that to you!"

Lacy put her arm inside his and sang to him. "*Send me the warmth of a secret smile, to show me you haven't forgot…now and forever, always and ever, little things mean a lot.*" Everything changed.

Lacy pulled Luke close. "I won't mind. If, if you kiss me more than you did her."

"What?" Luke turned his head and looked at her, astonished. She leaned over and pursed her lips.

"Wait!" he said. Luke looked down and to his left. "Look! Here's a little hiding place in between the lilacs."

He dropped his books and pulled her in, and wrapped his arms around her. Then he breathed in and kissed Lacy. Their first kisses were so light and so sweet. "O my," he said. Her eyes were closed. Her lips were waiting. The sweetest scent of perfume wafted up to him. He pulled her in close and kissed her and kissed her. He slowly trailed kisses across her face and down until he was buried in her neck.

"You're tickling me, Luke!"

"I love your perfume," he said, refusing to stop kissing. At last he ran out of breath. "Now we are both butterflies."

Lacy said, "I didn't think you'd dare. But I'm glad you did!"

She pulled him down and kissed him again and again, murmuring, "Once is never enough," after every kiss. Luke blushed.

Lacy stepped back. "Wait a minute. What happened to Sophie? She's not still around, is she?"

"Are you kidding? She stopped seeing me because her father heard Sophie talking to her mother. He thought Sophie was avoiding him, he got upset, and he scolded her. 'You're too young to be seeing any boy alone, especially an older student. I don't care if he's an honor student. He is causing problems. I don't want you with any problems.'

"Was that it?"

"The following Monday Mr. Tucker spotted me standing there after school. He rolled down the window and asked me a few questions. I don't even remember what he said. Or what I said."

He sighed. "Sophie was crushed. So was I."

Lacy said, "Were you embarrassed talking with her dad?"

Luke shrugged his shoulders, "Heck, yeah."

"Do you embarrass easily, Luke?"

"Heck yeah." Warily, he looked over at her. "At a Saturday night party for older teens, a taller girl holding a cigarette in one hand and a cold can of Schlitz in the other hand confronted me. I had been there less than twenty minutes. She was so rude, saying, 'You don't drink, you don't smoke, you don't run off in the corner with a girl? You're still in kindergarten.'"

Lacy squeezed Luke's arm as he went on. "The next Monday at school, some of the boys heard about it and came up to hassle me. 'What did you do this weekend?' Harry yelled to me across the room. 'You went to church, sat with your family, and went home for Sunday dinner?'

"Everybody laughed. I smiled and shrugged my shoulders."

"You handle embarrassment pretty well," Lacy said.

"Seriously?" Luke frowned and looked away.

Lacy looked worried. She knew something Luke did not want her to know. She sighed and said, "Did my dad ever embarrass you, Luke?"

"Nothing big," he said bitterly, pausing a moment. "He took me aside after church one Sunday a while ago. He raised his eyebrows, and quietly said, 'Luke, you like to sing. We could take you to Italy with us. So many singers came out of Italy.'

"I stood there staring at him. He said, 'Just get a couple new sets of clothes and ask your father for five hundred dollars.' Then he turned away."

"What?" Lacy exclaimed. "How could he ever do that?"

"I have no idea. I have never been so embarrassed."

Lacy gave him a quick sideways squeeze. "Never mind him, Luke. I make my own decisions. I don't want you to go to Italy with my family. They are so 'not you.' It would not be a dream vacation, more like a nightmare."

The next day as they walked home again, the last thing Lacy wanted to talk about was her dad and her family. She skipped ahead and then turned around. "Hey, Luke, I know you and your grandparents talk a lot. What's one thing your grandfather said that made a difference in your life?"

Luke looked directly at Lacy. "He kept telling me that Jesus said when someone hits you, turn the other cheek. So I celebrated my eleventh birthday in the hospital."

"What? Are you kidding me?"

"The hospital?" Lacy was stunned. "Luke, who hit you?"

"A classmate. My parents gave me a new bike. Beautiful Schwinn. Colin and I were riding bikes after my birthday party. He rode ahead of me through the deep sand at the lake near our house and his front tire got bogged down. I bumped into him. A total mistake. Unavoidable."

Luke stopped and Lacy stopped too. Luke grimaced in pain. "It was my spleen. He bruised it. I never felt pain like that before. Never have since."

Lacy stopped. "Couldn't they fix it in the hospital?"

"Back then they didn't have pain relief for kids."

Luke brightened up. "But when I was in the hospital and my dad came to see me, he kneeled down and prayed. He left me a photo I had taken in front of our house. He got it developed at Renneckars Drugstore. I carry it around.

"Dad prayed, "I know that you love me, Lord, because you protect the faithful and even the simple-hearted. Those who love their country and their family. When I was in great need, out on all those Pacific islands, you always surrounded me and saved me from countless injuries. I pray you heal my son and keep him safe from all pain."

Then he gave me this little note. "Let's pray this together," he said. "And then pray every day. It always worked for me."

"I read it aloud while he prayed. *Be at grace, my soul, for the Lord has been good to me. The Lord is with me. I will not be afraid. What can any person do to me? You are my helper and guide, O Lord. Turn my eyes away from worthless things and preserve my life according to Your Word."*

Double rainbow for my dad and me: God's forgiveness.

Lacy loved the photo and the story. "Your family is so special to me."

Luke softly sang this to Lacy. He loved his dad. *"'Oh Mein Papa, to me he was so wonderful, Oh Mein Papa, to me he was so good. Gone are the days, when he would take me on his knee, and with a smile, he'd change my tears to laughter.'"*

Lacy wanted to avoid tears. She never cried in front of anybody. She held Luke's hand tightly as they walked down the block approaching her home. Grass around her house greened in front, the apple trees and cherry trees blossoming in back. She changed the subject.

"But your grandfather and grandmother had a good influence on you too, yes?"

"Okay, it took me a while to see it. I finally realized the depth and meaning of my grandparents' love for each other when I saw Grandmother surrounded by a roomful of flowers during the celebration of their fiftieth wedding anniversary. I never saw so many flowers in my life. I couldn't even see the fireplace."

"That is so sweet, Luke," Lacy murmured and pressed close to him.

Luke was encouraged. "Then when other people left, she called me over. And she said to me, 'I know you have always loved the relationship your grandfather and I have. You asked me so many questions as a little boy, and I did my best to answer them. Now you are growing into a man. All I want to say is be careful with your heart. Save your best love for your wife. Don't give it away too easily.'"

Lacy looked away. Luke changed the subject. "I'm not totally sure what she meant. But Grandma Laura did much more for me than that. She played the piano with me as soon as my fingers could reach more than two keys. She taught me with such love and sweetness. It never seemed like hard work or hard practice. I learned how to play and sing her favorite hymns, and we sang together in church. Then she taught me how to write little songs of my own. That helped when my dad and I got going on singing together."

"We never went to church all the time," Lacy said. "You have three ministers in your older generation. No wonder you go."

She paused, trying to think of a last question before she opened the door and left Luke behind. "What's your favorite family memory?"

Luke's eyes were a little moister than usual. Finally, he said, "From back when I was a small child, Uncle Harold's robe and voice and presence were the closest things I've ever had to experience the Lord in person. I can't imagine any memory better than that."

8

At the end of tenth grade at Park Place Academy, Luke earned a key scholarship to a California Prep School in Palo Alto. Matt LaCrosse's former military commanding officer, also in Palo Alto, used his connections to get Luke into the prestigious Springfield Academy. The religion and academics of the Park Place Academy continued in part at Springfield Academy, which had earned immediate respect from colleges all over the country. Some teachers from both academies knew each other, were even related to each other.

Luke spent the summer after tenth grade working for the LaCrosse Furniture Stores, delivering furniture throughout the Chicago area. Luke developed great rapport wherever he went. People recognized him, knew his father as a war hero, and thought Luke was bound to follow in his father's footsteps. And through their religion courses Lacy had taught him a simple solution to making new friends and successful business contacts. "If you want attention and respect, you have to give it first. You can't make the second step." So Luke treated customers as if they were already friends.

Lacy spent months all over Europe with her family. She sent Luke postcards from Lucerne, Switzerland; the Black Forest in Germany; Cinque Terre, in Italy; Nice, France; and then London and Glasgow, Scotland. For the second summer, her family had figured out a way to keep Luke and Lacy apart. In addition to travel, Lacy spent parts of those summers in Spain. Her dad especially insisted she learn Spanish while completing high school. He wanted her to have special ability to manage one of his department stores in California where there was a high percentage of Hispanics. He would get the jump on his competitors.

Lacy returned from Europe and began her tenth grade at the Park Place Academy. School began earlier there. Her parents were happy Luke was no longer in her life. He had proven himself academically but he would never become a member of their upper-class society.

A week later, for the new school year in California, Luke had to travel. He began to board the train from Chicago to San Francisco. His family was at the station, sad to see him go. They would miss him and they knew Lacy would miss him. Lacy's older sister, Courtney, had also been accepted by Springfield Academy Prep, so Lacy got to come to Union Station as well. But Mr. De'Luca was there, obvious in his disapproval, upset that Luke had found a way to go to the same prep school Lacy would attend the following year. For the first time, Luke really understood that Lacy might become a distant star from his past, soon to be out of orbit. Or even out of his universe. The De'Lucas were driven downtown in their new, shiny, long white Cadillac. Matt LaCrosse drove his family down in a new blue Lincoln, given to him by his business partners.

The LaCrosses stood next to the Atchison, Topeka, and Santa Fe passenger cars as steam poured out from beneath the cars. They seemed unwilling to make a scene with a public display of affection. They supported the romance of Lacy and Luke as an unforgettable brand of teenage puppy love, but they expected no good-bye scene. It was hard enough for Luke to leave his two little sisters and his dad. It was much harder to leave Lacy. Her parents stood ten feet away. Mr. De'Luca made no attempt to wave, but Mrs. De'Luca looked at Lacy, then turned around and carefully waved to Luke, her hand hidden from her husband's view as they helped Courtney up the train steps.

Luke took a deep breath and walked up to Lacy. Tears pooled in her eyes. She handed Luke a little note on flowery paper. He had no note to give her, but he wanted to kiss her good-bye, no matter what. He felt resigned to a lost fate. He shook his head and looked down.

"My grandparents took a vow of poverty, and I'll probably never get over it."

She ignored that and looked up at him. "I'll never forget you, Luke."

"Good-bye, Lacy. I can't wait to travel on the train with you next year, when you come west with me." Luke turned and slowly began to walk away. He waved again to his mom and dad, his two little sisters. On his way to his train car, a movement caught his attention. There behind a dark concrete pillar, Lacy suddenly appeared, invisible to everybody else. She lifted her arms appealingly, her face upraised, her soft teary eyes blinking between swirls of curly black hair cascading down her shoulders. She was a year older now, and twice as beautiful. Her eyelashes quivered. Her eyebrows wrinkled in pain. "I'll be right here for you, Luke, when you come back." He stepped forward, sure she was going to kiss him goodbye. At the last minute, her father called out her name. He did not know where she was. She froze, and stepped back. Luke knew that was the best he would get.

The De'Lucas had turned to go. As Luke climbed the five steps up to board the train, on his last look around, he saw Lacy jump out from behind the pillar. A runner she was, and before he knew it, she was on a beeline and jumped up on the first step and then the second step. Luke heard her steps and turned around, shocked. Lacy grabbed the train car handle for support and passionately hugged Luke as she came up. He looked down, amazed, and she edged up against him, "first love" shining in her eyes. And then she kissed him. She really kissed him. Not a Chicago kiss. A Hollywood kiss, a romantic kiss, a long goodbye kiss.

Exhilaration surged through Luke's body. No train ride for him. He wanted to turn around, jump down, and dance with her. "One and two, three and four, we're going to get up and rock some more. We're gonna rock, rock, rock, around the clock, tonight."

She was gone, running after her parents.

Luke looked after her. Life was going to change. He could never come back to the home town that he knew. He would be different. Everybody would be different. But he jumped up, and swinging

66

through the doors, he sat down next to the window, hoping to catch one more glimpse of her.

When he glanced down, she was still there! Lacy raised her face to the window. Luke blew her a kiss. Right behind her Mr. De'Luca stared up at him, his look commanding Luke's lips to silence and his arms to lower. Luke looked away, disconcerted, and then he stared down Mr. De'Luca. He had never done anything like that before. Finally up in the train he had the advantage of height. Lacy stepped away from her father, blinked away her tears, waved twice, and was lost to view as the train began to move.

Luke took a deep breath. He immersed himself in the memory of that last kiss. The best he had ever had. As the train pulled out of the station and began its journey west, Luke came back to reality: *My parents are sending me away to a school in California. I have to give up both my paper routes. I can't follow my beloved Chicago Bears and White Sox every morning. No more dawns out in the garage, folding newspapers and sneak-reading the sports section with frozen fingers. No more Lacy to fill up the rest of my day. No more waiting in the little patch of woods beside the trail for Lacy to show up so I could walk her to school without her parents seeing us. No more soccer games with her at recess. No more carefree walks home for lunch. No more afternoon projects in the library. No more evening phone calls from her closet. No more secret meetings on the enclosed porch, surrounded by sweet-smelling pines, shrubs, and bushes nobody could see through.*

No more Lacy.

He might as well subsist without sunrise and sunset. It was like being in prison, living on bread and water, living without freedom. It might as well be a new planet. Life without Lacy. Luke slumped down for the forty-hour, two-day trip away from heaven and his "special angel," feeling as if he was headed to hell. He could not sleep. He felt like he was handcuffed to his seat and just stared through the window all night. The trip took forever.

Julie London's sweet song floated through him every hour. *"Now you say you love me, I can't believe that it's true, Why don't you cry me a river, cry me a river, I cried a river over you."*

In the morning Luke looked out and noticed the high northern road through the interminable corn and wheat and grasslands landscape of the upper Midwest. Then the Great Plains finally gave way to the rough, green, and steep Rocky Mountains, with all their canyons and rivers and winding railroad tracks. Luke started to pay attention and to enjoy the new country. By the time he spilled into the basins of Utah and Nevada and crossed the Sierra Nevada Mountain Range, he had accumulated maps from the stewards and spent time twice in the dining car. He started to eat again. And breathe again. The final hundred miles coming into San Francisco witnessed the transformation of a teen—at first lost in the past—now pulling into the harness as an adventurer, ready for something new. After all, he reflected, *Dad traveled west away from his family. He knew it might be forever, right into the most vicious war in the modern world.*

He jumped off the train and took the Springfield Academy bus out to the campus in Palo Alto, looking at scenery, wondering how cramped he might feel on campus in a dormitory room. He checked into the campus and got into his room early at the boys' dormitory. He tried to think of it as an adventure. He began doing his scholarship work immediately; sweeping and cleaning the dormitories and the classrooms assigned to him every day of the week. Even four hours on Saturday morning, the day he arrived. It was the only way his parents could afford to send him. Most of the other boys would arrive on Sunday. Luke had a small room partly under the stairs, built for one student and not two. Luke wondered if guys would say he lived in a broom closet.

He didn't care. He studied his class schedule and focused on success. He knew what books he needed, and he stood at the door when the bookstore opened at 8:00 a.m. on Monday. His classes began at ten o'clock. Just about everybody with whom he shared a sidewalk or a hallway knew everybody else. They may have spent one or even two years there already. Luke stood tall, walked like he meant it, and responded somewhat indifferently to the girls who noticed him and smiled. He was tattooed and branded with Lacy in his heart and his heart stayed on his sleeve.

He had turned sixteen by then, and Lacy's fifteenth birthday blossomed after Veterans Day. He wished he could go home for Thanksgiving, but there was no way. Christmas was highlighted on his calendar, and going back to visit his family was at the top of his list. He was sure Lacy would be there as well.

Mr. and Mrs. De'Luca had made it clear that Luke was to stay clear of writing Lacy. For God's sake allow her to experience life on her own, without Luke as a constant companion. They even said something to Luke's dad. *And Lacy went along with it.* Luke was all too aware of the power Mr. De'Luca had over his family. But he read and reread all the notes she had sent him the years before. Nobody could take Lacy away from him.

Thanks to her parents, Luke didn't see Lacy for his whole junior year, starting with his first Christmas at Springfield Academy. Every time he came home for a vacation or for holidays, the De'Lucas were either traveling or visiting family in another state. He learned quickly why many teenage romances flicker to an end. They don't flicker themselves extinct at all. Rather, unaccepting parents stomp them out. Thank God that his younger sister Jessica was in the same class as Lacy. Jessica knew what had to be done. She kept Luke updated at least two or three times a month. Most of the time, Lacy didn't know she was being "recorded." But sometimes, a sweet little note from Lacy was included in Jessica's letters.

Luke's mom and dad really encouraged him to move on and forget the De'Lucas. They did not want him mooning around and dropping off the honor roll. So he worked long hours into every night. He joined a school track team and ran every day, early in the morning and sometimes late at night.

He earned high honors for his first semester, thereby gaining new friends. Students respected his intelligence and his answers in class and on tests, so they gradually took him in and accepted him. He ended the entire year with honors and additional commendations. Of course Lacy graduated from tenth grade at Park Place Academy with honors, including awards for more plays and concerts she had starred in. Jessica kept Luke up to date on that, just as she had done all year.

9

The time finally came for Lacy to travel to California. After she arrived at Luke's prep school that sat above Palo Alto between San Jose and San Francisco, she stayed in no dormitory, no place very near the campus. She was a guest in the former Wellington mansion. The De'Lucas took advantage of their business connections in California to house Lacy there. Their friends and colleagues, Mr. and Mrs. Dahl, had three sons and a daughter, Monica, who was Lacy's age. Mrs. Dahl thought Monica needed a good friend, so Lacy was invited to live in their mansion instead of the dormitories. The De'Lucas took every pain to make sure Lacy associated with the most refined crowd.

On campus, Lacy was very popular. She was a junior, Luke a senior. In the middle of football season, she caught the interest of the quarterback for Springfield Academy. But when Brandon heard some rumor about Luke and Lacy's past romance, he got jealous. One late fall day Luke and Lacy were talking on the school steps. Brandon drove up and parked his Mustang right in front of them. He dialed up his radio loud. Tennessee Ernie Ford came booming out. *"If you see me coming you better step aside, a lot of men didn't and a lot of men died."*

Brandon got out of his car and started to come around toward them. Luke pretended that Brandon was just having fun, that he probably knew Luke had sung since he was ten. So Luke smiled and sang, "*One fist of iron and the other of steel, if the right one don't get you, then the left one will.*"

Then both Lacy and Luke, who had sung together many times, ignored Brandon, and kept singing the next verse to each other.

Brandon, at a loss for words, slid into his car and roared off. Lacy smiled. "He probably thinks we're crazy."

"We are, no doubt," Luke said, giving her a hug.

Luke had many friends in his senior year. Lacy worked madly on making new friends who had already created their network the first two years. Lacy and Luke were both awkward, having been so close. Now they didn't know how to connect. Nobody in Luke's class knew Lacy. Separate peer groups closed around them both.

Her sorority sisters loved her high spirits and happy bonding ability and the prep school fraternity brothers adored her beauty. She charmed the California kids by making every person feel unique. A nanosecond flash of love from her eyes was all it took. Each person thought he or she was the only star in Lacy's sky. In Palo Alto, a place filled with descendants from western pioneers and the children of huge landowners and business moguls, her deeply personal approach made her special to everybody she met.

Lacy thought about Luke, missing him, his athletic form, his personality flashing through her mind, her imagination. She felt more centered with new friends. But she couldn't get her mind off Luke, now that she was away from her family. *Luke moves so quickly when he's on a mission, especially if his running competitiveness kicks in. He wants to get the task at hand done well, so he moves quickly, and remains focused. He's not as leisurely a walker as his friends. Instead, he's strong and sure in his step, very erect in military manner.*

She really began to miss him. *He stands upright; his shoulders pulled back and down, ready to face the world. He projects himself outward. She thought about how he dressed. Nothing like she was taught. He loved jeans, logo shirts, running logos, shorts before they were fashionable, the best running shoes he could find. He was casual but meticulous. She remembered how Luke and she sped around the soccer field to see who was fastest, who could score the most goals. They had races down the paths to the lake, the church, and the lilacs. Sometimes she could outrun him. How can we see each other secretly? she wondered.*

Lacy stayed in a third-floor bedroom in the Dahl mansion. One week Luke noticed Lacy covertly looking at him every day in the hallways. And suddenly, the next week she saw him behind the mansion one late afternoon. He signaled to her from the thick evergreen woods and trees behind the property's fences. And so it began. He raised one arm straight up over his head, and the other arm straight out to the side. His old signal. He created the big L that stood for Lacy and for Love. She couldn't wait. She put on her running gear and burst out of the back door, running down the steps like a cougar. She ran right into his arms. "Oh, Luke, I miss you!"

"I missed you more, Lacy!"

They had not kissed for so long, the first kisses were tentative, even exploratory. Suddenly they both reached out and held each other's faces, kissing so tenderly. Luke lifted her off her feet and wouldn't let her go. They both stopped breathing.

"Luke," she protested. "We have got to run together!"

"Oh," he said, gasping. "I forgot."

"Put me down and try to catch me!" And he couldn't.

When they ran the next few days, he sang his favorite song for running, *"You can knock me down, step on my face… but don't you step on my blue race shoes."*

From then on, in the late afternoon Lacy would run out of the mansion, down the steps and through the fences. She and Luke ran as long and often as they could. But they were eminently careful. There was so much to lose. Finally, they had found the way to connect more closely without anybody knowing. When Lacy went on the runs, they took turns being the lead runner. This is how they often saw each other. They made their way along the Skyline trail, which wound along a mountain ridge. They could look to one side and see Palo Alto, Santa Clara, San Bruno, and the other towns along San Francisco Bay. On the other side, the hills spilled toward Half Moon Bay and the Pacific. It was an incredible view that left them breathless every time they took it in. That didn't happen every time they ran, because fog often crept up the coast.

One time, they came upon a trail that fed into the Skyline, Luke's left hand holding her right. Joy propelled both of them along as they skimmed past beautiful evergreens, firs, and pines that smelled like Christmas. They particularly loved the redwoods. That day Lacy said, "The biggest redwoods can grow up to 300 feet and live for two thousand years."

Luke stopped, looking over at her. "Two thousand years? They were on earth when Jesus Christ was? Why aren't the big ones on the skyline?" He asked.

"The redwoods we keep running by are clustered together, all about the same height, right?" Lacy responded.

"Right." Luke panted and pointed. "Why do the forests look so bare out there?"

Lacy grunted. "You don't want to know. They took so many of the older trees here, firs, pine, and redwoods, and shipped them to San Francisco to rebuild the city after the earthquake."

Luke blustered, "And all this time I liked San Francisco."

Lacy and Luke arrived at a little clearing of meadow grasses and a few scattered live oaks. All of a sudden they spotted two deer. Lacy grabbed Luke and pulled him to a stop. The ears of the does perked up and their tails lifted, alert, ready to flee.

Luke stood trembling, holding his breath. Everything seemed to pause. The sky spun, his chest heaved, and the deer remained still as statues. Luke leaned his head against Lacy's shoulder next to her cheek. She leaned into him and kissed him ever so softly. Seconds clicked by. Their hearts took the moment into a lifetime memory. They never wanted to leave or breathe. God's grace descended like a fine mist onto their shoulders. They could feel it. They were connected to each other, and to the universe, in a mystical spring haze. Lacy whispered, "Now I know why you read Thoreau."

During his senior year, Luke trained for the Triple Cross-Country run—fifteen kilometers or 9.3 miles. It was the biggest and toughest high school race of the year. He trained extra on nearby forest preserve trails. Now the route took them down Meriwether Road, around Redwood Pond, and up Jericho Hill. Three miles later, they would catch their breaths underneath a big oak tree.

At one point, Lacy practically tumbled down a trail next to and paralleling Jericho Creek Road. "Nemo!" she yelled.

Gasping for breath, Luke yelled back, "Say what? You're yelling at me?"

"I'm not yelling at you!" Lacy looked over and smiled.

She called back. "I'm yelling at this trail! I am pushing myself."

She cleared her throat. "Nemo came from Scotland's motto: *'Nemo me impune lacessit*. Nobody attacks me with impunity!' This trail is attacking me big time."

"Are you kidding?" Luke teased her. "Nobody attacks you."

"Nobody defeats me either. Come on then!"

She went into a crouch. "See if you can defeat me."

She and Luke ran along the forest preserve trail, its feeder trails, and through the tall grasses. When they reached the rolling meadows, Lacy broke into a sprint. She flew out in front of him. Just when he got winded again, discouraged from being left in the proverbial dust, Lacy turned around and stopped, bent over, hands on her knees. Sunlight caught her fine black hair—more of an exquisite liquid maze than mere strands of hair—falling forward, then back, and then forward again. Her bright smile caught him from a hundred yards away.

She stood up, her chest rising and falling. "Coming?" she called, her voice full of affection. That one word helped Luke run faster. One word. One smile. He'd follow her anywhere. She made him think he could do anything, run forever, run across America.

They mapped out and ran the course together. Parts of it they had not run. Two-thirds of the way through the course, while cresting a long hill and descending suddenly around a corner full of trees and underbrush, they almost tumbled on a railroad track that came out of nowhere. Luke tripped and Lacy stumbled between the railroad ties.

Luke's heartbeat tripled when he saw Lacy trip across the silver rails, catching herself in time. Had she been injured or badly hurt, her family would have found out about it. They could find some legal way to enforce the order they had given Luke never to see Lacy again. And he would have never forgiven himself. Lacy recovered and pulled up savagely, steamed that she'd almost taken a tumble. She gave Luke a sideways glance, frowning in a way he'd never seen before. Her pride was scratched. She yelled at Luke, "Seriously! Train tracks to jump over?"

He yelled back, "I had no idea there were train tracks to jump over!"

He ran over close to her and grinned. "We'll really be in trouble if there's ever a train on the rails. If you hear one coming during the race, run back and warn me, okay?"

"Of course! I'll be ready." she said. She wasn't competing, but she would be there.

The week passed. Luke trained alone. Race day came, and the rain was so heavy the meet was moved a day back, with better weather promised. One thing you could count on with Pacific storms, Luke thought, unlike the Midwestern storms I grew up with. If it rains one day out here, it will be sunny the next.

The next day all the runners from eight nearby schools arrived at the starting point. Luke played over in his mind his coach's big warning: "Don't go out fast with the hotshots. Start slow in the rear of the pack. You are a Southern Pacific freight train hauling pig iron, like Johnny Cash sings, 'Pickin' up a little bit of speed, pickin' up a little bit of steam,' and pretty soon the hotshots will be coming back to you. And all you can do is keep pickin' up a little more speed."

The gun fired and the human tsunami crashed forward. Luke counted to twelve before he could start running in the back of the pack. He ran freely, with deep breaths to build surplus energy. After the first mile, wet nervous tension flew off his forehead. He looked at the runners' feet in front of him, keeping calm while avoiding the temptation to look ahead to the looming hills, which would intimidate him.

He paid heed to his hero, black pitcher Satchel Paige—who should have been in the major leagues, yet was honored for his play in the Negro Leagues. His famous warning: 'Never look back. Someone might be gaining on you.'

A mile into the race, he heard light footfalls alongside the running trail. Lacy burst into view, jumping over huckleberry bushes and startling a few runners. Two hundred yards ahead, she stopped, waiting for him to catch up. Runners stared at her. Lacy flashed her best smile and waved Luke forward, yelling, "Luke! Come on!"

His spirits soared and his feet flew. "You're running like a deer," she yelled. Lacy jumped just left of the trail, urging him forward with her body posture, stimulating him to his best effort.

Then she disappeared over a hill.

Luke caught up to five runners from Los Gatos running in a pack. They began heckling Luke. "Why do you need a *girl* to help you win the race?"

Luke yelled as he sped by, "She can outrun all five of you vatos."

They kept yelling, "Where's the rest of your team? We'll run you down like dogs on a rabbit!"

Luke picked up a little anger speed. He cleared his lungs with a "Hoo-ah!" three times to get rid of a searing stitch in his right side. The speed and pain made him double over. Only one-third of the race was behind him. He focused on everything on either side. *Looking ahead is daunting.*

Finally half the race was done. He steadily gained on runners ahead of him. The Los Gatos gang tag-teamed to see if they could get somebody up next to him, alternating lead runners and shouting threats that the brisk ocean breeze dispersed. Luke swore he'd never let them go by. He had never run against such an aggressive pack before.

As Luke approached the six-mile mark, he heard somebody running lightly toward him. Lacy burst into view, her face full of barely suppressed excitement. She came at him on his right, and then turned around and ran. She whacked him on the shoulder. "Luke, honest to God, there is a train coming!"

She glanced behind. "Beat the train to the crossing! You will catch all those guys napping!"

Lightly cuffing Luke to get him into high gear, she sped ahead, turning back to wave him on. "Kisses for coming in first at the finish line!" she yelled. She knew that would spark him, give him a new kind of energy.

He picked up speed, and got a terrible stitch in his side, and again yelled, "Hoo-ahh!" three times to get rid of the pain. This time two runners jumped off the trail in fear. Luke's eyes teared up from the wind and the fear and the pain. He crouched down, leaned forward, and rocketed around the wooded corner.

A red-and-white double-diesel Southern Pacific freight train exploded around the corner flying toward the crossing. Its noise and piercing whistle split his ears right after the engineer spotted him. Rhythmically shrieking, one freight car after another pounded toward Luke. And he knew there was no end to it. He knew if he lost the race with the train to the crossing, he'd either die or lose the ribbon.

Lacy already stood on the other side of the train tracks, furiously waving him on. He threw down four more desperate bursts of speed, feeling the ground shake as millions of tons of kinetic energy thundered toward him behind a screeching whistle.

"O no!" He lost his footing and started a fall toward the ground, more like a dive.

Lacy screamed as she saw Luke's shadow plunging toward the front of the locomotive. But Luke hurled himself across the tracks, heels over head, hoping to land again on his feet.

His parachuting-somersault worked, just as Bruce, a Korean war veteran, had taught him. When an attacking soldier thought he had an easy kill, Bruce took five steps forward, dove in a somersault to the ground, flipped back on his feet, and lunged forward to stab the enemy. It worked every time. It was fast, it covered twice as much ground, and it was safer.

Luke remembered the move just in time. As he flipped upside-down and over the tracks, the steep front edge of the train nicked him, enough for blood flow, but Lacy caught him, and hugged him. She wiped off the blood from the back of his head, and pulled him down to a crouch with her. "Look at the runners!" Fifty pairs of runners' legs pumped furiously up and down, running in place on the other side. Some hurled epithets at Luke beneath the cars, but he just laughed. Or tried to. Nothing came out. His lungs screamed, his throat convulsed, his legs withered. Lacy would have none of it.

"Come on, Luke! The race is not over! The clock is still ticking!"

Luke almost fell over again. Lacy leaned down and lifted him up. "Come on, Luke! You only have a handful ahead of you." He nodded. "The rest of it is a piece of cake," she said.

The pain in his side abated and he began running freely and easily, only because Lacy stayed right with him, stride for stride. She veered ahead on shortcuts and then cheered as he went by. Finally, toward the end, she took off on a dead run over to a large cluster of redwoods, behind the finish line.

When Luke flashed across the finish line in his traditional kamikaze sprint, he spotted Lacy, the tenth person down the chute, her long, curly hair windblown and glamorous, and her eyes sparkling. The most beautiful smile crossed her face. Fifty feet down when he turned around to come back, she held her arms outstretched to gather Luke in. They danced around the finish line. They didn't care who saw them. Photographers were there. *Who knew where they were from?*

"You won! You won! You did it!" She almost lifted him off the ground.

"Are you kidding?" Luke responded, lifting her off the ground, breathing in her fragrance. "*We* won. You made all the difference. My coach, my running partner, my cheering squad. And look at you! You didn't even break a sweat. You still smell…delicious."

Lacy pushed away and stood silent. "I hope Dad doesn't hear about it."

Her mood changed when the announcement came over the loudspeaker. Luke not only collected the first place trophy for his school, but also was given a first place ribbon with a burnished silver medallion to hang around his neck. He immediately gave it to Lacy. She walked away and Luke saw her tuck it into her blouse. She waved him over where they could be alone. Underneath the tallest redwoods they began to kiss and they could not stop. "Here we are, under the lilacs again," she whispered.

Luke was ecstatic. "You came out of a dream, into my heart," he sang, reciting the lyrics circulating on the radio. "You're sixteen, you're beautiful, and you're mine."

"I'm not sixteen, mister."

"It's the feeling of the praises, not the words, that count," he said.

No matter what her parents thought, he could win her. He had a future. He had proven himself.

* * * * * * * * * * * * * *

The next day, they hiked to their favorite creek. "Okay, make yourself comfortable," Luke said. Lacy relaxed on the soft creek bank covered with grass. He began to read from *Huckleberry Finn*, just as his dad had done to him, with so much bonding. He wanted her to feel as close to him as Mark Twain caused him to feel with his dad.

"Then we set down, and watched the daylight come, Not a sound anywhere, perfectly still, a nice breeze, so cool and fresh, and sweet to smell the woods and the flowers." He paused. *"It's lovely to live on a raft. The sky all speckled with stars."*

Lacy snuggled up against him. "I love you reading to me. Nobody ever did that for me."

Luke stopped. "Wait a minute. There's some note in the margin. It's grandma's. Must have been her book." He looked at the frontispiece. "It is! Published in... 1929." He looked on the last page. Sure enough, her signature was there. He went back to the raft scene and looked over at Lacy. "She must have been feeling the aches and pains of old age. Here's what she wrote: 'To grow old in heaven is to grow young. There we all advance to the springtime of life.'"

"Well then," Lacy murmured, 'we must be in heaven already."

10

Luke's graduation from Springfield Academy loomed a few weeks away. Luke and Lacy were out on one of their last adventures. Luke loved the adrenaline of high adventure, hiking in beautiful environments, and the challenge of making a lasting relationship with Lacy. Sitting on their favorite ridge overlooking the Pacific Ocean, Luke mused, "I love what this country means to me. This is America, where you can be anybody you set your mind to be. I see everybody as equal, even though your future and mine could go their separate ways. You've gone places I would never be invited."

Gloom drifted down on his shoulders. "Social and economic prejudice is most intolerable to me. Our Constitution says we are all equal. It does not divide people into classes. If we believe it, we will see it."

Lacy sat up straight. "You just might be surprised who I really am, and what I have on my 'To Do' list. I have my dad's De'Luca name, but I am not that De'Luca. I am Lacy. You better believe that!"

"Wow," Luke blurted out. "I've never heard you say anything like that. Maybe we are more alike than our families think. We both want to experience life on our own, see the world as we see it, and go on our own 'Road Not Taken.' Don't you think?"

"You are after *an adventure* that will change your life. I want to *be the adventure* that changes my life." Lacy looked right at him.

Luke stopped and faced her. "I don't want us to follow our own adventures forever, Lacy. I want to meet you at the end of the rainbow. I loved you the first minute I saw you at the beginning of the same rainbow."

Lacy looked away. Luke reached out. "Remember all the songs I sang, when I was learning guitar? Johnny Cash? 'The Boy Next Door.' That's you and me. You were the movie star who went away to find fame and then came back home to me. And I would sing, 'I walk the line, because you're mine.'"

Lacy looked away. "I had my doubts. I felt abandoned when you first went away to California. Except for Jessica I had nobody to talk to. I sang, *"Born too late, to be your baby…"'*

Lacy looked at Luke. "We don't sing songs anymore."

He did not know what she was thinking. So he tried something else. He looked over at Lacy. "When you were gone every summer, I followed all my favorite teams and athletes. Your parents frowned on all that low-brow stuff. You think Gale Sayers of the Bears, Minnie Minoso of the White Sox and Ernie Banks with the Cubs weren't good role models? They helped their teams, the owners, the fans. They made memories for millions of us, inspired us. Thousands of kids moved up, moved out, and made something of themselves because of those guys. They did more than just entertain."

Lacy said, "But I wasn't brought up with any of that."

Luke went on. "They did what they were created to do. Just like Mozart, and Shakespeare, and Moliere. I love reading good literature and good music. We both love to sing. It makes me want to rise up."

"I have gone to symphonies and musicals and plays. I agree with you, Luke."

Luke looked down. "I admit it. I have not gone to many of those. Another thing I love and you don't is boxing. I love boxing. Too blue collar for your dad? I have my heroes here, too. Muhammad Ali. Sugar Ray, even Joe Louis from decades ago. You had to be tough and disciplined for that. I want to be tough like that too."

"My dad encouraged me to be the player, not the spectator," Lacy remarked.

Luke laughed. "What a great quote! That's twice now you have upended me."

Lacy said, "I couldn't help it."

Luke went on. "Lacy, you and I read many classics together. Education is the great leveler. Poor people as well as the rich read Emerson, Thoreau, Hemingway, and F. Scott Fitzgerald. Who can say which mountain of excellence I am going to climb? Or you are going to climb. I will bet you will surprise your family down the road with your own decision."

"You better believe it!"

"It may be something you never thought of. Even with your family's wealth, you could be just as trapped in your options. Nothing is going to trap me. I may not *be* the adventure, but I am going to *live* the adventure I dreamed of, just as Thoreau encouraged us to."

Lacy's eyes were warmer, and her eyes fluttered in anticipation as she looked up to the right.

Luke pressed her. "I loved Doris Day in movies and in song. I thought of you every time I heard her sing "Once I Had a Secret Love", I woke up with that song in my heart every morning whether I meant to or not."

Lacy finally smiled.

"Your dad would never listen to that, huh?" Luke paused. "I'll bet he was never a teenager in love."

Lacy looked away. "Mom listened to it. I know Dad seems to be all business. But he worked himself up from an immigrant to a self-made millionaire. How could he stop now?"

Luke agreed. "I do respect his love for classical music. Thousands of songs have sprung out of Italy. And the Chicago Symphony touches my imagination. My dad listens to that kind of music on the radio every morning. We can't ignore it. But I can't say much about opera."

Lacy quickly responded. "I don't like opera so much, either. But the Chicago Symphony is magical. I love going to their concerts. I love going to plays in Chicago, too. My parents took us as often as they could."

"I never thought I could afford that," Luke said. "But I guess we could have gone. Dad didn't know anybody in those social strata. For sure I had no friends that went to plays or concerts."

Luke kept right on going, wanting to find more they had in common. He went on, "We were about the last family to get television. Dad didn't have time for that. Besides *Victory at Sea* documentaries, my dad actually loved James Garner in *Maverick*. Even *Mr. Peepers*. We both loved Huckleberry Finn, and Robin Hood. He started out by reading them to me. And then he would listen when I read them, just to share them back."

"I want you to read those to me, Luke." Lacy nodded, smiling, and looked toward the deer and wildflowers, maybe lost in thought. "My dad never had time to read to me."

Head down, Lacy shot Luke a sideways look. Happiness flooded through him. *At last!* He thought, then avoided her and glanced up. "Look! A hawk—soaring on the thermal currents. See the hawk? He's searching, too, just like me. He's flying, doing something thousands of birds and millions of people cannot do, soaring for hours. He is the master of all he surveys. The captain of his own ship. Only eagles soar higher. I may never fly up with your father's flock. But I will fly like an eagle some day."

"Why are you telling me this, Luke?"

"Because now I can. And very soon I cannot. I will be gone. And you may move on, flying at your own speed and your own level. I am not going to be trapped like my grandfather. Grandpa was trapped by the times and could only get into his second choice of careers, teaching, and then mainly high school supervision. He became a high school principal because they needed him, and because of his ability to discipline and to command respect.

"He could have been an officer in the Navy. He wanted to be a university teacher, maybe at the University of Chicago, and an author. He wanted to share knowledge at a much higher level. He wanted to be somebody. He wanted to be "a contender," like the boxer said in the movie, "On the Waterfront." His church and his family held him back. And then it was too late."

Lacy found a fallen tree, a grandfatherly black oak that had toppled during one of the harshest winter storms, and led Luke to it. "You could be anything you wanted to be. You love learning. And you are a natural leader. Maybe you'll become an owner of a chain of stores, or a teacher at a university, or a famous singer. Your dad discovered his talent."

Luke frowned. "But where will you be, Lacy? Your dad has other aspirations for you—being married to a lawyer or a doctor or owner of a company. You'll get a business degree and become a leader in management within his chain of department stores. And he will have an idea who you should marry. None of that has anything to do with me."

Lacy moved closer and slapped Luke on the shoulder. "How can you say such things? You don't know me. You don't know what my dreams are. Who elected you as a soothsayer?"

"I want to share this with you now, Lacy. I have been thinking about it a long time. You won't slap me when you hear this. Emerson says what I want to say to you. I want you to keep it. Someday you may read it and find out I am a soothsayer."

Luke opened his journal. "You know he was a minister who became a writer and a transcendentalist. He refused to be trapped. He is well known for his essays. But what a poem he wrote: just for you and me. I picked out the best lines."

He gave her a copy and read it through. Then he held her hands and summarized it, squeezing her hands with each phrase. "Give all to love...obey the heart...let it have scope...hope beyond hope... follow it utterly...cling with life to the maid."

Lacy listened and held up her hand. "Give me a few minutes. I'll read you mine."

She got up and moved a few feet away on that old black oak. Ten minutes later she said, "Okay, come over here, honey."

Luke jumped up and took his place right next to her. He thought she might sit in his lap, so close he was. She read her love message very slowly, looking over at Luke every other line.

> *"Give all to love;*
> *Obey my heart*
> *'Tis a brave mistress*
> *Let it have scope*
> *Hope beyond hope*
> *And far away*
> *Some fine day*

84

The years will fly by
And it'll be just
You and I.

She looked at Luke, suddenly tender and vulnerable. "We both see the end of the same rainbow. Luke, you're in me. You won't go away."

Luke took her up in his lap and kissed her. "I'm not letting you go," he growled. "I'm not going anywhere," she growled back.

Minutes later he loosened his grasp and murmured, "I want you to always remember this evening, Lacy. See the full moon coming up behind us, about to float down this ridge to the ocean right there?"

"Maybe it's just a land of dreams, but dreams can come true."

"Looking so beautiful and new, just like you."

Lacy leaned over and climbed back in Luke's lap. "You are so sweet. How can I forget tonight? We shared so many love morsels."

She kissed him so gently again and again. "You're like a box of Oreo cookies. I can't eat just one."

Then she leaned back and touched his hand. "Luke, have faith in yourself. Even though my family has other ideas, I want you to carry this poem with you."

Lacy handed Luke lines of a poem. Holding his hands, she closed her eyes and crooned,

"I carry your heart with me
Wherever you go
You're always my beau...
Moon River, wider than a mile
We're crossing you in style,
Some day."

They strolled back to the campus and her mansion, hand in hand. They didn't want the night to end. It took them a long time to say good night. They kissed until the moon dropped over the horizon.

Luke's graduation day felt like a denouement, not the climax of his high school years. It was strangely anti-climactic, coming three days after the semester was over. Here he and Lacy had attended the same prep school together during his senior year at Springfield Academy. At his graduation, Luke loved having his parents and his uncles there for the ceremony. He could not believe Lacy did not come. She could not tell him that her father had made appointments for her that week, and she would be travelling during the week. He understood her parents not coming But Lacy not coming?

The next week back in Glenview during a larger family celebration, Lacy and her family returned from their travels and came to the party at Luke's home. Over forty people showed up. His uncles gave little speeches, his dad proposed a toast. Even Lacy stood up in front of her parents and everybody and praised Luke for all he had accomplished. She knew more than anybody what he had done.

Mr. De'Luca managed to avoid Luke most of the time that night. But then after a few drinks, he took Luke aside and said, "Now that you are a graduate, you need to move on and let Lacy enjoy her senior year on her own. We have extracurricular things planned in the Bay Area next year, and we have European plans this summer. We want to introduce her to some other families we do business with."

"What?" Luke was blindsided. "What are you saying to me?"

"Luke, you can't afford to keep up with her travels, the social life her mother has planned for her, and the foreign exchange program I have planned for her."

Mr. De'Luca noticed Luke's stricken look. "You can go ahead and keep your friendship with Lacy. You've been friends since grammar school. But don't confuse friendship with puppy love. Don't let puppy love influence your adult decisions."

Luke bit his lip. He knew better than to challenge an imposing father figure. But he couldn't resist. "I can't believe I am hearing this at my graduation celebration."

Luke felt wounded, disoriented. He looked over at Lacy across the room and looked back at her father. He shrank back. "Why do you pick tonight to rain on my parade? Isn't the timing a little off?"

"I've been meaning to have this talk for some time, Luke. I've just been traveling and busy. I'm sorry I couldn't find a better time. But this is the only time I have left. I'm sorry."

He turned to go away. Luke stepped after him and tapped Mr. De'Luca on the shoulder. "Mr. De'Luca, excuse me, but I just can't do that."

Mr. De'Luca was astounded at Luke's behavior. Luke paused and took another breath. "Don't you think Lacy should be part of this decision? I want to hear it from her."

The gin and tonic spun a corkscrew into Mr. De'Luca's right temple. Two blood vessels pumped purple, and Luke saw he had gone too far. This wouldn't be Mr. De'Luca talking. It would be anger and alcohol.

Mr. De'Luca rose to his tallest height and jerked his head down once as if he was going to head-butt Luke. His lips curled. "Don't come up behind me. Or ever put your hand on me. We're done here."

He turned to go and then looked back at Luke. "And you are not welcome in our home."

Luke rose up on the balls of his feet, high and tight. "What you say has no bearing on my life and my decisions."

When Luke turned away, Mr. De'Luca strode over to Lacy. Taking her arm, he marched through the door without saying anything to Mr. and Mrs. LaCrosse. His wife followed her husband but she stopped and apologized profusely on her way out.

The next day, Lacy called. "Hi, Luke. I'm sorry I didn't get to say goodbye last night."

She paused and he could hear a little catch in her voice. "Luke, my father has given me a chance to go to Italy on a foreign exchange student program. I leave tomorrow. If we are lucky, we can meet again later this summer. Dad told me some of the things you said to him."

"And you believe him without checking with me? Without giving me the chance to explain my side?"

"I can't talk, Luke. I'm so sorry. I let my relationship with Dad go unattended for so long. I have got to catch up and give him some of the time I gave to you."

Luke felt the betrayal. "What you wrote me on our last weekend in California? What about that? Is that all nonsense? How can you do that to me? In a week or a month, you're going to be sorry you turned your back on me. You are going to wish you could hear from me. And maybe someday you'll make your own decisions."

There was a pained silence on the line. Luke gritted his teeth and hung the phone back on the hook, "Good-bye, Lacy."

11

After graduation, Luke was not ready to go to college, despite his dad's carefully accumulated trust fund. Nobody could explain it, least of all Luke in public. Secretly, without his awareness of it, he was hesitant to start college without knowing where Lacy planned to be the next year. He could ill afford to change colleges for many reasons.

Two weeks into the summer, Whitey O'Day, a classmate from Park Academy, totally surprised Luke. He offered Luke a chance to sing and perform starting with a gig on the Fourth of July. Whitey was a genius on the guitar, and had already made a reputation on the North Shore of Chicago. He possessed a confidence for getting gigs that Luke did not, because Whitey saw music as a full-time career. He made a name for himself at some of the same restaurants Matt LaCrosse had. Whitey also had an encyclopedic memory. He already knew over three hundred songs with all the lyrics. Luke was inspired. He even brought back to life his old skills by singing and practicing on his piano at home in the event that a bar or restaurant had a piano.

The summer sailed by. Whitey and Luke even played at resorts around Lake Michigan. People started to talk about Luke going into entertainment full-time, but he took working for his dad seriously. He worked more than eight hours a day delivering furniture at least five days a week, wanting to do his part to help with college costs. Even Mr. De'Luca respected that. When asked, Luke admitted that he was eager to learn the business as well. Maybe he would end up working for his dad (just as he predicted Lacy would). Who knew?

Luke never expected to experience peace with Lacy's family. Then he got a bombshell. The last thing in the world he expected. Mr. De'Luca personally invited Luke to travel to Hawaii with the De'Luca family the last two weeks in August. He approached Luke after church the last Sunday in July. "Luke, could I have a word with you? Let's go out on this little porch away from others."

It was the same porch Lacy and Luke had secretly met in! Luke was sure he was going to catch hell. But Mr. De'Luca reassured him. "I apologize for my intemperate words last spring. I'd like to make it up to you. We have our end-of-summer vacation planned, and we want you with us. We are going to Hawaii. One of our favorite islands is Kauai. Of course we will see Oahu and maybe the Big Island."

"Whaaat? Hawaii?" Luke was thunderstruck. "Me? You are asking me if I want to go? Your family wants to share Hawaii with me?" Nothing like this had ever happened.

"Yes, we do, Luke. You and Lacy kept an exemplary relationship. Very mature. Very impressive. I never heard one complaint. As you may be parting ways this next year, we want to thank you for your leadership and your goal setting. It just took me a while to catch up to you. In the last year many people told me all you accomplished before we even moved here."

Luke was speechless. Finally he said, "Well, I learned from my teachers all the miracles God has done in the past, thousands of years ago. But this is the first miracle I have ever experienced personally. I can never thank you enough for this, Mr. De'Luca. Your generosity is overwhelming."

"We appreciate the high standards you set for Lacy. You encouraged her in her education, her spiritual journey, her musical performances, and her participation in sports. Nobody here could have done that as well as you did."

"You will not regret this, Mr. De'Luca. Thank you so much. I just need to let this all sink in. I don't know what else to say."

"There is nothing further for you to say. The 17th of August we will meet you at O'Hare. Your father can drop you off. Your tickets are paid for. I get excellent business discounts, so don't even think about it. We have separate quarters, condominiums, and separate rooms on board ship. You will have time on your own, Luke, and no obligation to join in all our activities. Just come to Hawaii and do whatever activities and outings you want to do."

He held out his hand. "Will you?"

"Oh, yes, yes sir." Luke was truly out of breath. "And Lacy knows all about it? She's part of the invitation?"

"Of course! You have yourself a good day, Luke."

To Luke it was the best miracle since Japan surrendered.

* * * * * * * * * * * * * *

The first few days in Hawaii were heaven to Luke, better than being Huckleberry Finn with Lacy on the raft, better than being Robinson Crusoe with Lacy on the island, better than being the hero with Lacy in *South Pacific*. He was perpetually delirious, happy to be alive, full of 'happy talk,' enthusiastic about every meal and every outing. He could not imagine anything changing. They swam at a beach better than Waikiki, and rode the waves in an outrigger canoe on Maui. They visited pineapple plantations, and flew along the Na Pali Cliffs on Kauai. They always dined at classy restaurants, usually for three meals a day.

But then one morning Lacy knocked on Luke's door. "Dr. Russ Wilder just called and wanted to know if we'd like to take a short cruise on his yacht. I told him we would. Is that okay?"

"A yacht? The guy has a yacht?"

"He keeps it here. It comes with its own crew. We are just along for the ride. Come on, Luke, it will be fun."

A shock swept through Luke as he opened the door. *What kind of togetherness is this? Cruise on another guy's yacht?*

"Who is this Dr. Russ Wilder?"

They both stood there looking at each other. "Just a friend of the family. He's vacationing here with his girlfriend, Gina."

"What does he do?"

"May I come in?"

"Oh, yes, of course. Have a seat."

They sat across from each other, Luke on the edge of a large blue easy chair, Lacy on a couch with gentle yellow overtones.

"To answer your question," Lacy said gently, "he's very educated. Well read. I think he works for the Defense Department. And he has another family business. He can never talk about it."

"So he's not a surgeon?"

"Not medical. He's pretty far up the chain in the careers he has."

Luke's eyebrows rose, then lowered in a frown. "What do you know about him?"

"He never had a childhood; his dad had him working for the family business before he turned thirteen. He was very mature for his years."

"What does he mean to your family?"

"His dad and my dad were great business partners. Then his dad died suddenly and Russ had to take over the family business. Dad helped him a lot. Now Russ knows a lot of people; he has connections overseas. He and Dad talk things over when Russ is in town."

"But your family isn't just thinking about business."

Lacy blushed. "He's just a friend of the family."

Luke was astounded. "So he knew exactly how to contact you?"

"They must have told him."

"Didn't he think to ask if he'd be interrupting our plans?"

"Oh, no. He called Dad and Mom told him, 'We'd love to see you. You know we enjoy your company. And Lacy would love to see you and Gina. She's always wanted to cruise on a yacht.'"

Luke shrugged. "Okay, give me a few minutes."

Lacy patted Luke on the shoulder as she went out.

Sure enough, Russ sent a taxi for them, and they boarded his yacht right offshore, not far from Hickam and their apartments. From the start, Luke liked Russ. He was very tall, very intelligent, and very socially adept. He had a covert position. He worked with a Colonel and developed a CIA program, which related to Russian energy concerns and lack of sufficient food supply in the future. They had already found a way to get him a Russian honorary Ph.D.

Once when Lacy and Gina were chatting, Russ told Luke some of the books he had read. "I read five or ten books a week," he said quietly. "I have to learn two or three new languages and how to help poor, starving nations feed themselves better."

Luke was aghast. He hadn't read a book all year. "How do you do it?"

Russ smiled. "Just native luck. Nothing I did. They had me take an IQ Test and I measured 157. Who knows where that came from? My dad didn't even finish college. My mother never went to college. Colonel Kinder got me into the self-learning process, where I set goals and self-taught. I was always bored in school. I asked the teachers questions they couldn't answer."

They anchored off of Lumahai Beach on the north side of Kauai, between Haena and Hanalei Bay, and rowed into shore. It was all theirs—one of the most celebrated beaches in the world. Right away, Luke noticed something strange; it was practically empty. He wanted to celebrate this beach with Lacy. It was where Mitzi Gaynor "washed that man right out of her hair," in "South Pacific," both play and movie.

They pulled the boat out of the water. Lacy, Russ, and Gina disembarked and began to walk. The crew members asked Luke to help them pull the boat up a bit more, which he did, feeling as if he was just one of the crew.

He turned to catch up with the threesome. Ahead of them and around the bend were the famous NaPali Cliffs, shrouded with fog and low-lying clouds. Luke thought he was going to break out singing "Bali Hai." It seemed like magic in paradise. Then he noticed Lacy and Russ holding hands, walking slowly down the beach. It seemed to be no big deal to Gina, who walked to the right of them, minding her own business.

Luke stopped dead in my tracks. Paradise turned grey. *This is Lacy? He had read somewhere that wealthy people do such things. It shows they are cool and not possessive. Not small-minded like middle-class types. Good God, they are sophisticated. Connections and getting along with others is good for business and politics and Hollywood. When a foursome goes out to dinner, the wives switch places in the car or limo and ride with the other guy.*

And then, reality smacked him in the back of the head. *What kind of cool crap is that? If I go out to dinner with a buddy and my wife, it's my wife I'm gonna sit with. If I wanted to sit with his wife, I would have married her."*

Luke almost turned around to go back. But then he'd be a sore loser. He slowed down, put his hands in his bathing suit pockets, and dawdled along, not wanting to be part of that little group. He walked in the surf and counted the waves washing over his feet.

Finally, he looked up and they weren't holding hands. They slowed down and waited for Luke. Lacy began talking to Gina. Luke's thoughts were salty. *Here I am Mister Invisible. I have no money, no status, no class, and no career. All I have is a bruised heart. And that's all I have to give Lacy. It ain't pretty.*

Luke caught up. "So what is so interesting?"

Lacy caught the tone of his voice. But she went right ahead, "Luke, Russ and Gina are headed for a cabin Russ has in Durango. They want us to come with them. I've always wanted to go to Colorado. Don't you?"

"Some day, sure."

'Why not this week? This month?"

"I thought we were just doing Hawaii."

"Let's do both."

"How could we do that?" Luke just stared at her. *Russ can do whatever he wants? He found a way to get rid of me?*

Russ broke in with his white knight routine. "'No problem. We have a private plane with six passenger seats. It won't cost you a thing. And the cabin is mine. No big deal. Two stories. Plenty of rooms. I'm happy to share it."

Lacy was thrilled and excited. "Come on, Luke, it will be fun. We've never flown together on a private plane."

Even Gina got into it. "I've got extra bathing suits and clothes that will fit Lacy. And Russ has a whole closet full of things you can wear, Luke. Don't even think about it."

"Okay, okay, let me think about it…"

That had a lot to do with spoiling the whole Lumahai Beach scene where Luke had dreamed of walking alone with Lacy. *Who knew she would begin washing me right out of her hair on that very beach? Luke thought, we should have gone to the south side of the island and walked on Shipwreck Beach. That would have fit our relationship better.* They rowed back to the yacht, and all stood on the bridge together. It was like a foursome in high school. Each person had his or her own freedom. A twosome was gruesome.

Luke always wanted to sail past the Na Pali Cliffs with Lacy. Instead, they all sailed past the cliffs together, with Russ pointing out the landmarks. There was nothing personal between Lacy and him. Lacy just liked to have fun. When she was in a group, she was just a group member. Part of the group. But in Luke's soul and spirit, he thought Lacy and he were a twosome. If they were indeed part of this new deck of cards, he thought they were the only pair of aces.

They anchored at the Hanalei Plantation and walked ashore to a fancy restaurant with its own private brewery. The cool westerly trades blew between them again. The bar waiter came up and asked for their order. "You want a San Miguel beer, Lacy? One of our favorites," Luke said.

Russ said, "I'd like the Kona Coffee flavored beer."

"Oh, I want to try that, too," Lacy said. She was all smiles.

So Luke ordered a San Miguel, Gina ordered a Beck's, and Russ and Lacy savored their Kona Coffee beers.

Lacy sat indirectly across from Russ, and they spent the first five minutes talking about their choice of beer. Gina quietly nursed her beer. She even pulled up a book she was reading, some novel, and put it on the table, like she wanted to sip and read. By this time Luke wished he was reading a novel somewhere, by himself, where no characters could reach out and hurt him.

That was only the first day. It had to get better. On the fourth day, in the evening, as they sat in the lounge of a lovely floating nightclub, Lacy got up from the table and took Luke's hand. They began dancing, and she moved in real close to him, humming the song in his neck. He couldn't switch gears that quickly; he loved her nearness, but was still listening to the screams from his abandoned heart.

"Lacy, where have you been? I have missed you all week."

"You're not missing anything now, Luke."

They danced together for a heavenly half-hour. Russ and Gina sat together for a change. They danced once. Luke didn't see much happening in that relationship. But Lacy was finally dancing with Luke—the kind of togetherness he had anticipated.

When the second week from hell—formerly Hawaii—was over, and they had traveled everywhere on Russ's yacht, rowboat, car, and plane, Luke felt as if Lacy was Russ's as well. Did money talk in paradise?

When they said their goodbyes, they acted like more than family friends. Coming down in the elevator from the sky-high restaurant in Waikiki, Russ and Lacy faced each other in the front, while Gina and Luke stood silently in the rear.

Lacy's face glowed with love and excitement. She seemed overcome with the moment, focused on Russ. Luke had to admit Russ was pretty cool about it. He didn't take advantage of Lacy's gushing.

"I can't wait to come to Colorado and see your place," Lacy said.

Russ smiled. "Oh, you'll love it. We have plenty of room."

"I have never been to Durango."

Luke closed off from the conversation and thought about Bobby Darin's "Dream Lover." That was Lacy all right. She was just a dream.

That elevator was the slowest one he had ever been on.

He was pretty sure he would never forgive Lacy for what she had done to him the last two weeks. He couldn't wait to get the hell out of the elevator.

On the street, it got even worse. Russ was certain he was now Luke's good friend, and so was Gina. Russ and Luke hugged and both said, "Thanks, buddy, it was great to get to know you."

Russ and Lacy hugged for a long time. "Goodbye, I love you!" Lacy exclaimed, with as much love and passion as Luke had ever seen her show. *She just won the WTH award for the year. What the hell?*

Gina played it cool too. When they hugged, she said, "Love you, Luke; so good to see you."

Luke said, "Love you, too."

Russ said, "We'll call you when we get to Durango."

Lacy became the excited one who needed male attention. "We'll be waiting."

You'll be waiting, Luke thought. He asked her, "What was that in the elevator and when you said goodbye?"

She held her hands out. "Russ is such a great guy! A terrific family friend."

Luke grumbled, "It looks like he's more than a family friend."

Lacy said, "Well, didn't he show you he was a friend of yours, too?"

"Of course. He's very sophisticated."

Luke had enough. He looked at Lacy directly. "With a friend like you, Russ surely doesn't need a girl friend."

"Luke, you're out of touch!" Lacy was insulted, as if Luke was the offender.

Luke turned bitter. "You said that perfectly. I *am* out of touch. You don't touch me and I don't touch you."

They went home wordlessly to their adjoining apartments, opened their doors and went inside. What a difference from how the vacation started.

After a long night the next day came and Luke just sat on his bed. He knew Lacy was in her room waiting.

Then it happened. Her phone rang, and she pounced on it. She banged on Luke's wall. "It's Russ! Russ is on the phone."

Luke trudged out of his door, went next door, and entered her apartment. Lacy said, "Russ, Luke is here."

She looked up. "Russ says hi, Luke."

Luke went over and sat next to Lacy. Mr. Invisible. Lacy gushed on, "Oh, I'm so glad you called. We loved spending time with you."

As Russ replied, Luke was in suicidal shock. Luke heard nothing from Gina. Invisible. Gina probably wasn't there. She probably was a prop for Russ. And it was impossible for Luke to get a word in vertically.

Lacy bubbled on, "Russ, I just loved your yacht. Thanks for all you did for us."

She turned to Luke. "We just loved it, didn't we, Luke?'

"Yes, thanks so much, Russ!"

Luke got off the phone and went back to his room. Lacy went on talking until there was absolutely no blood left in his heart. He could still hear her bubbling away. His heart was bubbling away too.

After the call, he could not even talk to Lacy. *Some guy I thought was just a friend showed up, and Lacy threw herself at him—right in front of me. What a fool I was. Now I know. She made it easy on me, actually.*

Luke picked up a fancy kukui necklace he had bought for her. He knocked on her door. By now it was approaching the middle of the day. She opened the door in her adorable blue nightie. She still had it on.

"Luke?"

He off-handed Lacy his gift. "Here's the necklace I got you last week, to remember our times together."

She stood there, knowing he was leaving, her mouth opened in surprise.

"We're not going to Durango together?"

Luke shook his head.

"Are you going home already?"

Luke nodded. "I got my ticket from your dad. I'm leaving today."

She saw his face, empty of all love and tender emotion.

Her eyes widened, and sleep fled from her face. "What's the matter? What have I done, Luke?"

"Nothing you'd understand."

To avoid giving her the mad dog look, he turned away. "Goodbye, Lacy. Enjoy your*self*."

12

September arrived. Lacy entered her senior year at Springfield Academy. After attempts by mail to communicate with her, Luke realized there was no chance. He wanted to try again to apologize, to reconnect. To experience what they shared together before his graduation.

He traveled to Palo Alto and arrived at her sorority house with only one day's notice. Luke spoke to the casual receptionist standing behind a little counter to his left and then took a seat in the waiting room, nicely decorated: leather couches and chairs, tables of maple and cherry, better than anything he had seen before. Luke kept a low profile. Using his peripheral vision, he noticed two frat boys dressed well in sport coats and sitting comfortably, as if they were at home. Luke felt the stranger, all dressed up and nowhere to go. He felt as if he was alone on the stage with no Dave Delaney and no supporting audience.

Luke took a deep breath and in swept the magic fragrance of a different setting, a different planet, with aftershave, and perfume, quiet voices, laughter of anticipation of things to come. From the inner hall stairwell, a girl stepped down and headed his way. All of a sudden, she was right in front of him. Nobody he knew. *She's talking to me?*

"Hi, I'm Natalie," she said, holding out her hand, "Lacy's roommate."

Luke glanced at her, sprang to his feet, and shook her hand. "Hi, I'm Luke," he said. "I grew up with Lacy, went to the same school."

"I know," she said. "She's told me all about you. You had a wonderful childhood together. You both were in sports, and you sang together at times in concerts, and you went to the same church. You skated on a cold pond in the winter. You swam in the pond in the summer."

Luke was taken aback. Lacy and he had a wonderful childhood?

"Childhood, "he smiled. "Well, I guess that puts me in my place." He shrugged his shoulders.

"No, no," Natalie exclaimed. "I didn't mean it that way at all! I don't think she will ever forget you. After all, you were her first real boyfriend."

"Whew! That makes me feel a lot better." He then stepped back, stunned. He looked back at Natalie and was taken aback by his attraction to her. Natalie had the most kissable lips and the most beautiful blonde hair he had ever seen. It was feathered, or something like it. So delicate and feminine. He didn't know what to say.

She picked up on his attention. "Well, life goes on," she said, tilting her head and raising her eyebrows. "You never know what tomorrow will bring."

Natalie started to step away, and then turned back. "Oh," she said, "Lacy told me she will be down in a few minutes. You can visit a little until it's time for her to go to the concert."

Lacy had a whole new group of sorority friends in addition to a handful of frat boys anxious to get to know her better. She finally came downstairs with three other girls, dismissed herself, then turned toward Luke. He hardly knew what to think. She was so grown-up, so self-assured. Despite her welcoming smile, as she approached, her eyes seemed to change focus. She saw him as part of her surroundings, not as her first relationship, her first love, her first kisses.

Luke stood up, hands hung at his side, quelling the desire to gather her into his arms and "ride the storm out," pulling her back into the Golden Age of their relationship, forgetting all the years between. Lacy stopped a few paces away. And then she leaned forward with all social grace. "It's so good to see you, Luke," she murmured. "What brings you here?"

"*You,*" Luke wanted to say. Instead, he replied, "I'm checking out a few colleges and universities in the San Francisco area." He couldn't take his eyes off her. So he blinked and said, "Have you looked in this area or would you rather go back to the Chicago vicinity?"

"It all depends on where I may get a scholarship," she said, looking right at him. "And which one my father is favorable towards. He still wants me to go into business administration, but I am not sure. It seems limiting to me. My travels make me think of other careers."

Luke nodded. He didn't know what to say. His mind dwelled in the past, and Lacy's focus was on the future. Luke felt a little out of time and place, not just to him, but to her as well. So sweet and kind she was still, but a little removed, unable to share herself. Lacy kept the conversation on him, what he was doing, where he was going to college, how his casual singing career was going.

After a moment, she asked, "Do you still think about a military career?"

"Well, yes," he admitted, feeling out of place on this campus. He would have to be an officer for Lacy to keep him in her life. He wasn't ready for college. Luke felt awkward, talking about himself. His future was out of his reach at the time.

The little visit seemed a blur, a dream gone awry. He hardly knew Lacy anymore. She was gorgeous, more beautiful than he had ever seen her. And she still had a sweet smile for Luke when she said good-bye. It was the shortest hug he'd ever experienced.

He turned around and glumly, numbly began to walk out. Then he spotted Natalie in the doorway with two of her sorority sisters. Luke headed right for Natalie and began to sing, just as if he were on stage. He opened his arms and began serenading her, "I lost my true love on the river of no return."

His well-trained voice mesmerized the whole room. It rang out and rang true. He got down on one knee in front of Natalie, "gone, gone forever, on the river of no return," then hammed it up a little with the chorus, "waileree, waileree, on the river of no return."

Luke quickly rose to his feet and enveloped Natalie in a quick but romantic embrace. He said, "Goodbye, honey," and kissed her on the cheek before he disappeared out the door.

The movie's gorgeous scenery and its plaintive wail would run through his mind every day for a while. He went home and joined the Air Force with two close friends in the fall of 1958. He wanted to travel. To get started. To reach his own goals. No Lacy.

Yes, Luke wanted to get far away. He would save money during his duty, get the GI Bill, and go back to school. The University of Arizona had the best ROTC program west of the Mississippi. He would become an officer. And he would finally have a chance to become a pilot. He knew his family would be proud, happy, excited. And so would he.

He climbed out of *The River of No Return* after taking the Air Force charter plane to Lackland Air Force Base in Texas. He wanted a change. Little did he know.

Book Two
USAF

13

The first week of basic training at Lackland Air Force Base started out with death of all individuals. The Training Instructor's (TI) first task was to wipe out the individual clothing choices of the newly arrived "rainbow" multi-colored clothed recruits into one shade of Air Force fatigues. These dead seeds planted into the ground down in Texas had to go through a lot of mud before they could blossom into a good crop of wheat. That required a lot of yelling and verbal abuse. The training instructors reminded Luke of thunderstorm micro-bursts that wiped out the multicolored flowers and reduced everything in their paths to mud. The rain seemed to stick on the faces of some of the troops. They were unwilling to let the others see them crying. For most, it was the first time away from home. Luke had gone away to a prep school as a junior and had no problem.

Just the same, when the submarine emergency-dive horn blasted the barracks awake at 0400 hours, Luke still rolled over and fell out of bed. He had never been on a top bunk before. His dreams of Lacy turned into nightmares on the way down. As Luke swung airborne off his top bunk, he narrowly missed Chance's shoulders on the lower bunk.

"Sorry about that," he said as he thumped on the floor.

Chance looked up. "Not your fault. I forgot you were up there."

Sergeant Fisher stood atop the stairs at the near end of the barracks, flipping the ceiling lights on, the light blinding his recruits. Both his voice and body stood bolt upright. From deep down in his diaphragm, fierceness billowed up and erupted from between his half-clenched teeth. "Listen up, people! You have two minutes to get dressed, two minutes to use the latrine, and two minutes to fall-out for calisthenics. Get moving!"

Sergeant Fisher was a short, tough guy with broad shoulders and dark hair, the square face of a boxer, and the demeanor of a prison guard at a concentration camp. The room grew colder when he appeared. His toned muscles and lean physique bristled through his uniform, showing the kind of man who completed sit-ups, push-ups, and pull-ups before breakfast. His after-shave lotion exuded confidence; you could almost smell it. He leaned forward on the balls of his feet much like a prizefighter ready to throw the first punch. Luke half-expected him to start the boxer's bounce.

Luke followed the eyes of a recruit across the aisle, at the far end of the barracks, where Sergeant Reeves loomed. Reeves looked like a hawk ready to sink his talons into a warren of rabbits. He didn't have to say anything. Reeves stood tall with blond hair and a long face. His physical presence stood in for a sergeant's shout. He had a fighter pilot's calm self-assurance, standing a full head above everybody, with his head cocked as if to say, "I dare you to say anything."

Luke had been warned about Reeves. He appeared friendly, and then *wham*! You were the enemy. He spoke sparingly, but when he did talk, watch out. They headed for their lockers at opposite ends of the double bunk. Chance's bottom bunk faced the center of the barracks. Luke's top bunk faced the outside window covered in black. Through a slit on the right side, he saw nothing but black.

Luke reached into his locker with its odor of new clothes and pulled out his neatly folded fatigue pants and shirt, then scrabbled for his boots, one jammed with socks, the other with rolled under-wear. Dressing faster than he had ever dressed in his life, he stood erect, practicing the chest-out, shoulders-back-and-down posture the military demanded of all its personnel. Other recruits all around him could not keep up. Already the barracks had an unwashed wrinkle-the-nose smell to it.

At the long line of sinks and mirrors, Luke caught a glimpse of Chance standing next to him. He measured Chance at about six foot two, with black hair and grey-green eyes that commanded attention even early in the morning. Chance's thick, dark eyebrows were equally commanding.

The two rinsed their mouths, forgot their new crew-cuts and through habit ran combs over their shaved heads. Then they rushed back to their bunks. Chance grabbed his hat and asked, "Am I good?"

Luke took a breath, paused, and nodded. "You're good."

Fisher pounded down the center of the barracks, heels shaking the old wooden floors. Luke and Chance stood at attention, screwed into the floor like their bunk. They stood only seven bunk spaces down from the sergeant's office. Fisher stuck his chest out and got into Chance's face, yelling as loud as Luke had ever heard anybody yell at close quarters. "Hey, butthead! Did I say anything about socializing?"

He jabbed his right index finger into Chance's chest. "Where's your hat, boy? You step out of this barracks without your hat on your head, you are out of uniform. You understand me, boy?"

"Yes, sir."

"Don't 'sir' me. I work for a living."

Fisher turned to Luke. "You, slick-sleeves. Do you want to earn your stripe?"

Luke looked out from beneath his eyebrows. "Yes."

"Yes, what!"

"Yes, sergeant."

The sergeant jumped into his face. "Keep your eyes straight forward! Do not move your head. Do not look at me! I take that as a challenge. And you do not want to challenge me. I eat guys like you for breakfast. Poached eggs."

He looked around the barracks, searching for any violation he could detect. He appeared as if he would address Chance. Luke's shoulders drooped just a little as he slipped into a bodily sigh of relief.

Sergeant Fisher turned back to Luke, fierceness etched across his face. "With your issue of uniforms yesterday, all of you were given a one-page summary of military rank. You were to memorize it." Without looking at Luke, he commanded, "Airman, what is my rank?"

Luke looked out of the corner of his eyes to check. He saw four stripes, breathed in, and answered carefully. "Sergeant."

The sergeant got back in Luke's face. "Son, whenever you follow my orders or answer my questions, you give me the answer, and then you will address me." He paused and yelled. "With respect. I am not your mama. I am not your friend. I am your sergeant. Do you understand me?"

"Yes, sergeant."

Sergeant Fisher looked around the room, boring into the eyes of every recruit, all drill bit and jackhammer, sending the message to everybody. He stood at parade rest stance, hands behind his back, two feet in front of Luke. "Now that is understood, I want an answer. What is my complete rank?"

Luke stared straight ahead, froze. Surely, he's a sergeant, but what kind of sergeant? A close guess couldn't hurt. "Five stripes. Your rank is technical sergeant, sergeant."

Fisher's eyebrows flickered up in approval. "You got it right." Turning to the other forty-some recruits, he barked, "Make sure you understand how we talk here. You address me after any comment or answer you make. Am I understood?"

The whole second floor of the barracks rocked. "Yes, Sergeant!"

Fisher walked down the center aisle. "I want everybody to look exactly the same as the next man. Nobody is better than or different from his barrack-mates. Same shoes, same uniform, same cap, same haircut, same clean shave. This is a first for you sorry rainbows that came in here, all wearing different clothes and different haircuts."

14

Sergeant Reeves clumped up the aisle from the far stairwell. He yelled at the rest of the recruits in his distinctly southern accent. "Y'all don't make the same mistake those two girls did. You signed up to follow orders, to learn the military way of life, to do as y'all are told. Do not speak, or eat, or drink, or take a crap without us telling you."

He dressed down Luke and Chance with his eyes. "No talking for the rest of the day! Dress up and line-up, two by two."

Luke sighed silently to himself. He didn't like mistakes. He never drew attention to himself. Flamboyance was not his strong suit. But he didn't like being singled out, either. Who had that right? Oh, yeah, the drill instructors.

Luke's broad shoulders squared with an easy air of self-reliance. He and Chance spun around and lined up facing the stairs. Fisher began walking back up the floor to lead the men.

"Forward, huh!" Fisher barked and marched to the head of the line.

Twenty bunkmates and forty recruits flowed toward and then down the stairs. Sergeant Reeves brought up the rear. "Don't be walking," Fisher yelled. "You're in the Air Force now. I want to hear a heel beat. One heel beat. You will learn to march together. You will march everywhere."

Sergeant Fisher lined them up outside on that bitter September morning. Two rows of twenty, facing him. There were shadows everywhere, only two lights shining out from each barracks built forty feet apart. The barracks lined the street for as far as Luke could see. They were weather-beaten and unstylish. He guessed they were built before the Army Air Force became the Air Force in 1947.

Sergeant Fisher broke into Luke's reverie. "People, it's time for calisthenics. Side-straddle hop. Move apart so you don't get in each other's way. On the count of one, begin. Do as I do."

The sergeant jumped and placed his legs far apart, with his arms over his head, then brought his legs together and slapped his arms against his legs. "One-two! One-two! Three-four! Three-four!" That's one count! Nineteen to go! He did the four-count until he had twenty. Luke and Chance kept up with the sergeant, unwilling to be singled out again. But a muffled groan leaked out of a skinny guy in the back row.

"Okay!" The sergeant yelled. "This candy-assed recruit just got you twenty more! The second groan gets you twenty more!"

They hit the ground and did twenty more. Luke turned his head back in time to hear Fisher yell, "Hit the ground, girls! I want twenty push-ups right now. Your chest will hit the ground. If it doesn't, we'll have your foreheads on the ground. Push up as far as you can go. No halfway push-ups!"

The squad labored through the push-ups. Airman Second Class Davis, the sergeant's mean and tough assistant, walked through the lines, either yelling at or praising each recruit he passed. One recruit, Landon, froze at the top of his push-up, his arms locked. Davis leaned down and pushed Landon to the pavement, smacking his face on the pavement. "What's the matter with you? You got frozen elbows? Don't be stopping halfway. We don't do halfway here."

They bit their lips and tried to avoid grunting. They finished the second twenty, hoping for a short break. They didn't notice that Sergeant Reeves disappeared to coordinate his troops' arrival at the dining hall.

A minute later, Fisher yelled, "Troops, get up! Stand at attention!"

Luke and Chance stood up, breathing hard but now fully awake. The rest of the platoon staggered to their feet. Some looked over at the dining hall. Luke swallowed, mouth dry, dying for a cup of coffee, or anything with caffeine.

"Run in place, gentlemen! Run in place, knees up as high as your chest, and count with me."

As the sergeant raised his knees high, he cried out, "One." They all kept running in place. Eight steps later, the sergeant cried out, "Two!" Eight steps later, "Three!" Eight steps later, "Four!" Luke thought they were finished... but *no*. The sergeant marched them through a different pace, speeding to a count once every four steps. As they began sweating profusely, he accelerated the count to every two steps. Then it was a one count for each staccato step—"one, two, three, four; one, two, three, four; one, two, three, four!"

Three recruits fell to the ground, gasping. "Somebody pick up those city boys!" the sergeant howled. Luke and Chance and one other airman ran forward. Each grabbed a fallen recruit and yanked him to his feet.

"Get back in place!" the sergeant yelled. The whole unit huffed and hyperventilated as though it were one big dragon.

"Attention! Get in formation! Four lines! Square off!" The unit formed four lines with each recruit squared off with everybody in his line.

"Forward, march!"

Fisher began by stepping up front, and then fell back so he walked alongside the unit. He counted cadence as each left foot hit the ground. Sergeant Reeves marched two steps near the back on the right side. The unit marched down the street toward the dining hall on the left.

This time, Sergeant Reeves called it. "Left oblique, huh!" The four leaders in front, coached by Airman Davis, took off at a slant toward the dining hall. They jumbled into a parallel spot as they drew closer.

"You want to eat, next time you will do the oblique correctly! Do I make myself clear?"

"Yes! Sergeant!"

"I can't hear you!"

"YES! SERGEANT!"

When it was their turn, they marched into the dining hall in single file.

"Take your tray, hold it out in front of you, and sidestep down the line," Sergeant Fisher said quietly but forcefully enough for everybody to hear him. "And stand tall! That's all!"

"What does he mean?" the recruit behind Chance whispered.

"Watch that guy in front of us," Luke said while looking straight ahead. He didn't want Fisher giving him hell for talking twice in one morning.

"Where are the glasses, Sergeant?" one squad leader asked.

Sergeant Fisher snorted. "There's a stack of bowls right in front of you. Pick up the bowl and push the button to fill your bowl with milk. You have not earned your glasses yet. You will drink out of your bowls like dogs!"

Luke and Chance exchanged looks, their eyebrows raised. Who knew? *My uncles never told me about this*, Luke thought as he finished half his tray of breakfast, working through two heavily fried eggs, burnt toast, and greasy sliced potatoes.

Fisher moved to the front of the group. "Everybody up! Dump your trays into those barrels and get into formation outside."

Luke stared in disbelief. How could this sergeant, or any sergeant in the Air Force, be such a bastard? The whole platoon shuffled over to the waste barrels and dumped out their food, looking at it longingly.

"Get up straight!" Sergeant Reeves barked, bringing up the rear. "Line up and take this like men."

They lined up outside and waited at attention.

Fisher and Reeves stood in front of the group. Fisher brought his arms behind his back and leaned forward. "Men," he said with a tight smile, "there are a whole lot of people you will forget in your lives, but you will never forget Fisher and Reeves."

Sergeant Fisher took a step toward the group. "Your first duty is k.p. Before we teach you anything, we will train you to work for your food. Your mamas don't live here. Nobody is going to feed you and pick up after you. Starting today, you will earn your privileges." He turned around and pointed. "We have sixteen hours of peeling potatoes back in the kitchen. You're going to help feed a thousand men today."

"Yes, Sergeant! The yells came from every row. "Yes, sergeant."

During patio breaks outside the dining hall and outside each barracks, the airmen bought Cokes or Pepsis and relaxed between six-hour straight shifts. A roof of crossbeams and vines covered each patio, which contained a couple of trees and soft drink machines with benches here and there that nobody used. A radio played pop music. Most of the airmen knotted together in bunches and bantered about basic.

Basic training was a tough and challenging environment. Getting along with your bunkmate was the first part of learning teamwork. "You will work with whoever we assign you," Fisher said earlier in the morning. "And if you cannot get along, don't expect us to find somebody that fits your personality."

Luke and Chance drifted out of one group. Luke studied the ground and looked up. "So, where are you from?"

"You wouldn't know it. My family owns a farm outside a little town north of Chicago."

"Seriously? I'm from Glenview. Where did you fly out of to get here?"

Chance shook his head. "Some airport on the south side of Chicago. They took forever to bring up the plane and get us all boarded. What about you?"

"Same place. Amazing. I didn't notice anything. We waited half the night to board the plane. It was my introduction to the military routine of, 'Hurry up and wait.' Speaking of wake-up, did you get any sleep on the trip down?"

"No, but I knew how a sardine feels jammed up in a small tin with a hundred other sardines." Chance shook his shoulders as if they were still crammed together. "At least the sardines are dead. When we landed at Lackland, all down and dirty, they put us right into a regular day."

The next day, Luke, after ten straight hours of marching, plopped down on a break bench on a barracks patio—for ten minutes. For a moment, nobody else trudged over. Luke missed his family, his mom, her cooking. All of a sudden, he thought of Mrs. De'Luca, Lacy's mom. *Hmmm. Lacy's favorite person is her mother. I hope she doesn't follow her mom, from a middle class family like mine, who is trapped into the rigid wealthy family lifestyle. She does not have equal status for sure. She has no status. And I bet Mrs. De'Luca has hidden feelings with Mr. De'Luca trying to run Lacy's life.*

He frowned, sitting there silently. *Mr. De'Luca is going to want Lacy to marry wealth. His wife will be dead set against it. Hey, that's one thing on my side. Oh, maybe that's why she feels close to Lacy. Lord knows she can't talk to her husband about it.*

That evening, as he lay in the top bunk, he lay puzzled. *How did Lacy develop her interest in the lower class? Maybe it was the family of servants who came every day to do all De'Luca housework and child care? Oh, yeah, it's the whole family of servants they had, poor people from Jamaica, who loved her more than anybody in her family did. No wonder. That's it! And she'd never admit it. Love talks, and money walks. Love is more important to a child than a dad who spends all his time at work.*

We are just like the Jamaicans. In basic training, we are the most common people in the world. The sergeants make sure we know that. We are lower than a dachshund pup, or poop. She's going to Stanford, a top university anywhere, not just California. Her family is strictly Republican from the day she was born. They won't even talk about FDR. Truman was a low-life commoner. Maybe I just don't know her, just like she said. He finally fell asleep, and paid for it the next day.

The next day at around four o'clock, exhausted and not wanting to talk with anybody, Luke got another ten-minute breather at the break bench. He took a long swig from a Coca-Cola, frowning as he banged it on the table.

Why doesn't Lacy admit it, she fears committing too soon to a man who cannot maintain her in the manner to which she is accustomed. Why does she think about all the poor and sick in the world? Her family never sees that side. Is that just a way to avoid me? Here I am a total nobody in basic training, the best ego-leveler in the world. We are nothing. We are "slick sleeves," no stripes on our uniform, in between civilians and nobodies. And here she wants to go out and help people lower than me. She even talks about going out of the country and working in the Peace Corps some day. Her dad would never let her do it.

The next day, after twelve hours of peeling potatoes, he had a change of heart. *Okay, I was wrong. Lacy really is more concerned about the world community, in particular, thinking about elevating people out of poverty. Maybe it's her reaction to having life too easy. We may be more alike than I think. One week she kept talking to me about the Peace Corps. She had to write a big research paper in the library. Why did she pick that? That's all she talked about for a month.*

On Friday, he sat down again on the same break bench working over the Lacy puzzle. This time he mumbled to himself, *what was I thinking? The last time I saw her, she threw me away like a childhood toy. Since she was in high school, her dream was to live near her father's big department stores, outside Chicago. She will get some kind of business administration degree. And her salary and future would be promising. So where does that leave me? Her desire to help others may have been just to win independence from her dad. Give her the benefit of the doubt. Maybe she will do it on the side or when she retires.*

Later, after sixteen hours of k.p. duty and a rushed supper, right before the lights went out, Luke and Chance had ten minutes to talk. Somehow it stretched to twenty minutes.

Luke shook his head. "Remember those late nights when everybody else was asleep, and you could raid the refrigerator? A glass of milk and a peanut butter sandwich on fresh-baked bread?"

Chance nodded. "It makes me hungry just to think about it. And I miss standing at my bedroom window where I could look right out and see our horses in the pasture."

"You're lucky you lived on a farm. Was your dad strict like Fisher and Reeves?"

"Are you kidding?" Chance frowned. "Not at all. My dad cared first about his horses. His other animals came a distant second. I was somewhere further down the line."

"You're lucky. *My dad was a Navy Corpsman during WWII.* When he came home, he never wanted to see one more wound or one more dead body, especially if it was a young soldier. I don't know if he'll ever get over all that. It was either sing or go crazy, so he started singing, and when he got home and I grew up a little, he got me singing. And life was so good. We sang in places I never thought

I'd be allowed in. But later he was so involved in his businesses; he had no time for me."

Chance wanted to know more. "So what kept you going?"

"My little sisters. Jessica is only a year younger than I am. Rachel is three years younger. My sisters were such fun. Anything I did with them they treasured. I didn't see it then. They really loved me. If I asked them how they were doing or how they liked what we were doing, like riding bikes, or playing hide-and-seek, or swimming in the lake, they would actually say, 'If you are happy, then we are happy.'"

Chance said. 'You can't beat that."

"What are the chances of us hearing that now? I was so lucky and didn't know it." Luke scuffed the floor with his right foot.

Chance grinned. "Same with me. My sisters, my horses, and my girlfriend." He sobered up. "Ah, crap, but she dumped me, right before I enlisted. Some rich guy swept her off her feet. I tried to warn her. But money talks and the farm boy walks."

"My girlfriend's dad ruined everything for me," Luke said. "Mr. De'Luca. His new wealth is like giving a gun to a baby. The baby doesn't know the power it has. The baby doesn't really care. Babies want everything given to them. Who gave him the gun? Do wealthy people live in castles over in Italy or what? He went from swimming in the moat to becoming king of the castle."

He sighed. "I gotta give him credit, though. He is a genius in business. Lacy said it was the quality of Italian clothes and Italian shoes that made the difference. He and his brother came over with nothing but ideas and the willingness to work. And they brought with them real Italian shoemakers. They delivered on quality."

Chance grunted. "We thought only cowboys wore jeans. Dad said the defense industry stocked up on them because they discovered how strong and tough and lasting they were. I had jeans that lasted me over five years."

Luke said, "Somehow the De'Luca's cashed in on the American craze for blue jeans during the war and after the war. My uncle told me, 'It's better to be lucky than smart.'"

Chance guessed. "Maybe the defense workers came home and they got the middle class interested in jeans. Many of them were middle class."

Luke said, "Were there many dude ranches out West? Maybe the rich people discovered jeans there and came home looking for them. People always idolized cowboys."

Chance said, "I have no respect for rich people walking around thinking they are tough cowboys."

Luke said. "I hope you and I are rich some day, walking around in blue jeans. And I hope Lacy is in blue jeans walking with me and holding my hand."

Chance said, "That thing about absence. Maybe it will work for us. It's so close to Christmas."

At that moment, the lights went out. Sergeant Fisher did the yelling. "Airman Davis put you a test. He gave you ten minutes for talking. Nobody paid attention to it. You all took twenty minutes. So you will pay attention to this. No more talking! Get some sleep: You are going to need it. Sometime this week Reeves and I will plan a midnight hike."

15

Luke began to look forward to the last day of basic training. Other graduates had told him what to expect: an audible heartbeat, lungs full of long-held air, and anxious moments standing in front of the big bulletin board outside the classroom, waiting to see what would be posted. Both Chance and Luke heard from the grapevine that the Air Force could go back on the promises the recruiters had made. Many fellow recruits in adjoining barracks, men with whom they had marched, had been summarily detailed to Cook School.

"Can you imagine cooking for a bunch of GI's?" Chance said.

"I'd go AWOL the first chance I got," Luke said, laughing.

Finally, the day arrived. Chance nudged Luke and pointed to the top of the bulletin board. There, on a list with fourteen others, he found the names he sought: Chisholm and LaCrosse.

Basic Weather Observing School
Chanute Air Force Base, Illinois
Departure time 0500 Friday tomorrow: 17 January 1961

Luke shook his head. "When my recruiter told me I would get into weather school, no problem, like a dummy, I believed him. I think we were lucky."

Chance chuckled. "The life expectancy of recruiters is shorter than most."

Luke responded. "We're both lucky in this case. Chanute is close to your farm and close to my home as well. We can get back there once in a while on a weekend."

"We might see if we still have any clout with our ex-girlfriends." Chance shrugged his shoulders. "Who knows?"

"As one-stripers? I don't think so." Luke stepped forward, smiled, lifted his eyebrows, stuck out his right thumb and forefinger, leaving an eighth of an inch between them. "Lacy will tell me she cares this much, divided by ten."

Chance took a step back, a puzzled look on his face. "How could you know that?"

Luke frowned and looked away. "I told you, man. Her parents call the shots. In this case, I'm the target."

Chance reached out and smacked Luke on the shoulder. "It can't be worse than my situation. Paula fell for the guy whose money and glitter promised her more than I could."

Luke felt his own fire extinguish. He felt the grip around his heart softening. His shoulders dropped. "How the hell did that happen?"

"He had a '57 Thunderbird. I had a Ford pickup. He belonged to a country club. I worked with horses out in the country. Here's the choice: golf, your own caddy, drinks at the ninth hole, versus sweat, your own horse manure, and a beer to go, down the road. Uh, let me think." Chance began to laugh.

Luke threw back his head and startled Chance with a full belly laugh. "You could be a comedian."

"Yeah, and three thousand of them are out of work."

"So what will you do on weekends?"

Chance moved forward, dismissing the subject. "Help with the horses. Find out what happened to that cute redhead growing up next door."

"You are making that up!"

"No, I'm not. And besides, as far as Paula is concerned, it's mind over matter."

"What do you mean? What does mind have to do with matter?"

"I don't mind, and she don't matter."

Luke guffawed and slapped Chance on the back. "You made me laugh twice in the past two minutes. Stick around, bro."

Sergeant Reeves walked up behind them. "You two had better get moving. And get ready for cold-ass weather. You're leaving sunny warm southern Texas for a godforsaken Air Force Base surrounded by acres of frozen corn-stalks."

* * * * * * * * * * * * * *

Frost turned to snow in Illinois. Snow turned to ice. Fog crystals clung to dark thin windows throughout the weather training barracks. When January rolled into Illinois, so did the coldest weather of the year. On that first Monday, Sergeant Hamilton stomped into the leaky old World War II barracks at 0500. "Off the hock and grab a sock," he yelled. "At 0520, your beds *will* be made, you *will* be dressed, and we *will* march to the dining hall."

From the right side of the barracks came a groan. Sergeant Hamilton nodded, anticipating that response. He heard it all the time. He stood up even straighter and yelled, "Didn't you learn anything in basic? You have no life except the one we give you. You can't do anything unless we tell you." He turned to address the left side of the barracks. "And after breakfast, we *will* march to the weather school. On the way, we *will* learn how to make sixty-three heels hit the pavement at the same time."

Hamilton walked over to the groaner, now sitting on his locker. He stepped backwards, leaned back, and kicked up his heel. In a flash, he propelled his foot forward on a horizontal line, a rattlesnake strike, too quick to measure speed. Hamilton's boot stood motionless a half-inch from Livingston's face, his point made. "How's that for precision?" he said. "That's the kind of precision I learned, and that's the kind of precision I will teach you."

Like every other man in the barracks, Luke and Chance stood there with their mouths open.

The sergeant rooted to the floor on one foot and slowly lowered his shiny black lethal weapon. "Now you only have five minutes to use the head and five minutes to get those bunks made up tight. I want to bounce a quarter on that blanket."

Outside, Sergeant Hamilton assembled the trainees in rows of four. "I need two squad leaders."

Shivering, Luke, Chance, and two others raised their hands despite the cold. The sergeant nodded at Luke and Chance. "Your names!" he hollered.

"Chisholm!"

"LaCrosse!"

The sergeant pointed to Luke. "You, in front." Then he pointed to Chance. "You, in the rear."

They took their places, secretly stomping their brogans to get warm.

"Dress right, dress!" the sergeant yelled. Except for the outside man, three men in each row stuck out their right hands and stood an arm's length from each other. "Today before we march, I want you to convince me you are *serious* about your life in the Air Force. You will learn this one sentence."

Hamilton looked around and cleared his throat. "Boy, are we enthusiastic!"

He walked forward alongside the fledgling cold-weather warriors. He turned to face them. "Your turn!" he yelled.

An anemic chorus broke the cold morning grip. "Boy, are we enthusiastic!"

"I can't hear you!"

The response grew. "Boy, are we enthusiastic!"

"More emphasis on *we*," Hamilton commanded. "If you want to eat, you better get it right. Come on, you greenhorns! Rookies! Babies! Yell like men, for Chrissakes!"

Chance and Luke gritted their teeth and turned to their charges. "Listen up, people! Let the sergeant hear you!"

The whole unit roared in a single voice. "Boy, are we enthusiastic!"

Their yell burned the frost off the windows.

A small grim smile crossed the sergeant's face. He tried to hide it. "Forward, march!" he yelled.

16

They walked up two flights of stairs and marched into the classroom. "Take your seats!" the sergeant yelled.

They sat. "I'm Tech Sergeant Jacobs." Jacobs turned to his desk and picked up a stack of thick handouts. Walking across the classroom, he slapped six packets on the desktop of the airman sitting at the end of each row.

"Take one and pass the others down." The sergeant had a medium build, average height, and angular features, like somebody from the South who grew up hungry. His eyes were sharp and darting underneath beetling eyebrows so bristling that nobody wanted to piss him off. His perpetual frown ploughed a deep half-inch furrow between his eyes. The men sat quietly, paging through their handouts, subdued.

Back in the front of the classroom the sergeant cleared his throat. "You've been here a week. You've had orientation. Now you need to memorize these documents of basic Weather Observing School. Never mind paging through this, turn to the front where you will find the syllabus."

Along with twenty-eight others, Luke and Chance picked up their packets and glanced at the syllabus and readings for the first week. The atmosphere of the classroom squeezed them with its windowless age, faded color, dark lighting, and low maintenance. Pitched into a second-story corner of a sooty brick building, it seemed more like a hastily fabricated prison than an exciting repository of valuable weather information.

"Listen up, people!" Without a blink, the weather instructor plowed into his thought. "I don't know where you will be assigned if you complete this training. So I have to prepare you for every kind of duty station throughout the US. Do you have any idea of the mountains of data you will learn to earn your Specialty Code?"

Sergeant Jacobs yanked down a national map four feet high by six feet wide, the ripping and clattering sound reminding Luke of old blinds. As the map fluttered on the wall, he impaled it with his baton at each of the four corners. "At some point," he continued, all growl now, "you will be expected to know how to read a national weather map in QuickTime. You will be the one providing fifteen important pieces of weather data for your duty station. And you will know how to read all the information from the other stations."

He paced up and down in front of the class. "Follow along with me with your weather school packet. You need to get a sense of all we do." Then he waved his finger, as though admonishing them. "But before you leave today, return the packets. I don't want anybody to have an unfair advantage and work ahead of where we are."

"What?" The chorus of surprise rippled around the classroom.

"You will all do fine. Open your booklet and follow along: warm and cold fronts, their diagrams." He pointed at Chance. "Chisholm, look up at the map here. From what you see, what do you call that curved blue line coming down out of Canada across Montana? Note the sharp little triangles hanging down from it every half-inch or so."

Chance studied the booklet and glanced back at the wall map. "It's a cold front, Sergeant."

The sergeant gave a small nod of approval. He pointed at Luke. "LaCrosse, what do you call the curved red line coming out of the Gulf of Mexico and stretching up to Oklahoma?"

"A warm front, Sergeant?"

He frowned. "I asked you. Don't answer me with a question. Describe for the class what symbols you see hanging down from that line."

"I see round half-circles on the top of the line, Sergeant."

The sergeant stood near Luke's desk. "Good job. You observed what you saw, the half-circles on top of the line, not what I called it hanging down from the line. You called it right. Even though I gave you misleading information."

Jacobs pointed to Chance. "Now you call it. Is it a warm front or a stationary front? Tell me what you know."

Chance looked at his booklet and wrinkled his brow. "I know it's a warm front, Sergeant. I don't know about a stationary front."

The sergeant walked over to the other side of the classroom. "Pay attention here. You will learn how to record temperatures and the dew point. The dew point has nothing to do with morning plant perspiration."

Sergeant Jacobs's humor fell as flat as a man's hair and energy on a sweltering summer day. Except for Luke, who chuckled. "You will learn how to report pressure at sea level with milibars," Jacobs said. "Memorize that term." The sergeant walked over to an airman in the back row who seemed lost in the details and turned the pages for him. He sighed and pointed. "What the hell is the *L* there, airman?"

"Low pressure, sergeant?"

A storm of disgust erupted on the sergeant's face. "People, all of you, you will cease answering my questions with a question. Be bold, make a decision, and call it. If you're wrong and you're humiliated in front of the class, I damn well guarantee you won't make that mistake again."

He marched to the front of the class and smacked his desk with his pointer. "Low pressure is a key feature linked to inclement weather. You need to know it like you know your pecker." He looked at his watch. "You have ten minutes for break. Don't leave the area. Go outside and get some fresh air if you dare."

Jacobs didn't wait ten minutes to resume class. Chance and Luke walked back inside to hear the sergeant saying, "Looky here. This explains all the ways to explain the amount of sky cover. With full sky cover, visibility can go below one mile and represent danger to all our pilots. High pressure linked with good weather is marked by Ceiling And Visibility Unlimited." He smacked the desk with each letter. "C-A-V-U. Remember that. The storm is over. The tornado has passed."

He paused. "Chisholm, go outside on the balcony and tell me the sky cover in tenths."

Chance rose from his desk and walked out of the classroom to the balcony and stood next to the railing on the second floor, closing the door behind him. The sergeant continued his explanation of sky cover.

A minute passed. Chance opened the door. Standing by his desk, he raised his hand. "There is five-tenths sky cover, Sergeant."

"So half the sky has cloud cover?"

"Yes, Sergeant."

The sergeant nodded once. "Next, you need to learn wind speed in knots and wind direction, the symbols. See that little line extending out a half-inch from the circle in the middle of the weather station report? It looks like an *F*. It is pointing to the lower right on your page. That indicates that the wind is from the east-southeast. See the two little feathers or lines that hang down from the end? What do the two marks mean that make it look like an *F*?" He pointed to a stocky airman in the middle row. "Any ideas?"

"No, Sergeant."

"LaCrosse, your observation?"

"It must be wind speed in knots, Sergeant. Each one stands for five or ten knots."

"Which is it? I need *one* answer. Each longer line stands for ten knots. If you see a shorter line, it stands for five knots."

The sergeant walked toward the laboratory side of the classroom. "We have an anemometer right here, which measures the wind speed and direction up on our roof. Who volunteers to read it?"

Chance, Luke, and Jethro Biggs raised their hands. "Biggs, give it a try."

Jethro moved quickly to the face of the wind gauge. "Wind is from the north and wind speed is fifteen knots."

"Close enough."

After two days focus on atmospheric pressure, warm fronts, cold fronts, and winds, the class began work on learning the types and the makeup of clouds. They thought there might be a handful of them.

On the third day of class late in the morning, Sergeant Jacobs put his hands behind his back and strode to his lectern as though giving his students an assignment that, for them, would be impossible. He turned around and looked at every airman in the class. "Here's your first homework assignment over lunch. Study this list of all twenty-seven types of clouds, with their pictures. Note the line drawings of the types of clouds. I want each row to get together and come up with the right names for the right pictures or drawings. Each of you, take a blank sheet of paper and draw those clouds with their names beneath them. Then check with each other in your row. Bring back one correct page for each row."

After the last morning presentation, the class sat down in the chow hall together, none of them hungry, all of them overwhelmed with the task. "Twenty-seven clouds. I can't believe it," Clark said.

"It's not just learning everything in that packet," Luke said. "We have to learn how to gather all the data, read the instruments, check the wind and rain gauges, and then plot fifteen symbols inside the diameter of a nickel."

Chance folded his hands out. "That's just normal type weather. Wait until all the data we have to learn about hurricanes and tornadoes."

Luke shook his head. "We haven't covered lightning strikes, either. You can't ignore them. Most people don't know zip about lightning."

"We don't." Chance drank his glass of milk and dumped his tray into the barrel at the end of the long table.

All the way back to class, the marching sergeant yelled at them repeatedly because they couldn't yell, "Boy, are we enthusiastic!" loudly enough. They filed into class tensely, and took their seats in silence.

Sergeant Jacobs moved away from the map on the wall and faced the class with a slight smile. "I was just fooling you about identifying all the clouds." His billowy, open-faced laugh seemed to be a green light for everyone in the classroom to join in. *The sergeant is actually human*, Luke thought.

The class responded with both incredulity and relief. A few students in the back began to laugh, and then the whole class erupted.

Sergeant Jacobs wagged his finger. "But I may not be fooling next time."

17

After three weeks, Luke and Chance were dismissed for the week-end with the rest of the barracks. "Report back here no later than 2200 Sunday." Sergeant Hamilton yelled. "You miss the deadline any Sunday; you get a disciplinary Article Fifteen. Miss three Sunday deadlines and you will be dismissed from weather school. You will be transferred to the cooking school."

Luke put on his winter uniform and overcoat and walked to Highway 51. After thirty minutes of standing by the roadside, a driver stopped and picked him up. The driver, a two-stripe airman, hunched his shoulders against the cold wind as Luke climbed in and shut the door. "Where you headed?"

"Glenview, northwest of Chicago." Luke coughed.

"I can get you up to Chicago. Where I let you off, I'll show you where to stand on the freeway around Chicago."

"Thanks!" Luke smiled and settled in the back seat, arms folded, trying to keep warm. "It's been a tough few weeks."

"They always are," the driver said. "I'm Andy."

It became the first of many hitchhike trips Luke took home. He never saw Lacy. And he stayed busy. Back on Chanute Luke and Chance assimilated more and more weather data with all its vagaries. One student named Brown came up to Luke after a major midterm exam that covered the whole first three months. "LaCrosse, you are a genius," he said.

Luke never forgot it. Nobody ever used that word in the Air Force.

* * * * * * * * * * * * * *

Three months later, spring came. With it, corn began growing around Chanute Air Force Base. Luke graduated and was sent to a high-level assignment, Severe Weather Warning Center in Kansas City. There he provided weather information from all over the country to forecasters. He quickly memorized 462 reporting stations, and plotted the weather for each station.

The first week, Luke studied his map and call signs, his confidence ruffled, his concentration scattered. He knew he'd remember the three-letter call signs for each reporting weather station. He took work home. He tried to stay late on the job, but the sergeant would not allow it.

Finally, in the first month, Luke got set on his own. One night, he scanned the national map, looking for cold fronts across the nation, from TVC to OHR to VCV (Traverse City Mich., O'Hare, Ill., and Victorville, Calif.) And so forth. This is what he needed to plot for each of the 462 stations. Each needed the same basic information:

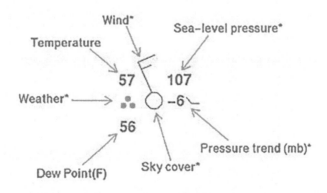

Sample Station Plot

The teletype weather data always came in a rush. Luke studied the messages and began his calculations. The term used around the world was knots, not miles per hour. Wind plotted in increments of 5 knots. The flag for the wind came out of the north-northeast at 15 knots (17 miles per hour). He plotted each term and digit with care, yet at lightning speed.

His brow knotted. *Dang! I made the five-knot bar into the longer horizontal line that stood for ten knots.* He corrected his mistake. The surface temperature was 57 degrees Fahrenheit. The weather with the three dark dots indicated moderate rainfall. Victorville, California, showed zero cloud cover, yet the inner circle was open. How could rain occur without cloud cover?

He checked the teletype. A correction had been transmitted; there was full sky cover. He penned in the dew point of 56 degrees. *This is the temperature at which the air is saturated with water. I must follow this,* he muttered, *very important for thunderstorm reporting.*

The barometric pressure trend forced him to think twice. He'd always known it to be measured in inches: 29.7 inches or below normally indicated a storm, while 30 inches showed good conditions. In the Air Force and the rest of the meteorological world, pressure was measured in milibars. He had memorized the equivalent: 29.92 inches of pressure equaled 1013 milibars, a much more accurate measurement. Here it showed a drop of six milibars, with a leveling out as indicated by a lazy L, no problem.

Two hours later, he completed the Midwestern and Western quadrants. One hour after that, the new teletype messages poured in on their scheduled three-hour interval. The staccato punching kept Luke alert and awake. This time, he began with OKC—Oklahoma City, the belt buckle of Tornado Alley. The sky cover was blacked in: clouds overhead.

To show the weather, he carved in a rough R-shaped symbol with a lightning arrow stabbing out of the right toe, instead of three dots. On top of the R was one dark dot: a thunderstorm with rain, an ominous change. This time, the wind rippled out of the west with three long horizontal stripes and one short horizontal stripe: thirty-five knots, equivalent to forty miles per hour.

He raised his eyebrows. *This is bad! This could bowl over a ten-year-old child.* The pressure trend, which had already fallen sixteen millibars, continued to drop with no sign of leveling off. Luke began adding further symbols for the twenty-seven different types of clouds at three different layer levels: nine low-level clouds from five to ten thousand feet; nine mid-level clouds from ten to fifteen thousand feet, and nine upper-level clouds, which hovered at fifteen thousand feet. He began to draw a bowl-shaped symbol for an L5 low-danger stratocumulus cloud layer, but then spotted the L9, the dangerous cumulonimbus cloud on the verge of becoming a full-fledged thunderstorm. He drew the symbol of a teakettle on the lower part and the handle on top of it. He watched the pressure falling and looked for the right symbol.

Walking down the hall after one of his shifts, Luke caught the attention of an officer and a forecaster. He saluted. "Sir, may I ask a few questions?"

"Once you tell me who you are," the forecaster said, his eyes peering at Luke, not sure of his intent.

"I'm Airman LaCrosse. I plot the national weather maps."

"What can I do for you? Wait a minute. Shouldn't that be the other way around?"

Luke scuffled his feet. "Yes. You are right."

The forecaster looked forward, trying to remain focused on the eastern seaboard forecast he needed to update. "Well, what is it?"

"Back in Broken Arrow, Oklahoma, a tornado struck and I was scared beyond polite expression. I was twelve."

That drew a smile from the forecaster. "You mean scared shitless?"

"Yes, sir. I didn't want to disrespect. A tornado struck Broken Arrow and destroyed homes all around me. People I loved were hurt and homeless. How have you been able to forecast tornadoes now, so we have more warning? Is there any chance you could take a few minutes and show me how you prepare a tornado watch or tornado warning?"

The man stood tall. "I'm Captain Jordan." He bore a similar appearance to Gregory Peck; a tall dark-haired movie idol of Luke's who starred in Westerns, World War II movies, and movies in the South as well.

Captain Jordan said, "When you get off shift, I'll give you the high sign. Be mindful now, this isn't normally allowed. But I do remember Broken Arrow. 'Wish we had caught it in time."

One day, Luke's sergeant discovered him in the hall outside the forecasters' headquarters. "LaCrosse, you are off shift. And out of place. Don't let me catch you loitering here again."

Luke stayed out of his way. After each shift, he would descend in the elevator and walk back up the stairs. He slipped into the large forecasting room where maps, screens, and teletypes changed every minute.

Within a week, Luke could visualize long red lines for the warm fronts out of California, blue lines for cold fronts out of Montana, and surface wind speeds and directions over the Texas panhandle, contrasting to faster upper atmosphere winds over Oklahoma. He determined all of these readings from individual numbers and symbols. As he checked wind speeds and direction, he traced the jet stream dipping down from Canada or the Pacific Ocean at speeds well over a hundred miles per hour. He noted the effects of daytime and nighttime temperatures on major weather systems. Equipped with that all of that knowledge, he sat like an excited spectator and watched the storms building toward their peaks around 1600 hours, a phenomenon caused by the sun's rays and earth's warming with the subsequent moisture in the air.

Luke studied the tornado records the captain showed him and conducted research at the local library. As a longtime fan of the glamorous heavyweight boxing division, from which he filed the accomplishments of Dempsey, Tunney, Marciano, Louis, and Walcott in his data-gathering mind, Luke was an accomplished researcher of both statistics and information that fed the larger story about the division. To Captain Jordan's amusement, he came up with tornado names resembling heavyweight boxing champions.

For a hundred years, nobody could beat the Haymaker tornado. It acted like bare-knuckle fighter Jack Johnson and boasted the deadliest tornado outbreak in history on March 18, 1925. Near St. Louis, Missouri, the Haymaker struck down and killed 747 people while injuring 2,027. Known for its wild swinging punch thrown with all its might, the tornado knocked out opponents one at a time, starting in Missouri, crossing into Illinois, and ending in Indiana. From that, it picked up the name, Tri-State Haymaker, after killing an additional 695 people while racing over 215 miles of land at speeds between 65 and 73 miles per hour, very fast for a tornado. Damages indicated the winds inside the tornado's funnel cloud exceeded 300 miles per hour. No machine could measure that kind of wind.

Another killer was the Brawler tornado, reminiscent of Joe Louis, who lacked finesse in the ring, moved more slowly, and lacked mobility. However, his raw power and ability to knock out his opponent with a single punch overcame the fourth weakness, predictability of his punches. On May 11, 1953, the Brawler tornado struck Waco, Texas, with a knockout blow. It killed 114 people, injured 597, and destroyed 1,500 buildings.

Beneath Luke's pointy pen and clenched hand, symbols for cumulus clouds turned into towering cumulus and then into thunderstorms. The winds increased and light rain became heavy rain. Hailstones could pelt the ground if the thunderstorm rose high enough. It all started with rain droplets formed around specks of dust, which then magnetized together and multiplied into raindrops.

They spread over and under the skies like a virulent virus: transparent pellets from ten thousand shotguns.

The drops would begin to fall, heavier than air, but then updrafts from the heated earth would toss the raindrops thousands of feet toward space, where they enlarged, multiplied and began their rapid heavier-than-air descent. Then another updraft shot them up even higher, as if they were huge basketballs of rain expanding by the minute, and a monster ball handler kept bouncing them higher and higher on a court the size of a thousand football fields. Meanwhile, the low-pressure system twirling counterclockwise around the thunderstorm caused the clouds to rotate and spin against the earth's rotation, getting larger and faster by the minute. From his plotting, Luke grew to understand that without thunderstorms, tornadoes could not exist.

From all his prior studies of tornadoes, Luke imagined how later, across the border in Kansas, the cumulonimbus mammatus clouds would form. Those huge pouchy clouds of greenish-black wrath would spawn a nasty litter of whirling tornadoes that snaked down to bite and poison the earth below. After the storm dropped all its rain and hail and spun off multiple tornadoes, it would cease its upward billowing, where the stratospheric winds at eighty thousand feet would then shear the top of the cumulus like a brushcut on a Marine. The huge cloud would turn into a gleaming white flat-top blowing straight out of the earth's atmosphere. But first, Luke could close his eyes and see it sparkling in the sunlight and peeking out of a distant western sky.

At 1615 hours on a Thursday, he raised his hand. The shift sergeant came over. Luke pointed. "This thunderstorm is dangerous and headed out of Cherokee, Oklahoma, toward Wichita, Kansas. Look at the winds and the rainfall." He pointed just ahead of the central activity. "Over here, the cold and warm fronts are colliding."

Sergeant Jackson grunted. "You better have something there if I notify the forecasters."

Luke nodded. "Yes, Sergeant."

18

The sergeant's heels struck the floor as if Luke was an irritation. Luke felt intense pressure to see the evolution and direction of every storm, and to make sure his findings were absolutely correct. Tight with concentration, he took care not to let his sweat drop onto his map.

Within an hour, the latest teletype indicated the thunderstorm and twisters had dropped down between Caldwell and Wellington, Kansas. Fifteen huge farms were hit hard, the far-reaching corn-fields flattened and crushed as if from giant footsteps, torn apart by hailstones the size of baseballs. But due to the warning, the farmers poured into their tornado shelters and their barns and the families avoided death and injury. But the worst part, at least twenty-seven homes in Caldwell had been destroyed, and at least fifteen homes were missing roofs and walls and trees. At first count, there were no deaths but over twenty people were rushed to the nearest ER, and fourteen people were missing.

Overnight, all but two were accounted for. The next day they were found dead underneath the so-called shelter of two oak trees. They didn't know lightning and large trees often attracted each other. Radio stations were jubilant. So many more could have been killed or injured. People in two counties in Kansas had dodged the cloudy bullets. Thank God the tornado threat, especially to Wichita, the third largest city in Kansas, had passed. The majority of citizens had been warned and protected below ground.

Captain Jordan brushed past the sergeant and congratulated Luke. "This helps make up for the disaster in Broken Arrow," he said as he looked at Luke's computations. "Let's keep on a roll here."

From then on the sergeant kept his peace.

Within two months, Luke could see his own improvement. After the forecasters learned of his former science projects on the history of tornadoes, they occasionally shared opinions with him. Luke told them about the Joe Louis Tornado, the longest tornado path from Missouri to Indiana. It stayed on the ground for seven hours and twenty minutes, just like its namesake boxer, who had the longest staying power of any fighter. He was a gentle fighter, but you didn't want to piss him off. Louis's attitude was good enough to reign atop the heavyweight division for twelve years.

Night and day, depending on his shifts, Luke studied for his advanced five-level weather specialty code. He passed with the highest score possible. Due to his outstanding record, he received new orders for Sixth Weather Squadron (Mobile), and a permanent duty placement for which he had longed.

With one of the perks available in military life, Luke caught a free flight in an old C-47 from Richards Gebaur AFB next to Kansas City, into Tinker AFB, outside of Oklahoma City. "The workhorse of the Air Force" required every passenger to wear a parachute. Luke was happy to be out of his small office in a Kansas City skyscraper evaluating other reports from out in the field. He would have "boots on the ground," and work to qualify for temporary duty (TDY) projects from which the squadron got its name. He would be face-to-face with tornadoes, stationed in places where tornadoes abounded and there were no reporting stations or Air Force bases. Excitement abounded.

Once settled into the squadron's dorm, Luke picked up his assignment from First Sergeant Sherry, a tall genial man recently back from duty in Korea. He handed Luke his orders and gave him a brief heads-up. "Sergeant Jones is going to want you to hit the ground running. Here's a general outline of your new assignment. Your duties: get those upper atmosphere helium balloons runs past 100,000 feet, follow a radiosonde which sends back all aspects of the weather which you will record for every foot of elevation. You won't be in an office. You will usually work in a tent or a Quonset hut. In addition, all runs are on set times. As a rule runs are set for every six hours. If conditions require it, runs are made every two hours. Even in calm weather at least one run per eight hour shift has to be made.

"You rawinsonde operators work rotating shifts, changing every two weeks. Most tornadoes kick up and drop down in the mid or late afternoons. We want everybody to get the chance to see a tornado overhead."

Luke listened intently. At last, he could focus just on tornadoes. He was eager to overcome the fears that had plagued his childhood when he visited Oklahoma.

The sergeant interrupted Luke's reverie. "Glad to have you aboard, LaCrosse. I want you to cut a *choagie* out to the South Forty."

Luke frowned slightly.

The sergeant laughed. "It's Korean for 'hauling ass.' Has a nice ring to it."

"Okay, I'll get my butt moving! Thank you, Sergeant."

Luke climbed on the squadron's bus shuttle, a battered blue Air Force bus from WWII. On the south side of gigantic Tinker Air Force Base, a military installation practically the size of Delaware, Luke found the squadron's Quonset huts, tents, and helium tanks. As he walked to the back of the bus, he saw Chance sitting on the back row with his hands on his head, happy to be out of the records-checking department where he had evaluated all the balloon-runs from out in the field. Now he was bound for adventure, and so was Luke.

"Hey, Chance! I forgot you were stationed here. Wasn't your first duty kind of boring? And now you're on duty at South Forty?"

The bus idled while the driver waited for more passengers.

"Luke, slow down, will you?" Chance straightened up, leaned forward, and jumped to his feet. "I hope we work out in the field. I hate being trapped in an office."

"Me too," Luke said, hands over his head.

"No more office. My sergeant knows I can improve things in the field, because I caught so many mistakes the guys were making out there," Chance noted. He held out his hand, and then gave Luke a bear hug. "'Great to see you! I heard about your last assignment. How did you get out of that city job?"

"Prayer, I think. How did you get out of yours?"

"Just lucky, I guess. The sergeant said I had proved myself at checking all soundings and finding the most errors, so I got detailed to go out and learn how to do it myself. He wanted me to show the guys out on projects how to do it right and not fall into the same mistakes."

Ten minutes and four miles later, the bus driver, Airman Second Holmes, called them to the front. Out the scratched front window he pointed. "See that big guy standing out there waiting for you? That's Senior Master Sergeant Jones. An Irishman. He can outwork and out-drink anybody in the Air Force. Double-time whatever he asks you to do. He has been in uniform since before the Army gave up the Air Force in 1947. There's nothing he hasn't experienced. Even the officers treat him as one of their own."

"Holy shit!" Their response was simultaneous.

Chance turned to Luke, worry lines running through his forehead like rows of corn. "This ain't gonna be no cakewalk. Everybody knows old Jonesie."

Ten minutes later, as they jumped off the bus, they eyed the big, bluff sergeant. He waited for them with a no-nonsense reddish face and piercing blue eyes. "LaCrosse, I heard from the Severe Weather Warning Center that you had a habit of naming tornadoes after heavyweight boxers. Give me an example. It better be good."

Luke thought a minute. "The Rope Tornado started out thin and wiry, hanging down harmlessly from the super cell tornado. Once energized, it turned into the Sugar Ray Robinson Tornado. He threw hooks and inside power punches. His jab was the busiest punch in the boxing world, thrown quickly with his leading hand. The Robinson Tornado smashed into Blackwell, Oklahoma, in 1955. Five years later, a tornado just like it hit Prague, Oklahoma. Then just last year, another tornado like the Sugar Ray killed sixteen and injured fifty-eight in Leflore, Oklahoma."

Sergeant Jones grunted. "Okay, you've done your homework. Now tell me about Oklahoma's worst years for tornadoes."

Luke smiled. "In 1959, seventy tornadoes struck Oklahoma. In 1960, a total of ninety-eight tornadoes touched down in that year. In boxing terms, the tornadoes made some towns kiss the canvas, knocked down face first onto the ground. You know, these newer tornadoes were unfair and dirty fighters. They used illegal and intentional head-butting, swinging their heads from left to right or up and down, causing serious damage. Towns were obliterated, with winds careening right and left."

Sergeant Jones held his hand up. "Okay, okay, I've heard enough. I wanted numbers, not dirty fighters. You talk too much." He frowned intensely. "I expect you to be as good at launching balloons as you are at making up civilian stories."

Now he shook his head. "It's about time you got here. You both are in the Flight B training class." He grunted, turned, and pointed. "Get out of my sight. Go to that Quonset hut and report in."

Tech Sergeant Stillman set out their first two days of work. "Watch these three guys and how they launch a balloon and follow it for two or three hours. Ask all your questions while you have the chance. Do this for two days, and then you will do it all yourself and earn your pay."

He looked down at the duty roster. "Chisholm, Chance," he growled and looked up. "Whenever I use the word *chance* in talking, don't _ever_ think I am talking to you. For example, if I say, 'You don't have a chance to get it right,' I am not talking to you. I never use first names and you better not either."

Training energized Luke and Chance, whether they spent time outside in perpetually windy Oklahoma or in a Quonset hut. One day, they finally had the opportunity to do it all—complete a successful balloon launch. They noted down all the surface weather and calibrated the baseline for the recording instruments inside the Quonset hut. They ran out to the twenty-foot-tall helium tent, selected a balloon, and attached it to a helium tank. Luke filled the balloon while Chance twisted the knobs governing the helium flow.

The paper-thin balloon swelled to six feet in diameter. "Okay!" Luke shouted. They stopped filling the balloon and tied it down.

Weather Tech Turnbeau stood near the Quonset hut next to his GMD (Ground Meteorological Detector), with its inwardly curved circular dish tracking the balloon, its radio signals, and its weather every minute no matter how far or how high the balloon rose. While the operators worked inside the Quonset hut, the technician remained outside.

As he stood next to the 150-foot-high pole wind indicator, Luke called out: "First flag, surface wind direction from the southeast."

"Got it!" Chance yelled.

"Second flag 80 feet up, wind direction from the northeast."

"Copy that!"

Luke called once more. "Third flag 150 feet up, wind direction from northwest."

"Got it." Chance yelled. "What the hell is with the three wind directions in the first 150 feet?"

So alerted, Luke called back, "Hey, this is Oklahoma, remember?"

He shook his head. "We have a serious weather front coming in, maybe two."

He yelled over to the technician, "Yo, Turnbeau, keep that GMD tracking. The winds are all over the place and they might rock your dish."

"I'll track it up your butt."

Luke and Chance took the Rawinsonde recorder from the Quonset, its baseline in place. They ran out to the helium tent and tied the instrument to the balloon with forty feet of rugged string. Chance held the balloon carefully as he walked to the center of a small field next to the tent. Luke held the Rawinsonde and proceeded to a point twenty feet behind Chance.

"Go!" yelled the sergeant.

Chance held the balloon high and sprinted ahead, thinking, *oh man, if this balloon hits the ground, I'm a dead Indian.*

Luke ran closely behind. Both knew how fragile their equipment was; the balloon could break anytime. The Rawinsonde also could get bumped and lose its baseline values; it was set to measure air pressure, temperature, and humidity. As soon as they thought the balloon could climb despite the strong surface winds, Chance would yell, "Release!" and let go of the balloon's neck.

Luke ran at an eighteen-knot speed, holding the white plastic object, just six by six inches wide and eight inches high. It had a transmitter tube attached below and a tiny parachute tucked in above. Equipped with a radio transmitter, the Rawinsonde instrument continuously streamed data so the GMD could record the changing locations of the Rawinsonde as well, giving Luke and Chance the wind speed and direction.

Luke had to run until the balloon snatched the delicate instrument out of his hands. *Oh, man, if I stumble or let it go too soon, it will smash into the ground and we will have to start all over again.* Chance yelled, "Release!"

The damn thing almost blistered his hands as Luke yelled, "Release!" Both balloon and Rawinsonde were aloft and blown away into the clouds. Chance and Luke ran into the Quonset hut with Jerry Rainwater and began computing and drawing up winds and directions until over an hour-and-a-half later the balloon popped at a hundred thousand feet.

"That's your first release," the sergeant yelled. "Don't think they are all the same. I want at least twenty releases and data collections before you go out in the field on a project where you are on your own and think you know everything."

In a little over two weeks Luke and Chance had learned the teamwork needed for a successful month of error-free atmosphere sounding. Both men felt comfortable enough to begin answering questions from other Rawinsonde operators, some of whom were being retrained. They felt ready for those out-of-state projects.

19

Chance and Luke brought more variety into their routine-driven lives with their weekend adventures. Chance met Gina, who had sneaked out on a Saturday night to meet new people at The Embers Glow, a popular nightspot for the Sixth Weather crew. She caught his eye with her red dress and high heels, even though she had brought a friend and they sat quietly at a corner table. It was so easy to walk over with Luke and ask if they could sit down for a minute. Gina refrained from bar drinks. She sipped on a glass of Seven Up. So did Julia. Luke and Chance had mugs of Coors Beer.

The girls started out with all the questions. It was like a church social, not a bar where the guys came up and tried to initiate talk to impress the girls. Gina and Julia learned about Luke and Chance's childhoods, where they grew up, and where they went to church. They got to know each other and before you knew it, they were up dancing, as if it were a church social. The girls knew the guys were new to Oklahoma and had met few local friends.

As the evening drew to its low-key close, Gina asked, "Why don't you come to our Church tomorrow? We have an ice cream social afterwards. We're at the end of the main street in Midwest City."

The next morning Chance and Luke rolled out early while the rest of the barracks slept in on a Sunday morning. They were eager to leave the sleepy base. At the Southern Baptist Church, they met Gina, now in a pretty tan dress, a bit conservative, who stood waiting in the foyer with Julia. In the daylight Julia's startlingly blue eyes brought out the colors in her sky blue blouse and dark blue skirt. They introduced the boys to the usher who promptly guided them to a section on the right in the front. Luke was impressed with the down home pastor who had great command of scriptures showing love to the neighbor, of going out of one's way to help, of even visiting those in prison, all of which mirrored the love of God as well.

After the service, people informally gathered in the assembly hall to visit a bit. The first thing the girls did was to introduce them to Mr. Warner. Luke and Chance shook hands with Mr. Warner as Gina said, "Meet Luke and Chance, the two upper-atmosphere weather operators. In the Air Force they are LaCrosse and Chisholm if you ever need to contact them. These two are in Sixth Weather Squadron, and they send big helium balloons up in the atmosphere to find signs of tornadoes before they hit.'"

Julia smiled and added, "Somehow they find winds and clouds up there that give them an idea of the coming weather. They call Oklahoma 'The Belt Buckle of Tornado Alley.'"

Mr. Warner was delighted with the term. He laughed and said, "Unfortunately, that is all too true."

Gina said, "Mr. Warner's ranch was almost destroyed by a tornado. They never found all the wreckage from the roof, or the three cows."

Mr. Warner wasted no time matching their profession with his concern. "Boys, I surely want to know more about tornadoes. I seriously need more advance warning."

The man wore heavy boots, jean overalls, and a curly beard, as though hiding his warm nature. "Gina told me before church that your Sixth Weather outfit travels all over the country looking for tornadoes. I'm glad to meet you. If you guys ever get warning about tornadoes in this area, let me know, will you? In high winds, neither my radio nor phone works well. I take it personally when I lose roofs and cattle."

"We'd be glad to let you know," Luke said. "We both like to run, too. We could get you word. Sixth Weather does plenty of balloon releases right on Tinker Air Force Base."

Mr. Warner smiled and nodded. "I need any information you can give me on how to protect against tornadoes."

He had a slight frown. "Wait a minute. Running isn't fast enough with tornadoes." He scratched his head, working his memory, then turned and looked them in the eyes. "You know, I just remembered a couple old motorcycles up in the hayloft. They've been stored there since the early fifties, when the former owner enlisted in the Army, served in Korea, and never came back."

"Wow!" Luke and Chance exclaimed simultaneously, distressed about the MIA hero but excited about the motorcycles.

"Killed in action fits better," Luke said. "Did you know him?"

"John Summers was his name. I knew him when he raced the bikes. A year after he went missing, his wife sold me the farm. If you are men of your word about giving me advance notice on tornadoes, come take a look at the motorcycles. They may take a bit of cleaning and fixing up, but John Summers told me he won a few races with them. He found a way to soup them up a bit. You could ride over here a whole lot faster than you could run."

"Thank you so much," Chance said. "I can teach Luke about motorcycles. I used to own one as a newspaper boy. When can we come see them?"

Mr. Warner looked down and nudged a clump of dirt off his left boot with his right foot. "Sunday's our family day. Come by tomorrow after work if you can. We live on that red dirt country road west of Tinker. Go out the west gate onto that road and turn left, then go south almost exactly three miles. You'll see our mailbox on the right out by the road. Just swing into our driveway. A quarter mile down, you'll see my big red barn on the right. Our farmhouse sits behind it. You can't see it from the road. We'll be looking for you men."

Luke reached out and shook Mr. Warner's hand again, marveling at both his generosity and his simple, explicit way of laying down exact directions to his house. "Thanks, Mr. Warner. We'll see you tomorrow."

Gina tugged Chance's hand, suddenly eager to move the conversation from motorcycles to her favorite topic, desserts. "Come over to my house. You've got to try my butter pecan ice cream. I made it myself."

Chance nodded and looked over his shoulder. "Come on, Luke. Homemade ice cream. It's a family tradition."

The next day, Mr. Warner greeted Luke and Chance in front of his barn, his overalls smudged from a morning of work. While following directions to the farm, they noticed the country roads, occasional ranches, and farms leisurely spread out beneath the warm sun. They couldn't wait to explore it all. Mrs. Warner waved from their front porch, with a little boy and girl holding onto her apron. Mr. Warner gestured toward the house. "That's my wife, Rachel. She's baking an apple pie for you boys. Come on into the barn first. Let's look at those bikes."

Luke and Chance followed Mr. Warner up a solid earth ramp to the second floor of his barn. Swinging the huge double doors on both sides, Mr. Warner stepped into the barn. The hay seemed to reflect gold in the sun, and the freshly cut planks on the roof shone brightly, in contrast to the dark and weather-worn walls and floors of the storm-damaged barn. He walked over to a dark corner and yanked off a surplus Army tarp.

The boys almost fell over. It was as though Mr. Warner had flipped open the top of a pirate treasure chest and they'd stumbled across old Spanish doubloons. The two motorcycles were as good as gold. "Are these babies what I think they are?" Chance asked.

Mr. Warner didn't answer immediately. His puzzled expression betrayed his lack of knowledge about the bikes. He thought Chance and Luke were disappointed. "The seats look terrible, I know. You'll have to replace them."

Chance and Luke looked away, unable to conceal their excitement. "It's not that," Luke said. "They may be classic models."

Mr. Warner focused on the desired outcome, getting the motorcycles on the road. "Come on, boys, grab one each and take 'em on down to the hose. I'll go get some rags and turn on the water. We can clean 'em up. I'm not a betting man, but I'm willin' to wager you an apple pie that you'll be able to ride those bikes home tonight."

As he walked out the door both boys said, "Tonight?" They both exclaimed. "You've got to be kidding."

They waited until he was outside the barn and then did a victory shuffle. Luke managed to stifle a shout rolling through his body. "What we have here are two vintage 1950 Indian Chief motorcycles in all their beauty!" Luke whispered quietly. "Sure they're rusty and haven't been ridden or cleaned for five years, but they are as good as a goldmine. We just have to dig a little further, clean them up…"

Chance nodded vigorously, "They're barn fresh, 1200 cc engines, and top speed over seventy miles-per-hour. But as long as Mr. Warner doesn't mind, we can get them souped up even more."

Luke agreed, his voice full of anticipation. "They're very big, strong, and solid. We know we can chase tornadoes and not get blown off the road."

Beneath the dirt-caked surface, the striking blue tint of one bike and the golden sheen of the other began to appear. The identification numbers read C-2022 and C-2023, so they knew the bikes were authentic. They were the eighty-cubic-inch Chiefs with telescopic front ends, two of the last real Indians. The Harley-Davidson fenders on both were bobbed, and the tires were still good. How could they get so lucky?

A half-hour later, their initial guarded optimism zoomed to hot-diggity enthusiasm. They filled the tanks with gas and held their breaths as they kick-started them. The roar of the bikes filled their ears with satisfaction and created huge smiles.

Mr. Warner gestured toward the open road. "Go on! Take 'em for a spin."

He didn't have to tell Chance twice. With a puff of dirt and a scream from the gears, Chance disappeared. Luke looked over at Mr. Warner, smiled, and took off carefully. When he exited the driveway at thirty miles per hour, Chance passed him going the other way, racing back into the driveway doing fifty.

"This is great!" Chance yelled as he went by. "Tornadoes, here we come!"

Luke yelled back, "No more boring weekends!"

An hour later, with miles of cross-country biking under their seats, the airmen sat on the porch eating Rachel Warner's hot apple pie. And ice cream if they wanted it. They did. Mounds of home-made vanilla ice cream covered the quarter-pie slices. Mr. Warner's kids, little Savannah and Willie, stood next to them, eyeing their plates, mouths open like a pair of baby birds.

"Didn't you get any pie?" Luke asked as he spooned a big bite of apple delight into one child after the other. Savannah and Willie shook their heads and smiled, unable to talk, mouths filled to the brim.

"Do you want some of mine?" Chance asked.

"One bite from each one of you is fine," Rachel Warner said, her voice cheerfully scratching its way through the screen door.

Chance leaned forward. "My turn," he said. "Come and get it."

The kids jumped up, ran over to him, and opened their little mouths.

Mrs. Warner waited a minute or two. When they had licked their lips for the last time she said, "Come children, we've got chores to do."

Luke and Chance both stood up. "Can we help?"

"No, no. You already have. I hate seeing things going to waste, like old motorbikes and fresh apple pie."

Luke smiled and said, "Thanks, Mrs. Warner, for the great treat."

Chance turned around. "Mrs. Warner, I grew up on a farm, and nobody could bake a pie as well as you."

They turned and moved slowly, full stomachs, across the porch and down the stairs. Walking the motorcycles back to the barn, they stood them up next to the front wall.

Mr. Warner came around the corner. "Sure you don't want to take them home?"

"We have to find a safe place to keep them first. Thanks, Mr. Warner. There is no way we can thank you enough."

"So keep the cycles here," he said. "My kids will enjoy seeing you again."

20

The next time Luke and Chance rode the Indians, they spent half a day roaring throughout the central Oklahoma countryside, practicing skills on dirt roads, wheat fields, and old washes. Stashing the bikes back in the Warner family barn, Chance and Luke hiked off the country road to the West Gate of Tinker Air Force Base, taking a shortcut through an adjoining field.

On the way home Luke spotted Possum Wash. It was accurately named, because once before he was accosted by an aggressive possum that had turned on him, baleful eyes glinting unexpectedly in the moonlight. But today the wash spread out before them twenty feet wide and ten feet deep.

"Who says I can't fly?" Luke said. He pivoted on the balls of his feet toward Possum Wash and took off at top speed with a final leap off the embankment. He windmilled his arms and whooped while soaring through the air, restricted only by the heavy jeans meant for country biking. Luke's tattered tank top fluttered up to his shoulders, while his dirty white Converse sneakers pedaled madly through the empty air.

For a moment, Chance thought Luke would remain airborne through some hidden force of will. When he hit the wash's soft sand and somersaulted, head over heels into an upright running position, Chance dashed to the edge of the bank and yelled down to him, "Hey, who said you could fly?"

Luke snapped his arms up to avoid a frontal crash into the opposite bank of Possum Wash. Caroming off the bank, he righted himself, wheeled off a one-hundred-eighty-degree turn and squinted toward Chance, shading his eyes against the morning sun. "I want to fly! My own wings, hang gliding, bungee jumping, or skydiving."

He took a deep breath and stared at the ground in front of him. A moment later, he grinned up at Chance. "And wouldn't it be something if I could ride a dust devil? Wouldn't it be something if I could ride a tornado? Even if it was only a hundred and thirty feet, like the Wright Brothers' first flight at Kitty Hawk?"

Chance howled and jumped into the wash, playfully knocking Luke down. "Are you crazy? Tornadoes can move a freight car. Tornadoes can carry an eighty-pound eight-by-ten-foot section of sheet metal across state lines. Do you remember Sergeant Kline telling us that about a tornado in Wisconsin?"

Chance hitched up his loose-fitting jeans and pulled down his faded gray sweatshirt. He leaned down and casually yanked Luke to his feet. "Get serious, buddy. We don't have anemometers that can measure wind speed in a tornado. You know they have to be at least category five hurricane strength, over two hundred miles per hour."

"You're looking at the worst possible scenario, bro. I've heard stories of people and animals getting little rides, no damage. Remember Dorothy and Toto? If it happened in a movie, it happened somewhere in real life. Come over and sit on the bank. I'll tell you about one."

With that, Luke leaped toward the east bank of the wash, found a ledge three feet above the sandy bottom, and catapulted himself up the rest of the way. A limb from an oak tree drifted over the wash from above the bank. Touching the bank and turning in midair, Luke descended and grabbed a seat on the edge of the limb, hands spread to his sides to cushion his fall. In one flowing motion, he smiled triumphantly, leaned down, reached out his hand, and helped Chance sit beside him.

"Don't you remember that early-fifties tornado in Arkansas?" Luke asked nonchalantly, as though he'd been sitting lazily up on the embankment all morning. "A cow was found dead up in a tree, a farmer was found alive on the roof of his barn, and his kitchen refrigerator ended up in the middle of the street. Before anybody could move, the refrigerator door popped open and a chicken flew out."

"Okay, okay, I guess it can happen." Chance kicked his heels against the bank. "Let's look in Oklahoma newspapers to see if it happened down here. It would be fun to get a free ride. But I sure wouldn't go looking for it."

"Maybe I'm someone special," Luke retorted. "You'll never know unless you explore it, give it a try. I'd rather find the tornado myself instead of sitting around waiting for it to come to me."

"Let me see if I can come up with a small epitaph for you." Chance closed his eyes and tilted his head in concentration:

> *Here lies a buddy of Chance,*
> *In a tornado, he thought he could dance.*
> *He waved his arms as he began to fly,*
> *His eyes grew wide when a horse galloped by.*

"I didn't think you could do verse." Luke grinned. "Reminds me of the last words of a redneck."

"What are they?"

"'Hey, watch this!'"

Chance laughed and came up with a second verse:

> *Luke prayed and said,*
> *'Please, if I have to fall, find me a river,*
> *I'll never again be a dangerous liver.'*
> *But God knew better than to give any hope,*
> *The guy would hang himself if he had any rope.*
> *So rather than hanging, he crashed on a slope.*

Luke shoved Chance off the bank. He tumbled down with no grace at all, not even bothered by the force of his fall.

They got back on the ledge and sat down. "Let me tell you a true story about Crow Boy," Luke said. "I know this story. I met Matthew Coyote at advanced weather training back at Chanute. He grew up on the Crow reservation in Montana and told me all about it. It was a family legend."

He took a deep breath. "In 1861, Crow Boy lay next to a river in Montana with no pulse, no breath, and no idea why somebody would try to drown him. He had been standing on the banks of Little Bighorn River, fishing for trout, his family watching nearby, when an adult warrior from another Crow clan rushed up and yelled, 'You little bird! You insulted me! Now you are going to die!' Neither Crow Boy nor his family was to blame. They had no idea."

Chance said, "Maybe the guy was crazy."

"No doubt. Indians are afraid of such people, and think they are possessed by evil spirits. So nobody stepped forward to help."

Luke went on. "Crow Boy held his ground, as he had been taught. His family, fearful of standing up to the mighty warrior, said nothing, not even his father. The warrior grabbed Crow Boy and flung him into the river. Seconds later, the warrior leaped onto the boy and held his head under the surface. As Crow Boy struggled to break free, his head bobbed out of the water. The warrior held him down again. One minute passed. Then another. The warrior heaved Crow Boy onto the river bank, gave his family a murderous look, and strode off, water flying from his arms and legs."

Chance exclaimed. "I'd have shot him with an arrow. Right in the back."

"He sure didn't earn any respect from me," Luke said. "Crow Boy lay as though lifeless. His family looked toward the warrior and approached, fearing for his life. It was too late. His mother and father carried him by the arms, and his brothers carried him by the legs. Sorrowfully, they lugged him out of their eastern Montana village. On the west side of a nearby mountain in the foothills, they placed him under a pine tree, afraid to bury him right away. The mighty warrior had warned them. Don't even touch him."

"Crow Boy awoke hours later and escaped into the wilderness. There was no way he could return to his village with that evil demon nearby. The messenger of death. He climbed to the top, on a promontory where he could be safe, alone with the sun and stars. He looked up and thought, *I can stay a boy and die out here. Or I can make it the time for me to get my vision and find my purpose in life. Next year is too far away. I will fast and pray this year to the Holy Spirit, to Grandfather, and get my warrior's name.*

"He sat on the mountainside, closed his eyes, and prayed for hours, his little leather bag of stones and fishhooks out of his pocket and on the ground between his legs. At the end of the day as he opened his eyes, death approached him, not in a murderous demon, but in a huge thunderstorm with lightning, crashing thunder, gusty winds, and hailstones hurled from the heavens. He ran back to where his family dropped him beneath the pine tree on the west slope. A voice inside told him to stay where he was. Hail fell all around him, but none came close enough to harm him. Nearby bushes and trees were denuded of their leaves, but over him the pine tree swayed unharmed.

"A black cloud hung from the thunderhead. Suddenly, it dropped lower and shape-shifted into the Big Dipper. Crow Boy heard the howling roar of Big Bear and thought the deity was singing a song to him. And then Big Bear reached down and lifted him up while still singing."

"What do you mean, Big Bear?"

"We call the group of stars Canis Major," Luke said.

"Four different times, Big Bear lifted Crow Boy off the ground in a gentle spin. When Big Bear stopped singing, he lowered Crow Boy back to the ground unharmed. But when Crow Boy dropped, he looked around and saw he had landed in front of a cave on the east side of the hill. He landed as Bear Child, the warrior's name given to him. He went into the cave to gather himself and clear his head. Black charcoal lay on the floor in the back of the cave, evidence of a fire pit used for many years. He picked up a piece of charcoal and drew a little bear underneath a big bear on the wall. His new name. Excited, he stood up, shook his head, brushed himself off, and walked back to the other side of the mountain on the west slope. Big Bear had indeed carried him through the air. The spot was more than a half-mile away, two minutes on a fast horse. He found his leather bag still lay on the ground, ten feet from where he had left it.

"Crow Boy's uncle arrived the next day to bury his beloved nephew. He fell to the ground when he saw Bear Child walking toward him. Bear Child sat down next to him and told him the whole story. They walked over the mountain back to where he had landed and he showed his uncle the drawing he had made in the cave. His uncle took him back to the village, where all the elders heard the story and vowed to protect him. "We will fight alongside you against any enemy, even those possessed by evil demons," they said.

"From that moment on, Bear Child led an extraordinary life. He had ridden on the tail of a tornado he called the Big Bear, who gave him his name. And he lived to tell about it. His story became legend, verified by all the elders of his clan."

"Run his most decisive action by me one more time," Chance asked.

"He jumped up to run for cover, but a still small voice inside told him to stay with the storm and to fear not. Hail fell all around him, but none came close enough to injure him."

Luke paused. "So picture this. Coming from the southwest quadrant, where all major tornadoes seem to start, the hailstorm had a black cloud hanging down in the middle of it. All of a sudden, the black cloud got bigger and swooped down in the shape of the Canis Major."

Chance couldn't help himself. "That's just what some tornado clouds look like, too. Remember the training films we saw on that?"

"Yes," Luke conceded, "but Crow Boy heard the howling roar of Big Bear and thought the deity was singing a song to him."

"He's right in the path of the tornado, and he thinks somebody is singing him a song?"

"Yeah, you and I might think he's in danger, but he doesn't. He believes he can communicate directly with nature, and nature in turn does the same. All of a sudden, he feels Big Bear reach down and lift him up while he's singing. You and I would call it the scream of a tornado."

"He got caught in the vortex? He almost dies from drowning, in water. He goes to the wilderness to gather himself together and instead, the tornado gathers him up to smash him into a thousand pieces?"

"No, no, Chance!" Luke raised himself up. "As Big Bear was singing, he lifted Crow Boy up off the ground four times, but only in a gentle spin. When Big Bear stopped singing, he lowered Crow Boy back on the hillside. Unharmed."

"He was okay? Don't you think it was just a vision he had? That he just dreamed it?"

"No, because when he got dropped back onto the ground from flying in the vortex, he landed on the other side of the mountain. Crow Boy wondered the same thing you did, until he proved to himself that he landed a half-mile away on the opposite side of the mountain."

"That sounds just like a story from the Bible!"

"Yeah, it does! And he led an extraordinary life from that moment on. That's what I want to do, fly up in vortex firsthand and live to tell about it."

Chance nodded. "I got it. He became a legend."

Luke thought of something. "Hey, remember Bruce Eggers? He and his wife were sleeping in their bedroom in Del City when a tornado struck without any warning. He slept on top of the covers. His wife slept underneath the covers. He woke up with two cracked ribs in a big mulberry tree outside his bedroom window. It was just as big as the one we're sitting in, but had more branches."

Chance nodded. "That was an incredible sight. We drove past all the wrecked homes and cluttered streets just to look at that tree."

"His wife was lucky. She got tangled up in all the bedcovers, flew up to the ceiling, and landed gently on the ground outside her window. But they both were airborne."

Luke swung down from his branch armchair and jumped out of the tree. It was a long fall. Below him, Chance heard a resounding *thunk*. "Come on, Chance, we can catch a tornado, a whirling dervish, or learn to fly a whirly-bird. They are both about the same. Crazy."

Chance looked at Luke and frowned. "What kind of goals are those? Flying in a tornado is no different from flying in a whirlybird.

They're both dangerous. Why would an Air Force wing nut want to fly an Army ground-pounder helicopter? You already said that was crazy. Are you crazy?"

Luke nodded. "You don't have to be crazy to be me," he quipped. "But it helps."

Chance was incredulous. "You love fighters and bombers. You're always listening to fixed-wing aircraft. You can tell what's flying overhead by the sound of the engines. Don't you remember marching in weather school, counting cadence and singing, 'I don't know but it's been said, Army wings are made of lead, I don't know but I've been told, Air Force wings are made of gold'?"

"Hold on, buddy." Luke sat up straight, arms clasped around his knees. "You already know I want to be an officer. You know I'm looking at the ROTC program at the University of Arizona, the biggest program west of the Mississippi. You know I want to do something in science and something in flying." He paused for a moment and took a deep breath. "But there's something you don't know. Nobody does. Let me tell you why I want to fly Army helicopters. With a helicopter, there are no natural born pilots. Anybody can fly a fixed-wing aircraft. A very small percentage of people can fly rotary-winged aircraft. And hey, I do love fighters and fighter-bombers, the F-4 Phantom, the F-104 Starfighter, the F-105 Thunderchief, and the B-58 that's worth its weight in gold. Even the B-52. It's ageless. That aircraft will last forever. Those planes fly above thirty or forty thousand feet. Even higher. They have no connection with the troops on the ground."

Chance sat next to Luke. "Okay, now we're both on the ground. You never told me about your fascination with helicopters."

"I drew pictures of helicopters all the time, beginning when I was five. Dad still has a whole album of helicopter drawings." Luke's tone grew more earnest. "I love helicopters because they're the transportation for so many infantrymen and Special Forces operations. They fly the troops in for the mission. They pick them up. They bring food, water, and ammunition. They come back while under fire and evacuate the wounded. They go on search and rescue missions. Talk about your ultimate support vehicles!

"Hueys can be ramped up into attack helicopters, with machine guns on deck, pointing out both sides. Helicopter pilots have saved countless lives. Just ask guys like Jerry Cahill, who was repeatedly pinned down somewhere behind enemy lines in Korea, what he felt when he heard the Hueys coming. All he heard was redemption. Salvation. God's mercy. He was rescued so many times. To this day, every time he hears any helicopter go overhead, he blesses that pilot. The chopper pilot is much more connected to the troops on the ground and the total Army mission."

The revelations were new to Chance. "I never gave it that much thought," he said. "There isn't the same ground troop connection or camaraderie with the F-4 pilots dropping bombs and napalm even on a five-hundred-foot-high strafing run. It's even worse with the B-52 pilots dropping twenty tons of bombs from fifty thousand feet."

"Exactly. The helicopter pilot directs fire on the enemy and helps the troops. He's more part of the real army. He has closer ties. He has sympathy and compassion for those guys on the ground. He takes them out on missions, and when the mission is completed, he flies out to bring them back. He'll do what he can to rescue them. If they're wounded, he will do his best to keep them alive. Don't you remember *The Bridges at Toko-Ri?*"

Chance grinned. "You made me watch that at weather school. Twice."

"Think of the helicopter pilots. Those two guys volunteered for a highly dangerous mission. Too dangerous. They landed their chopper in an enemy zone, which they didn't have to do, and got killed, shot to pieces, in a lousy, muddy, enemy ditch in Korea. They gave their lives trying to save one fighter pilot. That's what they were trained to do. That's what I want to do. That's what I'm going to do."

21

With the Indian motorcycles in hand, it was time for Chance and Luke to demonstrate their upper-atmosphere skills. They trained every day at Sixth Weather Squadron's South Forty. When they were in-between TDY missions out of state in Tornado Alley, they worked varied shifts: sometimes regular days from 0800 hours to 1600 hours, sometimes the night shift from 1600 hours to 2400 hours. Once in awhile, they also pulled graveyard, from 2400 hours to 0800 hours. As soon as they finished work, they switched on their ham radios to hear weather reports. They had to remain quiet in barracks, so they created different ham radio call signs and monikers and became volunteer weather reporters and recorders with a passion for finding the storm cells and chasing the twisters.

The airmen earned their stripes as US Weather Bureau tornado spotters, despite the Air Force's official disapproval of such work performed off-base. Luke's stint as a weather volunteer since high school helped. He also possessed John Park Finley's secret body of work, his scientific study of tornadoes. It was packed into his journals and stored in his memory.

Whenever they had time Luke and Chance ran through the countryside to the Warner barn. Mr. Warner was helpful mechanically, as well as a few of Luke's friends. They brainstormed ways to create maximum speed for the Indians with the ability to cover the most ground in the fastest manner. At the same time, the cycles needed to be tough, able to navigate through open fields, down country roads, over dirt paths, and across old horse trails.

If a tornado was reported and they were off duty, they pursued it, carrying along with them old, crackly walkie-talkies, along with ham radios and contacts for a network of other volunteer tornado observers. Chance connected with a ham radio operator out of Tinker Air Force Base, while Luke radioed in reports to a ham radio enthusiast out of Mustang, Oklahoma.

On the fourth of May, they anticipated an opportunity to spot a tornado in Roger Mills County, near the Canadian River. Their target area lay between Cheyenne on the Washita River, south of the Canadian River, and north of the town of Strong. They took the day off and raced out of Warner's barn early in the morning.

They whizzed west on Route 66 to Route 183 and swung north, big grins beneath their goggles. They shot up to Taloga and crossed the Canadian River, turning west and following the great loop of the river southward. "Dewey County had three tornadoes on April 30." Luke yelled as he rode alongside Chance. "I'm bettin' there will be action around Strong City today. I hope we can make it."

Chance looked over and tilted his head up. "We probably missed those. But I'm going to look up inside a tornado today. I can feel it."

South of Lenora and east of Camargo, speeding eastward, they spotted twisters in the distance, the open-faced sky and flattened horizon making the funnel clouds appear closer. They gunned their engines, hunkered down, and roared toward the billowing greenish-yellow clouds. Luke looked to his right and warned Chance right away. "There's a cold front coming in. It's going to pass on our right. See the roll cloud out in front?"

Chance veered right. "I'm getting under it. I want to see what Crow Boy saw."

Luke dropped behind Chance and called his Mustang contact. "Lex, tornado spotted at 1500 hours in Roger Mills County. Its width is narrow, but its path could extend for ten to twenty miles. It's 1545 hours, and we predict two tornadoes overhead at 1600 hours. We are two clicks south of Lenora and four clicks east of Camargo. Stand by."

"Roger, copy that," Lex answered. Luke jammed the walkie-talkie into his ear so he could hear above the motorcycles' roar and the howling winds. "I will notify the towers at Oklahoma City airport and Tinker Air Force Base."

"Be advised these tornadoes are northwest of Oklahoma City, but the system we see indicates tornadic cells will continue on a southeasterly path toward the city," Luke hollered.

Chance and Luke gauged the boiling clouds and rode furiously to intercept them. The winds were too strong. Their cycles were flung from one side to the other, and they nearly collided three times. After flying over a short wash, they skidded to a stop and laid down their cycles. They ran to one side of the wash, where two tree roots protruded from the embankment. Luke's rope-tying feats flashed through his mind, giving him an idea. If this tornado swept directly overhead, they could watch it from center stage. To do that, they needed to be fixed to the ground. After getting Chance's consent, he tied Chance to the roots with more tree-skinner knots than a five-ton limb or even Houdini could escape from: two running bowlines, a slipped buntline hitch, a sheepshank, and a tautline hitch. He left Chance's arms free. Then he tied himself up.

They cleared their goggles, reached into their leather saddlebags, removed their instruments—a barometer, thermometer, and homemade wind gauge—and adjusted their walkie-talkies. In the deep pockets of their riding pants, the old fatigues sewed doubly thick to save their legs from nasty scrapes, combat journals and sturdy cameras were ready for any free moments they might have.

The first tornado touched down a quarter mile away. Luke re-experienced the nightmare of his youth as the funnel barreled straight for them. He began to hear a thousand freight trains bearing down on them from all points of the compass. Shrubs, tree branches, grit, sand, and dust filled the air as they ducked down.

Chance pointed up and shouted, "Possum!" Luke watched an opossum flash overhead, disappearing in the debris thirty feet above them, and whirling into the twister's counterclockwise spin. Just as suddenly, the hundred-decibel noise from nature's loudspeakers ceased. They grabbed their ears in pain as their ears popped from the center's vacuum and accompanying absence of air pressure. Luke pointed to his barometer. "Gone down over one inch in five seconds."

Chance's eyes opened as wide as his goggles. Then he looked up and pointed. "Here we are, looking up the skirts of our first tornado!"

Luke thought he was inside a huge telescope that stretched upwards for a mile, twisting and turning. Its spinning black sides were filled with branches, boards, dust, grit, and debris, all whirling in a deathly silence.

Then the suction grabbed hold of them and flung them skyward, the ropes and the strong tree roots preventing them from launching into space. Eight feet up Luke yelled, "Look at our bikes!"

"Where are they? I can't see them."

"Out of the wash, up the bank, and under those bushes."

They grabbed each other by the elbows to stop slamming together. Chance looked into Luke's goggles, hoping to find sanity in his eyes. A desperate gleam shot out. "I'm going to live up to your name," Luke yelled. "I'm going to take a chance on flying."

Chance stared at Luke. In response, he flipped upside down, reached below to go head-over-heels and hand-over-hand, and crawled down his rope to the tree roots. Luke followed suit. With his legs wrapped around the tree roots, Luke grabbed his combat knife and severed one rope which looked to strangle Chance. His move proved hasty. The two vigorous upward slashes severed his rope. The winds screamed and dust filled Luke's nostrils. Before Chance could take a deep breath, a freak updraft snatched Luke up and away, unroped and unprotected. Chance couldn't believe it. The last thing he saw was Luke's thumbs-up signal. Luke's boots narrowly missed his chin as the twister kidnapped Luke and swept him away.

Luke spun down a familiar tunnel in an apparent death dive.

22

Luke awoke far away with split lips and a bloody mouth. He was jammed into the branches of a large mesquite tree. He painfully peered and calculated. Almost ten minutes had passed. The roaring passed over him as the other side of the tornado gave him a second punch with the resounding scream of a thousand freight trains. He swiveled his sore head to the right and hoped to see Chance sprawled out in close proximity. Chance wasn't there. Luke's bleary eyes traced the twirling rope ends dangling from his feet. The sulphurous smell of death permeated the air.

Back at the wash Chance untied his ropes and struggled to his knees, using both hands and feet to climb up the banks of the wash. When he reached the top, he couldn't move or feel anything. He was in shock. He tried to collect his bearings. Strange images flashed through his mind. Grasslands alternated with giant winter wheat fields, stalks slammed sideways in giant swaths, beaten down, never to rise again with the dawning sun. They looked destroyed, not merely defeated. Rows and rows of skinny golden soldiers, entire armies, held hands and bit the dust.

Where was Luke?

Distant stands of broken red cedar fell every which way, broken witnesses to the tornadic winds. Farther west, savannah-like forests dotted the landscape with trashed acres of pinon and juniper forestland. He glanced south, into the Oklahoma river bottomlands. Groves of cottonwoods, elm, and green ash groaned with twisted and broken limbs. Whole tree families were torn apart. Walnuts and pecans littered the ground.

Chance grew frantic. Maybe Luke landed to the east. There was nothing the tornadoes could do to harm the dense thickets and patches of post oaks and blackjack oaks, the "forests of iron," as one of his favorite authors, Washington Irving, had described them. Many a cowboy had lost cattle to such thickets, through death and injury.

His mind began to clear. Straight ahead of him, to the north, he saw a fresh oak hole seven feet across and seven feet deep. The tree's roots lost their hold on the rusty soil, leaving nothing behind but red oak stains scratching the small sides of the gaping empty hole. Looking at his instruments, it occurred to Chance that if he found where that oak tree landed, he might find Luke. Staggering west from the wash, he retrieved his Indian fifty feet away from where he'd laid it down and slowly climbed aboard. He stood up and roughly measured off a search area into ten sectors as the Civil Air Patrol had taught them. He sat down ready to kick his motorcycle to life. To save Luke's life. His butt hurt, but he had to sit.

As Chance slowly puttered away, the motorcycle motor protested the dirt and dust clogging its grimy intakes. He threw off his dirty goggles and squinted for signs of Luke. Brisk northwesterly winds behind the tornado's path blew all traces of teardrops away from his eyes. He couldn't help it. Questioning his own sanity, Chance demanded an answer. *Am I crazy or what? He makes a dare to me. And now he's gone.* A prayer floated through his consciousness. "Remember not, O Lord, the sins of my youth, nor my transgressions." If Luke was dead, it was Chance's fault. Luke rescued him, and then got whirled away himself.

He quickly covered four sectors with intersecting circles. Grunting in dismay, he retraced his circles within a huge figure eight. He was dizzy from all the bumping and scanning, his breathing tortured and uneven, just like his Indian's exhaust. Sector by sector, he advanced, bumping across broad open fields strewn with weeds, bushes, tree limbs, and storm debris. Halfway through his search, he began to imagine each far-off clump of debris to be Luke. Chance's heart pounded and his ears rang as he accelerated to the next clump, hoping to God he wasn't approaching an outdoor mortuary.

After a hellish hour, the walkie-talkie on his belt crackled to life. He gripped the brakes hard and came to a fierce halt, waiting for the dust to settle. Must be the ham radioman, raising him to see if he had survived. Chance lifted the radio to his ear.

It wasn't the radioman. "Chance, come and get me."

Luke. Chance couldn't believe it. "Where are you?"

"I can see your dust. You've been going in circles." His voice wavered. "Look over to your left at eight o'clock."

Chance grabbed his binoculars and scanned the point on the horizon. "You mean over to where that little wash is? With that funny looking clump of trees?"

"See the tree that looks top heavy? I got blown into it." His voice seemed to travel through the binoculars from another world. So distant.

Chance couldn't believe his ears. "And you're alive to tell me about it? Are you sure you're not calling me from somewhere else?"

"I didn't come all by myself. The minute I cut myself loose, I got slammed into an airborne tree. I loved that first feeling of flying. I was going super-fast. I was Superman. I got cocky. Just when I thought I was going to be Crow Boy I got knocked unconscious. "I'm bleeding, but I'm alive. I don't know how the hell I got here."

Chance held the walkie-talkie with his left hand and pulled up the binoculars with his right, trying to adjust them with his chin. "You mean you flew into a tree to ride a twister? You lucky dog."

"Are you kidding? I didn't mean to. The damn tree. I could have won your dare."

Chance focused on the small figure of the faraway flyboy while considering his comment. "Come on, Luke. You may be bleeding, but that tree saved your life."

Luke groaned. "What life? Come and pull me down, Chance. Look for branches going the wrong way. I'm tangled up in this crazy tree going sideways. All the ropes just make matters worse. I can't move. Come cut me loose."

Chance lowered the field glasses. "Are you okay? Did you break anything? I can't believe you did it."

"Yeah, I did it. I have no idea how I managed. I'm bruised up. I can feel that, but maybe no broken bones."

"I'm on my way, Crow Boy!" Chance dropped the radio into its pouch, lifted his feet off the ground, and squeezed the Indian for all its speed. Before long, he cut Luke from a wind-driven red oak youngster stuck into the belly of a mama oak tree. He pushed and pulled Luke through the branches, all the way to the ground.

As they stood beside the tree trunk, Luke lifted his head, scowled at the tree, and growled. "That hurt like the devil. Come on, Chance. Let me go."

Chance let him go. To his surprise, Luke fell down and kissed the ground. Startled, Chance almost asked him if he was okay. He got up slowly, swaying from side to side, his scalp still oozing blood, his shirt and pants torn and bloody. Luke gave Chance a strange look, as if to say, *some friend you are*, then thought better of it. He sighed. "God gives all bad golfers and some damn fools at least one Mulligan. I just got mine."

He kicked dirt onto one boot with the other, thinking about his ride. He shook his head and rolled his eyes skyward, mocking himself. He smiled. "I got a free ride, and I whooped it up for two freaking seconds. Then I didn't feel anything."

Chance shook his head vigorously. "You still made history, bro. Your mind couldn't handle all that fun. People pass out all the time during a dangerous fall. Lighten up, man. You're still in shock. You'll remember more details later."

He grinned and reached over to shake Luke's hand. "You did it. You did exactly what you wanted to do. You rode a twister and lived to tell about it."

23

News Clip: *Friday, May 5, 1961–*

Today, Oklahoma native Alan B. Sheppard, the nation's first successful astronaut, rode a rocket 115 miles into space, and celebrated a safe return 155 miles from Grand Bahamas Island, where he was picked up by Navy helicopters from aircraft carrier Lake Champlain.

While sitting at a Del City café, scratched and bruised, Luke drank four cups of coffee and read about Alan Sheppard's ascent into sub-orbital space and his safe, floating return into the Atlantic Ocean.

When he finished, he looked across the table. He couldn't help smiling. "Alan went a lot higher than I did and will probably go down in history as Oklahoma's favorite astronaut. But I'm telling you, Chance, I got a taste of what it's like to fly through the air. And I wasn't hiding behind cockpit windows."

Chance sat upright, his countenance a happy mirror of Luke's own. "You were the original open-air astronaut, Luke! Come to think of it, you were your own rocket ship."

"Let's hit the road, buddy. We're going to make a little history of our own this year. Any future association of storm chasers and tornado spotters will have us as charter members."

Chance snorted. "If we live long enough."

An hour later, Chance dropped his left arm for the manual signal to stop. Pulling over to the right on the dusty dirt road, he slammed on the brakes and fishtailed to a stop. A horsefly clamped on his neck, and Luke slid up beside him, goggles grimy with sweat and dust. "Ten o'clock high!" he shouted. "Twin-engine plane playin' tag with a tornado!"

Luke looked up and shook his head. "He's caught in the winds at the edges of the funnel cloud. He's trying to dodge and duck the updrafts!"

Chance swore in his native Cherokee vernacular. "He's playing with a broken arrow. He's twisting back and forth. You can't do that to a plane!"

"There goes his left wing!" Luke pointed. "He can't survive that dive!"

"We can pull them out of the wreckage." They hollered at each other as they hopped astride their Indian motorcycles and gunned the engines.

Flying north through patchy fields of wheat and hay, they left the Canadian River behind as they motored recklessly across the rough terrain. They took shortcuts whenever they could, looking up occasionally to gauge where the plane had taken the dive.

Luke thought he couldn't be more than five miles away. They'd covered the five miles. *Where's the smoke and fire?* His heart raced.

"What the heck?" Chance asked. "The wreckage should be right over this little hill and hollow."

Luke flew by, lifting his hands in stark disbelief. Two hundred yards further, he skidded to a halt and craned his neck in all directions. Chance rode up, popped off his goggles, and jumped off his belching steed. Hands on his hips, he looked around. "Tell me how we could have missed it!"

Luke shook his head slowly, calculations zipping through his mind like punch cards in an IBM computer. "We computed his elevation, his azimuth, his longitude, and his plausible rate of descent. He should have augured in right in this area."

Chance looked over and nodded.

Luke held his hand up. "*Mea culpa.* We didn't give the tornado its due. I've read about and seen a hundred things sent by Tornado Air Mail. Trees, cows, sheets of metal, whole houses in midair. We've just seen our first airplane swallowed up by a twister and hurled into the next county."

Chance nodded. "We have no idea how powerful a twister can be. We have no wind anemometers to measure such wind speeds."

Both of them sighed, their shoulders dropping in dismay, tiredness lining their faces, and travel clothes filled with wrinkles.

"We've got to go back east, into the next county anyway. We've got to warn people what's coming."

As Luke resumed his twister chasing, his mind calculated how to measure a tornado's destructive force. *Gale force winds, 63 knots, enough to knock a man down. Hurricane force winds, 75 knots, enough to propel a man a considerable distance . . .*

Five minutes later, Luke cruised to a stop beneath a shady oak tree. Pulling out a small clipboard from a lower pocket of his second-hand flight suit, he motioned for Chance. "Everybody I know thinks tornadoes are all the same," he said. "I just came up with a G-scale system to grade tornadoes. Let's figure on six levels. Starting with gale force winds of 63 knots, our weakest tornado is a G-1. The highest scale is a G-6, which could have wind speeds of 318 knots. The only force higher than that comes from an atomic explosion."

"How big is an atomic explosion?" Chance asked.

"The shockwave wind speed at Hiroshima was computed at 500 knots. It knocked over everything in a thirty-mile radius."

"So you add 51 knots to each G-Scale after G-1. G-2 at 114 knots, G-3 at 165 knots, G-4 at 216 knots, and G-5 at 267 knots."

Luke grinned. "You've got it. Let's start noticing the damage done and recorded from each tornado. We'll be able to figure what G-scale each tornado is, and people will have a clearer idea of what danger they're in."

An exciting realm of possibilities passed through Chance's mind. "Wouldn't it be great if our radars could catch a tornado on their scopes and identify it?"

By the time they reached El Reno, thirty miles west of Oklahoma City, the tornadoes had dissipated. "Look, Chance, underneath the anvil," Luke said, pointing east. The sun's rays reflected on the thunderstorm. *"Cumulonimbus mammatus!"*

"My kind of cloud," Chance said. "They look more like breasts than pouches."

Luke throttled down. "They're like pockets of saturated air. High concentrations of precipitation particles make the sinking air cooler than its surroundings—and there you have it. Breasts. That's where the mammatus comes in."

Chance frowned. "Why use such big words?"

"They say precipitation particles because they are two things, ice crystals and water droplets. Unequal distribution causes, say, twenty pouches to droop from one major cloud because the major updraft/downdraft motion has passed," Luke said. "I'd like to think the tornado is worn out."

Chance coughed once and looked away. "Those mammatus clouds scared me at first. I thought it meant a tornado was coming, not leaving."

They throttled down as they arrived in Mustang, Oklahoma, and stopped at a drive-through. "Why call these hamburgers?" Luke said. "I love beef. This is Oklahoma. There is no ham in hamburger."

They disappeared inside and went up to the counter. "Make that two hamburgers, please, and one large order of fries."

They picked an old red booth next to the window. Five minutes later the food appeared. "Why do they call these things French fries?" Chance picked up a crisp fry and popped it into his mouth. "They're just plain old American potatoes. There's nothing French about them."

Luke shifted on his seat. "Let's not quit the name game here. A chocolate milkshake, my favorite. Sure, there's milk in it, and chocolate, but what makes it indescribably delicious is the ice cream. 'Milkshake' just doesn't capture it. A Russian or a Frenchman would never understand our food."

Five minutes later, all food "inhaled," as Luke would say, Chance sat straight up. "Luke, look out over all that flat farmland. We've got incoming massive black clouds everywhere."

They ran outside. Luke kick-started his motorcycle. "That funnel cloud just dropped all the way to the ground. We've got trouble. It looks like a giant is blowing black smoke out of his mouth, trying to burn everything in front of him."

"I'm on it." Chance accelerated his motorcycle out of the drive-through. "We've got to move."

They roared eastward down the road below the belly of Oklahoma City. Chance looked back, only to see the tornado gaining on them. "We need shelter!" he yelled.

"Over here!" Luke barreled off the county road and down an old dirt road. Fifty seconds later, they rounded a bend to find three twisted dead trees hanging over and above a red dirt bank. Dead grass and two buckets lay in front of a lonely old building.

Luke ran his motorcycle up to the forlorn opening and jumped off. "I found this abandoned root cellar and tornado shelter last month. Come on in the back. It's deep into the hill. We'll be safe."

Chance scrambled into the abandoned shelter just in time. The tornado screamed up to the entrance. Luke rolled on the floor, hands over his ears, closing his eyes to the monstrous onslaught. Fear caked his memory and clogged his veins. The familiar nightmare returned. The war was back on and Dad was away. Nobody was left to protect him.

His eyes flew open. *I've got to save myself. I've got to save Chance.* He saw two piles of ropes in the corner of the cellar, with two ends tied to a huge yellowed root from a dead tree and the other ends twisting crazily out of the root cellar as if they had been stretched to their limits. Peeking outside, he found two beaten-up tennis shoes scattered outside. *Who could have been in this same situation? Who tied themselves down for safety? What happened to them?*

Chance grabbed his ears and shut his eyes. Sand, dirt, and debris swirled around the dusty insides of the abandoned shelter. The shelter sounded like an incoming squadron of B-52s. He tasted fear and smelled death.

Instantly, all sound and motion ceased. Something nameless and fearful knocked them over and sucked them straight up along with the roof of the shelter. The roof suddenly disappeared and they came to the end of their ropes, twisting and gyrating in midair, crashing into each other as the tornado's updraft sought to release them. At the edge of the property a clump of weather-beaten mounds of hay beckoned to them.

"Over there!" Luke yelled, spotting a mound of hay behind the shelter. Seconds passed. They felt like moths fluttering in a mineshaft, testing the air for poison. Before Chance could say anything else, Luke yelled. "Flap your wings, man. We've got to hit the hay!"

Like the happy ending of a bad dream, they crashed head-first into a hay mound. Luke climbed out and sat on the ground exhausted. Chance rolled out and pointed, then swooped over to a newspaper, still partly folded, where it lay on the ground twenty feet away, muddy and weather-beaten. "Check it out, Luke! Somebody in Del City is missing their morning paper."

"Either that, or the paperboy has one hell of an arm," Luke said. "A three-mile throw, at least. Where are the headlines?"

Chance read the right column on the first page: Friday, May 5, 1961.

"Four people were killed and 57 injured in the town of Poteau in eastern Oklahoma. Every home was leveled by a highly destructive tornado that swept through the area."

"That's got to be at least a G-4," Luke said, tucking the paper under his arm. "Let's see if we can follow the tornadoes. Let's check our maps."

They retrieved their motorcycles and performed quick post-tornado maintenance. The tornado had flipped them up, end-over-end until they landed forty feet away. However, they ran well. They opened up the saddlebags and plotted their next move. "Let's make sure our walkie-talkies are still working, Luke."

Chance dug his radio out of his saddlebag and checked; Luke followed suit. Pulling out their sets of maps, they compared their prognoses. Luke drew in a breath. "Do you see the pattern? Maybe twin tornadoes chasing us southeast? With a path five miles wide, one destroyed a dozen homes in Bethany and badly damaged a terminal at the Wiley Post Airport. Then the other, with a ten-mile width, slammed into Moore, directly south of us, hitting a radio tower and a barn."

Chance picked it up. "Then it destroyed another dozen homes. Large hail damaged crops in adjoining fields, broke windows, and wrecked a lot of car roofs and hoods. Twenty-six planes were wrecked at the South Shields Airport, and even a cemetery was destroyed." He looked up. "Let's get out of their paths. They came from the northwest and chased us southeast. It's late. We gotta get back to the base."

24

"It's a good thing we changed direction. Our spotter on the western border just gave me a heads-up. There's a flock of potential storms in the Texas panhandle heading for Okie City."

Six hours after Luke's remarks, they spotted the Sixth Weather's flagpole. In the distance atop the pole a triangle of three red lights blinked rapidly. They pulled off the road, tired, ready to go back to the barracks and sleep. But then Luke took his goggles off. "Tornadoes are coming and it's almost dark."

Chance replied, "Are you thinking what I'm thinking?"

Luke snapped his goggles back on. "Let's go! We gotta make sure Mr. Warner is safe."

They roared off, only a little gas in their tanks, and took a short-cut on the smooth road running alongside the railroad tracks, and then veered across two neighboring pastures. Finally, they bounced onto Meadowlark Lane where the Warner ranch waited two miles down the road. As they accelerated to maximum speed, the wind roared in their ears. It wasn't just their speed. Gusts of wind threatened to blow them off the road. Twice they almost collided. Once Chance veered off onto the shoulder. Both were sweating, anxious, tired, but determined. They knew how quickly a tornado can move, shift direction, go back up into the sky, and even make a U-turn.

Luke beeped and they swung into the Warner driveway. All the trees lining both sides of the driveway were severely bending as if the winds were beating their butts. When they came around a bend in the road, the trees on the left threatened them, swaying so closely as to graze their heads.

They drove faster and finally stopped with skids in front of the big two-story home. All the lights were off. The big barn loomed large in the back and to the right of the house. One of its big doors shook and stuttered against the other door. Chance took off on a run. "Luke, knock on the door! Get them down to the basement."

Luke yelled, "No way Mr. Warner is going down to the basement himself." He sprang up seven steps to the open porch. He slid up to the door and knocked, moderately at first. He didn't want to scare the kids. Nothing happened. He banged harder. "Mr. Warner! Mr. Warner!"

Nobody stirred. Luke banged on the door in a kind of Morse code so Mr. Warner would know it wasn't just because of the winds.

Finally, Mr. Warner turned on the porch light and opened the door. A gust of wind swirled around Luke and blew the door shut. He reached forward and pulled it back open. Mr. Warner blinked, his eyes opening wide. Luke was practically jumping up and down. "Mr. Warner, tornadoes are coming! They come knocking on your door right after me!"

Mr. Warner hesitated.

"Please believe me," Luke begged. "We just got the warning and we can feel that tornado. We came as fast as we could."

Mr. Warner shrunk back. "Not again!"

Luke was insistent. "But this time we can help! If you can get your family down to the basement, you and I can try something new."

Mr. Warner reached back and turned the inside light on. Luke shared his idea. "Come out and get your tractor. I'll get the other tractor. We drive the tractors up the ramps and park them outside right next to the big doors. We could stop the roof from being sucked up and off."

Luke jumped off the porch running, through the garden and to the pasture, where a tractor was parked. The wind screamed, filling the air with dust, dirt, debris, and branches, and anything else that could be ripped from its earthen moorings. Luke put his goggles back on and tied his bandana in place. A few minutes later, Luke and Mr. Warner revved up their tractors and crazily putt-putted forward as fast as the tractors could go. Luke drove up the earthen ramp to the big north entrance and wedged his tractor sideways against the two doors. Mr. Warner drove up the other ramp to the south entrance and wedged his tractor against the doors.

They both ran down the little slope into the first floor of the barn. Mr. Warner led the way to the east side and down the corridor with the six stalls for the dairy cows. Inside each stall was a contented cow munching on straw. "My cows are safe!" Mr. Warner exalted as he ran past. They could not even hear the storm winding up. He and Luke ran right down the corridor and out into the pasture, battling furious winds. Mr. Warner ran in circles to see if any of his cattle had taken shelter near the barn. Luke turned in circles yelling Chance's name as loud as he could. The wind practically stuffed the words back into his mouth.

Mr. Warner doubled back from the pasture into the west side of the barn. The opening was low, and he ducked his head. The big standing room for his cattle was empty. The big gate hung open. The air was still and it stank. He came running back into the pasture, gesturing wildly and yelling into the wind. "My cattle are gone!"

Luke sprinted over to him. "You have eight, right? All the stall gates were open?"

"No. No! We just penned them behind the one gate. They hate stalls."

Luke yelled, "Chance ran down here to check on your cows. He's got to be here somewhere."

Mr. Warner yelled, "They must all be out in the pasture! Fifty acres! Luke turned to run up onto the pasture and the fierce wind knocked him down. He rolled over and over again. Mr. Warner crouched down; his big frame more of a test for the wind, and ran over to Luke.

As he was pulled up, Luke exclaimed, "That wind is blowing over sixty miles an hour. Enough to knock a man down." They both braced themselves and struggled up the little hill, looking for the cattle. The faraway galloping of hooves thundered toward them. They could feel it in the ground.

The staccato beat got louder. "Chance is out there, I'll bet you," Luke yelled. Off to their left out of the dust and debris a small herd of cattle was being propelled right toward the barn. Behind them screamed the swirling winds of the outer ring of the tornado, picking up larger and larger objects. Along with hay and straw, pieces of fencing cartwheeled by, tumbling end over end overhead. They both knelt down, afraid of being trampled, or blown over, or sucked up into the blackening sky. The cattle began streaming by, as if they were floating. Suddenly one appeared, and then another. Mr. Warner let out a whoop and began counting as they galloped past, their eyes staring wildly, their mouths gaping open in terror. "Here comes number three! And four!" Out of the melee pounded two more. "Five! Six!"

Luke ran over. "There's two more coming! But where is Chance? Maybe they stampeded and he's out there bleeding."

Mr. Warner felt his confidence and his strength coming back. "We'll know in a minute," he yelled, his mouth next to Luke's ear. Luke stood all the way up, braving the tornadic swirls of dust. He yelled, "Chance! Chance! Chance!" He thought the worst. Then he yelled again. *Chance needs to know what to head for.* Exhausted physically and emotionally, he bent down, elbows on his knees, head down, eyes closed and full of dust.

Then out of the darkness and the chaos, he could hear whooping, and yelling. "Hee-yah! Hee-yah!"

Who else but Chance? A steer careened by Luke, narrowly missing Mr. Warner. The last steer pounded toward them, driven by the devil. No! It was Chance almost standing up, holding onto the steer with his knees and yelling like a crazy man. He didn't even see them, but he was the cowboy of the herd. His steer jammed into the last of the herd and pushed them all the way into the barn. There was no stopping him. Chance fell forward and bounced off two steers, falling right underneath the other cattle. Luke and Mr. Warner ran up behind him, certain he would be tramped. The cattle just stood there braying and quivering, afraid to move. Chance took his time, got up carefully, and slowly made his way through the little herd.

He shut the gate and walked right past Luke and Mr. Warner. Then he ran out into the pasture looking up. The wind had abated. The dust diminished. "Come on!" Chance yelled. A minute later they stood together and Chance pointed. "Your roof is still there!" he yelled.

Luke and Mr. Warner stood there, speechless and motionless. When Mr. Warner looked over, Chance stood next to Luke. "Well, Mr. Warner, your barn and your cows and your cattle are all safe.

"I guess we are about even now. Thanks for those motorcycles."

25

The next weekend, the two were out on patrol again. Luke waved and pulled off the road. Chance came up behind him, revving and throttling his motorcycle.

"Chance, look out! We have tornadoes to chase."

Rolling north on Air Depot Road, Chance and Luke cut over to the North Canadian River frontage road for two miles before finding the level ground on the road running parallel to the railroad tracks. They tried to angle closer to the twin twisters they had calculated to head northeasterly. Far to their left, more than a hundred oil derricks were blown over, an entire chess set swept away by Paul Bunyan's hand, the derricks scattered across the flat tableland.

Luke motioned for Chance to pull over. They stopped, feet on the ground, removing their goggles in disbelief, staring at the distant wreckage. "Can you imagine what those things weigh?"

"I can see why roofs get torn off. How can a tornado's implosion cause a whole field of derricks to get knocked over? Each one must weigh five tons."

They watched the trees and buildings bowed over, victims of a funnel cloud that appeared to be traveling just above treetop level. "That must be cutting a wide path of destruction," Luke said, taking in both the awesome display of nature and its inherent danger to them.

Chance got out his field binoculars. "There's a concrete block-house that just got demolished. Can you believe it?"

The frontal cloud changed course. Now it headed toward them, dark and snarling. Their engines howled and screamed as they accelerated. They bounced crazily in front of the black behemoth, their compasses pointed toward the small towns of Spencer, Jones, and Luther. As they sped past Spencer, two funnels formed in their rear-view mirror, reaching out and bumping each other. One roof after another hurtled into the sky, as if a strip of land mines were exploding behind them, and advancing.

Once they reached the outskirts of Jones, less than a mile in front of the twisters, they waved down the first police car they saw. The officer rolled down his window, figuring their request would be as innocuous as asking for the nearest filling station or diner. The officer had black hair, longer than average sideburns, and a complexion similar to Chance's, a few shades darker than Luke's. He wore sunglasses and a heavy frown. He sighed and shrugged his shoulders downward with a resigned, *oh well, it's part of my job*. He waited for them to talk.

They tore off their goggles. "Sir, we are licensed tornado spotters from Sixth Weather Squadron at Tinker," Luke said. "There's a tornado right behind us. Please call your supervisor. Sound the warning siren immediately. Get everybody into shelters, basements or root cellars."

At first, the officer appeared skeptical, but then he read the intensity in Luke's eyes. He turned up his radio and picked up the microphone. "This is Officer Gregory. Be advised: sound the tornado siren. We've got two minutes to hit the shelters."

Within seconds, a siren began to wail. Scanning the horizons they saw rain drifting to the northeast. Looking southwest, they noticed a black low-hanging cloud. "That cloud is too close to the ground, Chance. You know what that means!"

The officer took the cue from Luke. As he sped away, he shouted, "Thanks, boys! I'll round up the townspeople, alert the high school, and help the folks in the retirement center. You better follow your own advice."

Two hundred feet down the road, he slammed on his brakes and backed up, rolling down his window again. "We only have one squad car on duty. How fast can you guys ride to that hill to the east of town?" He pointed. "Emerson School is on the northeast side of that hill. Grades K through six. They will never see the tornado coming. But they do have a storm cave right above the school. Hurry! Get them into that cave!"

Chance and Luke fishtailed and raced to a shortcut over the hill, riding through fields and an adjoining baseball diamond. They arrived in less than two minutes, ditching their bikes on the front steps, then sprinting through the front doors and down the hall until they saw students.

Luke yanked the door open and yelled, "Tornado in sight! Free lunch for the first one in the storm cave! Teacher goes first."

Luke looked back. "Chance, check other classrooms and offices, I'll round up everybody I see here."

The teacher was petite, with white, almost blanched skin, reflecting her Scottish or British heritage. She had a striking billow of brunette hair. "I'm Nora MacLean. I'll take them to the cave. You bring along all the stragglers."

She disappeared out the front door, leaning down and shepherding her kids in front of her like a high wind through grain.

Within two minutes, they were all packed into the storm cave. Miss MacLean conducted a head count. She counted again: thirty-three kids, two teachers, two secretaries, and a spindly principal with a high forehead and black-frame glasses. Nobody knew where the janitor was. The principal tossed Chance an old rope he had carried from his office. "Tie down that storm door and both of you hold tight to that rope. Wrap it around yourselves if you have to, but for heaven's sakes, don't let the tornado take that door. It won't stop until all of us are up there howling in the wind."

Chance followed his directions without a word. Nobody could have heard him anyway. The noise outside was deafening, the wind shrieking and whistling through the door. Three times Chance and Luke were both lifted off the floor of the cave, but Miss MacLean and the principal held onto them until the noise abated and the howling ceased. The principal, Mr. Everly, unwrapped the rope around them and cautiously opened the door. Struck by a ray of sunshine, they crowded out of the cave.

Below them, the whole school building was gone. Nothing remained but fragments of the foundation. Mr. Everly and Miss MacLean organized the students into small groups and canvassed the school property. What remained of their cars appeared as scraps here and there in neighboring wheat fields a half mile away. Scattered schoolbook chapters were later found in the next county, some fifty miles away.

One of the students came upon a lifeless body, three hundred feet away, clinging to a door knob, his hand still locked in a vice grip. "I found Mr. Starkey!" the student screamed as he ran toward his teacher. "He's lying near trees right where he used to eat his lunch! I think he's sleeping!"

Miss MacLean rushed up to Luke. "Keep the children right here. I'll go see for myself."

When she came back, she walked past Luke to count her children again. "He's not sleeping," she whispered, casting her eyes downward. "But all my children are safe—not a scratch on them, thanks to you two."

Led by Officer Gregory, twenty cars retrieved the children. Every car that drove past Chance and Luke, the family members waved and screamed, "Thank you! Thank you!" Seven dads jumped out of their cars and rushed up to the two storm chasers to thank them. Chance was glad to be sitting on his motorcycle. Nobody could hug him. Luke thought the procession would never end.

Finally, Officer Gregory drove up and got out of his squad car. "Come on down to the courthouse," he said, shaking Chance's and Luke's hands over and over again. "Not even one of the kids went missing or got hurt."

Luke said, "God's got his arms wrapped all around us."

"Johnny Cash! I love his Christian music," the officer said.

"I wish we could have helped Mr. Starkey. We just didn't know where he was. Did he have family?" Chance asked.

"No. He sure wanted one. He just couldn't find the right person. He loved kids, though. We always thought he'd make somebody a good daddy." Officer Gregory looked away.

He started to go, and then turned around. "I'm not kidding," he said. "I know the mayor wants to thank you. He's going to give me hell if you don't come."

Luke reached out to shake his hand good-bye. "Thanks, but we need to check on one other possible tornado. Give us a few minutes."

26

Chance and Luke followed the procession of cars for a half-mile and then pulled off the road into a grove. Luke showed Chance a map. "This tornado could be regrouping and heading right for Luther. Let's take Hogback Road or the railroad bed and see if we can help them out."

"Let's go railroad."

"You got it."

They arrived at the county sheriff's office just in time to watch the tornado touch the ground and bounce up, completely bypassing Luther. The deputy on duty was a ham radio buff, with his own equipment as well as the sheriff's police dispatcher. Luke jumped on and checked with his Sixth Weather contact, Mitch Turner, who was in touch with another ham radio buddy out of Shawnee.

"Here's what you want to do," Mitch told Luke. "Look at the map. See Luther. Then grab Route 177. You want to head south to Tecumseh, southeast to Holdenville, bypass Wewoka, do a dog-leg into Calvin, and continue southeast to Stuart. Take the railroad shortcut east through Haywood. When you get right above the big Army ammunition plant, go east to McAlester, then continue east to Wister and northeast to Poteau. They got hit with one tornado, and we think they are going to get hit again. Nobody believes us. If you can get your butts down there, check out the skies and the patterns. Give them the warning they may need. Over."

"We're on it. I'll check back with you when we get to McAlester. Chance has Cherokee relatives who live there. I got family in Poteau. W3CIY, over and out."

"W3AJB, out."

On the map, the trip looked easy. Making the journey proved to be something else. The Oklahoma countryside had been transformed into debris as far as the eye could see in all directions, houses, barns, garages, outbuildings, all gone, to say nothing of numerous uprooted trees. They pinned their walkie-talkies to their ears and tried to keep up with the storm. From Lincoln County to Seminole County to Hughes County they rode, already aware of countywide damages in the millions and certain to climb. Past Tecumseh and close to Wewoka, they stopped at a dusty church where they heard a Good Shepherd pastor try to comfort families who had lost loved ones. One quote at the very end got to them. "Grief is not a bad thing in life. It reminds us that this life is not all there is here for us. Grief can be a chance for God to reach down, touch us, and comfort us."

Chance got up from the back of the church, pointed to his temple, shook his head, and tucked his walkie-talkie back into the toolbar hanging from his belt. He was not ready for such talk. They hit the road.

Luke started to worry about Lorraine and Scott Westby, who had become family to him. Westby was a master sergeant in supply who gave Luke a month of work when there were no openings for upper atmosphere weather operators. Scott and Lorraine had invited him to dinner when he first arrived at Tinker Air Force Base. Their two cute little kids, a boy and a girl, took to Luke as if he was a long-lost uncle. Before he knew it, though, Westby completed his twenty years and left Sixth Weather for the family farm outside Poteau. He'd grown up on the farm, and his folks needed him. His older brother had gone to the Air Force Academy, become a test pilot, and later commanded a whole Air Force Base. Instead of coming home after twenty years to run the farm, he'd continued climbing through the ranks. Now he was a general with no intention of retiring.

Metal signs for Route 270 lay along the roadside, ripped apart like cardboard. Outside Holdenville, they talked to a highway worker at a truck stop, a man with a bandaged nose and a bruised forehead, whose truck had been picked up by a tornado. "I got tossed around like a bowling ball," he said. "I am not driving anywhere. You should see my truck. It landed square down on the passenger side. Thank God it was not my side. I'd have lost an arm instead of breaking my nose on the other door."

Riding through Calvin, they watched firefighters move an injured man from the second-story bedroom of his home, where he'd been trapped. Two men were bringing him down a ladder, very slowly. The man was unconscious. Chance and Luke stopped to see if they could help, but by the time they got off their motorcycles, the rescue was finished.

They crossed into Pittsburg County, heading for McAlester. North of the Army ammunition plant, firefighters carried the bodies of a man and his wife from the rubble of their home. The wind had devastated farmhouses and surrounding tree groves. A local high school suffered massive destruction, with building after building leveled. Flying debris pockmarked cars. On the other side of McAlester, a car lay overturned with its lights and radio on, its engine running, and no driver. Crossing into Latimer County, they drove past more evidence of casualties, with ambulances and fire engines whizzing past or stopped alongside the road. In Wilburton, they saw two victims from a destroyed home lying on stretchers with ambulance on the way. The police officer told them, "They were found dead on the hillside behind the home, both still lying on the mattress. We don't know what killed them. No visible damage."

A search-and-rescue team showed Luke and Chance the basement of a home that was totally destroyed. "Home is gone, but the family had the good sense to build a basement," the captain of the team told Chance. "Grandparents live nearby," he said. "Otherwise they'd be like everybody else, staying in a church somewhere." He added, "Our search-and-rescue dog got injured rummaging through this house, looking for survivors. And they had already gone."

Beside an overturned car in front of a house, people tried to collect family photos scattered all over their front lawn.

They finally crossed the line into LeFlore County, close to Poteau and the Westby family farm. The skies were black and green, full of spiteful gusts. Riding a motorcycle was foolish. The unrelenting damage was nauseating, enervating, and exhausting to see. It never let up.

They rode into Poteau. There is no way to explain what a tornado can do until you see it firsthand. Roofs crumpled, bricks scattered, and trees split in half with no limbs remaining, just bare trunks devoid of leaves, fruits, or blossoms. Luke looked not into the face of death, but death's most vengeant scowl. People sat by the side of the road in front of their wrecked homes, staring, shocked, crying, their heads on one another's arms. A few lay face down in the mud, both hands pounding the soil in anguish. The vengeful tornado rubbed all of the smiles, grins, laughs, hopes, and dreams from their faces and hearts in a flash.

The property damage only added to the morbid shadow creeping inside Luke's head and heart. Indoor tennis courts stood without skylight panels; they'd been ripped away. A stuffed bear sprawled atop a pile of broken wood outside one apartment. A speed limit sign, torn in half, blocked part of the road. A mattress clung to a treetop. A convertible lay where a house and a garage once stood. The car looked like it had lost a rock-throwing fight against a pack of angry shepherds.

People scampered around one wrecked house after another, calling for their little kittens. Nearby, Red Cross workers gave a small assembly of Civil Air Patrol members their instructions on how to conduct visual surveys of tornado damage.

Chance pulled Luke over to the side. "You were right. This had to be a G-4."

"All these people suffering and we can't seem to be able to help them." Luke shook his head. "I feel terrible myself, and nothing has happened to me."

Chance nodded. "I have a bad feeling about the Westbys."

"I do too. Let's skip dinner and get the heck out there."

Luke couldn't imagine how Scott and Lorraine and their two little cherubs, Cody and Angela, could have survived this carnage.

His fear surged out of his stomach and almost overwhelmed him. Black bile burned his esophagus. *Wait a minute. Cody must be ten and Angela eight by now. Cherubs no longer. Maybe they won't be so helpless.*

They rode through Poteau and arrived at the long driveway. The big wooden sign identifying the Westby ranch was gone. So were the trees lining the driveway, their trunks and limbs axed like stalks of raw yellow celery. Red alert alarms pulsed through Luke. His heart rate stuttered and shot upward, filling his ears. The Westbys were three miles from a devastated town, far beyond the reach of neighbors who might have noticed their predicament. The sky lowered, and so did Luke's forward motion. The heart-pounding sound turned out to be Scott's horses loose in the fields, five huge Percherons charging toward the motorcycles.

They gunned their engines, not waiting to be trampled. The wall of noise protected them. The horses sat back on their haunches and reversed their headlong flight. Chance and Luke rolled down the long driveway, screwing on their most impassive faces to strengthen themselves for what they might see. Debris lay everywhere. The big two-story barn was gone; its huge timbers broken and twisted. Luke saw the familiar two-story farmhouse, built around the turn of the century. The first floor was intact, but the ceiling and second floor were gone. No sign of life.

Luke was overcome by terror. Righting himself, he jumped off and ran toward the house. There was a basement. That meant hope. However, Cody's and Angela's bedrooms stood on the second floor, separated by a stairwell. Scott and Lorraine occupied the big bedrooms on the east side. *Could they have survived flying through the air? Did they escape in time to hide in the basement with its big storm-cellar door?*

Luke ran straight to the storm cellar door, with Chance on his heels, and leaned down to open it in the secret way Scott had shown him. It was jammed shut. "This is a good sign." Luke knocked on the door. "Cody, Angela! Can you hear me? It's Luke, your Uncle Luke!"

He waited, then knocked again, and held his breath.

Seconds later, he heard a faint tapping. "Cody! Angela! Unlatch the door. We're here to help!"

A clinking and scratching sound preceded a tentative lifting of the huge door. It opened about an inch. Chance and Luke seized it and lifted it wide open. At the bottom of the steps sat Cody, holding his sister, who lay limp in his arms. Luke rushed down to embrace Cody and in the next minute Chance had pulled Angela into his arms.

"Cody, are you okay? What happened to her?"

Cody held Luke tightly. "I found Angela pinned under a fallen beam. We were rushing downstairs after the roof peeled off our house. Daddy always told me to head for the basement at the first sign of a tornado. We almost made it. Just as we got to the basement door, the stairwell we had just run down collapsed above us."

He pointed across the basement. Debris covered the opposite stairwell. Luke gasped. "How did you both get down here through all that stuff?"

Cody started to cry. "If I had let Angela go first, she never would have gotten hit. She was lying under a whole wall. I thought she was going to die there."

Luke reassured him. "But you were there to save her. She couldn't have lifted that beam and wall partition off of *you*. How in the world did you do it?"

"I don't know. I knew she couldn't breathe. I just had to do it. Daddy told me that once a mom lifted a whole rear end of a car up to free her little girl lying underneath. He told me sometimes God gives us superman strength, just like in comic books. I hoped he was right. I lifted so hard, I must have conked out. I woke up on the stairs and she was free. But she wouldn't talk to me. Is she going to be okay?"

Chance looked up. "I just checked her pulse, her breathing, and her eyes. Don't worry. I can feel her breath and her heart rate. Everything is normal, and her eyes haven't fallen back in her head where I can't see them."

Luke hugged Cody. "That's a good sign, buddy."

Chance worked on Angela, talking gently to her, rubbing her forehead, rubbing her hands. He looked up again. "She just has a bump on the back of her head, Cody, and a few bruises across her back where the wall crunched her. You did a super job getting her free."

Cody was inconsolable. "But I couldn't help Mom and Dad. The lightning struck, Mom yelled, and I ran to pull Angela out of her bed and get down to the basement. When the roof flew off, I think Dad and Mom and their fancy bed went with it. Every time I close my eyes, I get that picture. I hope I didn't see what I just saw."

Luke held Cody tight. The boy closed his eyes, spilling out his grief. "I think I saw the last of them. I don't know where they might have landed. They are not in the house, because if they were, they'd have been down here with us, just like we practiced."

Cody shook his head. "I've just been down here taking care of Angela, just the way Dad taught me to. But I haven't done a very good job of it. I couldn't even remember how to open the storm door. Thanks for coming to save us, Uncle Luke."

"Don't say that. You saved Angela. Look, she's responding to Chance."

The girl's eyes flickered and then opened, all big and blue and scared. She looked up at Luke, and her voice floated up to him so softly. "Where am I, Uncle Luke? Did you die too? Am I in heaven? Is this an angel holding me?"

"Whoa, girl, I'm alive and so are you, and so is Cody. The man holding you is my best friend, Chance, and he's no angel yet."

Concern knotted her baby-smooth brow. "Then where is Mama? Papa?"

"We don't know yet. But we will find them, don't you worry."

Chance nodded his head. "I'll stay here with Angela. You and Cody go back to our bikes, get flashlights and our walkie-talkies. Bring me mine, and I'll call for help. See that stack of blankets on top of that chest over on your left? Grab two blankets for Scott and Lorraine. I know you and Cody will find them."

27

Ten minutes later, Cody and Luke traced a search-and-rescue pattern to pace the thousand acres of corrals, fields, meadows, and pasture that made up the Westby farm. Creeks ran at both edges of their property, close to a mile apart, with groves of oaks and cottonwoods parading up and down the creek beds. Huge meadows filled the front of their property on both sides of the long winding driveway. In back, across a huge meadow, lay the beginning of the foothills and too many trees to count.

"Cody, with that image of your dad and mom disappearing above you, do you have any idea which direction?"

Cody thought a moment. "Maybe over and behind the barn." He pointed. "That way. I saw them up in the air, out of the corner of my left eye. I came flying out of my bedroom and down the hall to Angela's room. Can we check the big barn first, both stories? I hope I can find them in the hayloft. Let's look in all the horse stalls, too."

"Cody, in case your mom and dad are lying out in a field somewhere, let's call in the horses, just to be safe."

Cody gave out a shrill whistle, just like his dad. All the family horses picked their way through the debris and stopped in front of them. He and Luke tied them up in the stalls that still appeared safe. They counted the horses quickly: six Percherons and six Morgans. All accounted for.

Five minutes later, Cody and Luke scrambled through fences and began their sweep of the northeast pasture. "Mom! Dad! Mama!

Papa!" Luke thought they might respond more quickly if they heard one of their children call.

Chance called on the walkie-talkie. "Luke, help is on the way. We got search and rescue and the Red Cross coming. Let me know if you get lucky."

"Good going, Chance. How's Angela?"

"She's a baby tiger. She wants to come help find Mama and Papa."

"Okay, come on along when search and rescue arrives. We're in the northeast pasture. Cody thinks they may have floated over this way."

Cody and Luke moved carefully toward the creek on the right, hoping that the surrounding trees and bushes might have broken the falls of Scott and Lorraine. Then a sound, a low moan, and more broken moans.

Directly ahead.

They rushed forward, their flashlights blazing. They scoured the underbrush lining the creek, looking for Lorraine. She wasn't there. They circled back. "Mom! Mama!' Luke could hear Cody's breaking heart through his little voice quavering in the darkness.

Little life sounds seemed to echo around the glen at the edge of the meadow. Luke stopped and put his fingers to his lips, and Cody held his breath. Luke mouthed to Cody, "Did you hear that?" He nodded. Hope began to dawn in his eyes.

Ten feet to his right, Luke saw a telltale ripple in the high meadow grass. Walking together ever so slowly, each foot poised for a moment above the ground before they set it down, they advanced cautiously in the direction of the half-moans, half-sighs. Luke saw the bare form of a woman lying face down in the meadow, her head turned to the left. Lorraine! Cody hesitated, fearful of finding his dear mom already floating out of her body just as she and Papa had floated out of their home.

Luke walked forward and gently placed a blanket over Lorraine's naked body. Then he knelt down, his hand under the blanket. He gently moved his fingers over her upper back, checking for abnormalities in her cervical vertebrae. He leaned down next to her face, willing her to breathe and reach out to life, and hoping to feel her breath ever so slightly on his cheek.

Luke bit his lip to keep emotions in check. "Lorraine! It's me, Luke. Cody's right here with me. Are you okay? Can you hear me?"

Her eyes fluttered open. "I can hear you, Luke. Thank God you're here. Cody, honey, please put that other blanket over me. Is Angela with you? Did you get to the basement okay?"

"Yes, we got to the basement. Angela's back at the house. Luke's best friend, Chance, is taking care of her. I think she has a bump and a headache . . . she's okay."

"Wonderful. I know you took care of her. Ohhh . . ."

She passed out.

Luke radioed Chance with the good news. Cody needed more confirmation than that. "Did she really see me, Uncle Luke? Is she still breathing?" He held his breath.

"Yes, Cody-man, she is okay, and she knows you're here. I think it's safe to carefully roll her over. Her neck seems intact. Come sit on the ground and lean over to your right. When she awakens again, she'll be in your arms, looking right up at you."

Cody's tears stopped.

Luke took his time as he turned Lorraine over so she could breathe more easily. Pain crossed her face every time she inhaled. He needed to tell Cody, even though it might alarm the boy. "Cody, I'll bet your mom has some broken ribs. She might have a collapsed lung. They often go together. Let's be very careful so we don't puncture her lungs or any vital organs."

Cody nodded, holding his mama carefully. Lorraine flittered back into consciousness. Her voice was so weak; Cody and Luke both leaned down to hear her. "I remember getting ripped from sleep. The roof came off as our home exploded. I felt like Scott and I were just rag dolls tossed around by a violent swirling wind. Every second seemed like an eternity. The life I knew and the home I lived in was blown to smithereens."

"Mom, you don't have to talk."

"No, honey, I want to tell you this. I was sure I was going to die. In my last moments, I remembered going over to visit our ninety-year-old neighbor just yesterday. I took her some coffee brewed with our chicory and a few fresh vegetables from our garden. She was so happy to see me. Everybody knew her as Aunt Betty. I was so happy I visited her. It was something I always wanted to do."

"Mom, you'll be able to do that again. You're not going to die."

"Thanks honey." She struggled for the strength to speak again. Her voice cracked. "Luke, Cody will take good care of me. Please, please."

"Of course! Help is coming for you, Lorraine."

She held out her hand. "Wait. I remember bolting up in bed, awakened by a terrible loud noise. I yelled for Cody to save Angela. I tried to wake Scott, but he's a sound sleeper, and then the house started falling apart.

"I knew Scott and I were going upward, but the sensation was like going down a huge hill on a roller coaster. I thought this was the end. I knew I was going to die," she murmured. "All of these thoughts started rushing through my head. All the good times. All the things I haven't done yet. My whole life. Then somehow a feeling of peace came over me. I just put myself in the hands of God."

"Don't talk, Mama."

"I must have crashed into the ground somewhere on our property. I had grass and dirt in my mouth. My chest and ribs hurt so badly, and I was shaking from the cold. I began crying for help, but then I couldn't breathe. I could hear Scott somewhere crying for help. I was so relieved to hear him."

She paused, the details coming back to her in fragments. "Both of us wear glasses. They were on the bedside table, and I just know our glasses are gone. He won't be able to see much. Please go find him!"

She pointed to her right. "I think I heard something from over there."

"I'll be right back, Cody," Luke said.

Luke moved as quickly as he could. Eighty feet away, he found Scott, unconscious but breathing, his pulse rapid and weak. He radioed Chance. "We just found Scott. When search and rescue comes, get help up here in the upper meadow right away. Lorraine goes in and out of consciousness. Scott is more seriously injured."

"They just left here and are on their way."

"The way Scott is lying on the ground, all torn and twisted, I'm sure he has broken a leg or ruptured his pelvis. It looks as if he landed more on his hip."

"The ambulance is here. They have stretchers. They're on their way right now. Good going, Luke!"

On the way to Poteau Hospital, Lorraine heard the driver talking about two ambulances bringing tornado victims into the emergency room. Chance and Angela rode in the other ambulance with Scott. Lorraine frowned up at Cody and Luke, in a voice sleepy with medication and pain. "We're not tornado victims. We're tornado victors. We're still here."

28

Life settled down after all the storm chasing. Luke and Chance continued to deploy up and down Tornado Alley. By February, tornadoes showed up in the Gulf States first. By May, the tornadoes seem to hover over Oklahoma, hitting the state an average of eighty times in that month, and clobbering Texas and Kansas while in full swing. Tornado Alley stretched up through Kansas, Missouri, and into the Dakotas. While there, Luke and Chance marveled that they could run forever in the cool, dry climate on the roads surrounding the Grand Forks AFB.

Each "flight" or group of usually ten or more operators and technicians drove out separately or in a convoy on a new mission. The flight was self-sufficient with one master sergeant in charge and little interference from home base. Luke and Chance spent three months in Kansas and three months in North Dakota. They worked out of Grand Forks AFB, where the United States operated missile silos to protect against an over-the-pole Russian attack. They also supported B-52 flights far above Tornado Alley, down to the Barry Goldwater bombing range in Arizona and back, a twelve-hour roundtrip.

Luke and Chance drove the big weather van out to Castle Air Force Base in California to support the B-52 wings gearing up and training for a possible conflict with Russia. During off hours, Luke was chosen to drive his sergeant around. Should the sergeant get a second DUI, his career would be over. Luke was happy to help the sergeant out. He was the most even-tempered supervisor Luke ever had. They took a trip to Yosemite National Park, the redwood forests, and to a half-dozen bars. While he waited in the car, Luke spent hours writing Lacy. He had no idea if she got the letters. He just wanted to keep in touch.

On a crazy Monday in January, Flight B received emergency orders to get back to Tinker Air Force Base. In three weeks, they would be deployed to Tutuila, American Samoa. The Air Force and Army had less than a year to test out their nuclear weaponry, rockets, and thermonuclear devices before implementation of the October nuclear test moratorium to which the United States and Russia had agreed. Luke and Chance found a map, trying to figure out where they were headed. Tutuila was an exotic name. They learned it was an island not more than fifteen miles long, its capital city Pago Pago spread along the shores of a most beautiful harbor that filled the crater of an old volcano.

Luke couldn't contain his enthusiasm. "Holy hell! We are going to the South Pacific. My dad played songs from that musical all the time when he got back from the Pacific. I read everything I could about Polynesia, like Melville's little known novel, *Typee,* the first romance novel out of the South Pacific. And Michener, too, his book on the South Pacific…I have dreamed about the beautiful native Polynesians, and those getaway romantic islands. I call it "the golden triangle of Polynesia," from Hawaii down to Fiji and New Zealand, eastward to French Polynesia and Tahiti, and then northward back to Hawaii." He ran his finger along the map to show Chance.

Chance shook his head. "Get real, Luke. You're not going to have time to get to know anybody down there. We work maybe eight to twelve hour shifts, and twenty-four-hour shifts every so often. Sergeant Jones said we gotta stay close to our campsite. It's on the other side of the island from Pago Pago."

Not only did twisters keep Luke moving, but so did the Air Force. Soon after the tornadic outbursts that nearly claimed Chance and Luke's lives, they deployed for a dangerous island life underneath upper atmosphere nuclear detonations. The rockets were dated, and the nuclear bombs were untested…

During Luke's Tornado Alley duties, he had written Lacy at least twice a week. He took heart in that, even though she did not respond. He was keeping her in his life and in his thoughts—even while performing dangerous duties. He hoped she was reading his letters. He forgot how she dismissed him at Springfield Academy when he went to visit her. Now in a university, Lacy had to start at the bottom and make a new set of friends. But she still actually thought of Luke from time to time. Sometimes at night the pain squeezed her until she woke.

Meanwhile, Lacy had completed her foreign exchange program, had traveled around Europe and returned for college at Stanford University. But she traveled back and forth, working part-time at her father's department stores throughout Chicago and sometimes in San Francisco, whenever she had vacation. Now she was departing Chicago, walking toward her United Airlines waiting area at O'Hare, waiting to head back to San Francisco. What are the chances of their meeting, you may ask yourself?

Luke sat waiting his flight at O'Hare. He might be gone up to a year. He was excited but wary. The scuttlebutt on thermonuclear testing was nothing but dangerous, with untested hydrogen bombs and unproven out-of-date missiles to send the bombs on their way. And he would be on some of the same islands where they blasted off, or underneath their flight paths. There he sat at O'Hare wishing he could see Lacy one more time.

Luke got nervous. It was past time for boarding. Maybe he didn't hear the call. He jumped up from his reverie and ran out of the American Airlines waiting area of O'Hare. He rushed around a corner into the main corridor. Lacy was hurrying down the main corridor in the opposite direction.

He and Lacy literally ran into each other. Lugging his heavy duffel bag, he looked down and saw silver high heels. When they collided, Luke had to prevent her from being knocked off her feet. Luke dropped his duffle bag and grabbed her. He didn't notice who she was until he caught a whiff of her favorite French perfume. A vision of lilac hedges where they kissed flashed through his mind. Then he received a face full of her long, silky dark hair. They were almost cheek to cheek. There was no mistaking it. Luke had never even dreamed of such a meeting.

Their eyes locked. He instantly recognized her elegant nose and beautiful eyes and clouds of black hair so beautifully arranged. He could not believe his eyes. He looked away, and then he looked back. He sucked in a breath and peered again at her unforgettable silver-toned eyes. "Lacy! Are you okay?"

"Luke! What are you doing?"

Flustered, he stepped back and picked up his duffle bag. "I didn't mean it. I just thought if I hadn't caught you, you might have fallen."

"No. What are you doing *here*?" Hurt and accusation shot out of her eyes.

"I was home on leave."

Her eyes became black glaciers. "I haven't seen you for over two years. Why didn't you have the courage to come see me, or write me?"

Luke felt that old hurt creeping into his heart. "What are you talking about? I wrote you almost every day for a year. You never answered one letter. I was sure you married some family friend. Plus, you were never home, always away."

"What are *you* talking about? You have to explain this letter writing thing."

"Well, are you married?"

"No. Are you?"

Luke looked down, silent as a windless snowstorm. Finally, he shook his head. "What do you think?"

"Why didn't you call then?"

"I did call, every week for some time. You never answered the phone. Your parents always told me you were out, or that you were working or on a trip of some kind. They never took a message or asked for my phone number."

"What?" Lacy stepped away, aghast. She adopted a more conciliatory tone. "Come on, Luke. I had no idea. Come sit in the lounge and have a drink for old times."

Lacy took his hand and led him across the corridor. Then she let go, extended her arm, and pointed to a little table next to a window.

It overlooked two of O'Hare's longest runways. As they sat down, Luke couldn't even look out the window, much as he loved planes.

Lacy sat across the table. Her beauty filled up the whole room and struck Luke silent. Her black hair tumbled down her shoulders. Her white blouse filled out and accentuated her elegant gray suit, mirroring the magnetic color of her eyes. *She is even more beautiful than I remember*, he thought. *And changed.* From the youthful appearance he last saw, her face shone forth with a more refined and precious cameo look. She was self-assured and mature, surrounded by massive waves of hair. *This is a jewel placed into an even more beautiful setting. Lacy's crowning glory.*

She leaned across the table. "Can you give me a break, Luke? You left me."

Something about the way she tore into him, just like the night a tornado tore through his house, scattering his security, his sense of belonging.

The waitress sailed over. "I hope I'm not interrupting . . . What can I get for you?"

Relieved, Luke looked up and said, "Please bring her an Old Fashioned. And Old Style lager for me, my last chance to enjoy it."

Lacy nodded to the waitress and then sat in silence, waiting. The waitress returned promptly and set the drinks down.

Lacy took a sip of her Old Fashioned with a frown. She leaned forward. "What happened to you and me, Luke? What happened? Just because you and Dad got into that big argument on graduation night, you thought everything was over between us?"

Luke shook his head and drank almost half of his mug of Old Style draft beer. "No, your dad made it clear that everything was over between us. You just stood there."

"You graduated and you just left. I still had another year of high school."

"I went home to work, and every break you had, your family took you to France, England, or Spain."

"You just disappeared."

"I never left you. Didn't you hear me? I wrote you every day and sent you a packet of the letters twice a week to save postage. You never once answered me, so I threw my pen out the window."

Doubt the color of night and the thickness of thunderheads darkened her face. "You wrote me every day?"

"Yeah, for almost a year."

"You're saying that because I have no way of proving you wrong."

"Really? If you don't believe me, talk to my sister Jessica. She worked for your mom every Saturday, even though your parents had professional help. Jessica needed the money. She vacuumed, took out the trash, tidied up the kitchen, and helped your mom with gardening, flower pots, even the yard."

Lacy sat back, willing to listen. The frown slipped off her face.

"If she hadn't been working that day, she never would have seen a big rubber-banded bundle of letters hidden in a shopping bag," Luke continued. "She told me she said, 'Mrs. De'Luca, are you sure you want me to burn everything in this shopping bag?

"'Yes, Jessica. Put them all in the incinerator. It was time I cleaned out my front hall closet. Away up on the top shelf in the back, I saw that bag of personal letters. I asked your father about them, and he said he didn't need them anymore. That he was just saving them. I don't know what they were.'"

Pure puzzlement etched on Lacy's forehead. Her lips pursed together. "How did Jessica know who wrote the letters?"

"She recognized my handwriting, of course. And instead of burning them, she hid them in the evergreens in your backyard to pick up later. She folded up newspapers and burned them so it looked as if she burned my letters."

"Why would your sister save the letters?"

"I always confided in her. She knew I had written you every day. She knew how painful it would be for me if she just went and burned them."

Luke shrugged. That entire period welled up on him like a haymaker punch. "You never made any effort, so what difference does it make?"

"Wait a minute, Luke. If my parents were mean enough to hide your letters from me, they might have been mean enough to tell me things that weren't true."

She frowned and looked away, trying to remember. When she gazed at Luke again, her voice trembled, and remorse rimmed her eyes. "I shouldn't have listened to them, Luke. What they told me, combined with silence from you, broke my heart. When they confronted you after that weekend, they told me you said, 'Don't worry about Lacy and me—it's just puppy love, two kids who don't know anything about life. It's not going to go anywhere.'"

"They told you that? That's what your dad said, not me!"

"I know, now, Luke." She began to tear up. "They told me other things as well." She shook her head, lowered it, and then met his eyes. "How could I have doubted you?"

"I wondered that myself for about a million years." He drained his mug and looked at his watch. "We were in love for two years, young or not. You could have given our love more respect, more credibility. You could have taken the love of your parents for granted, but not my love for you." He stood up. "My flight is leaving in fifteen minutes. I have to go, Lacy. I'm on my way to the South Pacific. Please don't look at any of my letters. They will just make us feel worse. I'll give Jessica my okay to burn them."

"No, Luke! Please don't! I will read them. I will answer them."

Luke forced a pained smile. "Good-bye, Lacy. You don't even have an address for me. I've got to catch my flight. I'll be out of the country in three days."

"I'll get your address from Jessica. I promise!"

Luke grabbed his duffel bag and started to run for the gate as the last call for his flight blared over the O'Hare intercom.

Lacy jumped up from her seat, cutting off his forward momentum. "Remember when you were leaving me for the first time? And I jumped up on the steps of the train?"

She threw her arms around him and kissed him in front of everybody, the biggest close-mouth kiss he'd ever experienced. The kind of kisses he dreamed of with Lacy. Luke felt as if he had been swallowed up in love and with love, his soul soaring painlessly through that little tunnel people see when they go through their near-death experiences. His loneliness disappeared. And then he came back to earth.

Lacy kissed him again, this time a gentler good-bye kiss. "Remember this, Luke. I never forgot your kisses. And I will find those letters." She walked away ten steps, turned around, and smiled. "I knew you were watching!"

She walked away again. She looked back, flicked her skirt, and, while turning the corner, kicked her right foot behind her, just as she had done before. It always drew his attention to her cute butt.

Luke reached the gate and boarded the plane, his mind spinning like a tornado, his thoughts flying out like tossed debris.

Could it be?

Book Three
SOUTH PACIFIC

29

Chance and Luke peered out of the porthole windows of the Air Force C-54. Maui and Molokai shimmered in the sea southeast of Oahu. The Hawaiian Islands were as beautiful as they'd ever imagined the most enchanting archipelago in the western hemisphere, as Mark Twain had described them when he found the warm paradise of the Big Island in the late 1880s.

Twenty minutes later, they approached over Pearl Harbor and landed on the civilian airfield. After touching down, they taxied interminably—about twenty minutes—until they got to Hickam Field.

While civilian passengers were receiving their traditional welcoming leis a few miles away, nobody greeted Chance and Luke at Hickam. However, the famous easterly trade wind threw its arms around them and the pikake and plumeria-laden air caressed their faces.

Somehow, they made it to their barracks. It felt like a dream.

The Hickam barracks slept four people to a cell-like room. The yellow concrete walls outside were still riddled with bullet holes left by the Japanese during their infamous sneak fighter attack that plunged the United States into World War II. They were left to remind everyone who saw them: "Vigilance!"

The bullet holes drew a scenario through Luke's mind: *Sunday morning and the Japanese fighters are firing into a building full of innocent, sleeping Americans.* He noticed the cannon fire every time he walked into the barracks. The room was so small that once, when he jumped off the second bunk, he landed in Chance's overseas trunk. However, you could feed whole armies in the dining hall.

Away from Hickam, Hawaii spread her *aloha* spirit through the hearts and imagination of her two newest occupants. Huge misty cloud murals swirled high across the deep blue skies. The ocean surrounded them with its power and depth and also its dreamy serenity. It renewed Luke's faith in nature—there *was* a Garden of Eden. Sure beat all those fractostratus clouds in Illinois, all that cold weather. Yet, the thing that struck him about Hawaii was the Aloha spirit itself; everybody got along, playing music, caring about very little. Even the word "aloha" resonated with harmony.

Three days later, they departed for American Samoa. Their luck held. They stopped at Kanton Atoll with its oppressive humidity, often over 100%. Despite the weather, they always played Pacific cutthroat volleyball (win at all costs) once the sun began to descend. They ate heartily from a wide smorgasbord of South Pacific fare: fish, rice, breadfruit, fish, coconut, taro root, rice, pineapple, and a whole lot more. From overseas, they feasted on peas from California, tins of biscuits from Australia, and corned beef from New Zealand. The brass always compensated remote-site personnel with immense stores of food, beer, and soda.

After dinner, one of the men put Alfred Newman's "Ports of Paradise" on the stereo. The perfect initiation into the Pacific romantic mystique. Chance and Luke listened to the whole record, surrounded by moist, breezy darkness and the crashing of nearby waves, transported by the enchanting native songs and enticing instrumentals. Any romantic would have been hooked. Luke stayed awake far into the night listening to the record over and over until the words were branded into his heart. He wondered if island romance could happen to him. "Ports of Paradise, I'm sailing home to you, back to my moonlit memories, of an island love."

A week before their squadron took off from Kanton Island, another transport C-54 crashed and burned on takeoff. There were no rescue units or hospitals anywhere near the island. All passengers and crew perished. Chance and Luke held their breath. Their squadron lifted off from Kanton Island all right, but then the C-54 lost an engine. An hour later, they shut down the second engine. They limped 500 miles out of their way to a repair facility in Fiji. The entire time, Luke could see the second engine on the port side leaking a slipstream of oil. And the crew was only too happy to tell them the ocean below teamed with many more sharks than any other flight they had taken.

Chance nudged him. "If we lost those engines on takeoff, we might have been food for the sharks."

"I hate when that happens."

They spent three days in Fiji, perfecting the unique Pacific volleyball tactics that all natives had, and waiting for replacement engines from Los Angeles. The Fijians are known worldwide for their dazzling smiles. Luke also experienced the famous Fijian smile. Nobody can match the dazzle of a Fijian smile. Or the lasting effect. The same could be said about *kava*, their prized ceremonial drink, served with a coconut shell dipper. One night, Luke gamely helped the gang drink sixteen cupfuls, only to see the dishpan refilled again. He was sure he wouldn't be sick for years; it was so medicinal. He realized something right away: Don't ever try to kiss a Polynesian after you have been drinking kava. It numbs your lips and tongue. You can't feel a thing. But the smiles make up for it.

Once the new engines had been installed, they made the short flight to Samoa. They crossed the International Dateline. It was Friday the 13th on the day they left and maybe doubling the bad luck associated with that date. But Luke knew good things were coming. Seeing Tutuila from the air was like hovering above a vision. It made a dramatic visual statement as high as the mountain island itself.

They landed on Tutuila. Jumping off the plane, Luke gazed with astonishment at the huge mountain chain that ran down the middle of the eighteen-mile island, a natural volcanic spine. When the squadron received a few indestructible jeep and weapons carrier leftovers from World War II, they took an eight-mile drive, full of new sights, jungle scenery, rural villages, and a hundred scents and smells they'd never known. The native Samoans smiled and waved. So did the airmen. For Flight B of Sixth Weather Squadron, this promised to be the best mobile weather duty-station ever.

The Rainmaker Hotel awaited them along the waters of Pago Bay. The weather-beaten appearance of the huge grey building reflected its World War II construction. But Polynesian hospitality within made all the difference. It felt well lived-in. Its large, informal dining room featured eighty-six rooms and large porches around three sides. While quartered at the Rainmaker, they enjoyed their extra per diem pay and luxuriated while waiting for the tents to be finished twelve miles away in Leone.

Luke also met a few friends at the Rainmaker, including Olivvy. She enchanted Luke like the gold nugget he had dug up on the outskirts of a California ghost town. He even wrote a song about it. Everybody clamored for her attention. The waitress hugged people from behind if they were complimentary and behaved themselves. She always smiled. She was also very pretty. Her long black hair, slim figure, and narrow face were atypical of pure Polynesians, who tended to be thicker bodied. She always wore long white skirts or dresses. One day, Luke saw her legs, which shocked him; she hadn't adopted the American custom of shaving. But that didn't stop him. Olivvy was everybody's friend, just like Lacy. Luke had panned for gold in California and Nevada. Exciting. Anticipatory. But no matter how beautiful the location, it was painful to keep panning when the promising mountain stream appeared wherever he went, but only gave him only one nugget per year. No goldmine for him upstream. Luke dreamed of a woman who would be his golden nugget every day. He wanted a one-man woman without eyes for anyone else.

Three days after arriving in Samoa, Chance and a mutual friend, Gunnar, took Luke around to the Island Moon Bar. They drank a beer or two. Luke straddled a bench to watch Winnie, a pretty Samoan girl, and a sailor with a rather repulsive motion and expression sharing an island dance. The sailor was a drunken, mean-eyed German.

As Luke continued to watch, Winnie ended the dance and sat down right between Luke's legs. She faced Gunnar's back, and Luke felt her sweet presence. She talked to Gunnar now, quietly, unaware of her effect on Luke. He didn't hear what she was saying, but he was entranced with her form, her beauty, and her innocence. Winnie was slim, well proportioned, sharply featured, beautiful, wild, and playful. Her unkempt long hair made it appear that she just rolled out of bed. Gunnar was trying to reform her. That was his word, and the word of his friends. She seemed to respond to it. He carried an archaic sense of chivalry.

Gunnar and Winnie set up some kind of rendezvous, and then she jumped up and left. Gunnar, Chance, and Luke walked out slowly, taking in all the exotic women, adding their Technicolor mysteries to their memory cells.

Back at the hotel, they feasted on a Samoan smorgasbord: three kinds of fish, fried pork, breadfruit, sliced taro root, a few salads, constant side bowls of rice, various vegetables, and fried bananas for a delicious dessert. While they ate, Luke's curiosity took charge. "How did you meet Winnie, Gunnar? What did she do to interest you?"

"Oh, the first night I got here, I went to the Island Moon. I was drinking a beer and trying to figure out who was who. Some of those queer Samoan *fafafeines* look just like women. They even have a flower behind their ear."

Luke said, "Olivvy told me their name means they want to be a woman. And both sexes wear the wrap-around *lava-lava*, so it's hard to tell."

"If you notice their breasts, you can see they are flat-chested. Strange customs, huh?" Gunnar pointed out. "At home, those kinds of guys keep to their own bars and don't flaunt it. But anyway, some foreign sailor was on the dance floor with Winnie. She looked young and innocent. The sailor was trying to get her to practically make love to him on the dance floor, in front of everybody, for God's sake." Gunnar shook his head in disgust.

"So what did you do?" Luke asked.

"I wanted to clobber the guy. But I'm a foreigner, too. New here. So I got up and cut in on him. I didn't really want to dance, just get him off her case. If my looks could kill, he'd have been dead on the dance floor."

"So what happened?"

"Well, we started to talk, and she was so much fun, playful, and happy that I began to enjoy dancing with her. And the sailor did not leave, so we danced for a long time. I could not believe my watch when I finally came to my senses. That is how it all got started. My girlfriend back in Minnesota would have left me for good."

Winnie, the lively Western Samoan native with Chinese blood, set her sights on Gunnar Swenson. One thing Gunnar understood well: where he was from, they didn't have women like this. He slept in one of the inside rooms at the Rainmaker Hotel. Because Luke arrived on the island later, he had to sleep on the porch of the hotel only feet away from the breezes and the gentle slapping of the waves in Pago Pago Harbor.

During his fourth night at the Rainmaker, Luke was awakened by a gentle hand on his chest and tickled by the touch of long, black tresses. It was Winnie, looking for Gunnar at two in the morning. Bending over Luke, both of them very slightly dressed, she startled him. In a low, throaty voice, she said, "I want Gunnar. Can you get him?" Luke didn't understand why she asked him. Perhaps she was afraid to go inside the hotel.

Almost every night thereafter, she floated in and awakened Luke. The vision of her appearing out of a dream, rubbing his chest gently to awaken him, would haunt him during the following days. She seemed sweet, gentle. She moved like the breeze, noiselessly. The overpowering scent of pikake followed her. Guys sleeping five feet away on either side of Luke never heard her, saw her, smelled her, or touched her. She wanted only him to help her. He always got up, went in, and awakened Gunnar.

While Luke tried to go back to sleep, Gunnar would take her out to a little bench by Pago Pago Bay. Luke could see them in the distance. He was always talking to her, trying to help her change her ways.

Before midnight, Winnie danced and made all the rounds of the Pago Pago bars. She was not a one-man woman until after midnight. Gunnar and Luke joked about her being a love-aholic, a woman who got high on love and could only drink love to excess. Then in the wee hours, she'd feel some type of lover's remorse. She'd come to see Gunnar, who would remonstrate with her.

30

Brenda Lee's song, "I Want to Be Wanted," floated through Luke's mind off and on. It had since the surprise meeting with Lacy at O'Hare. He sang it softly, just as his dad used to do. And he sang many other songs, memorizing them on his time off. Music from KOA, the radio station out of Oklahoma City, came on over one channel from 0200 to 0400. Luke learned from it. One line haunted him. He imagined Lacy singing it back on the mainland.

"Where is this someone . . . somewhere, meant for me?"

During Luke's first months in American Samoa, two hospitable Samoan families willing to share everything adopted him. Any time he had off, he left Camp Leone with the sodden WWII Army tents pitched in the jungle with small clearings, but near a few open fields. The Quonset huts for weather and communication work sat next to an old WWII runway, built and used as a half-way point to transport planes to the far Pacific for air battles with the Japanese. Huge cargo planes like the C-123 lumbered in and parked while unloading, at least one propeller and engine quietly rumbling. It was a pacifier for the crew. They did not want to shut down and then be forced to stay due to engine or battery failure.

Luke would walk down the forest and jungle road to Leone, a seaside village. So on his way during the day, he often met a few sweet Samoan girls. Normally their families protected them, and men in uniform could not associate until they had proven their character. But Luke had already proven himself. The first thing they noticed was his stepping into their little white church in Leone one Sunday and listening to the singing. He quietly looked for a hymnal in the back row. But the singing was all in Samoan. He felt foolish jumping from the page on the left in Samoan and the opposite page in English.

All of a sudden it was Sunday again a few weeks later. Luke waited by the *Fa'aita fale* by the seaside, all dressed for church. Eti, the oldest son, came over from the small *fale*. Similar to the main *fale,* it consisted of the same thatched roof on poles, the same mandamus mats over crushed stone on the floor, and the same lack of privacy. Eti was ready to go to church and brought a *lava-lava* for Luke to wear. Chance, their other adoptee, was working shift at the Leone airstrip. Luke wasn't wild about the *lava-lava*, a colorful wrap-around skirt, but if a husky man like Eti could wear one, fine. So could he. It was *Fa'a Samoa*, the way of Samoa.

Eti brought a Sámoan Bible to church, and Luke carried his English version. Eti showed Luke where the minister was reading, and he followed along, suddenly missing the easy lessons in English in this Samoan Christian Congregationalist Church. He kept finding the passages in his Bible only to be nudged by Eti to go to the next passage. Luke felt a little lost when the service was over. He looked to his left and spoke in a low tone to Eti. "What was his main message? I could not follow it all."

Eti answered quietly. "The preacher is saying the Samoa we see now is losing its innocence. Families hear about the United States and so-called civilization, and the young adults are leaving this innocence. Joining the Navy is one of their favorite escapes. Then the shallow tourists and Americans are coming and want to stay, to teach our children, to run our schools, to build new hotels, bring in more vacationers, and make more fish-processing plants. They are taking our innocence away and replacing it with greed and money."

Luke winced. "I am part of that?"

"No, no, no," said Eti. "You love our country the way it is. You do not want to change it."

"*Fa'afit'ai, Eti*," Luke said. "You made me feel right at home."

He couldn't wait to hear more singing. It didn't matter if he didn't know the words. The devotion and the beautiful voices said it all for Luke. He turned his head away and looked to his right. He caught the eye of a beautiful Sámoan-Tahitian woman all dressed in white, singing with the most devoted look on her face.

He looked at her again. She sang. *So innocently. So sweetly. So devotedly.* Luke whispered to himself, "I love this island and these people. I want to be part of their innocence and culture. I am so lucky to be here."

He leaned over again to Eti. "Who is that beautiful woman?"

"Talia. It means she shines, she illuminates with the light of the sun and the moon. And guess what? She's a teacher. Perfect!"

"I have only one question: is she married?"

"No, she is a teacher. When the Education Office chose her to go to school and become a teacher, her getting married was not an option. She shines in the classroom and illuminates the children's minds."

Luke shook his head in awe. "Do you think she may need a teacher's assistant?"

Eti looked closely at Luke. "You are already hooked." He leaned in. "If you want to meet her, Luke, you can learn Samoan. Every vowel is sounded. I can teach you."

Luke looked at Talia. She was singing the Samoan version of "Amazing Grace," one of his favorites. He knew that just as a rainbow was inexplicable to Luke's little blind friend, Alpato, so the beauty of the singing and this beautiful woman would not translate to anybody back home. Angels in the highest heaven would not sing any differently.

He couldn't help but look at the woman as she sang the verses. It felt a love song – directed at him. Really, though, it was a love song to Jesus. In between his stolen glances, she studied him quietly, curiously, while she sang only four feet away. When they both looked at the same time, her eyes shone with softness. Luke swore it was not his imagination.

He knew the historical generosity of the Samoan and Tahitian culture when it came to love and affection. Could he go talk to her? He hesitated. Everybody will notice. Her innocence was that of a child, Luke surmised, probably like the little children she taught. But she was just as old as he. And she invited him with those soft dark eyes, on the same morning as the sermon on innocence and family. She did not look away as most *fa'afines*, or Polynesian women, might.

He could not imagine leaving her at the church. When the service was over, he walked back down the aisle right next to her, hoping nobody noticed. Her hand brushed up against his.

Outside the church, Eti introduced them. Luke was overcome with shyness. He had never been so close to a beautiful native woman, and an educated one at that.

"*Talofa*," she murmured. She turned and faced him. "I am Talia, cousin to the Fa'a'ita family."

"*Talofa*, Talia, I am Luke."

Her eyes glowed. "You said my name right."

"Can you please tell me how you'd say my name?"

"You are Luka. Here, your name ends softly. I like it. And you are adopted by the Fa'a'itas, too." She smiled. "You might one day become a Samoan."

"How do you know I am adopted?"

"I know the Samoan custom. I have eyes. I have seen you before. Do you talk to them in Samoan?"

"No. I am slow at learning the Samoan language and culture. Most of the family knows English better that I do Samoan, so they accommodate me."

Eti spoke up, "Talia is a teacher." He made it like an invitation. His voice dwindled off.

Talia turned toward Luke and decided to take a chance. "I can teach you the Samoan language. I do it every day. We have only fourteen letters in our alphabet. Our words are soft. A little like Italy. Our words end in vowels, never in harsh consonants."

Luke leaned forward. "Please, will you give me an example?"

"Your name is a perfect example. We call you Luka. Paul is Paulo. Your friend Timothy is Timoteo. Chance is Chance-uh." Then she looked down, a little embarrassed. "But I tell you too much, just like a teacher. Perhaps you don't need a teacher."

Luke spoke right up. "No, no! I need a teacher! I am only here for maybe four or five months. I love your island, your customs. I want to learn all I can."

Eti said, "We have a small guest *fale* behind our family *fale*. You can learn back there and Talia can teach, and we will let people know she is teaching you. I will tell them you are writing a story about Samoa."

Luke reached out and squeezed Talia's hands and then squeezed Eti's hands.

"My first questions. What does your name mean? And may I see you this coming week?"

Talia smiled demurely and said, "Of course, I have two names. And they fit together. Talia. We pronounce it Ta-LEE-ah. It means to wait, to anticipate in some way, the birth or return of Jesus. And my last name is Susulu. It means to shine, to illuminate."

Her smile proved her name and love poured out between her lips. "And yes, *ioe*, you can see me."

Luke said, "Your name makes me think of the three wise men following a bright star, looking for Jesus."

Talia burst into laughter, soft and melodious. "So you read the Bible. Good!"

She held out her hand, soft, brown, full of life. "It was so nice, *manaia*, to meet you, Luka."

Luke would not let go of her hand. "What does *manaia* mean?"

"You pronounce it mah-NAY-yuh, and it means nice, pretty, good manners."

"It was so *manaia* to meet you, too," Luke said slowly.

It wasn't long before Luke and Talia were off shift and this beautiful woman would sit with him under the palm-thatched roof, protected from the almost daily rain, and teach him her language. The rain made everything more intimate. She took her duty seriously. She leaned forward as he sat cross-legged on the ground, her lips and mouth close so he could hear and see her. Samoan women speak very softly, especially after passing the marriageable age of eighteen.

In the coming weeks, Talia had no idea of the effect she had on Luke. She dressed better than most of the native women, but she still often wore a lava-lava wrapped around her from shoulders to calves. When she leaned forward, he saw the most beautiful curves. She was intent on her teaching. Her natural innocence and unconscious attitude toward sex and intimacy was different from anything he had ever seen or read about. She was just "all there" for him; talk about being emotionally present! Luke had no idea how long he could last. He was drawn to her in such a magical way.

And they met every week until the third month had passed. She cooked for him; they had meals together, she even taught him how to dance. And he kept learning. The more he learned, the more he yearned. And Talia did, too. They began by kissing each other good-bye after a long hug. Luke began bringing her little gifts. She gave him books and drawings she had made, and even special seashells she had kept since she was a child. And she played little games with him. Luke would show up at the little guest *fale*, and Talia would be gone. This was not like her. Luke worried at first, and then he slowly walked up the path to the family waterfall. She surprised him every time, hiding behind a palm tree, dressed as a younger playful woman, not a teacher.

31

Luke wrote a story in his journal about Talia. He wanted to remember everything. He wished he could send the story to his little sister. But Jessica was a friend of Lacy's. Jessica would not handle it well, unless Lacy was already married. Maybe she was. The letter writing between Luke and Lacy seemed almost nonexistent.

He began. "Her last name means to illuminate or shine. It was only natural that Talia became my teacher too. I learned that coconuts are a daily delight. That people still carry two big buckets of water over their shoulders to their *fale*. That fishing is a daily necessity. She showed me angel fish, barracuda, gelatinous jellyfish that feed on algae in the coral reef. But now she said they have to import canned mackerel, bread, and something else I can't remember. She took me to the American Samoan tuna canneries, huge canneries with four thousand Samoans working there, many from Western Samoa. American Samoa supplies almost all the tuna to the United States. Tuna boats from California spend most of the year down in the South Seas where the tuna are thriving.

"While diving with me, she warned me about the moray eel that anchors itself to the reef, breathes with its mouth opening and closing, but when it bites it never lets go. You carry a knife underwater and bring up half a moray eel, or you drown. She showed me a Samoan friend with huge scars on his forearm. She fed me so many kinds of fish I lost count.

"She fed me coconuts in a hundred ways. She fed me mangoes, papayas, tapioca, cocoa beans. She drew maps so that when we were together and free in the future, we could hike up the tallest mountain on Upolu, 6,094 elevation, and then have the fun of eating lunch at the bottom of a nearby waterfall with its 180 feet streaming from the mountain far above.

"I learned that Samoans put their garbage and refuse on top of a raised platform so the wild pigs can't get at them. I learned that their *umukai*, an above-ground rock oven, produces the most delicious meal in banana leaves filled with mackerel, coconut cream, bread-fruit, and bananas. In fact, nobody can describe the meal.

"Markets are open here and there any day, selling almost every-thing, with continual social opportunity and interaction. Men arrive at work wearing a *lavalava*, a business shirt, and carrying a brief-case. On Sunday, everybody wears white, and everybody goes to church. Church lasts most of the day. There are Catholic, Methodist, Mormon, and other churches as well.

"There are two *tala* for every American dollar. She told me each family has a grandfather, chief, or *matai*. Each village selects the vil-lage *matai*. And there is the paramount *matai* who has the last say. Some things never change in Samoa, based on the family unit. She taught me any word with 'g' in it was pronounced *ng*. You say the capital city as *Pongo-Pongo*, even though it's Pago Pago."

"Talia showed him how each side of an island is totally differ-ent from the other side: the leeward, and the windward. One has the rocky outcroppings and blowholes. The other has warm sandy beaches and easy fishing. Away from the towns on the south side of Tutuila, the little communities on the north side still live the idyllic life in the *fales* built with thatched palm leaves. Samoans have the best smiles this side of Fiji.

"Samoan customs and civilization can be traced back to 1507 B.C. Tutuila, Savai'i, and Upolu are the three biggest islands, and Upolu is called the isle of kings. Robert Lewis Stephenson built his home there. It was the least populated of the islands, and the island with the most spectacular mountains and waterfalls. Stephenson was known as Tusitala, the teller of tales."

Luke remembered her songs and dances. He was so happy in anticipation. On the way home all the way up the hill from the ocean he sang and tried to dance through five of his favorites. He did not care who saw him, or how poorly he danced compared to Talia's. He started and ended with *MinoiMinoi-A*, wiggle-wiggle, get up and dance! Move your body. Such an adorable song, every singing group claimed it. Luke owned a Samoan record in High School, and "MinoiMinoi-A" was his favorite! Talia taught him all the words, and he loved watching her dance. She taught him *Mo'e-mo'e Pe-pe*, the "p" pronounced softly like a "b", a tender lullaby for babies. She sang it to him.

She carried on, teaching him *La'u Lupe*, contrasting two images of death with the Samoan flight of the pigeon, and the European plucked rose. She taught him "*Sau La'u Teine*," about a serenader knocking at the door of a beautiful Polynesian. She explained the Hawaiian influence travelling to the dance halls of Pago Pago. The one he loved the most, "*Oka'oka La'u Honey,*" was so rhythmic, exuberant, fun—and a bit silly. The singer compares his lover to the most highly prized foods in Samoa from the early 20th Century.

Luke's awareness of his mission coming to an end rose meteorically, like the nuclear missiles on Johnston Island. One evening, as the sun was setting over the swelling Pacific Ocean, Talia stood up and put the lessons and the books away. "Let's go for a walk, Luke. There are too many people right here."

She faced him and pulled back her shoulders, intent on Luke seeing her posture. She knew he had longed to touch her every day. She looked out toward the Pacific Ocean. Then she rose up on her tiptoes and pointed. "Can you hear the ocean? Can you see the ocean waves rising and falling? Can you feel the ocean's bounty and promise?"

Luke shook his head and smiled mischievously. "All I can see is your waves rising and falling. I can't even see the ocean." He laughed, hoping she would not be offended. All he could see rose and fell about two feet away. Her blouse moved with love and affection in a most natural way, so much the South Sea Islander. The bountiful breasts from her Samoan blood, the curves and slimness of her waist and hips from Tahitian blood. He was overwhelmed. Captivated.

Taking his hand, she floated down the beach to a grove of short and sheltering palms, away from the streets of Leone. She had the most natural feminine walk, her feet moving lightly and firmly in the loose sand, her hips naturally swaying, proud of her body posture, happy to be the woman she was. She knew Luke was looking at her, eating her up, almost every step of the way.

Talia finally stopped, far down the beach, underneath small palms, and in between a few sand dunes. She laughed. Such a soft and breathy sound.

She stepped closer to Luke. "I have a secret I cannot keep to myself any longer."

"You have talked to me about everything. How can you tell me a secret?"

"You are the only person I can tell this secret to."

Luke looked at Talia. "I'm a *papalagi,* a stranger here. How can you tell me a secret?"

She took both of his hands and looked at them. The ocean heaved soft swells into the beach nearby. Taking a deep breath, she slowly raised her head and looked at Luke.

Her lips parted. "*Ua here vau ia oe,*" she said. "It means 'I love you' in Tahitian. I have loved you ever since you came to my village. Ever since I first saw you."

Luke was speechless. All that struggle with Lacy from one year to the next. And here stood a woman who loved him right now, in the present, and had from the moment she saw him. She had no family to push him away. Her only family was the aunt she stayed with on the outskirts of Leone. Her original family lived on Upolu, a neighboring island, belonging to New Zealand. He knew nothing about them, and she never talked about them.

He couldn't take his eyes away. He was in love the minute she looked at him and told him that. But he was speechless. All he could do is enfold her and kiss her face, her neck, her hair. He couldn't stop. "I love you so much," he murmured. "Show me how to say 'I love you' in Tahitian, the way it sounds and not the way it is spelled."

Talia nodded her head slowly, and said, "Watch my lips. I will go slowly.

"*Ooo-ah hair-ray va-ow-ee-yah oy.*"

Luka repeated it.

Talia said, "Now you know it. I can see it."

Luke blinked, tears in his eyes. "Nobody ever said it like that to me."

"I know I surprised you. I surprised myself, too."

Talia giggled and started to walk away. Turning her head, she said, "Just think about it. You will know it and if you close your eyes you will feel it."

She couldn't resist the moment. She came back and took him by the hand. "I love that family of Poasa and Eti and Vee. I am so glad they adopted you."

"I am so glad, too," Luke said. He stopped, hands on his hips, thinking. "They have shared everything with me. And now we have shared them."

He reached out and pulled her in, hugging her and holding her and caressing her.

Talia said, "Come, I want to share the ocean, the shoals, the waves, the sands with you."

She moved away. It was up to Luke. She had told him her deepest secret. Would he follow? Luke caught up to her and took her hand. "Will you show me your waves and your shoals?"

Talia laughed in the most lovable way Polynesian women laugh, so full of love and innocence and emotional presence. It didn't bother her at all. Such a natural, breezy laugh. "You are so funny. Thank you for what you said to me. The trouble is, many of our words sound so same and are so different."

She reached to the spot they had been walking toward. Luke didn't even notice. Then she stopped, sank down, and gently pulled Luke down. "Come down to me," she said. "Feel the breezes, the swish of the ocean waves." She turned and showed him a gentle sand dune facing the ocean, invisible to the village, a scooped-out depression perfectly shaped for two. Luke felt in the grip of some filmy aphrodisiac he had never experienced. *Is it the ocean? Is it the island?* He couldn't move.

He stopped. "You have loved me for three months?"

"That's why I came to church," she murmured. "Sitting as close to you as I could. I could not wait any longer."

"You were so beautiful to me. I didn't dare talk to you. I don't speak Samoan well at all."

"I know, Luka." He loved the way she said his name. She made it sound three times longer.

Talia said, "And that's why I took you away tonight."

Talia was sitting almost in his lap. No, it was more like he was sitting in her lap. Her eyes were next to his, his lips touching hers. She leaned up and put her right arm around his shoulder and pulled herself close to him with her other arm. Together they sank into the soft sand. And she covered him with kisses, raining them down on him, her beautiful black hair breaking and folding over his face. Luke sank into the soft sand, sure he was dreaming. He floated on for minutes, in heaven at last.

The Talia leaned back and stood up. "We have to go back," she said, pulling Luke up. "You need time."

Luke shook off his bewilderment. "How did you know?"

"Your heart has been touched. Your mind needs to catch up. Americans needs this. They don't believe love can come so quickly and as easily as it does in Samoa and Tahiti."

She took his hand. "Right after church, we will meet and come back here in the late afternoon. Pray to God, think about it. I will do the same. We will see if we are innocent enough, if God is on our side. Not all things of the heart can be touched in one night."

"Okay," Luke breathed. "Next Sunday I will open my heart and see."

"Close your eyes first," Talia asked, touching his shoulder. A minute later he heard footsteps in the surf. "Now, turn around."

Luke followed her request. He heard the slip of clothing and felt something touch his heel. Curious, he waited a moment and turned back to see her.

He heard her voice at the same time he heard a splash in the slow surf. There Talia stood swaying to the beat of the ocean waves. Hands on her hips, naked and as innocent in the beginning as Eve, she said, "Follow me, Luke, and let's walk in the water."

When Luke saw her, he thought she was going to walk on water. He ran through the lapping surf, skipping in the water. She took his hand. "Stop looking at me, Luke. Look at the lagoon. You will never see water this sweet and innocent, so warm and soft."

"No wonder," he said. "I will never see a girl as sweet and innocent, soft and warm, as you. It's your lagoon."

Talia stopped and kissed him, pulling his hands in to hold them to her heart. Luke kept them up, long after she had let go.

And they walked together, with all the time in the world. The sand was smooth, no shells, no rocks, no crabs or small sea creatures to nip at their toes. She sang softly to him and made him sing the songs that she had taught him. Life was good.

After walking and talking until the stars stood still, they came ashore and headed for home. They reached the center of Leone. The village slept.

Talia whispered. "We will follow God to church, and after church, we will follow love."

Luke turned and held Talia for a long time, murmuring and kissing her in the neck. "I can't wait," he whispered. "But every day will be so long. Every night I will dream of you."

Talia kissed him for a long time. Polynesians kiss with a natural and innocent passion that no Americans could ever imagine. Probably never could. Luke floated all over the road going east back to camp. Talia walked on the road going north, past Three Brothers Shoals, past the outskirts of the town.

32

Talia and Luke stayed at the church after services, visiting with others in the congregation. By now they had accepted Luke as one of their own, with similar devotions and ideals. Luke enjoyed all the people dressed in white who came up to greet him, all the families that came together, all those who noticed Luke singing their songs and reading his Bible next to Talia reading hers.

Then they went home to Eti's and Poasa's and played games with the children. Luke read them stories he had written about his childhood. They loved hearing about his winter games, skating on ice, playing hockey, cracking the whip, competing in races. Not to mention snowball fights, and making snowmen and snowwomen. They could not imagine ice and snow. In the South Seas and Samoa, they had sun, rain and a lot of it, rainstorms and flooding, breezes, and typhoons. They had mountains and beaches. Their competition including rowing the fastest outrigger canoe, swimming across the bay, playing cricket in a few ball fields, and fishing.

The family had a good lunch, normally not big breakfast eaters. They prepared three kinds of fruit sliced up along with chunks of breadfruit, taro root, and fish delicacies. The boys began to prepare the below-ground rocks for roasted pig. Luke and Talia relaxed with an afternoon nap, staying out of the direct sunlight. When they awoke, they each had a cup of Samoan coffee, with the traditional adjustment: plenty of cream and cane sugar.

They meandered down the beach where they played in the little waves, and then kept going down the shore for a half-mile, beyond a rocky point where few were willing to travel. With awakening anticipation, they clung to each other as they approached their little sand dune behind a curve in the coastline. They sat down carefully facing each other, and then edged themselves closer, pulling their sandy bottoms even closer to each other. With arms slowly outstretched they leaned forward and held onto each other, finger-tipping each others' face, sweeping their palms across each others' chest, and finally kissing gently and repeatedly as long as they can breathe.

Like an enclosed campfire, their kisses begin to gather warmth and intensity, pulling them together, each one becoming more and more passionate. Talia curled up in Luke's lap and began singing to him. Her eyes were glowing, her lips so enticing. "Amazing Grace" in the Samoan language is even more humble and heartfelt than the American version. "I once was lost, but now am found, was blind but now I see." It was the first time Luke ever heard it as a love song. He imagined them being in the whitest, softest church on the island, full of the whitest-clothed Samoans, as innocent and child-like and as devoted as any two could be.

When she sang the Samoan lullaby, *"Moe'moe Pe'pe,"* she held Luke as tenderly as any woman could treat a man, as if he were her baby, holding him softly in her arms. Luke began kissing her, interrupting her song of love. Her cradling arms and voice circling around him had such sweetness. She was part of the ocean, always there, always life-giving, always present. She had the Samoan gift of living completely in the present moment. The past was gone, the future far away. There was just today. Just this evening. There was no hurry, no urgency, just gentle ocean waves and soft sea breezes. This is why romance is so spellbinding to the rest of the world. No beginning. No ending. Her songs had no end either, but plenty of interruptions, all good.

It seemed about a week later that she leaned him back and kissed him on his face and neck so gently that he might not notice. She sang a song about a Samoan pussycat, with the same kind of love pet owners have. Sunset came, followed by nightfall. This was the most comfortable time for Polynesian women to become intimate. They lived daily in an open community with open *fales*, and only night-time promised privacy. Talia leaned down again and kissed Luke's eyes and eyebrows. When he kept them closed, she soundlessly rose above Luke, and unwrapped her *lava-lava*, twirling it downward as if it were a fishing net. Which it was.

When he opened his eyes, he felt warmth and gentle pressure on his hips and abdomen and saw her bare stomach and felt her strong legs around him. While he centered his gaze on her beautiful mane of hair, she leaned forward, reached her arms back to untie her halter-top, and tossed it behind her, floating in the sea breeze. Instead of a flowery design, Luke saw nothing but firm dancer's breasts leading up to well-formed shoulders and a beautiful neck. Dancer training in Tahiti begins as a workout and ends with firm bountiful bodies. Talia's clothing was gone and all her natural beauty and innocence surrounded him. Clothes were a later invention of mankind. He reached up, ever so carefully, and touched her softly, affectionately, as reverently, just as he would touch rose petals, or frangipani blossoms. She was cupped, caressed and pulled down toward Luke.

"I love you too," she murmured. "I know you love me."

"Feel the soft seas," she said. Before he knew it, Talia carefully moved aside, leaned down and shifted him around. Luke's clothes disappeared in whispers somewhere on the crest above their sandy bed. She lay next to him softly, breasts swelling, her body innocently inviting, full of South Seas romance. "*Fa'a Samoa*," she said. Her body sparkled in the early moonlight, showering him with love's power, as they surrendered passionately to each other, immersing Luke in the Polynesian guilt-free attitude. Making love was as natural as ocean swells, falling rain, and climbing coconut palms for breakfast.

Luke could not keep his hands off her, sliding his arms around her, moving his hands up and down her back. He slowly brought his hands back and forth around her hips and that little shelf above her bottom, and then circled them in front around her tight little belly button.

She softly, suddenly took in a breath and said, "Luke, we can have all night, just like the tide."

He could hear the soft pounding of the waves as the tide came in. He could feel it. As it washed over him, he could not tell if it was his heart pounding or the surf. Waves lifted him up and seemed to flow over him. Then a wave rolled up and stopped, rocking him in its natural motion, caressing him, and surrounding him. Luke could feel it becoming full of the warmth and moisture of the crest. The wave crested over him, paused, and slipped back. When the wave would sweep over him, he squeezed back or he might have gone under. He felt the gentle pressure of another wave coming forward. At times he thought he was sleeping or dreaming.

Luke heard Talia say something playful about waves. Waves were never one thing. Breakers on the beach had always fooled Luke. He liked to play a little game with the ocean. Lying on the beach and daring the ocean, he would see the inches-high front of a wave sweeping toward him. He would roll to his left, but then a second wavelet would still sweep toward him with its own little sounds. If he escaped that, another wavelet would sweep up the beach from the right.

"There's no escaping it," Luke thought, as he was dreaming and drifting on the beach. Then he felt the ocean rocking him back and forth in the surf. There was just a flow, no stopping the ocean and no stopping of anything. Even the breeze played on them with its own waves. Talia leaned down from above and squeezed him. He thought she was part of the ocean. Then she said, "Are you happy?"

"Are you kidding?" He squeezed her, and held her, and she could not get away.

Talia kissed him. And then she shook her finger at him. "Just remember, tomorrow, you are innocent."

"What? What do you mean?" Luke couldn't help frowning. *Why would she bring that up?*

Talia said, "This is my gift to you, the ocean's gift to you, a gift of a thousand years past and present. I am happy to give this gift to you. That's why we call it, 'a happy time.'" Nobody will be cross with you."

Luke sighed. "It's the happy time, as you call it, the happy time I always wanted, without knowing what it was." He caressed her. "You fill up my heart. There's no room for anything else. I don't care what happens tomorrow."

Luke felt they would never be two again. Just one. Talia flowed over as gently and firmly as a wave until she lay over Luke. "And tonight," she kissed him, "tonight you will be happy for a long time. This is love from Tahiti. Lovemaking is the same as eating together, or swimming together, or sleeping together, or floating on the ocean together. We don't do anything in a hurry and never with a bad feeling."

Luke was mesmerized. "Can we go live in Tahiti? We will love where everybody lives like you. Why would we live any place else?"

"No, no. You will be happy right here." Talia stopped, her body holding him in. She chided him. "You are doing what I want to make happy. I am doing what I want to make happy. God sends love everywhere, all the time. Love is free like the ocean and the wind and the clouds. Just like the weather. It is a gift when it is wet and rainy. It is a gift when it is hot and sunny. It is a gift when it is dark and quiet. Down here we are created to use this love. Our ancient gods make love as well."

Talia pressed on. She went forward, ahead and then back, part of the ocean, one wave after another, giving herself to him. Luke sharply drew in a deep breath, suddenly aware of the need for his passionate response. He became part of the ocean too, and the breeze, and the ocean fragrances. He followed her and gave himself to her, and became part of her. Once Talia sat up as they crested a wave. Again and again she leaned down and held Luke's face against her heart comforting him and surrounding him with her curves.

Sometime after midnight and before the tide change, Talia turned into a Tahitian tsunami, rising up from the bottom of the sea as if from a nearby volcanic eruption, lifting them higher and higher and gaining speed as they approached the opening in the reef. They clung to each other for safety and security as they rushed through the narrow opening. The wave rose for a final crest, and then crashed into the soft and peaceful lagoon. Luke and Talia were set free, floating in delirious pleasure on the silvery waters and gliding softly toward the shore.

When Luke opened his eyes, they were floating above the scoop of their beach bed. Minutes later they felt Talia's lava-lava spread out for them below. Talia quavered in delight minute after minute, just as fulfilled as a baby's mama, happy, out of breath, singing little snatches of her favorite songs. Soon they were curled up beside each other, listening again to the ocean, feeling the soft night breeze. So happy. So free. So full of peace and contentment.

Then Talia kissed him, leaned over him, and out of her halter-top she pulled out a beautiful feather from a seabird. She softly blew on it, stroked it against her cheeks left and right, and then stroked her breasts as slowly and as softly as Luke had done, with the happiest smile, sighing with pleasure. "This is fa'a Samoa too," she said, as she began, slowly, tantalizingly moving the feather, stroking and brushing Luke up and down, over and across, until she had dusted him all over with heaven's petals. "Now, it's your turn," she said, handing him the feather. "This is not a dream. It's just a beautiful ending that many do not know about." Luke seized the exotic bird feather and started on Talia just where she had ended on him. He took his time, quiet and mesmerized. She caught her breath when Luke said, "This is as much fun as our whitewater adventure."

"Can we have another adventure?"

...Time drifted by as it always does with Polynesian romance. But an hour later, Talia stood up. "I better make sure you get back to your camp," she smiled. She reached down and pulled him up. "Otherwise, the tide will come in and we won't leave until sunrise."

As they walked back, she sang songs to him, and made him sing some choruses with her.

But when she said goodbye at the rainforest crossroad, she slowly moved her hands up and held Luke's face so tenderly. "Remember this, Luke; you don't owe me anything, no promises. I gave to you. It is *fa'a Samoa*. Our ancestors taught us, 'To give—only to get—is not giving,' and, 'to give—without—expectations—is giving.' Whatever happens to me, whatever happens to you is not up to us. We had heaven for three months. We will always have that."

Luke burst out, "Why are you saying this? I am not leaving yet. You are teaching and it is not the end of the year. How do you know the future is not in our hands?"

Talia frowned only for a moment, and then looked up. "Luke, we don't know anything about what happens next. We have been so lucky. But I may not see you again. And you may not see me again. I have not told you everything. If my family finds me here, and then finds out about you, there will be trouble. They had big plans for me. Samoan traditions are still their life.

"But I ran away to our home country, New Zealand. I wanted to teach. And I became a teacher.

"I did not want to get married."

Luke drew back in surprise and in pain. "Why can't we think about tomorrow?"

Talia sighed. "You will be leaving Samoa. We know that. You cannot take me home to America.

"And I cannot take you home to Upolu." She threw her arms around Luke and kissed him as if there was no tomorrow, as if she might not see him again. "Remember this, Luka. If you are happy, I am happy."

Luke couldn't let her go. He said, "I will never forget this day. I will never forget tonight. I will never forget you."

She turned to go. "And I will always remember you."

She looked back. There was an ocean of sadness in her eyes. "Someday when I am talking to my children, and you are talking to your children, we will say, "'Long ago and far away I lived the dream. I was the dream. But I am so glad I came back and had my family. I am so glad you all were born.'"

Luke stood, dumfounded. "What do you mean, Talia?"

"We dared to love, even though we had to leave."

"I will find a way back," he protested. "We just started."

Talia only got a few feet away, and she turned. "You will not be able to find me, Luka. I am so sorry."

Luke stopped dead in his tracks, speechless. Talia searched for the Samoan idiom. "But you will always be with me and in me at the top of my heart."

And then she was gone. Luke trudged home back to his tent in the jungle near the old runway. Safe and secure—tucked into his heavy Bible sitting in a tray at the bottom of his travel trunk—he dug out a prized photo and prayed over it.

> *I know you love me, Lord, because you do not send down your wrath on every little mistake I make. You love me, Lord, because you do not keep score of all my sins and then berate me whenever you get a chance.*
>
> *I know you love me, Lord, because you are slow to lose patience with me. You love me, Lord, because you do not treat me as an object to be possessed or manipulated. You love me, Lord, because you use circumstances of my life in a constructive way for my growth.*

> *Talia and I in our hearts created a home in you, Lord.*
> *We are strong, we are family, and may we stay family forever in heaven.*

33

Talia was right: anything could happen. The next day, Captain Jack Mills piloted the C-123 cargo plane as he had for years, flying back and forth across the Pacific, ferrying men and food and equipment and machines from one island to the next. Whatever was needed by the Air Force. He touched down on many an island. The next day he called Luke on the ham radio. When Luke reached the communication shack, the radioman held out the earphones. "It's private," he said.

"Luke LaCrosse here."

"Captain Mills. We spoke on one of my flights out of Hawaii. I thought you might be interested to see the damage from these nuclear missiles and nuclear explosions," the captain said. "I think a guy named Chisholm told me about your concern for the preservation of nature and native cultures. You quoted Henry David Thoreau, I think. These natives, what's left of them, need somebody who can make the world know what happened. I land tonight and take off tomorrow. You are welcome aboard as an ACM. Over."

"Thank you, sir. I will report in tomorrow before takeoff. I'll ask Dutch Schultz to take my shifts. The flight sergeant can live with that. We're doing twelve on and twelve off. What is your destination? Over."

"Kwajalein, and we're gonna make an unofficial stop on Bikini Atoll, so you can get a firsthand view of the world's first nuclear disaster. Over."

"Roger that, captain. And how many miles are we flying? Over."

"As the crow bait flies, two thousand three hundred miles and ten hours. Piece of cake. Already done a thousand today just from Hickam. Over and Out."

The next day, Captain Mills did the "wheels up" at 0600 hours with Luke aboard. Luke rode up in the cockpit. "I'm glad we are finally above sea level," Luke said. "It's nice and cool up here."

"I wouldn't notice," Captain Mills said. "All I do is take off, fly, and land. I have the most boring life."

"You know, truck drivers are only supposed to drive so many hours at a time," Luke said. "You're gonna have to pull over to the side of the road and park later on today."

"Pulling over is easy. It's taking off again that's hard. That's why you're here; keep me awake. I left Hawaii at 1300 yesterday to pull in here before 0500. It'll still be light for a long time. We're crossing the International Date Line halfway there."

"I'm glad we wingnuts don't have any initiations like the Navy does when you cross over the line," Luke said. He leaned forward in the ACM seat behind the pilot.

"Maybe we can make one up. Like scrub the wing with a toothbrush."

"I hate when I get blown off the wing without a parachute."

Captain Mills laughed. "Hey, are Dakota and his girl, Moana, doing okay?"

"Say a prayer. I'm hoping they get together before the Mormon missionary snags her. Her family seems to favor the missionary."

"Bird-in-the-hand kind of thing, huh? He's there, Chance isn't."

"Roger that, Captain. Speaking of disasters, what can you tell me about the nuclear disaster out here?"

"Let's start at the beginning. Our first atomic bomb explosion in New Mexico was codenamed Trinity. People in nearby Truth or Consequences thought the sun came up twice that day. A blind girl one hundred and twenty miles away saw the flash."

"I can believe it," Luke said. "Our heavy goggles make the sun look like a little pinprick of light. But when the missiles detonate, we can read a newspaper with those goggles on. It's god-awful bright."

The captain shook his head. "It gets worse. We are Joint Task Force Eight for nuclear testing. The whole thing goes back to Joint Task Force One in 1946. The Navy wanted to prove that it had ships that could both take and survive an atomic blast. The mission was to carry out the atomic bombing of an array of our Naval Fleet. We detonated one in the air, 'Able One,' then one in the water, 'Baker.' Eighty-six of ninety-five ships were contaminated by a mile-wide dome of water. That's why I call it the world's first nuclear disaster."

Luke shook his head. "Why would we expose nearly a hundred ships, forty-two thousand men, and a raft of islands to radiation?"

"You know what Bob Hope said, don't you? 'As soon as the war ended, we located the one spot on earth that hadn't been touched by war and blew it to hell.'"

Two hours into the flight, Captain Mills yelled, "Look way down to your left! In less than an hour, we'll do a bootleg landing on Bikini. I have to drop off crates of top-secret medical supplies. I'm gonna need your help."

"Glad to do it. I need the exercise."

Captain Mills landed on a crushed coral landing strip. They taxied down to a collection of Quonset huts, corrugated metal half-domes on the sand. They looked comically out of place in the tropics of this island, one of the largest in the atoll. Five natives sprinted out to help them unload. Engine number two, as usual, remained running.

When they finished, Luke stood under a trio of palms and talked to the Marshall Islanders. "Here, have a Ni," said the local foreman, a Melanesian with dark skin, a curly beard, and a palm-frond hat.

"You mean a Ne-Hi?" Luke asked.

"No, Ni we call a young coconut, not pop. Our favorite drink."

"Thanks. How many islands in Bikini Atoll?"

"Thirty-six, minus two. The bombs made two islands disappear and turned three others into sand bars. They moved a hundred and sixty-seven of us off Bikini first."

"Did you notice any radiation sickness?"

The leader adjusted his palm-frond hat. "All over the Marshall Islands. Radiation burns, then miscarriages, then thyroid cancer and leukemia. That's why you bring us medicines. Some of us came back. But we can't eat much."

A second native said, "We always say, 'Radiation—no smells, no color, no touch—but don't eat the coconuts.'"

"And don't eat fruits and vegetables," added one companion. "And don't eat the fish!" another yelled.

"Before your Navy came in and detonated two bombs in 1946, life was beautiful," the leader said. "We had white sand islands full of coconut palms over a turquoise sea, with fish and sea turtles everywhere."

Luke nodded, taking notes.

He continued. "You didn't stop there. In 1954, you exploded a much bigger hydrogen bomb on Bikini. Fireball four miles across." He gestured, eyes and arms wide open. "Mushroom cloud a hundred miles across in five minutes. We say monster bomb causes monster babies. Then from twenty miles up the nuclear fallout began. Our beloved islands began to rain back down."

He made the sign for square. "Nobody noticed us. The men on a nearby Japanese fishing boat, the *Lucky Dragon*, had radiation injuries, and the whole world heard about it. Why didn't people hear about us? Many women on islands all around us have given birth to babies with injuries. Deformed, sick, on Rongelap, Likiep, Ailuk, and other islands your officials said were not affected by radiation."

Luke thought of Chance and Tiara, or Moana and Dakota with a deformed baby. He shuddered. "What's being done?"

"All of us in the Rahk chain have lost either wives or babies, or whole families. That's why we came back. We have nothing left to lose. Clouds of money are coming soon, the government says. Handfuls for each person. But a million dollars cannot replace Bikini. And nobody can replace our families from the past or our families in the future."

"Come on, Luke!" Captain Mills yelled, boarding the plane. "Haven't you got enough material by now? You want to get sterile? We're due in Kwaj in less than an hour."

Luke turned to the natives. "I will never forget you. I hope my country doesn't either."

"Here," said the leader. "Take some Ni with you. It came from far away. No nasty surprises in it."

After Luke boarded, Captain Mills kicked his plane in the ass and they flew off Bikini. "I can't get away fast enough," the Captain said. The island receded in the distance.

Luke felt a disease spread from his stomach throughout his body during the ride to Kwajalein. Even his toes. *Great God in heaven! My hero Henry David Thoreau will never forgive me for being part of this. But I am going to be part of the healing of the islanders, not part of their death. I promise you that, Thoreau.*

Bitter tears ran from his eyes as he leaned over in pain. Captain Mills averted his face for the same reason.

34

When Luke returned to Tutuila, American Samoa, there were no signs of and no word from or words about Talia. The school year was over. There were signs of heavy rains. There were no stars in the sky. No natives on the beaches. No magical fragrances.

The generals up at Hickam Air Force Base scheduled a whole new set of nuclear tests. The former operation was critically damaged by poorly built missiles; too many unscheduled explosions, casualties, and some airmen blinded by unexpected explosions.

Luke immediately got orders to get a military hop to another island, Rarotanga, to substitute for an airman with a strange illness who was sent to Hawaii. He loved the island and made a note to come back another time. The time dragged for Luke. He tried everything to contact Talia.

Then back on Tutuila, there was still no sign of Talia. There was dust in the air, but still no stars in the sky. The magical fragrances around Leone were gone. One person missing and it seemed as if the whole town was deserted. Luke was heartsick, lost. He looked everywhere, walked everywhere. There was nobody at her aunt's *fale* on the sea either.

He went over to the Fa'a'ita *falé* many times, knowing something had gone wrong. Eti and Poasa were gone to Upolu, and did not want to see Luke. He came back every day, and others in the clan were out fishing somewhere or in the jungle looking for a wild pig. Luke volunteered to harvest coconuts and breadfruit from the family plantation, and three little children went with him. For that day, he was happy.

For a week, whenever he could, Luke sat in front of the Fa'a'ita fale all afternoon. Finally, the matai of the family, the grandfather, took a hand on the last day. Before the usual family worship time, he walked out to speak with Luke.

He sat down, legs crossed, Fa'a Samoa, in front of Luke. "I am so sorry that my sons will not talk. They are heartsick about Talia. They are forbidden by her family to talk to you. And they know they cannot help. They are too sad to see you. Anything they do will not go well for Talia."

"What is it? What could change our world so quickly?" Luke was acutely puzzled.

"Talia's uncle came from far away Upolu, not Savai'i, and not Apia, the capital city. You know those two main islands of New Zealand called Western Samoa?"

"Yes," Luke said, "I went there secretly myself with my friend, Chance."

The matai, grandfather, head of the clan, continued, "Talia was promised to another long ago by her father. But an educator from New Zealand wanted her to become a teacher. Secretly, he found a way to spirit her away from her family, get her to New Zealand, and sponsor her in education. She got her teaching degree. We were so happy. We don't get along with her family. They had no idea of her secret. They gave her up for lost. When she began teaching in New Zealand her supervisor was happy, but in less than a year, she sorely missed the Samoan people.

"She went through the authorities in Pago Pago and won a position here in Leone, American Samoa. She came back here and began to teach. She took our last name. She did not marry, and she did not have children. Here everybody loves her. But in Western Samoa, girls do not do that. They shame their family.

"And you know, even here in American Samoa, people thought Talia had passed the age of being marriageable. She was much older than eighteen. Somehow, her family looked in Pago Pago but never thought of her being on the other side of the island here in Leone.

Word got around about this teacher who never got married, and her uncle became suspicious. He came over to Pago Pago and insisted the education authorities tell him the truth. He even threatened a lawsuit, unheard of on the islands.

"When her uncle finally found her, two weeks ago, with the threat of violence he took her away. She will never return. The customs are different. Her life would be in danger if she escaped again. She is lucky her family took her back."

The *matai* took Luke's hands. "We found out yesterday that she was forced almost immediately into the marriage ceremony with no preparation, no celebration, and no other family."

Feeling great sorrow, Luke said, "It's more of a punishment than a traditional ceremony. I can't imagine her living in such a relationship."

The *matai* remained silent, and then he spoke. "But nobody can see her. To protect the family's good name, she must stay in the marriage."

Luke went ahead, "I want to go over and get her, rescue her! I cannot risk the charge of AWOL, absence without leave, or desertion. Then I could never return. But still I have to see her one more time, to make sure what you say is true."

The matai insisted. "That's the worst thing you could do."

"Why?"

"They can still use tribal law and put you in jail. They could say you kidnapped her, that you sexually assaulted her."

"How can I possibly believe that?"

"She is in Western Samoa, not American Samoa. You are not protected. We know what's going on. They plan to go back to their old traditions, to break free from New Zealand."

Luke put his head down for a long time. "That is not the life she taught me," he said. "That is not what she believes. She taught me the ancient way."

The family *matai* reached over and held Luke's hands. "I am so sorry," he said. "Even if you tried to kidnap her, it would not work. Trust me. Eti and Poasa are just heartsick about it."

The *matai* handed Luke a well-used piece of paper. "Luke, read along with this as I say this prayer in Samoan."

> *Jehovah God, Creator and Savior, Divine Design*
>   *Itself,*
> *You are my treasury of compassion who bestows*
>   *within me*
> *Supreme inner peace, beyond anything my finite self*
>   *can see.*
> *You love all beings without exception,*
> *You, the source of my happiness and goodness,*
> *You alone are my guide on the path to heaven.*
> *I will follow you only, God, and cast aside my*
>   *wicked ways.*

Luke sighed. "It is tough but I must face it. I cannot do this alone. I will pray every day."

The matai said, "Talia taught you how to talk to God, how to pray in Samoan. Think of all the strength she had to do what she did. She gave up her long-term family future for three months of heaven with you."

It took Luke a long time to leave. He just sat there on the ground. He could not feel any lower.

Hours later, he stood up. "*Fa'afit'tai*, thank you, Grandfather." The little piece of paper with the prayer on it dropped behind him.

"Take it with you," the grandfather called. "It will bring you peace."

Luke picked it up, shook his head, and began to walk away.

"Talia wrote that for you. Talia will always be with you," said the *matai*. "She knows she cannot leave. She will find peace wherever she is. And you must do the same. You owe it to her, and you owe it to God."

The next day Luke came back. He stepped off the road, the ocean at his back.

"Luka, my son!" The *matai* called to him. "I have a message for you. She sent me a messenger, Lotu. You don't have to go to make sure."

The *matai* beckoned to him. "Talia says to tell you—she will survive. She will stay with her family. Some day she will teach again. Some day when she has raised a family, and she is old, she may see you again. But not until then. If you ever loved her, you must move on. She has. And you know she loves you."

Luke nodded. "I will survive, for her. But this will take a long time."

The *matai* said, "One more thing. She knows what you do not know. She knows you love another from your childhood. She knows. She knows about Lacy. And she will not be happy until you are married to Lacy. It cannot be anybody else."

Luke dropped his head and trudged back to the Air Force camp. It took him a long time to believe Grandfather's last words. But he knew down deep that Talia loved him, would always love him, and would not be happy until he was married to Lacy. And neither would he.

35

In the next month, Luke kept away from all romantic thoughts. Every day Luke gritted his teeth and attended to his job, doing extra shifts, cleaning up the camp site after rains, unloading cargo planes, and even helping Sam the Chinese cook make the most delicious midnight biscuits, ready for breakfast the next morning. A week went by. Two weeks. He refused to let any emotions into his life. They were lethal to his health.

Then early one morning, he heard Brenda Lee's song on late-night radio out of Oklahoma City. Thank God for KOMA. At two a.m. its radio waves carried across half a continent and an ocean to America Samoa... *"I'm sorry, so sorry, that I was such a fool."*

Luke thought both he and Lacy should be singing this lyric to each other. Since the surprise meeting at O'Hare, their communication proved sporadic. For one thing, it was something at which they had never been good. In addition, his address changed, the cargo plane flights were poor mail carriers, and at times they both were so busy they didn't write. Lacy had the wrong address more than once and Luke never got the forwarded letters until back in Hawaii. He was pretty sure Lacy was involved now and then with other relationships.

How could she not be? She matched Talia in beauty and intelligence, and she moved in high society. And he had to admit he had not been attentive or consistent. O'Hare was only one stand-alone meeting. And for sure he had been totally involved with Talia.

He thought about Lacy and hoped she was listening to the hit record and thinking about him. It was amazing to him that Talia was insistent about Luke finding his way back to Lacy. How many would be willing and able to do that? Here on the islands he sang, *"All alone am I."* Both doors to love were closed to him. He tried prayer. He found himself willing to do whatever it took to become worthy of Lacy's love again.

He often ran down to Three Brothers Shoals, sitting on the beach, praying for relief from his eternal loneliness, an outcast of his camp longing for love. The sea shimmered six feet away, covered with white foam, the incoming waves sudsy on the trough and frothy on the crest. He looked at the stars and back to the sea. He gazed at the Milky Way, feeling its attraction just as if it were calling to him with silent voices out of the past.

He thought of his childhood memories with Lacy and wondered if she still looked at their favorite stars and galaxies, just as they used to. He scanned the sky with rusty binoculars, and a chant began lapping on the beaches of his mind: Antares, Sirius, Rigel; Antares, Sirius, Rigel. He was homesick for the mainland and picked out the red, white, and blue stars. The moon slipped across the heavens with slow grace, and he felt the merging closeness of sea and sky, a twilight embrace, him caught in the middle, drowning. Brenda Lee's voice floated through his mind as did thoughts of Lacy, *"You can depend on me, though you say we're through."*

The dark shadows on the moon carried names of enchantment—The Sea of Dreams, The Sea of Nectar, The Sea of Fertility, The Sea of Tranquility. He couldn't see them well from the mainland, but the closeness of the ocean's islands to the equator brought them into view. Luke longed for the full moon to bring Lacy back to him. He would be ever faithful, ever constant in the heavens, ever holding her in enchantment. He would sing to her, *"Mistakes are part of being young, but that don't right the wrong that's been done."* He had to win Lacy back.

Maybe she's singing, *"Will you still love me tomorrow?"* The message comforted him.

"God has plans for my happiness," he told himself every day. If his feeling for Lacy continued to grow and Talia got what she wanted—Lacy and Luke together, he could envision hope for the future.

It took Luke a long time to muster up the courage to tell Chance and Dakota about Talia. They had wondered about it, but kept it to themselves. He explained it the best he could, not easy when he had to use gestures in the darkness of a tent. Dakota and Chance both agreed.

"We're just naturally curious," Chance said. "Here's a beautiful woman who wanted to teach you. And she did, right out in the open. You got to learn the language and all the best of her culture. We never took that opportunity. You couldn't help it if you both fell in love."

Luke nodded. "And I guess I ain't much better than anybody else. Nobody would believe me if they saw me in that little fale, talking to her any day we were free, and I said we just talked."

Chance nodded. "Yeah, but naturally, Luke, why would you just talk to her?"

Dakota shook his head. "Lighten up, man. Your favorite uncle would retell you one of his favorite stories. Here's Luke who went to confession three weeks in a row. The first week he told the Father he could have gone home with a long-haired brunette last Saturday night, but he didn't take the chance. The priest nodded. Luke asks, "What will be my reward, here, or in heaven?"

The priest says, "Perhaps God will give you more pasture for your cattle."

The second week he told the priest, "After church I could have taken a ravishing blonde girl home. It would have been just us. But I didn't take the chance."

The priest nodded. Luke asked, "What will be my reward, here, or in heaven?"

The priest thought for a moment. "Perhaps the barn will become filled with a few more of your favorite Appaloosa horses."

A week later, Luke told the priest, "This time I could have stayed all weekend with a beautiful Polynesian girl in her home on the ocean, her whole family gone to the farmers' market for two days. I just couldn't take the chance."

He nodded. "So what will be my reward for that?" Luke asked.

The priest's human nature got the better of him. "A bale of hay, you jackass!"

All three of them guffawed, Luke the most of all. His gloom washed away. But at least two of the other airmen in the tent woke up and yelled, "Shut the hell up! It's two in the morning!"

Dakota leaned over and said sotto voce, "At least you won't be singing Buddy Holly's song to her, *'All my love, all my kissing, you don't know what you been missing, O boy . . .'*"

Luke said, "You both know I am allergic to hay. What else could I do?"

36

Luke thought about Lacy for weeks. Late one night, he sang along, *"I-I-I wish that we were married, so we'd never, never, never, never say good-bye."*

The next day, he received a letter from his little sister, Jessica. He grabbed it and carried the letter out into the nearby jungle. When he read it, he swore, and threw Jessica's letter as far as he could. It hit a palm tree and landed in the mud. Thinking better of it, so as not to insult Jessica, he strode over, stooped down in the mud, and picked it up. She had written to tell him of Lacy's impending engagement—of course to someone else. He trudged back to the tent, strode across the room, and slammed it deep into the depths of his footlocker, kicking his locker and swearing to himself. From Jessica's letter, it looked as if Lacy hadn't remembered their pledge. He looked around, embarrassed but relieved that everybody was eating lunch at the dining hall. In the afternoon he played volleyball with both natives and servicemen. But he couldn't get Ben King's song out of his mind, *"When the night is come and land is dark…stand by me, stand by me."*

After a long, rainy night shift, Luke got to bed late and got up late, still gloomy. It was still raining. After lunch, the unit's informal mail clerk handed him a letter. It was the first letter from Lacy in what seemed like years. He sat on his bunk and read.

Dear Luke,

Don't fall out of your palm tree. I know you think I took a vow of silence with you. It's been a long, long time.

I must apologize for being so protective of my dad. You hurt him and me deeply by what you said. He was just being a dad: "Nobody's good enough for my little girl." He shouldn't have said those mean things to you either.

I am sorry things went glimmering, as F. Scott used to say. In the years since we split, I found to my regret that I've never met anybody who influenced me as much as you did. So why are you there and I'm here?

Well, almost nobody. I'm writing you because of the pact we made down at the stables. You gave me your little notebook on 'Angel Talk.' I gave you a poem. We said that, before we crossed over the bridge (to marriage) and left our past behind us, we would contact each other no matter what, no matter where, no matter when. We owed it to each other because of our childhood dreams and plans. You were so sweet. I'll probably spend the rest of my life telling my children about you.

So here it is, sweetie. Before I say yes and I do and we will, I owe it to you, and you're hearing it from me first. We are announcing our engagement next week. Any objections? As they say during the big ceremony, please let me know. This is your last chance to make a case for us, for you and me. Because I still do carry your heart in my heart.

Talk to me, Luke. Do it for old times' sake. No matter what, as your uncle used to say, even at the end of a rough conversation, 'We still love you.'

Your favorite teen angel,
Lacy

After reading her letter for the fifth time, he tucked it in his shirt and trudged through the mud and cinders to camp. He walked directly into the chow hall and enjoyed American food that day for a change, thinking of Lacy while spooning in his favorite navy bean soup, and munching a grilled cheese sandwich. Dutch Schultz sat across from Luke and Chance, talking about going back to college in Indiana after his discharge. Dutch was heading back to his family place outside Muncie. He and Chance began to argue again about their favorite rivers. Chance bragged on the Maumee River, and kidded Dutch that the Mississinewa came from the mouth of a drunk. "Nobody in his right mind would name a river that," he said. "Originally, it was a whole sentence, and that one long word is all that's left."

Dutch grumbled, "It's because you're too ignorant to learn it. You are my motivation to go back to college."

Finally, Luke got Dutch's attention. "I just got a letter from Lacy for the first time in ten years. Okay, in ten months. She's about ready to run off and get married."

"Oh, great," Dutch said, the smile leaving his face. "You can't do anything about it down here. "What could you do?"

"All I can do. Sit down and write her. I've got something to tell her, too. It's funny how it all came together like this. She won't forget this last letter, just like I won't forget hers. I ain't gonna be too sociable for the next couple days."

"That ain't nothing new. When you finish, I'll have a bunch of cold beer waiting, buddy."

Luke tried to write on his bunk. An hour later, he took the camp jeep and rumbled out to Island Fever Reef. He sat on the beach beneath a palm tree. The ocean comforted him, flowing and splashing rhythmically, relentlessly, constantly cleaning whatever it touched. The breeze floated around him; the air became tinged with red. The setting sun painted a bright silvery path that stretched from the water into his heart, bathing the clouds in its glory. The molten sun collapsed into the ocean like a huge weather balloon. The waves lulled Lacy out of his life.

He wrote anyway:

Dear Lacy,

I got your letter. I did fall out of my palm tree, like a crazy coconut. Anguish and happiness to hear from you filled my heart. "Lacy still cares! Lacy remembers our past." We even traded blood on it, remember? Little cuts between our right thumb and forefinger and we shook on it. Our hearts' blood touched and mixed. And we held hands that way until the blood dried. Tecumseh and Black Hawk couldn't have done it better!

When I re-experienced our pact, so long ago in our secret church porch hideaway, I thought of our innocent, loving hearts, together so long ago, and the void that stretched out after it. I can't say there has never been someone else.

But I'm finally going to lose you. It's all new to me, Lacy.

I'm ninety-nine percent sure I can never have you. I'm never going to have whatever it is your family expects. I don't want ever to win you and then find that you can never be happy with me. I love you too much to do that to you.

So, Lacy, are you sure this guy loves you and has a long history with you, like I do? In a marriage, friendship is a key element. We have always had that. Do you have it with him?

I will never forget that you are so passionate with goodbyes.

Twice you surprised me and overwhelmed me back in Illinois.

This is not a passionate goodbye. I don't know why you say goodbye, I say hello.

We still love you, too,
Luke

When the Tuesday cargo plane arrived a few days later, and they loaded it, Luke's letter sat in the man-sized mail sack—along with its sender. It's about as crazy as you can get. Luke formed the plan with Guido, the squadron's funny man, who, it seemed, could do anything and get away with it. The additional crew member's spare oxygen mask and oxygen bottle were missing from the cockpit of the old C-123. Luke carried them, in case the mail sack was not leak-proof.

Luke needed to return to Hawaii to see if there was a way to hitch a ride to O'Hare. His mission—to prevent Lacy from getting married. The heavily loaded C-124 rumbled down the short island runway but the pilot had waited too long to take off against the rising tide. The runway was four hundred feet shorter than the standard. Luke felt the vibratory shaking and protest of the mighty engines.

Takeoff seemed to take forever. It felt like the pilot was reenacting the five-mile taxi from Honolulu International to the Hickam runway. He heard the pilot and the crew calling out to the fat heavy metal bumblebee, "Come on! Come on! Lift off! Lift off!"

A frantic wail came from the cockpit. It was the copilot, Jerry. "We're going to hit that wave! Oh my god, Oh my god! We are going to flip!"

Those were the last words from the cockpit as the heavy plane somersaulted in the ocean, burrowing in nose first. Those in the rear of the aircraft banged against the ceiling and were flung forward. Fortunate, because in the tail section, heavy equipment broke free, flew into the air and landed on the ceiling. The aircraft sank in deeper water beyond the shallow shelf around the island. Both pilots and the crewmen up front died, their seatbelts still tied tight. The rear bay of the plane opened into sunlight and the vast expanse of the sea. The sea rushed in and caromed back out with the mailbag. A riptide from the deeper waters pulled Luke and the mailbag out to sea, far from anybody's sight. Besides, nobody was looking.

The inverted plane proved convenient for the rescuers. The bay opened into sunlight instead of sand. The search and rescue effort focused only on people.

37

A few days later, Luke's parents received a mysterious telegram from one of his on-site sergeants forwarded through headquarters at Hickam Air Force Base:

> *On an unofficial and unauthorized Air Force flight out of Palmyra Island, Airman Luke LaCrosse, #16646053, may have been blown out of a malfunctioning cargo door in a freak accident. The C123 cargo plane failed to achieve lift during take-off from Palmyra and crashed into the ocean at the end of the runway. After two days of searching, we were unable to find his remains. There is only an extremely small chance that he was not on this flight. He will be listed as MIA: Missing In Action.*
> *—Chief Master Sergeant M. Turner*

Matt LaCrosse called Sixth Weather Mission Control in Hawaii. The commander took the line. "Good morning, sir. I am sorry to report that there was a plane crash off Palmyra Island. Your son, in all likelihood, was on that plane. We were unable to find his remains. There is a serious undertow on the east end of the atoll."

Among Luke's siblings, Jessica heard the bad news first. She and Luke enjoyed a close relationship. He had left the ham radio set to her and taught her how to use it. She kept it in the attic.

The next day, the LaCrosses attended church, sitting in the fourth pew from the front on the right side of the church, on the right side facing east, as they always did. Mrs. LaCrosse remembered how the huge stained glass window, designed by Luke's artistic grandfather, had always fascinated her. She wondered if he would ever again see the window and its divine way of sprinkling sunlight into the image. She thought of the times when Luke had sat next to her, holding her hand, whispering questions about mountains and rivers and the well carved into the huge window. Tears trickled down her face. Her heart wouldn't let him go. *They must be wrong. Luke is still alive. I just know he is still alive.*

Mr. and Mrs. De'Luca sat in a back row beside the exit. In warm weather, Lacy, her sister and brother were the first out of the church, avoiding the smoke-filled lobby where people visited after the sermon. Lacy was home for a few weeks.

Jessica kept track of the De'Lucas and watched carefully to catch Lacy when she emerged from the side lobby exit. Jessica worked to compose herself as she approached Lacy.

She saw Lacy escaping out into the beautiful, rectangular courtyard ringed on three sides by flowers. Jessica was sure Lacy was thinking about Luke's graduation ceremony so many years ago in the courtyard. She saw Lacy standing next to the closed-in screened porch and was sure Lacy might be thinking about her and Luke's secret meeting place.

Lacy, lost in reverie, stood with a frown creasing her forehead. Jessica walked up with a similar expression. Jessica and Lacy didn't have a great deal in common, but Jessica had an agenda. Despite the De'Lucas' upward social level, distancing them from the LaCrosses, Jessica wanted her brother to find happiness. She carried a box of poems, letters, and short stories Luke had written Lacy but that Lacy never got because of Mr. De'Luca. Mrs. De'Luca intercepted them and stored them for a long time in her own bottom dresser drawer.

Lacy couldn't avoid Jessica, or her frown. "Hi, Jessica! What's wrong?"

"We think Luke is missing. Mom and Dad got a telegram."

"I thought Luke was on Palmyra Island."

254

"He was trying to get off Palmyra."

"What happened?"

"The telegram from Hickam Air Force Base said Luke is officially missing and presumed lost at sea."

"What! How could that be?"

"On an unauthorized flight off Palmyra Island—maybe he was coming here? We've heard you're about to announce your engagement. Maybe he knew it, and knowing my brother, he probably wanted to talk you out of it. He wasn't on Palmyra. They looked everywhere for him. We called and everything. They couldn't find him. They waited two days before they notified Dad. We found out yesterday."

Jessica took a deep breath. "I know we have this hidden agreement to never talk about Luke, especially after you called him ancient history!"

"I'm sorry I said that. It's just that last year, you brought up a relationship that Luke and I had begun when I was in seventh grade. Puppy love!"

"Lacy, he just saw something special in you first."

"Let's not talk about it."

"I know something that might interest you, speaking of ancient history. Luke wrote a poem in 1954 about you when you said your good-byes at the train station."

"That was years ago. What's the big deal about that?" Lacy looked crossly at Jessica.

"The big deal is he sent it to you along with a poem he wrote for your college graduation in 1962. He sent them and many others and you never got them."

"He told me that when I saw him at O'Hare Airport. I found it hard to believe. How do you know that?"

"I happened to be at the right place at the wrong time, for your mom at least, at the incinerator in the back of your property. Your handyman was about to burn a big stack of letters with Luke's handwriting. He lugged out two wastebaskets and went to get another. I saw the letters addressed to you and trapped a few wasps in the old bellows we use to make fires burn better. The wasps chased your handyman across the yard while I grabbed the letters and emptied the waste basket."

"Where are they?"

"Stashed underneath a false top in Luke's old high school trunk up in the attic."

"Why in the world are you telling me this now?"

"Because everybody else thought he'd gotten over you a long time ago. So did I."

"Of course, he had. When I went to Springfield Academy in 1955, he was a senior and I was a junior. Despite my family's renewed efforts, we fell right back in love and had a marvelous year together. Then Dad and he had a final brouhaha at the end of the year after Luke's graduation. Dad told me some of the things Luke said. I couldn't believe Luke could say that, but he wasn't here to defend himself."

"Luke said it was much more than that. He said your dad told him, 'You could never give her the life she is used to, you could never make her happy. When Lacy gets married, you couldn't even afford to fly to her wedding.'"

Lacy gasped. "All this time, I thought Luke just breezed out of my life. My family thought I was such a fool. But Luke told me all about the letters! I didn't believe him."

"He never breezed out of your life. You flew out of Luke's life. You were always traveling. You never breezed out of his heart, though. He remembered your twentieth birthday, your twenty-first birthday, and a few more as well. Like your graduation from college in 1962."

"My twenty-first? Not that year, he didn't!"

"Come on over to the little porch. We have more privacy." Jessica pressed on. "Yes, he did write to you. I couldn't help reading them. I'm sorry. He wrote you a beautiful card with a story about your birthday. Everything he wrote made me realize he grieved over you for years. Neither of you even spoke to each other when you were back here? Had you hurt each other that much?"

"We each thought the other had. I don't want to talk about it. I've really got to go, Jessica."

"Seeing is believing. Here are the poems he wrote you. And the cards too. You might as well have them. Let me know when you want to pick up the letters. Some day you might ask your family what they did with all the letters Luke sent you."

Jessica sat quietly while Lacy read Luke's poems and cards. Then Jessica's words sank in. Lacy was stunned, incredulous. She looked up at Jessica. "What could have happened to Luke? Could he have died? Gone AWOL? He could never go without leaving me a last word. He told me we would meet again."

Lacy reached out to Jessica. "Let me go home with you. Please, please, I want those letters now."

Out on the back porch at Jessica's home, Lacy plopped down next to Jessica, with none of the lightheartedness Luke's home provided for her. Lacy started reading Luke's letters, and had to stop. "I will take them home. I can't do this anymore." Luke's letters were in her lap, smudged with tears washing up one sweet memory after another.

She stood up. "Do you mean it? Luke might have been coming here to rescue me?"

Jessica stood up and hugged Lacy. "When we find Luke, we are all going to look at things differently, aren't we?"

"Do you think that he still cares that much?"

Jessica was firm. "Of course I do. Don't you? Can't you feel it?"

38

Much to the Air Force's relief and embarrassment, they found Luke in an airtight mailbag floating in shallow water on Island Fever Reef, alive, two days after they called off the search. He had regained consciousness but had sustained injuries and relied on the oxygen from the plane. A hospital plane transported him to Hickam.

Behind the Hickam hospital walls, Luke struggled with holes in his memory and his life. He awoke in a strange mood from recurring nightmares of his worst fears, the inability to breathe, the close confinement, and fear of drowning, his worst fear. Burning to death in a plane crash? No problem. It ain't going to happen. Being shot? Never occurred to him. Sucked up into the eye of a tornado? Been there. Done that.

But claustrophobia and water in the lungs—nothing could be worse. And that is exactly what happened to him. In his hospital bed behind closed eyes, he saw an old WWII dock, its wood worn smooth from the waves. He looked out on a blue-green lagoon, a cruise ship leaving the dock, him not on it. He couldn't move fast enough. There was an outrigger canoe alongside the dock, rocking in the waves, smiling brown faces. Seagulls shrieked in the velvet-soft trade winds. Why was he on the dock? *People are waiting for me. Who are they?*

A sense of urgency gripped him. Some decision should be made. What was it? *What in the world was I doing? How in the world did I get here? Am I getting out of the Air Force? Or going back to college? Was there a wedding?* His mind was a confused mess. His brain swelling had receded, but the cracks in his skull were still there.

Another set of images, a dream vision, haunted him, with Lacy and her beauty. When she disappeared, a whirlpool of despair swallowed him. *Why did the dream vision come to haunt me every night?* He circled back again and again to find the answer.

An orderly brought him breakfast, fresh pineapple and a South Pacific soufflé. The nurse checked his vital signs and walked him to the patio beneath the palms. He sat in a white wicker chair. *Isn't there something I usually do? Something?*

His appointment with the trauma specialist proved frustrating. "The crash into the ocean has nothing to do with my state of mind," he told the shrink. "It took me a while to remember that. But I have nowhere to go. My tour of duty is almost up, and I have nowhere to go. What the hell! I should have died in the crash. I told you about Lacy, the girl I've wanted all my life. She just wrote me, I think, and said she was getting married . . . right before the plane crash. And I have no life to give her. Her family is very wealthy."

"So that's why you tried to get to Hawaii as parcel post?" The doctor smiled. "We have to see if we can avoid any punishment you earned. Once you fly above that, you may accept your loss and get on with living. Finish your tour of duty, not a year behind bars. Go back to the mainland and start a new life."

"Get on with life?"

"Look, Luke, you do not know if she got married. She may have been waiting to get a response from you. That was the vow, the agreement. I know you wanted to present a protest, or do a rescue in person. But in her eyes, you did not respond."

Luke's voice dropped. "We fell in love in junior high. Then we were separated for a time. When she completed ninth grade, her parents insisted that she not go stay at Park Academy where I could secretly see her. They did not want us to get together again. So for one year, she lived as a foreign student in Spain. She picked up Spanish as a second language, so her dad's company could be represented in South America. She also completed her sophomore year of high school.

"Then her junior year, she came to Springfield Academy. Her parents knew I would graduate at the end of the year. So it was safe. I was a senior, she was a junior. She gathered friends like bees do honey, both male and female. But eventually, we got together again. We really kept it below the radar. We found other secret places to meet. We kept the romance on low. It was a wonderful way for me to complete high school. She had another year to go...."

He began to pick up the pieces. It was all coming back.

"We came back together in high school, where she had a million friends. But we always had secret meeting places at first because everybody said she was a baby, or that she was out of my league."

The doctor smiled and nodded, happy to finally hear from Luke.

"In my senior year, she gave me a poem by e.e. cummings. I still have it in my wallet. She said she carried my heart in her heart, a secret that nobody knows. She said she would never let me down."

At the end of the week the doctor smiled and reassured Luke. "Your brain and body are recovering nicely. But you can't lie around out here living in the past, forever broken-hearted. What you need is new direction, new purpose. Follow your service commitment and enjoy your healing."

"Sir, it's a one-in-a-million shot. You get Lacy out here, and I'll start living again. It would be a miracle. I'd consider it a sign."

"I'll look into it. It is not my purview, you understand. What's her full name? Tell me where she is. Perhaps I can reach her without letting her family know."

"She's back in college. Lacy De'Luca. Getting close to finishing college. What month is it? What day is it? What year is it? Maybe you can say you're from the University of Hawaii, and you want to talk to her about a graduate scholarship. She, or especially her family, will never let her come here just to see me."

"I'll see what I can do. I won't promise anything."

"Thank you, sir."

That night the same nightmares flashed. At 0311, he awoke with a start. *Lacy, her face, her smile, her long black hair billowing over him.*

Then she leaned down and whispered. He opened his eyes wide, trying to unravel the mysterious vision.

It didn't feel like a nightmare. He blinked. He focused . . . *Lacy!*

She leaned over and whispered, "Why don't you heal, so we can get married?"

He beheld her beautiful aristocratic nose, long black hair, cameo face. Lovely green eyes. Wait, were those flecks of gold in her eyes? Yes. Lights of love danced around her. "The whole town's talking about the Jones boy, the Jones boy, the Jones boy," she sang softly in a whisper.

"And I just happen to be the Jones boy. And I just happen to be in love."

And then Luke sank back onto the bed into the darkness.

At 0730, he rolled out of bed. Where was *Lacy? That wasn't a dream. She was here kissing me, singing to me.*

Wasn't she?

He looked in the mirror. "I know you."

Luke jumped into the shower. A Mills Brothers song came back into his mind, and he began to sing it for the first time in a decade. When he shaved, two weeks of stubble disappeared. He put on shorts and a fancy Hawaiian print shirt and walked down to the hospital restaurant. Everybody stared at him. He ate breakfast and bought a newspaper. He walked back to his room and left a note.

He walked up to the open-roof front lobby of the hospital and sat beneath a twin palm tree. He waited for Lacy all day, and the next day, and the next. The following day, he bought a journal and a pen in the gift shop and began writing again. He borrowed an e.e. cummings book from the hospital library and read in the lobby. When he called the doctor's office, they said he was on vacation.

The next day, he purchased two leis and strung them around his neck, one for him, one for Lacy.

Luke wrote Lacy three letters and left them at the doctor's office. He could wait no longer. At 7:00 p.m., he went back to his hospital room and fell asleep dreaming of the foreign lands he would visit after his Air Force tour was over. There was the counterinsurgency project, and with it, a weather observation position on an island off the coast of North Vietnam.

He hummed, *"The Jones boy, the Jones boy, he just isn't the same somehow."*

39

On the day of his release, Luke got up, showered and shaved, wore his best clothes, packed his AWOL bag, and was on his way. He crossed through the outside courtyard and walked underneath a huge banyan tree. Something was different. A woman from the mainland with no flowery island blouse or skirt sat on a bench with tree branches curving down and attached to the ground. He blinked. Then he stared. He couldn't believe it! It was Lacy! For the first time in months, he broke into a run.

Lacy.

He stopped three feet away from her. She smiled her marvelous smile, surrounded by a heavenly glow. For all he knew, she did just descend from heaven. "I have always wanted to say, 'Aloha,' Luke," she said, looking up at him as if they'd never been apart.

He stopped dead in his tracks, his heart ceasing to beat, his breath held and his lungs motionless, afraid to scare the heavenly image away. The last time he'd seen her, in the night, he'd sworn she was there. *I heard her singing to me, but she wasn't there.* Luke rubbed his eyes to make sure he wasn't seeing another vision.

He looked down at his AWOL bag, trying to remember what he was going to do if he saw her again.

He looked up again. Only inches away, Lacy smiled at him.

"Lacy—if it's really you, hug me."

She wrapped her arms tightly around him and pressed her lips to his ear. Her words poured out. She couldn't stop. "I'm so sorry,

Luke. Jessica brought me up to date with your letters to me and your accident. You knew more about what would make me happy than I did, or my whole family did. The thought of the ocean swallowing you up, and your being gone forever out of my life, shocked me. I had to stop what I was doing. I left my fianceé and my studies and my family behind, Luke, darling." She hugged him and kissed him a thousand times.

Luke nodded with every phrase she uttered, tears of relief rolling slowly down his cheeks. His chest shuddered. Long slow breaths whispered the feelings of his heart.

"I can't talk. And I can't let go of you, Lacy. Holding you is the best thing I have ever done in my life. You held me for a few seconds at O'Hare," he said.

He couldn't help thinking, *who am I to her? What about Russ? He's been hanging around Lacy for years. My father doesn't own the biggest construction company in Chicago.* Then he said, "You're just a dream. You must be a dream. You never answered any of my letters."

Lacy said, "No, I'm not. Dreams do not take you to lunch. I'll make up for the letters. I didn't know what my parents had done until you crashed into the brink. And Jessica set me straight.

"I am taking you to lunch. Come on, Luke!"

They walked hand in hand into a brightly colored Hawaiian bar down by the ocean. They sat at a table outside and luxuriated in the cool breeze and the fragrance of pikake, roses, and orchids. The waitress strolled over in shorts and a halter-top, Luke ordered mai-tais and shrimp for an appetizer.

The waitress responded, "We just catered a luau. Would you like roast pork and poi? It's our special."

"Perfect!" Lacy said. "It's my treat. You get dinner for lunch."

Luke said, "Thank you, honey."

He thought a minute. "Lacy, if you don't like poi, I'll eat yours. It's an acquired taste. I'll get you fresh pineapple instead."

"Whatever you say, Luke, is fine with me." She squeezed his hand. "What can we do tomorrow? Tell me some places we can go that you can take me."

"Okay, first thing in the morning, we'll walk up to the Punch Bowl cemetery. You cannot imagine a better view, a better vista. Then we'll go out to the Arizona Memorial. They just opened it up. I'm so excited to see it all. The USS Arizona burned when I was only two years old. I saw it later when I first came out to Hawaii on the way to Samoa. I saw the original video. What a terrible sight, what a catastrophe, watching all that smoke and fire, and then seeing the whole ship disappear into the sea with its crew of over a thousand. And on a Sunday morning!"

"This time you don't have to see all of it alone, you sweet thing." Lacy leaned over and kissed him. "Oooooo, here comes our food. I love pork. My dad bought the best pork roasts for Sunday dinner." Lacy leaned forward and picked up a fork, and she deftly twisted a mouthful of pork from the huge platter between them. Luke imitated her.

"Dip it into the dish of poi, Lacy. Just try it." Luke dipped his second forkful into it and raised it to his lips, "Mmmm. It tastes good as a sauce or topping."

She took a bit of the poi by itself. "Okay, I tried it. You can have mine."

"I didn't expect you to like it. No worries."

He stopped and smiled at her. "Did you ever see them roast a pig in an underground oven?"

"No. Doesn't it get all dirty?"

"Luke burst out laughing, the first time he had laughed in months. "No, no. They wrap it in big Ti leaves completely and it's surrounded by hot stones, and then covered up with dirt. That's why it's so tender and moist. No *tea* leaves, as in English tea. The Ti leaves in the tropics. They're as big as palm branches."

Lacy said, "Well, I've always loved the side dishes. They do different things with rice out here. The vegetables look familiar, but they taste different… better."

Luke needed to sharpen up. "Do you mind if I order some good Hawaiian Kona coffee?"

"No, I love coffee. My family always loved coffee."

"You never had to make it for yourselves, either, did you?"

"No, but I learned how when I went away to college."

They enjoyed the leisurely lunch just being together. Luke couldn't keep his eyes off her.

While he was just sitting there taking her in, Lacy stood up. "Where can we go, Luke?"

"There are apartments for families of the patient right next to the hospital. They don't know I have left yet. You rent one apartment and I'll rent another unit right next door."

He just stood there, looking at her. She put her hands on her hips. "Aren't you going to go?"

"Yes. Sure. I'm afraid if I blink twice or tap my heels, you'll disappear."

"Luke, the sooner you get going, the sooner I can start the healing. They say hands-on works best."

"I'm gone." He disappeared. In less than an hour, he got his key, unloaded all his gear into the little apartment, and rushed over to where Lacy sat in the shade of a twin palm tree.

Lacy stood up and hugged him until he couldn't breathe anymore. "I love being here, Luke. Our childhood days were so perfect, so together. We had our own little world and it was enough." They walked hand in hand down toward the beaches.

"My universe decreased by half when your father found ways to put us at cross purposes."

"Mine too, Luke. I can't just toss away my father."

"I know. I hated tossing away my life."

Lacy said, "Now you and I are marching to the beat of a different drummer. I grew up with beautiful homes and horses and travel. I love beautiful art and pictures and museums. But I loved reaching out to people. I want to make people's lives better, richer. I spent two years in the Peace Corps. Some say I could make it in Illinois politics. I could make a difference."

"Lacy, you've got to bring me up to date."

She said, "After you left our Prep School, I enjoyed more leadership posts in my last year. You know I started college at Stanford, didn't you? All alone was I. You were gone."

She looked at him. "That summer after my first year I attended a finishing school in Spain."

"Yikes, Lacy. Where did all that come from?"

"My father. Who else? He wanted to see me as a successful executive with worldwide possibilities. Personally I wanted to spend a year in Italy. I would meet all the De'Lucas."

"That's quite a little jump from your role as 'Daddy's little girl.'"

"Well, everybody has to grow up some time."

"No offense intended, Lacy."

He stopped. "By the way, why in the world are you out here talking to me? I'm Mr. Nobody in your new world. Just call me Nemo."

"You were Mr. Wonderful in my old world, Luke. When you get out of the Air Force, who knows where you'll land? You have always been somebody special, somebody who will become admired and followed."

They found a hotel and restaurant right on Waikiki Beach. They sat together looking out at the surfers and swimmers. They feasted on grilled mahi-mahi and traded fresh memories like exchanging one lei of flowers around each other's neck for another. After fresh pineapple for dessert, Lacy got up and opened her arms. "How sweet it is to break bread with you, honey. Come on, let's go for an evening walk."

As they walked, they reminisced the days of their wonder years, because there seemed so little they had in common in the present. When they returned to adjoining apartments, they had the hardest time saying goodnight. Lacy turned and kissed Luke just as they had done in high school, and went inside. It wasn't enough. She was holding something back. Luke must have stood at her door for an hour. He couldn't bear to leave her. But he couldn't bear to push himself into her new life yet. Little did he know she was right on the other side of the door.

The next day they went to a sweet little place for breakfast with fresh pineapple and mango, the usual rice for breakfast, and a fresh catch of fish from the ocean—red snapper.

"Lacy," he said, "imagine us back in that little closed in porch freezing to death, trying to keep our hands warm with paper cups of hot cocoa and nibbling on Mom's homemade sugar cookies. Isn't it heavenly to eat in paradise together?"

Her eyes flashed pure love to Luke for four-one hundredths of a second—the time it took his favorite heavyweight newcomer, Cassius Clay, to hit his latest opponent. If Luke blinked his eye in either case, he would have missed it. When he looked up, the pure love was locked in.

It was a miracle. For the next hour Lacy was twelve again, or maybe thirteen—she was all Luke's, not some sophisticated graduate student from a noveau riche family with millionaire connections.

They took the long walk up to the Punch Bowl cemetery, and after lunch they took the boat out to the USS Arizona. Lacy was so interested in Luke, his family, and his family military traditions. He wanted to know all about the countries she had visited, what she had learned, who her friends were. They sang songs they used to sing. They recited poetry they used to send to each other.

The following day delivered on its promise of paradise. They awoke to doves on the window sills of their adjoining rooms, and had breakfast of fresh pineapple and mango and eggs Benedict out on the beach. They swam at Waikiki, played in the gentle waves, and lunched at Ala Moana beneath its famous banyan tree. They surfed on the bigger waves in a fourteen-foot outrigger canoe, complete with six native oarsmen, sailing in on a wave for over half a mile. And that night they sat in the sand and listened to Don Ho in person. Luke was on a cruise ship of love he didn't ever want to get off. He wanted to cruise around the world forever.

A day later, they rented a car and drove to the Hanalei Plantation, seeing all the sights, taking pictures, walking on beaches, and eating lunch under a grove of palms. They sailed over to Kauai, and took the boat up the river to the Fern Grotto, where so many people got married. They climbed to the top of a lighthouse on the coast and spent the night looking up at the stars and out on the ocean. They talked about a future... *their* future. They talked about starting over in Hawaii, far away from their families. Luke thought there was a chance he could get an early release and stay in Hawaii. They could set up for a new life.

They were bonding, and the boundary lines separating them in the past were melting away. All those lonely days out in the Pacific with only memories vanished into the balmy air surrounding the lighthouse. In their place vibrated the hum of a hundred honeybees making a beehive in his heart, healing all his wounds.

One morning he woke up and couldn't see the future. He thought about all the love he had experienced with Talia every day. He got up and looked out the window. He couldn't get Talia off his mind. All he could see was Talia, the ocean, the past. He shook his head, and closed his eyes. "Lacy, I can't get ahold of our future."

"What do you mean?" She came up behind him and hugged him. "Our time together here has been the best chapter of my life. What could possibly be wrong?"

"The last time we were here in Hawaii, I dreamed of the best. Look what happened. We had our first crash-landing."

He turned around and saw her disappointment, and her sadness. "I was thoughtless of you back then, Luke. I really was a spoiled child. You did not deserve that."

She took a deep breath. "Can we talk about it now?"

Luke thought back to Talia and all she gave him and all he gave her. He turned and looked out the window again. Talia was totally his. And despite their being apart, Talia would always love him. Polynesians live with the ocean and on the ocean and they live by the ocean. The ocean never changes. It is always there for its island inhabitants. *That's Talia. She will love me her whole lifetime. I have no idea if Lacy will. We have had so many ups and downs, backward and forward. How do I know Lacy won't change by whoever she is with?*

Luke sighed. "I'm sorry, honey. What I want to talk about, I can't talk about. I'm not ready. And I don't think you're ready either."

"How could I not be ready? I dropped everything and came out to be with you. I was ready to be completely with you." Lacy started to cry.

Luke gathered up his courage and gently held eye contact with Lacy. "I need time," he said. "I wish I could tell you. But I don't want to hurt you. Not after all you've done."

269

His voice broke and his lips quivered. Sadness filled the whole room, every molecule in it, and they both started to cry.

"Luke, I am here with you in Hawaii," Lacy insisted. "Can't you feel it? I'm not part of your nightmare in the ocean. I am not part of that disaster. This is me, Lacy, the one who still loves you. You could have asked for anything. We could have made love every night." She cried and cried.

Luke's body went absolutely still. He agonized over the dilemma. *Now I really don't deserve Lacy. If I talked to her, and told her the truth about Talia, it would break her heart, and at some point, I will have to tell her. And then everything will be over.*

"We need to get your strength up," Lacy said gently as she kissed him all over his face. "I can kiss away all your tears, honey."

She stepped back and looked closely at him, slumped over. Her eyes glistened when she saw his condition. "Luke, are you okay?"

He couldn't talk. "I so don't deserve you."

She listened and could not hear him breathing.

Finally, she murmured, "Now don't take this too far. But I'm not doing a thing until I know you're whole and healed and happy."

"I need time," he said. "There is so much I have to do. I have to make something out of myself. I'm barely started."

Lacy could not handle his reply. It was so unfeeling, so insensitive after what she had just said. She started to cry. "You came back to rescue me and crashed into the ocean. And I came out to rescue you and I'm crashing into the ocean. Do you really want to do that, Luke? Didn't you hear what I just said to you?"

He looked at her, unable to speak.

Lacy put her hands up to her eyes to stop the tears. "I left everything back there. Now here I am in the present. What more could I do?"

Luke took her two hands and held them. "Thank you so much, Lacy. We had so much fun together. You gave me hope." He brought her hands up to his lips and kissed them, so carefully, so tenderly.

Lacy smiled through her tears. "I owed you for the last time we were in Hawaii."

"Well, I owe you for this time," Luke said gravely.

There was a knock on the door. "Mr. LaCrosse. This is Jeremy from the front desk. You have an important call from your commanding officer. Pick up your phone, give me a minute, and I will patch you through."

Luke let go of Lacy and went over to the desk against the wall. He picked up the phone and waited. He listened for the connection. "This is Airman LaCrosse, sir. At your service."

The louder than normal voice on the line began in full mission-ready focus. "This is Colonel Mosely. We need you badly on the Nevada Test Site. You serve three months back there, I can get you the extra pay, separate rations per diem, travel pay, you name it. Your old battle-buddy Chance Chisholm needs you out there. He's run into some personnel problems on the site, personality conflicts with a small Army contingent. There is something else going on there. He can't talk about it and I can't do anything about it. But I think you can. You're my best hope, LaCrosse. Can I count on you?"

"You can absolutely count on me, sir."

"That's a yes?"

"Yes, sir. I am ready."

The Colonel said briskly, "Pick up your orders at Base Operations at Hickam tomorrow morning at 0400. You'll be on your way before 0600 hours."

Luke repeated his orders. "Thank you for giving me this opportunity, sir. You will not be disappointed."

He hung up the phone. *Thank God for duty.*

Luke shook his head. "I'm so sorry, Lacy."

"I heard it all," she said. "Goodbye, Luke. I have to go now."

Lacy kissed him and left. When she got to her rental car, she opened the door, fell into the driver's seat, and started to cry. She threw the keys on the floor. She felt so alone, so unanchored. She cried and cried, seemingly unable to unwind all those years and memories. She felt unable to grasp the future. *What should she say to her fiancé? What will her parents say if they hear about her trip to Hawaii? I expected Luke to be more of a rock once he saw me. Once he knew I was his completely. And all through my trip to Hawaii, I thought I was the rock. And I wasn't.*

40

Luke got his new orders from headquarters, the wheels were up, and he was on the cargo plane headed back to the Nevada Test Site for full duty. As detailed in another story, within a month he saw Chance through all the complications and earned a commendation award from the State of Nevada and a promotion from the Air Force as well. Everything began to shape up for him. The underground nuclear tests were much easier to work with than the live missile detonations.

Just as Luke got set to get out, go to college, and catch up with his life, he got surprise orders to go back out to the Pacific. His sergeant said, "The Colonel said three months. You still owe us two months." Luke did not want to go back to Samoa. Back where he had found Talia and then lost her. It was the last place he wanted to go.

Back stationed at Camp Leone, life dragged on for him. Sergeant Rogers put him back in charge of taking men into Pago Pago on Saturdays and Sundays—any weekend when there were no nuclear tests up around the Marshall Islands. He brought a dozen men in, parked the wepo, (weapons carrier shuttle) near the ball field, and went for a walk. He was an empty shell from the ocean with no life inside him. His Air Force adventures were behind him. All he thought about was starting college. A month went by. It rained.

He strolled through Pago Pago and eastward all around the harbor, remembering Talia and all they did in the ocean and in the lagoons and on the beaches. The beautiful harbor might as well have had Talia's name on it. She was so calm and protected, nothing like the ocean with its typhoons and fearful waves and riptides. Peace and tranquility floated around her and inside her, just where he wanted to be.

Two hours later he ended back at the wepo to get his canteen and his camera. He wanted to take just a few more photos for his memory album with Talia. This time he headed toward Faga Toga, toward the west. Across the field someone waved to him. Even from where he stood, she was magnificent. He stopped, wondering who she was, willing to meet her.

"I know you, Luka! Remember me? I'm Natal'ia."

She began running to him, more like floating across the green field. Luke looked down, not wanting to seem interested as she smoothly approached him. But he was impressed she knew how to say his name Polynesian style. "Wait," she said, reaching out to him with both arms. "I have seen you with Talia. Then she disappeared. I was jealous of her. And I wanted to meet you. And dance for you. Then you disappeared."

She smiled. Her smile had everything in it. And she was still dressed in her dancing costume. "But I never see you in the places I dance."

"I don't go there. I have to stay clean and dry to take the men back to Leone in the middle of the night."

"Look at me now, Luka," she said and posed, arms outstretched, standing on one leg and extending the other leg behind her. Luke drank it in. He couldn't help it. Then he looked down, a little embarrassed. "I'm sorry I didn't know your name. I think I did see you dancing once."

Natal'ia laughed. "Natal'ia is my stage name. Nobody remembers to accentuate the second syllable. It's so elegant, just like *Tá'li'a*, don't you think?"

Luke laughed. "Not just the name," he said. "I admire your costume."

She gave him a sideways demure look. "Aren't you going to ask how I know you?"

Luke said, "My papa always taught me to celebrate the present moment. I need the present moment so much right now. I am happy.

I am happy you remember me. Happy you are here. It does not matter how you knew me before."

She came up close to him, so beautiful and bountiful, knowing he couldn't take his eyes off her. "Luka, you look so sad. Come with me." Natal'ia stepped forward and gave him a warm open hug, something he had not felt for a long time, something that brought tears to his eyes. He couldn't believe it. He could feel the silk of her dancing costume underneath her blouse and the warmth of her breasts, hidden to most, but not to him. And she wouldn't let him go. She took his hand and he walked with her as if he was in a dream.

"Come and sit on the bench by the bay and talk to me," she invited. Luke had no choice. She sat sideways, asking him questions, and answering some of his. All Luke could see was Natal'ia in all her splendor. He was tongue-tied. It appeared as if he was looking down, but his peripheral vision was mesmerized by her curves and her costume. When it was time for him to take the men back to the camp, she got up and walked halfway across the field holding his hand.

Natal'ia came from Tahiti, just as Talia and Moana had. She wanted to meet men who didn't just think of her as a dancer. She knew about Luke from her friends in Pago Pago. She knew he loved people for who they were, not for what they could do for him, or with him. She knew he loved little children. And she knew he would care for her and respect her as a woman, just as he had with Talia.

Before she let go of his hand and turned around, she said, "Will I see you again?"

Luke smiled and took her in, only with his eyes. "I bring the men into town at least two times a week."

She leaned in and kissed him just as if they had known each other for months.

It didn't take long for Natal'ia to be drawn to Luke. Not even two weeks had passed. To her, he was such a gentleman. He had grace and intelligence. He cared for her, and he cared for her deeply. He never pressed himself on her. And she knew about Talia, she knew the pain he lived with. She begged him to confide in her, talk to her, and take comfort from her.

Finally, late one night when Luke got someone else to drive the men home, Natal'ia leaned over and took him in her arms. She whispered, "I can help you with your emptiness. I know a way to make you float in the air like an albatross. You will float until you find the one you really love. And you will not be sad and alone while you are floating."

Luke drew back a little. "How can you do that?"

Natal'ia smiled and squeezed him. "You will know. Just follow me."

She sounded like somebody from the South Pacific. Magnetic and gorgeous, she walked with him and talked with him on the shores along Pago Pago harbor. She danced for him on the hidden beaches and taught him how to dance with her. She was entirely different from Talia, but she made an impact on Luke whenever he came into town. Luke began to fear that the force of her impact would evaporate him—similar to the nuclear test explosions. Every quiver in her eyes and her lips captivated him, just as she knew they would. More than once, when she ate lunch with Luke in her happy, carefree fashion, she leaned over and carefully brushed off his lips. And then she kissed him quickly and drew back before he tasted her. He knew how a honeybee felt, perched on the petals of a flower full of pollen, looking down into a delicious prison. Her rose-shaped lips were soft and intent on their target, but they hadn't reached his heart yet.

The day came when she couldn't stand it any longer. "Come to the secret cave," she said, "and then your heart might follow. It won't hurt you. Besides, you will love to get away. We have no privacy at the bars and restaurants and beaches here."

The day arrived. Luke walked across the ball field. Everybody swam in the bay, cooling off. He went to his favorite store, known all around the Pacific, and bought some shirts for his friends, for the "getting out party" he would have back at Tinker Air Force Base on his last day in the Air Force. Then he stopped at the post office and looked at the names above the letter boxes, hoping to remember Samoans he had known months ago.

Natalia walked up behind him. "You won't find what you are looking for here."

"You caught me," he said. "You are right. I won't find it."

She pulled her shoulders back, and took his hand. "Come with me."

Luke tried to avoid her hand. He didn't want to be seen with her that way. Natal'ia moved close and pulled him out of the post office. Her perfume enveloped him, her long hair caught in the breeze, floating over to touch chest and shoulders. Her closeness was more than magnetic.

Luke moved away a half-step, a bit startled. He walked over to the bench by the bay. "Do you want to sit here like we did before, and talk?" He was perspiring in the sun. It was muggy and debilitating.

"No. It's far too hot here. The cave and its beach are always cool. And quiet, with a mountain breeze." She took his hand. "Come, I have a canoe. Can you paddle? I will take you across the bay where it will be quiet. See over there?" She pointed to the other shore. Luke squinted.

She bumped into him. "Come, I will show you. It is a mile at least. We're lucky there is only a little breeze, and the harbor is quiet. No big ships coming in today."

She found the canoe with an old outrigger on the left side. "Did you know they used to call Savaii, Upolu, and Tutuila the Navigator Islands because Sámoans make such wonderful canoes?"

"No."

"Sámoans made the best canoes, and they sailed all over the Pacific. That's one reason for their islands to be called the Navigator Islands. They found the island I grew up on, far north and west of here."

Finally, Natal'ia grew quiet. Luke fell into the steady rhythm of their paddling. They reached the other side of the harbor, and Natal'ia jumped out to pull the prow of the canoe up on the beach. Luke dropped the paddle inside the canoe, and together they dragged the canoe beyond where the tides might pull it back into the harbor. Nobody was in the area. The harbor was quieting down, the people settling in for supper.

"Where to?" he asked.

"Follow me. We walk up this trail until we get to a little cave on the front of Mount Rainmaker. You can almost see it from the other side of the harbor. It is an outer island custom to know about and use this cave. It's almost unknown to the Samoans."

Luke followed her up the jungle trail for about a mile. Birds cooed their evening songs. Once in a while, they heard a wild pig snorting in the underbrush. They climbed over some rocks and turned to the right beneath a huge tree. He saw a cave with inscriptions around its mouth. In front of the cave lay a sandy area, about fifteen feet in diameter.

"Sit down," she said, crossing her legs in front of her and pulling her feet toward her lap, her knees jutting out to the sides. She wore an orange and white checkered lava-lava with a matching halter top. She pulled her hair into a long ponytail and wore lipstick and rouge, unlike many Sámoans. Luke's friend, Sela, had told him that Natal'ia's ancestry was primarily French Polynesian with solid traces of Samoan. Luke already knew that.

"There is an older woman who has noticed you," Natal'ia said. "She has taught me in the old ways of Melanesia. She has watched you in the past months and wants to save you from falling down the same path all the *palagis* go."

She paused and took a deep breath. "You can be a promise-keeper. In your eyes, we see a man capable of great love and devotion to one woman. But we also see a hunger in you that might lead you off the path to happiness. You are trying to save yourself for such a woman, but here in Oceania there are many reasons for happy times. We don't like it when the sailors come and take our love. But what can we do? Women must obey the men. Especially because of the old custom, many still think sailors fell from the sky."

She patted his hand. "Keep listening. But once you take blossoms from our women—who wear a flower over their left ear if they are available to a man—you will be tempted to move from blossom to blossom, from woman to woman, like a bee who cannot stop for only one flower. We see men losing their hopes and dreams. They don't understand our island love. They look only at the surface. They do not see the real gift God can give us. They think island women are like free money floating from the sky. Pick up as many bills or blossoms as you can. But Americans don't earn them. They gather them only to throw them away."

"I know," Luke said. "I have seen this many times. I am stuck driving the men into town for beer and women almost every week. Soon they must drink more beer to have a good time. The next day, they are not happy, like spoiled children."

"It's so strange. Free love in Polynesia is taken for granted by sailors or the Europeans or Americans."

Natal'ia shifted her legs, and Luke's glance followed the gentle movement of her ankles and her knees and her thighs. He couldn't help it.

"I can teach you how to love a woman. I can save you from going from woman to woman. Once you make love like the ancient custom, you will never want to waste your time with the usual flower blossoms. It will also make you save yourself for the one woman you love. You will never again have a friend like me. You won't need another woman until you get married."

Did I just hear that? Luke was puzzled.

"Don't wander away from me, Luke."

Natal'ia spun a story. "Far away and long ago, on an island we have legends about, a young island princess was taught to keep away from boys. She had an older woman watching her. When she became marriageable, only the smartest and strongest suitor was selected for her."

She rose and walked to the middle of the sandy area. "You will see why we need it sandy." She untied her ponytail, showering her shoulders with her luxuriant black tresses. She untied her traditional lava-lava, slowly and delicately unwrapping herself, pulling it away from her body, displaying her beautiful sculpted legs and saucy bottom, mountains and valleys, shadows and highlights, the sweetest hints of hidden places. With a ceremonious movement, her clothing floated to the ground behind her. Nobody saw the lava-lava touch the sands.

Luke was sure he was dreaming or hallucinating. But now she sank slowly to her knees, spread apart in the sand, her toes curled in toward each other, her feet resting on their outer edges. Reaching her arms behind her, she unhooked her halter top and extended her right arm out, dropping her top neatly next to her lava-lava. In one fluid motion, she rose to her knees and bounced back on her toes, leaning toward him and playfully tempting him. "Come here. When nobody is looking, we do this island dance, very close, and then I put my arms around your neck, and put my legs around you, like this, crossing ankles behind you."

So Luke stood up and Natal'ia pulled him. She leaned gracefully back, arching her pelvis and leaning her head down until it almost rested on the sand. Every part of her body sparkled in the sun; there was nothing he couldn't see. She was so entrancingly natural. Luke shivered with anticipation. Her skin was so golden, her body stretched out in the most appealing way. Then he frowned. She was enticing, but it seemed impossible to hold her close.

Nevertheless, his desire to hold Natal'ia and to press together with her grew stronger and stronger. He was in no position to make a choice. Her body had beckoned him; her moist and gleaming skin pulsed through his bloodstream, overwhelming his arteries and veins, synapses and nerve endings, coating his skin with an enticing film of love.

He leaned, off balance, entranced, mesmerized, speechless, fighting back an overwhelming urge to sweep onto this soft beach like a runaway wave. She said, "Wait, Luke. I promise if you let me show you how to make love in the ancient custom taught by our priests from long ago, you will be able to save yourself for the woman you love and want to have a family with. You will not want to waste your time with the usual flower blossoms.

"You must understand," she cautioned, "You will not remember how we did this. And you can never repeat this. That's how the ancients created it. But you will be satisfied and floating until you find your partner and marry her."

Her body was bent like a bow.

And that's all he remembered. Luke held on tightly for a long time, giddy, floating first on ocean waves and then caught by the wind and tossed far up into the sky, higher and higher. He felt like a moist raindrop falling and then rising back up in the cloud and then falling again. He was in a thunderstorm that wouldn't stop. He was breathless.

How could anybody survive this ride?

Finally, he felt himself falling, falling, falling, and then he found himself landing lightly down. Natal'ia was right next to him. He was surprised the sand hadn't turned to glass. One minute passed into another until at last his breathing was deep and full. He felt as if he had just climbed Mount Manga, 2,140 feet high, and knew he lacked the energy to climb down.

Natal'ia made it clear once more. She lay on her side, curling around him, talking to him.

"So, we're just looking out for you. Otherwise, you'd never leave the island to get married or to get an education. And you would pine away in sorrow because Talia cannot be with you, or you would go from one lover to another. We can see that in your eyes. It's the call of the Pacific. No man understands it until he is here and somebody loves him and a family takes him in."

Luke looked over at Natal'ia curled around him. "If anybody can do what you said, it's got to be you."

She wrapped herself around him again. He murmured, "Okay, okay, I got the message. I can feel it. I can wait. I can feel it. I can wait . . . I can wait for you, Lacy."

He drifted off, murmuring, "Lacy...Lacy.'"

Natal'ia's eyes softened. Then she caught herself before love caught her. "*Manuia*. Good luck for you. This woman you are saving yourself for, she is very *laleilei, very special.*"

Two hours later, she woke Luke up. "It's time to go, sweetie."

Her clothes seemed to just wrap around her. And Luke's too. As they walked to the canoe, Luke felt light, happy, floating, and relieved. He had just experienced a personal, emotional, physical kind of thermonuclear explosion without any deadly radiation. The radiation from this detonation was of another kind, warm and hot and life-giving.

They paddled across the harbor, pushed by a breeze. He could hardly hold the paddle. When they hit the shore, as he pulled the outrigger up and turned to say goodbye, Natal'ia caught him by surprise and kissed him.

"This for me, saying goodbye," she said. "This is not for you." She hugged him one last time and wouldn't let him go.

She drew herself up. "Now you are healed and ready. You will not pine for Talia. And you will...wait... for..."

"Lacy," he said. But all he could see, hear, feel, touch, and taste was Natal'ia. Her perfume floated behind her, but her fragrance covered him and protected him. He would be safe.

41

Swimming against three-mile-per-hour currents on the ocean floors anywhere in the Pacific was impossible. That was all life had for Luke. And all he could see. But finally! Time surged by like the currents flowing off the Kerguelen Plateau of Antarctica. Not the average three miles per hour, but at least six miles per hour and maybe seven. They are the fastest ocean-floor currents in the world. Sixth Weather Squadron's work with the atmospheric wind currents included some necessary studies of deep ocean currents and surface ocean currents. Luke knew that once he got out of the Air Force he would be swimming with the Kerguelen currents.

So the day came that no enlisted man forgets. Luke's tour of duty was almost over. Luke flew from Samoa to Rarotonga. He had to wait a day, and then flew to Hickam, a 2,000-mile trip in a C-23 cargo plane, noisy, empty, and offering nothing but a cargo net for a seat. The cruising speed of 225 knots gave him time to look at nothing but ocean forever. He got out his worn copy of Carl Sandburg's biography of Abraham Lincoln. Only Lincoln's struggles and the tortures of the Civil War had kept Luke's mind off the endless miles sitting on a cargo net or on the cargo itself when flying across the Pacific Ocean. He deplaned at Hickam and immediately signed up for a free flight home.

An hour later, he boarded a C-54 going to Davis Air Force Base outside of San Francisco. He stayed overnight at Davis, and finally arrived at Tinker in a "Super Con," an Air Force Constellation passenger plane, going home in style. He spent the last day and night off base at Bricktown in Oklahoma City with all his Sixth Weather Squadron buddies. Try as they might, they didn't come close to sampling all two-hundred-fifteen draft beers on tap.

The next day, the Lieutenant gave Luke his Honorable Discharge and military ID card. Luke saluted for what he thought might be his last time, and Chance drove him out to Will Rogers Airport. Chance asked, "So how long did you serve?"

"Three years, nine months, and one day. Then the Colonel extended me three months. It's all good," Luke said.

"I'm glad he did. I couldn't have succeeded at the Nevada Test Site if you hadn't shown up."

"Great minds think alike," Luke said. "Thanks for all you did for me. And all the good times and good flights we had."

"Believe me, it was my pleasure and God's blessing," Chance said. "And I truly hope you find a way to corral Lacy, seeing as you have nobody waiting downrange in the Pacific."

"I have a long way to go. Speaking of corrals, with her strength, she will still be a free-range wild mustang for a long time," Luke said. "No stallion will have the power to tame her, and she will always run as the lead mare. It will take time for us to run together, but I'll never corral her."

Chance shook Luke's hand. "That was a bad word choice on my part, Luke. I have somebody waiting for me downrange. If Tiara gives up her dancing, we will make a home together in Sa'moa. I'm through with Chicago winters."

Luke raised his eyebrows. "That's another story."

It was only eight hundred miles to Tucson, Arizona, and for Luke and his eighty-thousand mile tour of duty, he was sure he arrived about ten minutes later. He was a civilian for a few days when he began school at the University of Arizona, but joining the Reserve Officer Training Command (ROTC) by the end of the week gave him a new military ID. He didn't tell his Air Force buddies that he had chosen the Army ROTC program. He had his eyes fixed on his lifetime Army helicopter pilot's dream.

He took courses and programs that could get him through college in three years. That was crucial in his catching up to Lacy. The university had an academic scholarship waiting for him, as well as the pay an ROTC student in good standing could earn. Luke did his part. He knew he had let Lacy down. She came all the way out to see him, maybe to rescue him, take care of him if he needed it. She risked everything for him. And he didn't come through. He didn't believe her. He hadn't believed in "them." At this point in his life in Arizona, he was sure she didn't either. But his full romance and history with Talia could have ended with a Polynesian marriage. It didn't.

But had she known or had he told her, Lacy would have regretted coming to Hawaii. In fact, she might have hated him and have never wanted to see him again. And the worst part—he had given up on his dreams of them together. What kind of life or strength or hope could he possibly give Lacy? He knew he had a lot to prove, mainly to himself. He didn't expect Lacy to keep in contact, and he had his mad pursuit of goals just as she did.

But he understood repentance, God's forgiveness, and reformation. He needed to make a new life for himself. He needed to catch up. He prayed every night for a long time, looking at a special photo from his collection.

> *"I love you, Lord, because you have heard my voice both silent and spoken in all the myriad times I lost faith in myself and didn't believe. I understand the Psalmist who constantly referred to his enemies. A hundred times a day, I can fall victim to those enemies, the negative voices and emotions sown in the years of my childhood.*
>
> *You heard my cry for your confidence, mercy, and salvation. Because you turned your ear to me countless times, I will call upon you as long as I live.*
>
> *Only you can heal spiritual diseases. You are full of compassion, graciousness, and righteousness."*

The healing warmth and beauty of God's protection.

A year later, Lacy and Luke had yet to meet again. He was not ready. He wanted to match her efforts. He was so thankful that Lacy had taken a year out in a work/study program, joined the Peace Corps, and served brilliantly in Jamaica, moving up the chain of command until she was an assistant director and administrator. Besides winning her independence from her father, she had earned many credits in her business administration major at Stanford University. She was two years ahead of him in college.

Lacy as an advanced junior had resumed her studies. Jessica carefully kept them both in touch, a little bit here and a little bit there. She wisely took a long time to tell Luke that Lacy had given her engagement ring back to Russ. Jessica realized that both Luke and Lacy suffered from the Hawaiian vacations they had ruined. Even now, two years later, they were still bruised.

Luke was now a sophomore at the University of Arizona. After nine months of excellent performances in his regular classes, he plunged into a full summer program. He had no time for anything but his studies. He took accelerated courses, and due to his experience in the military and his excellent writing skills, he was asked to join a recruiting program as a part-time ROTC student/teacher, helping students improve their skills in other ROTC programs. He travelled to the most promising universities in the West.

One night at Stanford, Luke sat at a big table in the library, while waiting for his group and the full-time military professor to arrive. He casually watched another writing group of older college kids. Among sixteen students, there appeared to be a professor and a librarian, and one startlingly attractive woman. She sat at the end of the next table over, almost out of his view. Her teacher handed out packets to each student.

Do I know this girl? he thought. *She reminds me of Lacy…*Long curly black hair, not just strands coming out to die, but the thinnest liquid strands—something alive and glistening—flowed down and curled around her shoulders and below her neck. *Wait a minute! Lacy!*

He couldn't take his eyes off her, so to read his prepared lessons he held up his notebook in front of him. He held a pen in his hand and laid down his notebook at times to look as if he was making changes.

When the professor and the other group of airmen came to his table, Luke seemed preoccupied. They were in Army fatigues, and they all looked the same. He hoped it wasn't the same for him. He nodded to them as they sat down, somehow a quick count of a dozen. They showed him a measure of respect. His had rank, medals, and ribbons.

"I got here early to get caught up," he said. "I'm working on something right now. I want to finish it before I read it and get you all a copy."

Nods came from all sides. The professor handed out a stack of papers, and they were handed around the big table. "Here's the impromptu assignment. Let's work on this first," he said. "Luke, let me know when you are ready."

Luke looked as if he were writing. He picked up his clipboard to catch the light as he corrected his copy. The rest of the time, he looked off in space, as if concentrating. Okay, it wasn't space. He couldn't take his eyes off the Lacy look-alike. She wore a violet sweater, accentuating her slimness. She had the most distinct and luxuriant eyebrows, matched only by her eyelashes. Her nose had the refined look of a place higher up the DNA coils, showing strength of character and individuality, reminiscent of a Michelangelo classic. He had never seen her wear this clothing style.

Luke was transported, breathless. Minutes seemed like hours. There breathed a live classic, with movement free and flowing. He shifted in his seat a few times to watch everything she did. She lived with grace, composed, and complete in herself. But she smiled easily and leaned forward, attentive to those around her. *She thinks first and talks later. When she has something to say, it is worth hearing. She does not talk to fill up time or hear her own voice. She floats through people like a lilac fragrance. She had a way with people. That's got to be Lacy. But Lacy matured. She can cast honey on the waters and calm the sea. She gets along with everybody; they look at her with love and respect.*

She always makes the effort. And if somebody makes a worthy statement, her smile has exceptional effect, her attractive mouth showing rows of well-formed bright white teeth, all in a small and attractive semi-circle. On her right nostril, a tiny silver star lay almost hidden, easy to miss. He had not seen that before. *Neither had her father,* he was willing to bet. Her natural skin tended toward an olive color; she wore little if any makeup and no lipstick. Her oval face was proportional, surrounded by massive waves of hair. Compared to a sea of round faces and square faces, she stood out, impossible to ignore, exciting to focus on.

Once she caught Luke looking and flashed a warm, dazzling smile, though she seemed unsure if it was him, *as if, how could he be here?* Luke tried to stay out of her line of sight, but watched carefully. Occasionally, there appeared a slight vertical line on her brow, perhaps processing her desire to understand the speaker. She had small, well-formed ears with long silver earrings hanging down. Her fingers were long and slender, and her voice was unmistakable, both smoky and bright. Clear as a bell, full of love and innocence and youthfulness, a voice so unusual you want to hear it again. She had a touch of an accent, unidentified, maybe something brought back from Jamaica.

On her left hand was a ring with four silver bands apart yet connected. Her right ring finger had a similar group of four bands of a copper color. Those were new to Luke. When she talked, she tilted her head a little upward, sharing her thoughts kindly, casting them above her listeners. She was in sharp contrast to others who talked looking down or away.

Beneath the wave of hair on her brow, her eyes were harder to describe, hidden between her luxuriant eyelashes and eyebrows. They were a warm and soft shade of green, hidden a bit, atypical, a color seldom seen. When she got up to leave the room for a minute, she came around the table, naturally attractive, slim in waist, long legs shapely in jeans. She flowed away from the room with an easy purposeful stride and disappeared into the hallway. Luke almost stood up. He knew Lacy's stride.

When she returned, Luke noticed she had relatively short fingernails, small for the length of her fingers. At times, she folded her hands, fingers clasped together. She had Navajo symbols on a long-sleeved sweater, a black background with grey symmetrical patches with the Navajo symbols. The sweater went perfectly with her dark black hair. Her clothes were vintage California, always on the verge of new fashions. Luke thought she shopped in San Francisco, not Chicago. She looked young but displayed the maturity of a woman ten years older.

She had a totally striking smile, entrancing when she flashed it. The smile transformed both her and those around her. By this, Luke knew it was Lacy. *She had a female version of the unforgettable Jay Gatsby smile—like a sunrise bursting over the horizon, with the assurance that the world has no limits, that anything may be accomplished, and that anybody can be won over if you are persistent enough.*

Come to think of it, her smile was brighter than the sun—more like a thermonuclear detonation two hundred miles up, which first casts an astonishing white light from one end of the Pacific to another. And then the aurora borealis dances back and forth behind that astonishing detonation of white. She had a universal smile, one the Fijians are noted for.

Just then, the professor asked Luke to read his chapter. He handed out copies to the others and to the professor and began to read. His assignment: to show the importance of a family history of serving in the military. He began with the most important commanders in U.S. history and cited the percentage of those who had a family history of military service. He gave short bios of a handful of national heroes, and then concluded by citing his own family history in the U.S. Armed Services. He gave vivid and colorful descriptions of events, battles, and even cited strategies. LaCrosses had fought in the Revolutionary War, the Civil War, WWII, and Korea. He gave an impressive example:

Major LaCrosse was an attaché to General Lee. He knew that General Lee practiced Henri Jomini's military theories. Jomini's first offensive principle had a consistent drive to seize the initiative. General Lee understood this. The leader must know how to take the offensive and then keep the initiative. He showed it in the battle at Chancellorsville. General Hooker had the advantage and a well thought-out battle plan. But General Lee reacted quickly and caused General Hooker to draw back and lose the initiative. General Lee used Jomini's second principle, the maneuver principle, and maximized positional advantage over the enemy. He ordered Lt. General Thomas Jackson to conduct a flank attack, and took advantage of General Hooker's lack of action.

General Lee used Jomini's third principle of the massing of forces, throwing the mass of his army against only a part of Hooker's army, inflicting heavy losses on Hooker's army by surprise and through advancing from three sides, forcing Hooker to yield the battlefield and ultimately to retreat.

Luke concluded that General Lee was by far the better tactician. He also concluded that the Union was lucky to have prevailed, given all their generals who never practiced the Jomini principles. To prove his theory, he gave over five historic examples of failed initiatives and lost battles. Then he updated the class with many generals and admirals who came from military families and had distinguished themselves in the twentieth century: The MacArthur's, the Patton's, Senior, Junior, and Patton III. And there would be others coming, such as Benjamin Davis, Senior and Junior; Creighton Adams and son; William Caldwell and son. All the students around the table were mightily impressed and even more so, the professor.

"Mr. LaCrosse," he admonished, "You have a sterling military career ahead of you. Don't ever take your foot off the gas pedal." Finally, he predicted what the future might hold for youngsters in a military family.

The response from his table was not deafening, except in a university library. The librarian got up and headed toward Luke's table. The professor held up his hand, shushed the group, and the librarian turned away. The professor asked the class, one at a time, to go around the table and give Luke a response or critique. Luke gave each student his full attention, and thanked each one as they spoke to him. The professor said his thank you's but Luke was not listening. The class, all of a sudden, was gone. Everybody had left the table.

Lacy's class was almost over. What next? Luke frowned. Lacy had made the last gesture in reconciliation by coming to see him in Hawaii. Yet her behavior in Hawaii with Russ the first time seemed inexcusable. She had broken his heart, and then he had broken her heart. *Who is this gorgeous, gracious, and educated girl-turned-woman? Could she come back into my life?*

Tonight, she for sure didn't choose or plan to see him, and he for sure didn't choose or plan to see her. Luke closed his eyes for a moment. *Maybe this is a gift, an answer to my prayers. Purely to be enjoyed in the moment. No past and no future. I don't care if she doesn't talk to me tonight. I'm happy to be in the same room. Even with my eyes closed, I can still see her, hear her, and feel her presence.*

When he opened his eyes, some of her class still sat at the table. Lacy was gone.

Luke went back to where he was lodged for the night. He found a comforting photo and prayed.

I know you love me, Lord, because you are slow to
lose patience.
You love me, Lord, because you do not treat me as
an object to be
Possessed or manipulated.
You love me, Lord, because you use
Circumstances of my life in a constructive way for
my growth.

42

In his junior year Luke won the opportunity to compete for the ROTC Army Combat Diving Program at U of A. He had no idea how he was recommended until the sergeant in charge told him. He had excelled at every level in ROTC and in his academics. Luke was so immersed in going forward he never thought about any opportunity in combat diving. He was in the damn desert, not Key West or Maui. He trained during the school year at the University's Olympic pool, and travelled to Coronado Island to compete for placement in the Army Combat Diving School in Key West.

Luke took notes throughout the class, and wrote up the story more than six months later. He wanted to write it in the first person because he knew his success would help and even motivate others to take the challenge. Nobody from the university's ROTC program had ever graduated as a combat diver.

One Man's Story: Luke LaCrosse

A song floated through my mind: "*Now it begins, neddles and pins… the big hurt.*"

I looked up. It was time for the dreaded tank test. Sergeant Hoops and his imposing Special Forces demeanor and no-nonsense shades appeared above and in front of me. Only Hoops had the timer watch and whistle to start and finish the exercise. Nobody else could wear a watch, least of all us. I couldn't even monitor my progress, as I did in my running days.

"LaCrosse, ready?"

It was a challenge, not a question. I swallowed and nodded. "Yes, Sergeant."

Hoops walked down the line, prepping the other three ROTC cadets. "Okay. men. Give me your best five minutes! I want to see your hands above water at all times, you got that? Starting . . ." he glanced at his watch, "NOW!"

Ninety minutes of physical training drills, plus a mile swim in a cold ocean, left me totally chilled and muscle fatigued. I pushed off from the side and began the dreaded tank tread test, my feet scissoring front to back, my hands above the water, trying not to bob up and down. With my first surge of exertion, I fought past initial fears and nervousness. Still, it wasn't long before my legs began to ache and my lungs began to burn. *One . . . two . . . three . . . four.* I measured my water strides mentally each time my feet reached their furthest point from each other and then changed positions.

By the fourth day, two fellow cadets, along with ten others from across the country, had already been sent home. How could I keep up? The water was cold, the air was cold, and I was cold. I set my jaw and steeled myself. *Do the task or stay down trying.* The sergeant's voice from earlier instruction zipped through my consciousness.

The day before, two instructors dove in and pushed two cadets to the pool's bottom during the fifty-meter underwater swim. Both cadets began to float to the surface. "Don't even think about coming to the surface unless you have completed your assignment," Hoops told them.

I glanced at the pool's deck. Sure enough, defibrillators and oxygen tanks sat against the wall. Trained Army Special Forces medics were on hand for CPR, resuscitation, and any other emergencies. *Woe to the man who needed them. I might as well cash it in.*

I closed my eyes for a moment, shutting out images and thoughts of failure. My mask began to fog up slightly, alerting me to change my breathing. I looked up and over to Sergeant Hoops, hoping for the one-minute signal, knowing I would not get it. The sergeant saw my disbelief through my mask and frowned. "Keep your hands above the water!" he yelled.

All of a sudden, the twin eighty tanks, weighing close to a hundred pounds out of water, seemed to pull me backwards and down. My feet screamed with pain, my bruised foot muscles and ankle tendons protesting against the weight of the huge eighteen-inch Navy SEAL flippers. Still, I pushed forward, then backward, scissoring toward that impossible five-minute mark.

"Get a-hold of yourself!" Hoops commanded. "Assume you got one minute down. So take one minute at a time. Not one test, not one day, not one hour. Just one minute at a time."

I continued in a tortured monotony, kick after kick after increasingly uncomfortable scissors kick. Every second felt like thirty. I went back to counting: *one . . . two . . . three . . . four. Time to close my eyes . . . I remember now . . . body immersed in water, checklist flashing through my mind: Coronado Island . . . Twin eighty tanks strapped tight . . . Frogman flippers on snug . . .twelve-pound lead weight belt on tight . . . Seal bubble mask on tight . . . Life vest on tight, lollypop string puller accessible for sergeant's-only instant inflation . . . Tread water . . . scissors kick . . . hands above water . . . Five minutes . . . FIVE MINUTES!*

Nobody would ever understand the pain involved. Nobody I know has been in a position where you can't quit, you can't call in sick, and you can't beg the boss for mercy. My basic need to breathe motivated me to push my legs harder and harder, to a place they've never been pushed. Nobody sets himself up to be tested to his limits, because nobody wants to face failure. This is what the Army's doing. On our own, we would not do it. The Army needs to know they can count on us to get the job done. So I'm either an A student, or an F—for failure. Pain has nothing to do with it. Can I live with pain and get the job done? Can I will my body to do what must be done?

Hoops' voice flashed through my mind again. "There's no social promotion here, it's 'Get it, or die, GI." My feet flailed ponderously through the water, my neck arching, my hands trying desperately to stay above the surface. My eyes were on Sergeant Hoops. Two days before, during my timed exercise in the pool, Hoops had walked across the deck toward me! He had glanced at his watch and pretended to start blowing the whistle. And then he smiled and walked away.

I hope he doesn't do that to me again.

Fear squeezed my gut. I felt a tremendous need to relieve myself. I fought the childish urge to excuse myself and climb out of the pool. *I've got to go, sir,* I imagined myself saying to the sergeant, as if urinating in the pool were a possible death penalty infraction. Of course, the sergeant would let me go. *Wouldn't he?*

Shaking my head, I came to my senses. I noticed Sergeant Hoops' glowering face and push-off motion with his huge hands. "Get away from the edge, LaCrosse!" he shouted. I only heard him faintly, as if he were on the back end of a dream.

I'm gonna make it to halfway, and then I'll go to three minutes. I can't let everybody down. Jensen and Todd had already washed out. Ventry was being swallowed up by the water; no hope remained in his eyes.

I'm all we've got left. I've got to do it.

Count, count, count, I reminded myself. My lungs ached and gasped in their dual effort to remain fully inflated for life-saving buoyancy and to gulp in life-saving oxygen. My ragged throat threatened to spasm. My hands constantly wanted to dip underwater to help the rest of me stay afloat.

Suddenly, I swallowed water from bobbing down too low and began coughing and gasping, trying to clear my freaked-out lungs. "Keep your hands above the water, or you start over!" Sergeant Hoops yelled.

Excess water pooled around my eyes. I had no idea if they were tears of defeat, or a reaction from the coughing.

Count . . . count . . . count.

I looked through my foggy mask and saw Sergeant West in the pool, easily treading water as if he didn't have a care in the world. West was my lifeguard. Of course, Hoops wasn't going to dive in to help; he was keeping time. To my right, Ventry struggled, fatigue pulling down his body, courage propping him up. I almost swallowed another lungful of water. *I'm not swallowing any more.*

Where did all this pain come from? My legs, my legs, my feet. *Feet, don't die on me!* I've never done anything this hard before. I've never failed at any strenuous activity I tried before, whether it was soccer, track, running the high hurdles.

Who was reaching for the edge of the pool? Someone was panicking, totally losing it. The sergeants wouldn't respect that one bit.

I felt like I was going to fall over backwards. Sergeant West assigned somebody to pull at me from behind, trying to harass and annoy me, trying to make me give up. The tanks dragged me down. They were much heavier than we were told. *I've got to use my hands. It's that or die.*

I carried on, heart pounding out of my chest, lungs exhausted, legs leaden and growing unresponsive. I sensed Sergeant West's disappointment in me. He could see me with my hands threatening to go underwater.

I'm not quitting, I'm not reaching for the pool's edge. I'm not giving up. I'm not going home early.

I opened my palms and began moving my hands in forty-five degree arcs, back and front, to stay upright, to keep from going under permanently. It worked. *Maybe I can get my breath back.* It didn't work that way; instead, it produced the opposite effect. Instead of just my legs using the limited oxygen, my arms were drawing upon it as well. My breath increased, if that were possible. How can I keep this up?

Everything was so cold. The air had already chilled my bones. The ocean hovered at fifty degrees, about the same temperature as the pool. We wore only T-shirts. *Am I still upright? Where's the sky? Sergeant West?*

All of a sudden, Hoops blew the whistle! I can't believe it. I did it! I never thought I could. I flapped my arms to keep above the water. Sergeant West helped me out of the pool. He could hardly do it. Hoops walked over with a disgusted squint, looked down at me, and yelled, "You almost lost it, dog. I am not monitoring your next test."

It was the hardest thing I had ever done. I went to the rest room whether I needed it or not.

But within ten minutes, I got to my feet and walked out to face the sergeants. "I'm ready for the drown-proofing drill, Sergeant Hoops," I said.

"See you tomorrow, LaCrosse."

I went home and collapsed. I didn't even make it to the bed. I have never gone to sleep that early. But the next day started at 0500. I had to get up at 0430 am.

The next day, I marched up and reported in. "I'm ready, Sergeant West."

"I'll believe that when I see it. Burfield's your buddy, so get to it," Sergeant West replied. "You know the drill, Burfield. Don't cut him any breaks. Tie his hands, and tie his feet . . . tightly. Get him back in the pool."

I thought I could do it, after yesterday's success. But after ten seconds my heart already pounded. There must be some trick or technique I was missing. Why didn't they teach it? I heard one of the sergeants talking about an egg-beater kick, where you kick figure eights sideways, not up and down. Why hide the technique? I seethed at the unfairness of it all. First, five minutes of scissors kicking with tanks on, hands out of the water. Now two minutes of treading water with hands out of water and no gear.

I can't stay upright any longer. Was I really falling backwards? The tanks and lead belt were pulling me down. Were there magnets on the bottom? Everything around me slowed down. *I must be floating, or am I still falling?* Everything was so easy now. West was just floating around next to me. Seconds went by and I thought they were minutes. I was losing my ability to breathe. I was shocked, but not panicked.

Out of the corner of my eye, I saw Ventry by the side of the pool watching, his face twisted, his eyes opened wide. *He thinks I'm in trouble.* He kept staring at me. I couldn't see east. I couldn't see west. I couldn't breathe.

For God's sakes, Ventry, don't give up! I can get back to the surface . . . Just give me a few minutes. I'll get my strength back and finish the job. I'm not giving up, Sergeant West. I'm just resting, sir. I'm seeing these beautiful colors, yellows and blues and greens . . . I never noticed them before. Can't be the sunset, but it reminds me of two or three . . . I can almost touch these colors.

Then my feet hit the bottom of the pool. I must be hallucinating. *Is that somebody down here? He looks a little like my dad. It couldn't be. This apparition looked pale. I couldn't touch him and I could see through him. He put his finger to his lips, pressed them together. "You will be okay. Don't breathe. Just let go." So I lay on the bottom. I am not leaving and losing. I'm not going up."*

A swarthy hand grabbed the lollypop, pulling the cord. My life-saving vest inflated, lifting me off the bottom of the pool. Next to me swam Sergeant West, diving in to save his student. He propelled me to the surface, swiftly unhooked the tanks, and began slapping me. "LaCrosse, breathe! LaCrosse, breathe!"

After a few slaps and shouts, I opened my eyes and gasped for breath. Air! Blessed air! The colors faded, and I gulped huge drafts of air, trying to clear the slow-motion dreams away. I still felt as if I were in a dream, unable to move, detached from my body. Never did I feel so tired. The pain was worse than death; it just went on and on, without any mercy.

Sergeant West peered closely at me. "Now get out of the pool! Nobody's gonna do it for you."

I felt foolish and awkward, trying to regain use of my limbs with the coordination of a baby just learning to swim. I slowly swung one arm over the other on the side of the pool, dizzy, exhausted, trying to get to the ladder, which seemed a hundred feet away. I clambered out of the pool and swayed at the top. My mind and body operated at two different speeds. "LaCrosse needs a buddy! Get over and help him with his gear!" West yelled.

Burfield, a cadet from Wisconsin, rushed over and grabbed my elbow. Slowly, I stumbled over to a bench to reach my gear bag. Burfield helped me remove my gear, slowly, one piece at a time, each piece presenting its own pain when I took it off. It took ten minutes.

"Get out of my sight! Sergeant West yelled. "Come back in ten minutes!"

All that remained were my swimming trunks. "Even if you don't have to," Burfield murmured, "head for the men's room."

He didn't have to say it twice. As he held open the door into the restroom, I staggered over to a bench and plopped down onto it. I was surprised my legs were still attached.

"Stay here while I watch the door," Burfield said. "I'll get your gear."

He brought it in and got me back in my gear. He tied me tight and cast me off the ladder. Sergeant West gave me the thumbs up. And I thought I could do it. And I did it! The sergeant must have known. I got it together! I made it into the final ten candidates for the Key West Army Combat Diving Qualification Course!

He ended the story there.

* * * * * * * * * * * * *

That summer, Luke went to Key West and qualified as the first ROTC student at the University to become a registered Army Combat Diver. The scuba bubble tattoo on his upper right arm proved his prowess as a graduate of the Army Special Forces Combat Diver Qualification Course. The motto of the school was, "In sharks, we trust." From the oceans, stealth missions of Army Combat Divers were designed to support the ground troops.

At the Special Services graduation ceremony, Sergeant West shook Luke's hand. "You made it. Seventy-three started and twen-ty-seven finished. Most of those Special Service guys were in the pipeline for two years waiting. You were the only one of ten ROTC students who made it. You did it the hard way. Not many come that close to lying on the bottom and drowning without giving up. You never gave up. You earned your nickname, Stone Cold."

"Stony," he said with a slap on the back, "I never saw anybody so calm in the face of failure and drowning. You earned the nickname."

Sergeant West smiled. "You really hung with our motto, 'It's better to drown than to not get the job done.' Next time we meet, and it's not in the roles of instructor and student, the first beers are on me."

43

A year later, Luke graduated from the University of Arizona. The university awarded him a unique bachelor of science degree in Leadership – with Honors. He was now ranked with outstanding students adept at leading teams, making difficult decisions, and effecting change. In addition, he was an officer, a second lieutenant. All in all, it was a gigantic leap from being enlisted. The elite Army Special Forces Combat Diving credentials opened up more opportunities for leadership. Finally he had a bachelor's degree in leadership; he was a military officer, a second lieutenant, and a member of the Special Forces. But his outstanding academics and qualifications led to an even higher opportunity. His name appeared on a list for the Army Aviation Training Program in Fort Wolters, Texas. Helicopter School! The only person not surprised was Luke himself.

When he was given the opportunity to attend helicopter flight school, Luke gave the credit to God. It was exactly what he wanted to do. He did not want to experience combat from fifteen to forty thousand feet, pretty much unconnected with the ground troops. He used his mastery of a Bell helicopter trainer as a prelude to deployment with the UH-1 Iroquois. Months later, his family came for his graduation as an Army helicopter pilot at Fort Wolters, Texas. The whirlybird tattoo on his upper left arm proved him a master in the air as well as in the water. It matched up with the Special Forces tattoo on his upper right arm. The words inscribed on the new tattoo, "Above the Best," showed Luke's support for the troops on the ground. The UH-I Iroquois, named after the Indian Nation, had been in service for years, but after 1962, its nickname, "Huey," phonetically from UH-I, stuck.

Immediately Luke went to the advanced school for combat, the primary aviation school at Fort Rucker, Alabama. He had studied every facet of the helicopter. The Huey was the first turbine-powered helicopter, developed by Bell Helicopters at the Army's request to be a medical evacuation and utility helicopter. It had the cargo capacity to carry fourteen troops or six stretchers with a medic. It developed later as a gunship, with two door gunners equipped with M60 fully automatic machine guns.

In aviation school Luke learned the fascinating history of the versatile Huey. In 1966, the helicopter's engines were placed with a bigger Lycoming engine with more power. Now, inserting and extracting troops into hot landing zones, Luke delighted in the characteristic "Whump, whump, whump" sound that came from the two-bladed rotors, especially during its descent into the landing zone and turning in flight. He loved hearing the Huey when he was standing near on the flight line, first the scream of the jet turbine engine, then, the blades' slow turning. The blades would start spinning, each one visible. Luke would see the tail gunners in the open rear bay, the tiny windows of the pilots, and the big double windshield. He slowly ratcheted up the rpm, the blades just a horizontal whirlwind, and then he pulled pitch and roared into the air. The Huey leapt off the ground and tilted forward to gain speed and then lift.

Luke couldn't wait to be at the controls without the instructor in the back seat. As a pilot, Luke had been trained to know the Huey's complete systems like the back of his hand. He had an appreciation for the redundant hydraulic-driven pilot controls, consisting of cyclic, collective, and anti-torque pedals. He knew the cyclic, or "stick" controlled pitch. The anti-torque pedals changed the pitch of the tail rotor, which controlled the yaw while counteracting the torque created by the main rotor. He studied his manuals late at night so he could attain an aircraft commander's knowledge of the helicopter.

Luke had more time at the controls than anybody. Any time some student was ill, Luke stepped up to take his place. His graduation from Fort Rucker was his fourth graduation since he left the Air Force.

Two months later, he got his first deployment. First Lieutenant Luke LaCrosse stood in front of a mirror in the officers' quarters at Bien Hoa Air Base in South Vietnam. After a long day of combat, the hot shower shaped him up for further briefings. As he shaved, his upper body gleamed in the overhead lights. The scuba bubble tattoo winked back at him. His upper arm muscles caused ripples in the helicopter tattoo. He could do anything.

Luke started out with "A" Company, Twenty-Fifth Aviation Battalion, and part of the Twenty-Fifth Infantry Division. He hoped to work with his buddies in the 229th Assault Helicopter Battalion, First Cavalry Division. As a rookie pilot, for the first six months of his deployment, he flew MEDEVAC missions, landing in drop zones, picking up the wounded, and flying with all due speed as an air ambulance back to the hospital on the main base. He also ran Ash and Trash missions, single ship resupply assignments, bringing food, C-Rations, and water to troops.

From MEDEVAC missions, Luke trained to pilot the Hueys as troop transports. Luke moved up as a pilot, and aspired to become elevated as aircraft commander, no longer just a pilot sitting next to the aircraft commander. He would fly slicklifts, or unarmed helicopters; later, the term was shortened to "slicks".

Pilots had to fly fleets of Hueys in formation, sharpen their troop insertion skills into the landing zones, and then land under fire to lift the troops back out. The fleets might consist of three, six, or even ten Hueys.

Luke struck gold and within three months he became an aircraft commander of a newly developed version of the Huey gunship, where the two bay doors were removed and replaced by two rear gunners with machine guns, making the Huey an open-door aircraft, the first of its kind.

Every day he looked forward to the Huey vibrating through his body, the beat of its blades drumming through his imagination, stoking his adrenaline. He knew that troops on the ground waited for the sound that no other helicopter emitted. He knew he, his wingman, or platoon brought feelings of relief and salvation to those troops stranded in the jungle.

One time, a combat sergeant dragged one of his men out of the jungle over to the Huey, lifted up the gut-shot soldier, helped two others to climb aboard, and then poked his head into the cockpit. He said, "Captain LaCrosse, in the past a gut-shot soldier would die on the battlefield, and now, who knows how many wounded men you have saved. There's nothing like the sound of a Huey."

The next day a soldier climbed aboard with his battle buddies and told him, "We must think of you as a savior. I keep hearing guys saying, "Jesus, he's finally here! Thank God Almighty!""

Luke, said, "I thank God Almighty, too. I am in exactly the right place, at exactly the right time, and doing exactly what God intended me to do."

Later, after another fourteen-hour day, back in his bunk trying to calm down, he thought, *I wonder if Chance remembers me talking about this. This is way better than chasing tornadoes back in Oklahoma.* He still couldn't sleep, so he wrote Chance a short letter, wondering if he'd ever get it. He'd never know how that one letter got Chance planning a get-together for Luke and Lacy at an up-coming Sixth Weather Squadron Reunion.

Luke, his unit, and fellow unit cohorts saved lives daily. In past wars, most of the wounded died on the battlefield. Hueys made the difference. The helicopters gave the troops equal power with the hidden North Vietnamese Army, sweeping Americans to safety at a moment's notice. They lightly embodied the Native American warrior motto, "He who fights and flies away, lives to fly another day."

Luke focused on nothing but his Huey and his missions. He knew every detail of his Huey. Its fifty-seven-foot length demanded a certain size landing spot in the jungle. And the spot often had to be big enough for three Hueys to land. He took advantage of the climbing speed of 1,755 feet per minute, avoiding enemy gunners with his characteristic swoop upwards. As a pilot, he knew how to use his two 7.62-mm M60 machine guns and his two rocket pods and 2.75-inch rockets. As he stormed into the landing zone, hovering only for a moment ten feet off the ground, Luke's tubular skids slammed a trademark "equal sign" into the soft jungle soil. In addition, the helicopters could hopscotch across Vietnam and catch the enemy unaware.

Luke took his general support primary mission seriously, but he belonged to a unique group of pilots who worked to enlarge their missions. Besides aeromedical evacuation and cargo transport, they added search and rescue. They also schemed to do more air assault and coordinated artillery support from behind the lines. Luke varied between red, white, and blue teams. The red teams were attack Hueys, the white teams were reconnaissance or observation Hueys, and the blue teams were the troop transport Hueys. Luke began in the blue team, but almost immediately he proved his excellence as a red team leader, providing protection to the ground troops whenever the enemy overwhelmed them. From Army Combat Diving School, he had learned the absolute value of working as a team where one mistake going solo could kill the whole mission and put the other pilots at risk.

There was no rest for Huey pilots. Day after day as MEDEVAC pilot, Luke had to take fire and stay until the wounded were all loaded. Every mission left so much blood on board his aircraft, so many cries and murmurs of the wounded, that Luke wondered if he'd ever be able to lead a sane life back home. His lurid dreams always had wounded warriors in them. Sometimes his Huey would be shot out of the sky, with all aboard killed except him. He'd awaken with a start and shake his head. Day life was almost as bad as his nightmares, which did help him appreciate daytime combat flying.

44

One day, after six months of combat flying, they paused before they dropped into a hot LZ (Landing Zone). Luke was aircraft commander in the first Huey, Captain Arnold the aircraft commander in the second Huey. As Arnold hovered, he yelled, "This sonofabitch might have three canopies, LaCrosse! I've seen this before and it was a disaster. We lost Hueys and wounded soldiers. Who in the hell inserted troops into this cluster? You go first this time."

Luke had to find a hole between trees three hundred feet high. He pointed and shouted into his mike, "Opening at one o'clock low!" He eased the Huey through the gap and hovered again, anxiously looking at the fuel gauge. He scanned the surrounding jungle to find a hole through a lower canopy. He pointed and shouted again, "Opening at nine o'clock low!" Luke carefully squeezed the Huey through a seventy-foot-wide gap and hovered again. Captain Arnold was one canopy above him.

Luke yelled, "Son of a bitch! We are a hundred feet off the ground and another canopy of trees below has branches that need trimming."

Luke anticipated the enemy rounds to smack him in the butt. He gave the twirl motion, and rotated his Huey in a circle.

"Here's the LZ!" Luke shouted. He maneuvered his Huey down through the last canopy and slammed it onto the ground. The minute it landed the helicopter took multiple rounds from the enemy forces surrounding the Army platoon who had called in the rescue.

Captain Arnold's Huey came down right next to him. Three rounds came through his windshield. The third round killed Captain Arnold instantly. His pilot grabbed the controls. The Huey rocked and began to tip.

Luke's Huey took multiple rounds in its fuselage. He had no idea why it was Arnold's last day and not his. Arnold had family, a wife, and three boys. Luke's crew picked up the wounded for both helicopters while taking fire. Luke yelled, "Let's get the hell out of here!"

With his crew's help, he lifted and maneuvered the Huey between the canopies. Leaning out the right door, one crew member yelled, "You have twenty feet over here!" The other crew member peered out the left side. "No room here!"

Sweat poured from inside Luke's helmet and dripped off his nose. He beat his way through the canopies and roared back to base. He had another load of wounded and shell-shocked troops delivered to the hospital. He was tired of being shot at, tired of all the wounded and dead piled into his helicopter day after day. He wanted the Huey with machine guns. He spent four days training a replacement pilot who had just arrived and knew little about jungle combat flying.

"We first used the Huey primarily for medical evacuation. But before long, we had missions of transport, airborne battlefield command and control, artillery fire support co-ordination, and search and rescue. Later, we used it for troop insertion into the battlefield or extraction from it. Now I am flying as an armed escort. In the beginning, our Little Bears flew slicks, meaning we were not a helicopter gunship. We had no rocket pods hanging off our sides. We had no cannon or mini-gun pods hanging on the bottom or on the nose of the helicopter. So the sides of the Huey were smooth and slick."

Luke kicked at the ground. "We are trying different ways to make the Huey into a gunship. I will be flying a model called a Nighthawk. We had a machinist install a mini-gun on the Huey that was so powerful it would begin to fall apart after fifty hours flying time. Thousands of rounds fly out every minute. We finally could protect our troops from ambush."

"The CO of the 229th Assault Helicopter Units of the First Cavalry Division put in a request for me. He had just lost a couple of pilots. Maybe their deployment was complete. With First Cav, I started out as a pilot in the right front seat, and then moved up to Aircraft Commander. I know you'll ask me what I wear. It's a two-piece flight suit, Nomex—fire-retardant pants and shirt. I get to wear a .38-caliber revolver. And we sawed off the M-16 infantry rifle so it would fit in our cockpit. So don't worry, in case you do, because I can take care of myself in the air and on the ground."

Luke knocked on his CO's door. "Sir, I have seen enough wounded and dead to last three lifetimes. And I want to fight back. I want to kill the bastards that killed my fellow A/C. I can save more troops' lives by taking the enemy out. I want to take action. I can't do MEDEVACs anymore. Let me get somebody else's blood on my bullets. I can't stand seeing any more American blood spilled."

His CO nodded. "I thought I'd see you in here today. I knew you and Captain Arnold were close."

"I learned a lot from him. He showed me tactics I never heard of."

The CO stood up. "Okay, LaCrosse, you are in Bravo Company. You are ready. And they need you."

Luke flew as if there were no tomorrow, as if he were invisible, on the edge between foolhardiness and disciplinary action. He was madly exhilarated and knew it had to do with Captain Arnold's death. Janis Joplin's song hammered through his mind in tune with his rotor blades: "*Freedom's just another word for nothin' left to lose.*"

At the same time, his heart remained on a downward dive, racked with lingering bitterness about his failed relationship with Lacy. At least three different times, they had taken the ride to the moon and come back separately.

He had joined the Air Force because he loved military planes; he had grown up next to a naval air base and he had always wanted to fly. But at the time he lacked the education to qualify for flight school. Besides, he wasn't a top gun person. He was thankful Spike, the command sergeant at ROTC, and Sergeant West in combat diving had pushed him to the breaking point. It was the turning point in his life. He earned that college degree. He'd gone to Combat Forces Underwater Operations down in Key West. He had become an Army officer and had worked his way up the chain. Now he had momentum. Lacy's family would have to drop their disdain and distance.

Luke took chances whenever he could, daring death to take him down. If there was one straggler in the troops waiting to be rescued, he never left. He circled the clearing and shot around the edges. If a fellow pilot was shot down, Luke would push his Huey in like a fighter jet, the Huey dangerously nose down, and take out the enemy while the MEDEVAC Hueys picked up the downed crew.

If Luke's crew had to land, jump out and help lift the wounded into the MEDEVAC Huey, he didn't care. He still shot the hell out of the enemy. The CO liked helicopters to form in groups of three on some missions: lead helicopter, left wingman, right wingman. One night after a weather-delayed mission and they finally got back to base, Luke told his right wingman, Captain Herman, "We just came back from the worst-case scenario, flying with zero-zero visibility. No ceiling, no runway visual range. We are supposed to fly with a four-hundred-foot ceiling and 1,600 feet runway visual."

Herman agreed. "Yeah, I was sweating flying too close to you. I don't like flying at night or flying in monsoons, when we are flying only on instruments. But the worst part of flying is communications. We are responsible for three radios and ten frequencies, for godssakes."

Luke said, "Here we are flying and taking evasive action while everybody in the world is yelling at us. As the lead aircraft, I radio you to change your direction, the aviation unit commander is warning me about enemy fire. The ground commander is yelling at me to hurry up, increase my speed. Who the fuck can do all that? Whoever put this program together has no clue whatsoever about flying."

"And don't forget all the other pilots are yelling out information on the enemy. If we listen to them all, we'd augur our aircraft in." Herman thought for a moment. "Check it out: When we circle the landing zone, firing, we are to count, 'one-thousand-one, one-thousand-two, and so on,' and then lift off. What the hell? What about the wounded troops who can't board below in time?"

Luke groaned, "We just wait and shoot. But my orders were to at least bring back the helicopter, and not get shot down in the landing zone where we add four more to the body count."

Herman growled, "I don't think that's operational procedure. The CO is covering his butt counting helicopters. He is a desk pilot, that's all he will ever be."

* * * * * * * * * * * * *

A month into his new role as aircraft commander, Herman asked his CO, "Whenever we have a seriously dangerous mission, why does LaCrosse always volunteer?"

"I don't know."

"Would you like to know what I heard?"

The CO frowned. "Not if it's scuttle-butt. It should be official, or closed-mouth."

"All I heard was LaCrosse saying, 'One death experience is enough. The only woman I ever wanted a family with is gone. And then, Captain Arnold, killed in action. He had a family, and it's gone. That's two. God will not give me a strike three. So I stay here and fly.'"

"Does it show on his past record?"

"Nothing that I can see."

Weeks later, Luke's Huey got shot up, bullet holes everywhere. One round glanced off the blade and ricocheted off Luke's helmet. He felt a little woozy and his pilot, James, had to bring in the aircraft. As they carried Luke to the infirmary, something dropped out of his right pocket above the ankle, where pilots carried a photo or a good luck piece. The medic reached down and picked up a photo. He looked at it a split second and then patted it into Luke's chest pocket. Luke's eyes opened. "What did you put in my pocket?"

The medic leaned down and said, "A picture of your wife, sir. It looks like you carried it around since your college days."

Luke frowned. "That's not my wife. It's the girl who got away, since high school."

He closed his eyes and turned away. Later that night, he dug up a favorite photo he had taken, and wrote another prayer:

> *Jehovah God, Creator and Savior, Divine Design Itself,*
> *You are my treasury of compassion who bestows within me*
> *Supreme inner peace, beyond anything my finite self can see.*
> *You love all beings without exception,*
> *You, the source of happiness and goodness,*
> *My guide on the path to liberation, rebirth,*
> *And enlightenment.*

> *You will bring me home to a place of beauty, like West Fork,*
> *Oak Creek, Arizona. Someday I will be hiking on this trail*
> *With Lacy, if you are willing and I am able.*

45

Back on his own bunk within the week, Luke reached into his wallet, brought out the old photo and the poem all folded up. In red ink on paper folded into scraps, Lacy's flowing handwriting reached out and touched him. It went something like this:

> *I carry your heart with me*
> *I am never without it*
> *You are whatever a moon has always meant*
> *And whatever a sun will always sing is you*
> *Here is the deepest secret nobody knows*
> *I carry your heart.*

At the bottom of the page was the date: February 14, 1956. Over ten years ago! *What the hell! It can't hurt.* He got out paper and pen. After two hours, he had written ten pages. When he read them over, he realized he couldn't tell that much about military operations. He remembered what his CO had reminded his unit: "Civilians have no idea what military combat life is like. Save military talk for your military brothers. Be cool and offhand when you write home, just like your fathers did in Korea or World War Two.

"This is not a popular war. Talk about how much you love the simple things in life, how you miss your home town, talk about the weather, and reminisce about your past with them. But don't share with civilians and don't scare the women!"

Well, he thought. *I've got to write somebody about this.* He thought about his former ROTC sergeant. Spike was once a Special Ops man who'd worked behind the lines. Just talking to him would help. Out on the base Luke found a straight, flat piece of wood that looked like an old high school ruler. He tore the letter into paragraphs, some for Lacy, and some for Spike. He pieced them together, one paragraph at a time, and had two letters in front of him.

* * * * * * * * * * * * *

Hi, Spike!

Hello from hell! How are you? Where are you? I hope you are not disappointed that I didn't get into the Special Forces, the Underwater Demolitions Teams. I got the chance to transfer to airborne, and I took it, much like the chance you gave me to get into Army Combat Diving. I'm flying Hueys over here in 'Nam, just as you used to fly into the face of death on the ground. I often think back on my life. I suppose it's because there's no guarantees on how long mine will be. Did you ever have such qualms or questions about life on the front lines?

* * * * * * * * * * * * *

To Lacy, he wrote:

Hi Lacy! Hello from hell. Where are you now? You likely have not kept up with me. I fly search and rescue helicopters in Vietnam. I have been here in the rain and jungles for over six months. It seems like six years, which is why I am reminded to write you. It's probably been six years since I saw you. If you are married and have any kids, just throw this away. (Not that you won't throw this away, anyway.) Time and calendars are too fragile to keep here in the heat and moisture. I will never complain about Chicago weather again. Things have changed from one universe to another. Being a combat pilot and commissioned officer has opened up new vistas for me. Army Aviation provides a good bridge to management positions. We do team playing, goal setting, pay attention to every detail, monitor the mental attitude of each player, and complete every mission no matter what. If we were a company, we'd outstrip all competitors.

I can't believe I still have this little poem you copied for me ten years ago. I think they were going to bury it with me. I fooled them, however. I am your Timex. I have taken a licking and keep on ticking."

* * * * * * * * * * * * *

Luke broke the letter into two parts:

When I first got to base camp in Vietnam, I had to get check rides from the standardization instructor pilots as well as a commander's evaluation. I started as a pilot, and knew I had to do well to become an A/C, aircraft commander. I flew all the time. The Huey was the helicopter for me, and for everybody else. They needed to know if I was proficient, or whether I'd be a sandbag, dead weight in the cockpit during combat.

I started by flying VIP missions, taking generals and colonels from one base to the next. Then I got to take a few generals out to the combat zones. We flew every day, rain or shine. In less than a month, I got detailed into a MEDEVAC platoon, and we went into combat zones all over southern Vietnam. Now let's just say I'm an armed escort.

* * * * * * * * * * * * * *

Luke saved his descriptions of the horrors of war for Spike.

Hey, Spike, here's the second part:

I saw so many horrible sights. We evacuated soldier after soldier after soldier and I knew many weren't going to make it. The worst times in my life involved personally leaning over a wounded soldier lying on the floor of my helicopter to make sure he was still alive. I couldn't get out of the cockpit very often, but there was such a sadness and sense of loss that came over me for each soldier in my care and transport. I can't fathom how much harder it is for doctors and nurses to watch grievously wounded soldiers pass away before their time, some before they've even reached full adulthood. Too many kids in this war.

Seriously, I came here all patriotic and full of fighting for my country. Now I see it's a thousand-year-old culture; it's so different from ours. I shouldn't say this, but I wonder whether we should even be here. All the guys that have been here a year say the main reason they get up and fly every day is purely to help and save the guy next to them, whether in the air or on the ground.

* * * * * * * * * * * * * *

He sketched out a rough map on the second page:

Here's South Vietnam. An inch scale is about fifty miles. To the left is Cambodia; we can't go into their airspace. There are four parts of Cambodia drilled into us: way up to the north is Fish Hook; straight west and a little bit south of that is Dog's Head, also known as Elephant Ear. Way south and east of that is Angel's Wing—west of us at Cu Chi. Right below Angel's Wing, on a horizontal parallel with Saigon, is Parrot's Beak. Check this out: Saigon is a big dot down in the right lower corner. About a half-inch above Saigon is a smaller dot, my main base, Cu Chi. Up a bit north-northwest, is Dau Tieng. I've been there many times. The huge base northwest of that is Nui Ba Den. It's on a three-thousand-foot mountain. All the rest of the area is jungles and rice paddies. Southwest of that is Tay Ninh. This is our area of operations: four areas altogether. We have four friendly places on the whole map. MEDEVAC missions were pretty safe. We had armed escorts.

Then I got into combat insertions and extractions. Those were more dangerous. We'd pick up a full load of troops and drop them off in mini landing zones—clearings, or bomb craters, or rice paddies. Extractions were usually hot; we knew we were going to get shot at. Insertions were trickier because we didn't know if we would get shot at and we had no idea where the enemy was. We flew a lot over the Mekong Delta.

You know what it sounds like and feels like to get shot at; now I do as well. When the bullet or projectile whizzes past me, I hear a crack! Or a sonic boom. And I know somebody I can't see is aiming from below. When a round hits our Huey, I feel it in the controls. A round coming through the cockpit or the radios is deafening! If a bullet hits the transmission or the rotor system, we know right away. The instruments record lost pressures and fluids, the hit blade whistles by our heads, and the Huey vibrates all over.

* * * * * * * * * * * * *

Hi Lacy, here's the third part.

You probably don't know much about my helicopter. A Huey has a crew of four: pilot in the front right seat, aircraft commander in the front left seat—they trade off flying fifty-fifty. Then you have the crew chief in the right rear seat, and gunner in the left rear seat. The crew chief takes total care of the aircraft, which is loaded with 1,800 pounds of JP-4 fuel and two M-60 machine guns with 1,500 rounds for each gun. Some of us have machine-guns in the open bays with gunners. We carry eight troops with floor space for plenty of equipment. We could take twelve people in addition to our crew, if we had open space. Our turbine engine gobbles four hundred pounds of fuel per hour. We could go from Saigon to Cu Chi on less than five hundred pounds of fuel.

If we'd get lost, then we'd tune into three ground stations and read the radio magnetic heading to each station—it's like an electronic compass. We'd draw three lines on our maps in the opposite direc-tion; wherever the lines crossed, there we were. So don't worry about us. We have everything covered."

* * * * * * * * * * * * *

It was time to wrap up with Spike.

"Our combat assault always began with artillery. We flew close to the Landing Zone area, sent the

hash marks, the clicks to the artillery, and they delivered the rounds from behind the lines, so to speak. Remember when I went to basic training one summer and they trained me to be an artillery spotter because of my math and physics scores? Now I have a special connection with the artillery units. When I call the targets in, I used some of the same language they did. Back at the base we had pounded a few beers together. They know I got some of the same training they did. I like to think our connection rained more shells down on the NVA than any other units. But I could be wrong. After the artillery barrage, we fly lead helicopter, or Nighthawk missions, to take out the enemy or protect the MEDEVAC Hueys when they fly into the landing zones.

So far, so good, Spike. I hope you get this. And if you have time, send me one of your famous short memos. Tell me if you had fears or doubts when you were in life-or-death situations. Did you ever go behind the lines over here? I can't really tell my family about such things."

You will always be my best sergeant,
Luke LaCrosse

* * * * * * * * * * * * * *

He also decided to sign off with Lacy.

Goodbye, Lacy. A fellow pilot told me I should write you. So if anything happens over here you won't think of me as just MIA. I owe you that much.

What about you? Bring me up to date. Do your parents still have Paul or somebody in the wings who they think you should marry? Do you have someone in the wings that you think you should

317

marry? Sixth Weather Squadron holds its bi-annual reunion in six months. Oklahoma City. You don't know anybody down there, except maybe Chance. If I ain't dead I will be there. Nobody will know you are down in Oklahoma, so you don't have to look over your shoulder. What have you got to lose?

You know I'm the first autographed photograph in your yearbook. And you are the first autographed photograph in mine. Don't look! It's Luke.

46

Luke mailed the letters. Three days later, he was back on duty. The doctors had confirmed there was no concussion, just a nasty bruise behind his left temple. Luke was A/C in the Bravo Company 229th Assault Helicopter Battalion, with three platoons. He was Yellow One—flight leader of a platoon of six Hueys. His new call sign was "Killer Spades," tougher sounding than his MEDEVAC call sign, "Dust-Off." He liked the base at DauTiang. He could lift off and take his place in a tight formation, one rotor diameter apart. He took pride in leading as they dropped into the landing zone. Every pilot had to keep his spacing when circling the landing zone, for inserting troops and picking them up later.

After months of insertion and extraction, Luke's Huey stayed too long over the landing zone where ten slicks had offloaded almost 150 South Vietnamese troops. He ran low on fuel and ammunition, and as he turned low over the jungle, an NVA machine-gunner punched a dozen holes in the fuselage, and hydraulic fluid leaked out. This required immediate ditching. He and his three crewmen were dragged through the jungle canopy. Luke's personal alarm drilled through his mind. His two door gunners were unprotected; both bay doors were gone. But the canopy cushioned the Huey's crash-landing. When it hit and rolled on its side, the rotors slammed into the ground just long enough for Luke to think he was losing his concentration.

Luke jumped out, hopped around the other side of the Huey, and helped the pilot, Captain James, and the other two crewmen out of the aircraft. He ordered them, "Move twelve feet away, guns pointed down. Take a position fifty feet north and ready your weapons. Take a quick look for our gunners, but stay down and stay close."

James, the crew chief, and the cockpit gunner broke low and ran to a spot fifty feet ahead of where the Huey was headed when it crashed. Luke stopped to plan. His perspiration dripped down his flight suit onto the soft soil floor of the jungle. He anticipated an immediate attack. The NVA were masters of stealth, moving and appearing as suddenly as the Native American Apaches could appear out of flat ground or a mesquite thicket. Luke dropped out of sight. He crawled and scraped through twisted metal back to the rear machine gun on the upward side. He checked for ammunition and pointed the gun in the direction where he thought enemy troops might appear. He draped himself over the gun as if he were the dead gunner.

Minutes later, four NVA troops dressed in black blinked out of the jungle and approached the Huey. Luke waited to make sure there were only four. They were twelve feet away; guns pointed downward, when Luke opened up and killed all of them with two ten-second bursts from his machine gun.

James came running out of the jungle. "LaCrosse, are you okay? Have you been hit?"

"No, that was our machine gun! James, contact home base with our coordinates. Get a clearing where they can do search and rescue."

"What about our gunners?"

"I'll get on that. They are going to need our help."

"Ten-Four." James stepped back into the wall of green and got on his radio.

Luke plunged into the jungle the way they had come. Fifty feet, a hundred feet, a hundred yards. He saw Sergeant Lancaster lying up against a tree, almost buried in the undergrowth. Luke gasped, ran to the sergeant and leaned down. He carefully checked for serious injuries, especially the spinal column and made sure of a neck pulse.

"He's alive! I can't believe it!" He gently lifted and pulled Lancaster's body away from the tree and out of the undergrowth. "Sergeant, can you hear me?"

There was no response. Just in case Lancaster could hear even if he couldn't open his eyes or talk, Luke leaned down and spoke softly. "I'll be right back, Sergeant. This is your aircraft commander. Your A/C."

He shook his head to clear his emotions and thoughts, and then looked up in alarm, as if more troops were coming. Instead of troops, over to his right and a few feet off the ground, he could see somebody stuck in the lower branches, a hundred feet away. Luke sprinted over to the body, thinking the worst. He jumped over thick underbrush. Above him, six feet off the jungle carpet, Sergeant Graham floated and twisted in a light breeze. Luke ran to the tree and began climbing up, using vines and branches to help. He had to be quiet, and he had to reach down from above Graham. When, grunting and feverish, Luke got high enough, he climbed out on a limb above and reached down for Graham.

As he leaned down, he spoke unnecessarily loud. "Sergeant! Sergeant! Can you hear me?"

Graham opened his eyes and looked up in disbelief. "Where am I?"

"You're here with me in the jungle. We are going to get out safe. Are you okay? Any broken bones?"

"No, just . . . dizzy. I'm all tangled up. I can't get out."

"Give me a hand, and I'll get you out."

Luke saw the sergeant's straps and jumpsuit tangled in the branches.

With his survival knife, he cut the straps and sliced away the branches.

"Hold onto the branches as we go down. I'll carry the rest of your weight." Pulling Graham into him, he laboriously clambered down the tree. When they reached the ground, he checked on Graham, who sagged against him.

"Can you walk?"

"Yeah, with a little bit of luck."

They staggered to where Lancaster lay, and Luke sat Graham down next to his unconscious gun mate.

James rushed through the jungle, bent over to avoid detection. He found Luke. "Search and rescue are coming for us," he whispered. "They are breaking off from another mission. We have to reach a clearing two clicks north. You take Graham. I'll take Lancaster. Wherever we go, they go."

Luke knelt down, carefully put Sergeant Graham over his right shoulder, and slowly stood up. He held his .38 revolver in his left hand.

"Well, come on, Lieutenant. We gotta do this thing."

Minutes later, they reached the clearing and heard the *Wop! Wop!* Wop! of the search and rescue Huey. It landed hard, its blades whirling. Two gunners jumped out and grabbed Sergeant Graham. Luke and Captain James gently lifted Sergeant Lancaster up to the medic and jumped aboard. The crew chief and the gunner jumped aboard last. The aircraft commander lifted the helicopter off the jungle floor and dodged back up through the canopies. Twenty minutes later, they landed at Bien Hoa Air Base.

After they unloaded the wounded and went through debriefing, they went back to their quarters. Luke didn't know he was wounded until he grew dizzy while sitting on his bed. Soon, he was in the infirmary with a concussion and a deep red wound crossing down his back.

Two days later, his CO appeared at his bedside. "LaCrosse, what are you doing in here? How did you get a concussion and still manage to get all six of you out of the crash site?"

"I got the concussion from bashing my way out of the Huey, sir. I don't really know how we all got out."

"LaCrosse, I'm not sure what to do with you. Your twelve-month deployment is up in the next couple months. I like what you're doing for us."

"Sir, if you get me into the AH-1 Cobra, I will extend for six months."

His CO smiled. "I hoped you'd come up with that option. Don't forget, you get thirty days leave between your regular deployment and your extended deployment."

Luke smiled. "Perfect! Just in time for my Sixth Weather Squadron Alumni Reunion."

The CO stood up. "Let's get going on the Cobra right away. When you recover, I'm rotating you over into our Attack Helicopter Cobra unit. That suits you better and suits me fine. It's the Delta Company. Call sign 'Smiling Tigers.'"

Luke sat up. "Thank you, sir. You won't regret it."

"You are going to have to get up to speed. The AH-1 Cobra is a full fighting machine. You can get your aircraft commander status back after you get your training. We need you to fly protection for our slicks, for troop insertion and extraction. You need more speed and maneuverability, and the AH-1 Cobra will give it to you." He handed Luke a manual. "Study this while you recover."

"Thank you, sir! I will recover ASAP."

During his recovery, Luke thought about the whole situation. He read everything about the Cobra he could get his hands on. While the Huey had made the theory of air cavalry practical, the Army had to be highly mobile all across Vietnam. There was no more standing and fighting long battles; nothing like Korea, where troops stayed and held positions at great loss. Fleets of Hueys could fight the enemy at the times and places of the CO's choice.

Luke frowned as he saw the problems. Unarmed helicopters would be too vulnerable to drop troops in the landing zone. What sitting ducks these wide warriors would be without artillery or ground support! The only way to make the landing zone safer was from the air. So Hueys were armed with machine guns and rockets and began to be used as armed escorts. However, the massive influx of troops in Vietnam had brought a new era of war from the air. The linchpin of all fighting was the Huey. And out of the Huey design came the AH-1 Cobra, built in all haste for better protection of the aircraft.

Luke's trainer came out of NETT, a unit that had trained at Bell Helicopter, and then come over to Vietnam to train Huey pilots in-country. It was a first. Warrant Officer Davidson started Luke's training with a sharp warning. "Toss out the book learning. You need to learn what we call, 'pilot technique.' It's on-the-job training. The Cobra will teach you. Experience will teach you. You need to get a 'control touch,' where you feel your machine, become one with it. You can't do a spilling flat. You need to know when you hover in this baby, you have more power, but you eat up more JP-4 fuel. We can't take on a full load of fuel because we are heavily loaded, heavily armed. Don't forget that, or you'll auger yourself in."

The next day, he admonished Luke before their first combat training mission. "Remember, your Huey can fly without hydraulics. They have one system. The Cobra can't. So we designed it with two hydraulic systems. Don't be confused about that in the middle of combat. And for God's sake, don't fly directly over our troops. Your gun is firing hundreds of hot rounds and dropping hundreds of hot shell casings. I don't want them dropping on our troops. Fly parallel to them if at all possible."

After training at the base, Warrant Officer Davidson rode with Luke on his first combat mission in a Cobra. Luke put the Cobra into a screaming dive at 195 knots per hour and then circled the landing zone with his wingman. Luke triggered all the shooting and rockets on the right, the Cobra wingman began shooting on the left of the landing zone, and then they continued in the "wagon wheel" until they thought they had blasted all enemy bunkers and foxholes around it. Then the Hueys landed and picked up all the soldiers in the landing zone.

After two weeks of solid training, Luke was ecstatic. He performed maneuvers that, up until now, only fixed-wing aircraft could do. He had more safety and battlefield effectiveness. Fixed-wing aircraft were often trapped in their revetments by heavy incoming fire. Luke learned how to quickly get airborne and unleash massive firepower with lethal accuracy.

There were three things he didn't like. As a Huey pilot, he was accustomed to, and relied upon, the extra eyes, ears, and firepower of the two door gunners. He fretted over the Cobra's soundproof cockpit, because it was extremely difficult for him to detect close ground fire from the NVA. In addition, the Cobra's ineffective ventilation air blowers turned the cockpit into a stifling cauldron that sucked in Vietnam's oppressive humidity.

What Luke really did like was the Cobra's natural speed of 171 miles per hour, which he sometimes pushed to 190. The Huey's max was 135 miles per hour, with a cruising speed of 125 miles per hour. Without rotors turning, the Cobra was thirteen feet shorter, and its rotor diameter four feet less. But it did have additional stub wings. Those, along with the slim silhouette and smaller shape, made Luke and his aircraft a much tougher target to hit.

The Cobra had a six-barrel Gatling gun, spun by an electric motor. It could fire 4,000 rounds a minute, but Luke carried only 1,500 rounds. The ammunition was belted together in clips, pulled into the gun by its rotation, which immediately declipped the bullets. Luke, like everybody else, fired the gun in bursts of ten. His rounds were explosive enough to be tank killers, but in Vietnam, there was no way to prove it—no tanks. The mini-guns were on his right; the 40-mm grenade launcher on his left in the M28 turret. He and Captain James formed the crew of two.

Luke received "intel" that the enemy had surrounded the landing zone. He called in the hash marks for the artillery and waited until they pounded the area. Minutes later, with Luke in the back seat and Captain James in the front seat, they lifted off in a Fire Team of two Cobras. If the landing zone was jammed up with NVA, they would call in the Hot Fire Team, a third Cobra. The flight to the target lasted only thirty-three minutes. Luke's flight had the lead on the Fire Team, so he approached and fired mini-guns and rockets into the left side of the landing zone. His wingman took the right side, and they flew in a fast and furious wagon wheel.

Like most of the US Military, Luke's combat sorties became more and more vigorous as 1968 rolled into 1969. His next mission, undertaken with another Cobra, was to escort ten troop-carrying Hueys of the 118th Assault Helicopter Company during a combat air assault. Luke and his platoon destroyed four enemy bunkers and fourteen sampans. He knew his Cobra's high speed and slim profile made it almost impossible for the enemy gunners to track and hit. They often ran for cover.

After weeks of combat sorties, Luke marveled that the enemy troops seemed reluctant to fire at the Cobras, probably for fear of retaliation from an almost invisible foe. They were used to firing at the slower, wider, and less-armed Hueys. Luke reveled in his new combat missions where he had increased maneuverability, zero loading, and higher speed. He struck his targets with a substantial increase in his dive angle and an increased speed in his approach. With Hueys, he never overflew his targets after a gun-run, but with the Cobra, he overflew targets regularly.

With months of combat missions under his belt, Luke and others did not limit themselves to the basic mission of protection. They continued to serve as armed escorts for the Hueys, but they also provided armed reconnaissance and flow-fire support. Luke twice diverted his flight to a search-and-rescue mission, where a downed crewmember from his battalion waited for him. He picked up a copilot, whose pilot had been killed, from a downed Cobra, and flew him back to base precariously perched on his open ammunition bay doors. The next week, he and eight other Cobras unleashed every bit of firepower to repel major attacks on the Saigon Air Base.

Luke's prayer was short but he prayed it every night.

> I know you love me, Lord, because in Your Word, You are acknowledged as the Maker and Creator of the universe: "The heavens praise your wonders, O Lord, Your faithfulness too, in the assembly of the holy ones. For who in the skies above can compare with You, Lord? Who is like the Lord among the heavenly beings?"

And he looked at the photo every time he prayed.

> You are my rock, Lord, always above me, always in the Skies. Your glory shines for me.

Luke checked his calendar. After a year of troop carrying, MEDEVAC rescue, and combat flying, his month long break was coming up. He would take a two-week R and R vacation as well. It was timed perfectly to the Air Force Sixth Weather Squadron's ten-year reunion. It seemed like a lifetime away, in a parallel universe. His first stop might be on the West Coast, but his destination was Tinker Air Force Base. He couldn't wait to catch up with Chance and his other Air Force buddies in the middle of Tornado Alley.

Thinking about his past, his mind turned to Lacy. He bowed his head. *I wonder if she ever got my letter. Couldn't be intercepted. Regardless, I'm coming home. What a miracle if I saw her in Oklahoma City. Either way, I'm coming back for some Cobra revenge.*

Book Four
THE REUNION

47

Sixth Weather Squadron Alumni Association held its reunions at the Holiday Inn outside Midwest City, midway between Will Rogers Airport and Tinker Air Force Base. Luke was back in familiar territory next to Tinker Air Force Base, catching up with old friends. At the first get-together, they sat in a huge room, hunkered down at tables filled from edge to edge with cold beer. Everybody revered the top man, Sergeant Jones. He had served in one kind of weather squadron or another since 1954.

Joe Kerwin served for the longest time in Sixth Weather—twenty years. He gave details on projects ranging from land and sea, at Christmas Island, Truk, Guam, Buka, Port Moresby, New Guinea, during the U.S. and British nuclear testing in the Pacific, and then during the following French nuclear testing. He had a project in Alaska to track the Russian nuclear testing. Joe said, "There was so much fog in Alaska, the Air Force flew C-130s and C-141s in a box pattern, dropping dry ice to transform the fog into ice crystals so our planes could land safely."

There were numerous photo-mapping projects Sixth Weather took part in, providing weather for the complete aerial mapping of the Pacific Ocean, South America, and Africa. Guys sauntered over to hear Joe Kerwin. Kerwin said, "At one time, the U.S. Air Force shot test missiles from Vandenberg Air Force Base on the coast of California, far downrange into the South Pacific, but they could not retrieve them for study and improvement. Concerned about their weaponry, they determined that the maps were wrong, not the missiles. That led to photo mapping and new maps, important for our security and missile defense systems. That helped us later. At one point on another deployment, I spent seventy-nine days aboard a ship, launching helium weather balloons. We needed exact coordinates."

"Any of you guys remember when B-52's from Barber's Point, Hawaii, flew over Christmas Island and dropped thermonuclear bombs, set to explode at 50,000 feet over our heads?" Herman asked. "The gooney birds on Christmas Island were blinded by the incredible light from the blasts, and we were detailed to shoot them out of mercy. I knew LaCrosse hated that part."

Chance spoke up from the adjoining table. "At Eniwetok, during the testing, a project buddy got coral poisoning from swimming on the reef. He developed a hole in his foot. The doctor on board told him, 'Keep it dry.' Some help he was."

When Joe was on a project on an island up in Alaska, he arrived to find our support radar did not pick up an enemy plane until it was ten minutes out. "You have a temperature inversion out there, maybe six thousand feet up," Joe said after making some of the upper atmosphere runs. "The radar signal bounces off it. You need to take your equipment up on that mountain," he pointed. "Russia is not that far away."

"I can't do that," the radar man protested, "I would have to leave my wife and kids."

"What's more important, your country or your family?" Joe responded.

"You can't do a thing when fighters or bombers appear ten miles out. They will be dropping bombs before your anti-aircraft batteries are even alerted. You must go up the mountain, above the temperature inversion."

"Ah, the Russians." Luke took a long drink from his beer mug and spoke up. "Whenever we spotted those Russian fish trawlers off the coast of Guam, we knew we had a bombing mission in Vietnam coming up. They could monitor our bomber takeoffs and warn the anti-aircraft batteries in Vietnam that missiles or bombers were headed their way. So when there were no trawlers, we knew there would be no actions."

Dakota said, "We were sent on a project at Chico, California, and another up in Alaska. We needed two trucks full of helium to fill one high-altitude balloon designed to drift for two days and capture radioactive particles and other classified data at sixty thousand feet. That balloon was one hundred twenty feet tall, compared to our usual five six-foot-wide helium balloons."

Luke said, "We had the same mission down in American Samoa. Our balloon was set for one hundred eighteen thousand feet altitude to catch the disruptions in the Van Allen belt right where the gravity lines come back into the atmosphere. We could monitor the damage to the Van Allen belt. It took us forever to fill that balloon at Camp Leone. Small groups of Samoans sat around the big launching field next to the runway to watch. They had no concept whatsoever of what we were doing."

Chance said, "Down on Buka Island in the South Pacific, our tents were so hot in the tropical sun the natives took pity on us. They built us shacks with palm branches which were much cooler. Why didn't we think of that? We did learn one cool thing though. When we were faced with warm beer, we used the fire extinguisher to make the beer icy-cold."

King said, "Remember how good the pilots were on those god-forsaken islands we were stationed on? The C-124s would drop us supplies because they could not land. No runways. Once on our radios we asked them, 'how accurate can you be?' They said, 'Put a red handkerchief on the spot you want your supplies.' We did, and they dropped tons of supplies dead on that red handkerchief."

Luke shook his head. "They had lots of practice. Look at all the places we supplied weather support: Christmas Island, Truk, Guam, Buka, Port Moresby, Alaska, Thule, and Greenland. Some places were so isolated."

Frank said, "We were so isolated our own government didn't know where we were."

Everybody laughed. Another guy said, "Most guys don't know that the Supporting Photo mapping Unit #1370 with airmen on board for seventy-nine days out of Alaska, measured high-altitude air samples. They found radioactivity at five thousand degrees Fahrenheit in clouds coming over the North Pole from Russia. They were doing serious testing. I hope our warheads have equal power to that."

"I hope we have superior power to that."

Dakota Duval pulled up closer to the table. "Many of us spent time on Johnston Island, with twenty-nine missile sites, and missiles shot toward us from Vandenberg Air Force Base as well. Remember? Those missiles had a five-hundred-square-mile target below Johnston Island, and all around us were Russian trawlers with all their electronic gear. Every so often stray radiosonde instruments dropped down on their trawlers by our weather dropsonde operators flying in B-29s and B-50s. No parachutes attached. From twenty thousand feet, they picked up plenty of speed."

48

Sergeant Jones (Clifford T., the Legend) got up and looked around. Everybody stopped talking. "The meeting's about to start," he said. "Don't go in dry. Get yourselves more beer, and get your ass over to the meeting room."

By the time they got to the meeting room all the stragglers and latecomers had shown up. Chance and Luke sat in the back row. Colonel Mosely stood at the mike, facing rows of hard chairs filled with Sixth Weather Squadron personnel. His impeccably coiffed silver hair brought out the contrast between the alabaster starchiness of his white shirt and his dark blue slacks. A black leather belt and a pair of black, square-toed Nando Orsini Italian shoes, bought during a vacation in Florence, completed his reunion attire.

Luke told Chance, "If any person could look as if he was in uniform while in civvies, it's the colonel."

"We have got to get some better threads, no doubt," Chance said. "I hope we don't have any visitors."

The colonel's smile radiated warmth. "Welcome to our first Sixth Weather Mobile reunion. I never saw very much of you while you were out on mobile missions, and I know you appreciated that."

The men laughed. Colonel Mosely went on. "But I always appreciated your ability to function independently as a flight or raw-insonde team wherever we sent you. I am glad I didn't need to go out on those missions."

All around the room the men turned to each other, talking for a moment about one mission or another, happy to be so recognized.

The colonel smiled. "We sent you to some places I wouldn't send my worst enemy."

Gales of laughter filled the room. Everybody had at least one screwball mission to share. Guys leaned over to tell their stories to each other. Within moments, names of key assignments rolled from the back to the front of the room on a tide of chatter.

The colonel gave them time to share. Then he looked toward the back of the room. "There were a handful of men who got stuck under Army supervision at the Nevada Test Site. I'm glad you worked it all out."

Chance, Luke, and Dakota all said, "We couldn't have pulled it off without you, Colonel."

The colonel continued. "We all got more challenges than we bargained for. But all's well that ends well, and you kept Sixth Weather's reputation untarnished."

Men up front responded. "What are you talking about, sir?"

The Colonel said, "We'll save that story for another day."

Chance mumbled, "The more we saw of wild mustangs, the less we liked people."

The Colonel said, "Shirley knows more stories than anybody. She's the secretary and all things come through her. Come on up." And he waved her up. Shirley took the mike, turned toward the audience, took a deep breath, and leaned forward. "Here's one of my favorite stories that most of you may not know. You weren't here at Tinker."

She adjusted her glasses. "Our first sergeant lived off Tinker before they put the quarters on base for enlisted personnel—and they had very few officer quarters either. Becky Davis and Madge Davis were schoolteachers in Midwest City, and they lived exactly across the street from the sergeant. He thought an awful lot of them. Their father, old J.T. Davis, was always pulling pranks on our "First Shirt" (First Sergeant). J. T. claimed he never pulled a prank on anybody. But we all hung out with J.T. because he gave lessons in pranks and could out-Bongo Bongo, who we all thought was the king of wild pranks."

"One time, the sergeant went on a weekend pass to Dallas and came back to Tinker. We had hung a sign on his old '48 Chevy. We were all hiding in the parking lot, watching. The bells began to ring then in our First Shirt's head. We could just see him thinking, 'Boy am I going to have some fun with this sign.' He saw us hiding and called out, 'You clowns get over here.'

"The sergeant said, 'Colonel Barnhart has just gotten his old Dodge painted. We think Clark painted it with some paint they had left over from something in the motor pool. We don't even know where it came from. It was gray paint, anyway, and believe me, it was something else. But it did look pretty good. They did a nice job on that car.'"

Luke scanned the audience. Some guys knew the story and hid their smiles behind their hands. Wives, girlfriends, and some other airmen didn't know the account, but they leaned forward to listen anyway. Luke noticed Ashcraft, and Grayson, whom he hadn't seen for years. They put up their hands in greeting when he caught their eyes.

Shirley held up her hand so the audience wouldn't get ahead of her and continued. "Colonel Barrow, the Fourth Weather Group commander, was coming in for a complete set-up and orientation from us so he could evaluate what had been happening in Sixth Weather. Colonel Barnhart was gonna pick him up at the base operations, and he had his car all shined up. That was a good-lookin' old Dodge.

"He didn't know that, in the meantime, we had put this special sign on the passenger side. The sergeant had us stick that sign on there with masking tape, and we never thought about the paint job. That paint was fresh, believe me! So, Colonel Barnhart drove down to base operations and Colonel Barrow came out there and got in. He sat on the passenger side, and he didn't say anything about that sign. Colonel Barnhart got in the driver's side and they rode back to Sixth Weather.

"We had lookouts who gave us the high sign, and we hung out in the parking lot again. And Colonel Barrow got out of the car, right in front of us, and looked over the car's roof, right at Colonel Barnhart. 'Say,' he says, 'are you displeased with this car?' Barnhart says, 'No, I'm not displeased with it. I like my Dodge.'

"'Well, how come you're wantin' to trade it off?'

"Barnhart replied, 'I don't know anything about that.'"

"Barrow then said, 'Yeah, well, there's a sign on it over here.'

"Colonel Barnhart walked over and looked at the sign. It read: *Will Trade for a Sow and Seven Pigs.*

"The colonel exploded. 'Those sons' a bitches!'

"We were all laughing so hard, falling on the ground trying to keep quiet. Colonel Barrow did his best to hide his shocked laughter. And Colonel Barnhart said, 'It's that damn first sergeant, that's who put that sign on there.'

"Then the colonel heard us all laughing. Have you ever heard Bongo laugh? Limbs break off of trees and birds fall from the sky."

"Colonel Barnhart called us all over. 'You men find the first sergeant and tell him to get out here and get that sign off the car.'"

Shirley looked off to her right. The audience howled, knowing that it wasn't just the First Shirt. "But wait! There's more!" Shirley's shout quieted the audience.

"The colonels marched into headquarters. We went over and got the First Shirt out to the parking lot. We pulled that sign off. But when it came off, all that gray paint came off with it!

"When the sergeant saw it, he said, 'Oh shit! Oh shit!' We howled with laughter. The sergeant was all shook up! The First Shirt ran as fast as he could to the motor pool. We followed him. He went over to Hammer and said, 'Have you got any more of that gray paint that you put on the Colonel's car?'

"'Yes,' Hammer said. 'Why do you need it?'

"'That's not for you to know! Give us the paint!'

"And Sergeant Sherry, the First Shirt, made us go over to sand and repaint the door before Colonel Barnhart came out again. We fixed that door up one minute before the colonel came back out with his visitor. They were on their way to the Officers Club."

From the first row, Colonel Barnhart jumped up in mock rage, shaking his finger at Shirley and Sherry and then at the whole room. "Why am I always the last to hear a good story?"

It took a few minutes to get the room quiet again. Shirley gave the mike back to Colonel Mosely. "And that was the story of the Dodge for sale."

49

The colonel took back the mike and gave it to First Sergeant Sherry. "I want shorter, funnier stories—not at an officer's expense!"

Sergeant Sherry reached out and grabbed the mike. "Okay, men, I think what the colonel means is to share a story about yourself, no brag, just fact, or just funny. And if you have a story about somebody else, that's liable to be even funnier."

Joe Kerwin came up and said, "I have a good story about Sgt. Jerry Yeager, who had the record for the fastest plotting of wind speeds and directions even if he might have been drunk."

Everybody laughed. Joe went on. "Jerry got arrested by a police sergeant in Gulfport for intoxication and was put in the weekend slammer. I found out about it and went in to get Jerry out. I made up a story that Jerry just had a death in the family, and that I would take care of him and get him back to the base. The sergeant and the jailer agreed."

Joe casually took a drink, enjoying his moment.

The whole room yelled, "Come on, Joe, what's the rest of the story?"

Joe grinned. "Then Hurricane Camille hit Gulfport with its hundred-mile-an-hour winds, heavy rain, and huge storm surges on the beaches. Jerry wrote that red-necked SOB a letter with no return address. "Camille—yeah, that will teach you to put a weatherman in jail."

"Here's one of my favorites." John Arno said. He a weather-man of Italian descent. "Americans always get this wrong. They think 'Domani' is a cool thing Italians say. *Domani* does not mean *tomorrow*. It means *not today*. And that's why Italians live longer with their wines and siestas."

"Why?" Luke asked.

Sergeant Arno said with a straight face, "When they say *domani*, they just don't care, they don't give a shit, and that's why they live longer."

Another howl of laughter went up. Some of the wives were shocked.

Chance got up. "You will not believe this, but it is true. Joe Kerwin, the ladies' man, lives in longevity. A long time ago, he asked his girlfriend back in Newfoundland to marry him. She said, 'No.' Sixteen years later, he met up with her again in the States, and she's not married, and neither is he. So he asks again, 'Will you marry me?' And she says, 'Yes.' You can't make this stuff up."

Kerwin laughed and shook his head.

Sergeant Epps got up. "Guys were doing all sorts of weather reporting, including *spheres*, where they triangulated lightning strikes. We were working with a forerunner of the modern Doppler radar, now dual-polarized. Other flights on the island are doing high-range navigation photo mapping. In addition to my other duties, I had to supplement the K-rations dropped down to us out on the islands. We had no landing strip.

"I needed fresh fruits and vegetables from the natives to augment rice, spam, peaches, pound cake, and cigarettes. After a couple weeks one of my men said, 'Why are you spending time with those dumb farmers?'

"And I said, 'What are you talking about, ya dumb shit? These guys are feeding you fresh food. Who's the dumb one?'"

Chance, Luke and Dakota were falling out of their chairs, like everybody else. They had often been on the same flights, the same missions. All had seen duty in Samoa, Johnston Island, Truk, the Marshall Islands, and the Nevada Test Site, among others.

Sergeant Runion got up. "In the K-ration tins, Sears provided the cigarettes, but they were of terrible quality. Sergeant Hardy here wrote Sears headquarters. 'Stop sending those cigarettes, or when we get back stateside, my men will never buy anything from Sears.' And Sears changed what they had been doing for years, all because of one sergeant."

Almost all senior weather personnel, Chance, Luke, and Dakota included, had the Specialty Number 25252 from the advanced training at Chanute Air Force Base back in Illinois. Some of the old-time sergeants like Jones had taught the course. Sergeant Jones had been in weather since 1953.

"Sarge, give us some more stories!"

Jones got up and told us, "In 1953, we could have taken out China. McArthur wanted to use small nuclear bombs when he got to the border of North Korea. Only a few of us knew that. Instead he got fired."

Before he sat down, he looked around and said, "Any rookies here who didn't serve in the nuclear testing out in the Pacific, get out to the bar, and bring back all the cold beer they have." Eight airmen got up and hurried from the room.

Jones said, "Come on, get up here and tell more stories. Or stay where you are if they are short."

Buck Bucklin said, "On Conan Island off Vietnam, we provided weather for our artillery—clouds, rain, wind. They'd get the grids and shoot."

Another weatherman, John Day, said, "We provided upper atmosphere balloon runs on board ship down near Tahiti. We were close to three French nuclear detonations."

Dave Trumbo said, "I saw those missiles flying through the air. They looked like flying bedsteads. A million bucks apiece for those losers."

John had plenty to say. "Down in Bolivia and Brazil, at Xingu, pronounced Cheengu, we had a runway with serious trees right at its end. We would back right up into the trees, rev the C-47 or the DC-32 and the trees are bent double. A C-130 usually grazed the trees at the other end of the runway when it took off. Sometimes, we

342

flew in an H-3, a piston reciprocating jet, a four-blader. We had to fly somewhere and make calcium hydrate charges to make hydrogen for our balloons. Every trip was an adventure."

Dave said, "We took a bus trip to Brazilia, two hundred and fifty miles. I thought Bongo was a crazy driver. These Brazilian drivers were off the charts. They could never get a driver's license up here. I was in the grip of death every other mile."

He took a long drink of Coors. Everybody followed suit. "In the Amazon River basin, we saw an anaconda swallow an entire cow. Nobody will ever believe it. I wish I had a camera; those anacondas can be twenty-eight feet long and weigh 500 pounds. I thought Gerry could bite off a manta ray's head until I saw that anaconda."

John Webb said, "Down in Corumba, we were out throwing Frisbees with the kids. In one day, the Frisbees were tattered up. So we wrote to Whamo and said, 'What's up with your Frisbees? Little kids out here throw it on the beach and one day later they are trashed.' So they sent us a hundred Frisbees."

Dave said, "At Tagautinga, only the village doctor had a car. A guy on a horse brought us milk every day, big jugs of milk. He'd pour them out into smaller containers.

"But at Camp Mercury out West in Nevada, they had cows and chickens in close range to the nuclear explosions. They tested them for radiation, and the cows ate the grass to see if radiation showed up in their milk. I'd much rather be in Brazil with that fresh milk."

Ralph chimed in. "Brazil. We had Navy pilots come in on the forest runway. The only way we could handle that was to imitate the aircraft carrier. We spread huge chains across the runway so the tail-hookers could come in and hook those chains. It seemed mighty weird at the time."

Bongo said, "Remember when the Brazilian planes went down in the jungle? Nobody could find them in such a dense tropical rain forest. Even para-rescuers could not locate them. That happened twice."

David Guenther told us he had worked at NASA, training astronauts such as Armstrong, Lovell, and Conrad. The astronauts had to know the winds. The four rocket engines blasting off and going up are significantly influenced by the wind speeds and direction. He worked with the lunar training model. He was one of our Sixth Mobbers who helped develop Doppler radar. He had gone up as high as any Sixth Weather Squadron member ever had. "The one thing I remember most," he said, "is how down-to-earth and how personable all these astronauts were. So easy to work with."

"Speaking of winds," one of the wives asked, "What are the worst wind speeds you had in Tornado Alley? Weren't they dangerous?" She was a newcomer.

"Here's the problem," Luke said. "The anemometer measures winds accurately up to 120 mph. But we knew we had recorded winds at 218 mph in other ways. The sonic anemometer measured wind gusts, but not the real deal."

Chance said, "But it was possible to see a circular pattern of trees blown over. Recently the fastest wind speed was measured at 318 mph. But none of our instruments could record that."

Kerwin said, "Now they have to measure tornado wind speed by the damage done, from the EF-1 to the EF-5 range. Some scientists say the wind speed in the vortex may reach over 400 mph. I don't doubt it."

Arno said, "At times, due to high winds, we had to release our helium balloons fifty miles upwind of where we wanted to gather data. At that distance our GMDs (Ground Meteorological Detector) might be five or six degrees off, and we'd have to re-launch."

Ed Skowron recounted his duty stations in Brazil, Argentina, Easter Island, and Chile—all with an eye to help other Air Force wings update the photo mapping. The Air Force wanted to correct inaccurate weather maps in South America and the West Pacific. "We had a refractive index sounding to compute refraction bends, which distorted the photographs and the moisture level that affected the bends," he explained. "Air Force C-130s and C-135s were pressed into service. We used dropsondes, weather instruments dropped from a weather plane, giving information all the way down to the ground. We had to do that over the forests of Brazil and Chile. The mountains were always dangerous, especially when we tried to cross over the Andes."

Bill King got up to describe a tornado. "A tornado is like a tiger; it can turn, twist, and lunge at virtually the same time." He gave incidents where that happened, especially to tornado chasers. "When the tornado doesn't look like it's moving, it's actually coming right at you," Gordon McCann added.

It was break time, and people got up to use the bathrooms and get more beer. Chance, Luke, and Dakota stayed in the back, and started adding up all the factors which develop into a tornado.

Luke talked about moisture, instability, windshear and upslope, approaching cold fronts, and dry lines of air. The dew point was the trigger—the temperature where moist air turns into water, five degrees less than the dry line. Dakota talked about how the most tornadoes spun out of the southwest corner of a thunderstorm super cell, and that the thunderstorm often was preceded by a squall line. Chance talked about the storm coming in with hail, indicating that raindrops had fallen and then been swooped up by the rising wind, then fallen again, then swooped up again, each time enlarging that water drop into hail that could reach the size of a baseball.

Those of them who had been at their mobile stations—with tents and Quonset huts—were close enough to observe the surface data and then the funnel cloud. They recorded as they watched tornadoes that whipped to the left or to the right when nobody expected it. They saw the tornado—how it can lift off and then swing its tail beside it, swinging back down to the surface. The weather chasers who died two weeks before the reunion had been driving in their storm-chaser trucks right alongside the tornado. They were sure it would stay on its southeasterly course. But it did a one-hundred-eighty degree turn and came right at them, killing them instantly. They were professional storm chasing scientists, not thrill seekers. Gordon and Tom Grace came up with something new. Sometimes tornadoes acted like an underground river, hitting the same town or latitude/longitude more than once. The record is four times the same place. And a tornado might have smaller ones all around it.

The five of them went out to the bar, bought a few more beers, and toasted the squadron, lifting their beer mugs high. Thunderstorms keep rotating up past 70,000 feet, with a beer mug top. When you see that anvil flat top, you know it has dissipated and is being blown away.

And so were the three tornado-eers. It was the end of the day.

50

The next day's events began after breakfast together. Those who signed up climbed into cars owned by the airmen and veterans who lived near Tinker. It was a great place to retire among friends and familiar surroundings, but not so great for avoiding tornadoes.

First they got passes and caravanned deep into the base where they had worked in and on "The Back Forty" where the squadron trained and ran upper atmosphere soundings continuously. It was home to so many of them. Then they trooped into Sixth Weather headquarters on base to say hello, and after lunch at a local restaurant in Midwest City, they drove down to the National Severe Weather Warning Center. It was now part of the University of Oklahoma in Norman, Oklahoma. That was the highlight of the day. The squadron got to visit so many weather laboratories in-house. They had experts who kept them abreast of all the latest developments in tracking thunderstorms, tornadoes, hurricanes, floods, thermonuclear detonations, and other scientific projects and missions. A handful of Sixth Weather members had already transferred over as employees immediately after their discharge.

Back at the Holiday Inn, Chuck Miller, the emcee, president, backbone, and sparkplug of Sixth Weather Squadron (Mob), began the meeting after dinner and during dessert and photographs. Luke and Chance, Dakota, and everybody else admired, respected, and loved Chuck. He was one of only two black airmen in the 4th Weather Squadron's history. He was half-Cherokee and half-black.

He stood straight and lean, handsome, soft-spoken, short hair, and stood a few inches below six feet tall. But his karma and demeanor made him appear like an NBA player.

In private conversations, we learned how he was discriminated against, what was said to him during his long career, how he tried to react-like a gentleman, and how his peers treated him. None of those negative aspects ever deterred him or changed him or made him angry or bitter. He was the perfect example of a man who crossed race barriers, moved up in rank, became a master sergeant who worked well with others and helped those beneath him. A natural leader. Nobody ever got in his face. He had that kind of strong but gentle influence on others.

But tonight at the meeting after dinner, Chuck took his time and reviewed the day's events, especially for those who had not taken the tours, and then he began explaining the next day's schedule, with the big final banquet, awards, and photographs.

Suddenly, Luke stopped listening.

He was sitting in the back of the meeting room with Chance and Dakota. Chuck stood at the lectern with the mike up in the front of the room. Ten feet to the left of Chuck, somebody beautiful stood in the doorway. Luke looked at Chance and almost fell out of his chair. "What the hell! What did you put in my beer? Jack Daniels?"

Chance laughed and jumped up. "Just a minute, buddy," he said, and rushed up to the doorway. He reached his hand out and pulled somebody out of the hallway. She nodded to Chuck and walked ahead of Chance. Some gorgeous woman, elegantly dressed even from a distance, walked straight down the aisle without a care about whether or not she belonged in this room.

Luke took a deep drink out of his bottle, and then took another drink. Was he drunk or crazy or both? That can't be who I think it is.

But it was Lacy. He hadn't seen Lacy in maybe six years. He got to his feet, swaying a bit.

Lacy materialized as if she had just walked through a wall. She floated down to the back row and pulled Luke down beside her. Luke stared straight ahead in disbelief. His lips moved. *I can't believe I just saw what I saw!*

Chuck knew about Lacy but noticed Luke struggling with reality. He turned to the rest of the room. "Okay, men. It's time to take a break and catch up with your wives and what-have-you."

All the men stood up with shouts of laughter. Chance winked at Lacy and leaned down to hug her. Luke turned around slowly, just staring at Lacy, as if he were living in a dream. "Lacy," he said, "Is it really you?"

"Well, Luke," she said, "Didn't you hear the man? You are supposed to catch up with your wives and what-have-you."

Chance fell over with laughter. Lacy frowned up at Chuck. "I've never been a 'what-have-you' before.'"

Luke finally regained his composure. "Lacy, you will never be a 'what-have-you.' For me it's just a, 'where-have-you-been-in-my-life?'"

He leaned over and kissed her. "I just wanted to make sure."

She kissed him back. "Now you know."

Luke looked at Chance. "Did you have anything to do with this?"

Chance said, "What did you expect? I knew how you felt about Lacy."

Luke, Lacy, Chance, and Dakota walked outside. They found a small grove of Australian pines clustering around four lawn chairs and a wicker table. Chance plunked their mugs down, half-full and foaming with Heineken draft. Dakota brought out a beautiful wooden bowl of nuts and snacks. Luke was still in a daze, staring at Lacy as if she had just petrified him with perfume. He hadn't sat that close to her in nearly a decade.

Lacy touched his arm. "I'm sorry, Luke. I didn't think it would be that hard on you. I must have startled you."

"It wasn't hard on me. Dying is not hard if you are going to heaven."

She kissed him and held his head in her hands. "Luke, thanks for your letter. I had no clue you were overseas and flying Hueys."

Luke avoided it at first. "You earned your degree in business administration, I think. That's all I know. You may be an administrator in your dad's business. Is that correct?"

Lacy nodded, made a face. "That was my father's idea, to prepare me to go right into his company's management. Since then I have had other thoughts. And I have done other things."

She reached out and took his beer away. "Come on, Luke. It's your turn. Chance told me you graduated from a ground-breaking program."

"I got lucky," he said. "They developed a new program at the University of Arizona, innovative, almost the first in the nation. A Bachelor of Science in Leadership. It fit in perfectly with the ROTC program. You'd have liked it: varied courses, like psychology, writing, negotiation, reading case studies, ethical decision-making, logic and organizational behavior. It wasn't administration, but it was leadership, the perfect degree for my career."

"Chance told me you got through college and ROTC with just about every honor you could get. I know you are an officer. And you are a pilot."

"I want to know about your program."

Lacy shook her head. "It's nothing new. You know me. I don't like being a carbon copy. Tell me a little more about yours."

Luke looked at her to make sure she was really interested. She looked right at him. Yes, I am interested.

"Okay," he said, "we integrate our life experiences, learn leadership styles and structures, and then create our own individual leadership profile. But also we have to function in cross-cultural contexts. It has to be evidence-based decision-making strategies, and we were given experiential learning opportunities…Well, that's enough."

"Hah!" Lacy said. "When I saw you presenting your paper in the Stanford library, I knew you were personally and academically gifted. More than I thought." Her eyes sparkled and she broke into a laugh, full of delight. "I fooled you!"

"I thought that was you at the other table! But I couldn't believe we could be in the same library."

Luke showed astonishment, and then began to laugh. "Chance, I can't believe you did set this up."

Lacy giggled. "I am sure my dad would be impressed with all you have done and become. But I'm sure his approval wouldn't mean anything to you."

When she said that, the pain and bite of his old grudge dissipated like a spent wave. Luke said, "No, I'm glad he would be impressed. Lacy, I let bygones be bygones. I have no quarrel anymore with your family. Your dad wanted me to be the best I could be. He is an extraordinary entrepreneur and manager of people. Besides that, I don't need anybody's approval."

"Luke, you really have changed." Lacy's face was crowned with happiness. "And Chance told me things my family would never hear about. You are close to being the only pilot awarded the Silver Star for heroism on the battlefield. He said it was one of the highest awards you can get. You jumped out of your wrecked Huey, grabbed the Huey's backdoor machine gun, took out the enemy on the ground, and rescued two of your crewmen."

Luke said, "Anybody else would have done the same thing, what we were trained to do. 'Leave no man on the battlefield.'"

Lacy said, "Okay, but I learned more. Chance told me you were awarded a DFC (Distinguished Flying Cross)—right Chance? Also one of the highest awards you can get as a pilot. You circled a downed helicopter with six dead men in it and fired everything you had at the enemy surrounding the Huey. A couple of your wingmen said you were on fire with your mission. You did things with your Cobra nobody had ever done. You almost ran out of fuel. And it was all for men who were dead."

Luke said, "Well, yeah. Our dead soldiers are even more important than our live soldiers. We have to rescue them. They cannot be dismembered or dishonored or dragged around and put on the enemy's news channels. That would just kill their families."

Lacy sat up straighter. "Is it true then? Chance said when that Huey crashed into the jungle on a different mission, you detoured from your mission. You circled overhead and protected that crew until our troops could come and rescue them."

Luke growled, "Chance, I'm gonna bust you up. Why would you tell her all that?" He turned to Lacy. "Chisholm doesn't have the brains God gave a billygoat. It's not what I did but who I am—the guy you took a chance on when you were fourteen."

"You took a chance on me too, Luke. Sorry, Chance. Misleading choice of words. Luke, we had many things in common, and I always imagined that we were growing on parallel paths, no matter where we were or who we were with."

"A long time ago, my unfounded jealousy probably sunk us in Hawaii. Now I know better and think differently."

"My unfounded jealousy probably sank us in Hawaii, too. I knew you had been in love with a beautiful Polynesian," Lacy said. She then reached over and patted Chance's shoulder. "Chance, you were so right!"

"So what did he tell you? What could he have said to get you here?" Luke was fired up with curiosity.

"For one thing," Chance said, "I told her you overcame your death wish with water. You almost drowned in Army Combat Diver School. She was there for you in Hawaii when you almost drowned off of Palmyra Island. But I was worried about your death wish in Viet Nam."

Lacy straightened up. "You remember, Luke, when you dropped me and left me in Hawaii, and went back to Nevada, I had the impulse to follow Mom's social mobility leanings. I thought of putting my career on the backburner and see what kind of marriage offers I could get."

She shook her head. "I still worked in my father's business. I started out in human development and personnel, and worked up to assistant manager of one store in San Francisco. I am in line for manager for a smaller store he has in Palo Alto. I overcame my impulsive nature and realized that the men who were interested in me were phony, shallow, and full of self-interest…"

"What do you mean?"

She went on. "When I walked through our Chicago offices and the secretaries thought I was out of earshot, I heard fragments of conversations, something about marrying the boss's daughter. My dad got a lot of mileage out of it, too. Guys joined the firm thinking I'd be their stairway to the top."

Chance got up. "If you two will excuse me," he said. "I don't think I'm needed here anymore."

Lacy and Luke laughed. "Hey, before you go."

He gave Chance a standing bear hug. Lacy joined in. Nobody wanted to let go. Finally, Lacy leaned forward and gave Chance a kiss on the cheek. "Thank you," she murmured. "You just brought me back to life."

Luke slapped Chance's shoulder. "She brought me back to life. And so did you. Damn! Now I owe you both!"

They all burst out laughing. Luke said, "Man, we have been through everything. Tornadoes, hurricanes, missile explosions, thermonuclear detonations, whitewater waves, hailstones, thunderstorms, anvil clouds…"

He paused, seeing if he missed something.

"Just don't tell me I'm the pot of gold at the end of the rainbow," Lacy said. "Thanks to my father, I've heard that once too often."

Luke smiled. "At least you don't have to worry about me wanting a springboard into or a hand up into your dad's businesses."

Lacy looked down, then away. "Speaking of springboards and pools, my family is going on a whitewater adventure," she said. "My father offered a whitewater trip to any California employee (and his family) who reached his or her goals for the fiscal year that ended July first. Three people did it. The Middle Fork of the Salmon was the top prize."

"Was it California because people there are more adventurous?"

"Yes." She smiled. "People in Chicago don't even know Idaho exists. Their getaways involve Lake Michigan on all shores. No canoeing with wind or wave. But nobody wanted anything to do with white water. So my family is going. The trip for five was already paid for. You've done it. You are part of the company. You know the rafters. And it will cost you nothing. Chance told me all about it. You've earned tons of leave. You could show me so many things I would miss."

She looked directly at him. "Luke, will you join us there? Will you come with me? You will see my family under different circumstances. They will see you as I see you now. You are the war hero. You're the combat diver. And besides that, Luke, we need you."

Luke stood up in pretense. "What? Are you kidding? I'm going to have to run another search and rescue mission? That is *one tough river*. Your family thinks they can handle it? A hundred miles of whitewater?"

Lacy stood up in her best indignant "so there" pose. "We got the best guides and the best company money can buy. Don't worry about that. Will you think about it?"

"You don't know what you're asking for. I'm going to have to do a lot of training up there to get my skills back. That river's nickname is earned. A Cobra, not even in combat, has challenges like 'The River of No Return.'"

He raised his eyebrows. "Well, sure, I'll think about it. I won't be the aircraft commander, so to speak, but I will be a pilot. I am not going as a passenger."

"I know that," she objected.

He teased her. "Have you ever realized our lifetime together had all the earmarks of a hundred-mile whitewater rafting trip gone awry?"

"How could you say that, Luke? Don't you remember the pools of still waters in between?"

"Yes, but I'm still skeptical of the headwaters, the parents who gave you birth when you emerged on earth."

They both laughed. "You're so funny," Lacy said. "I remember your old sense of humor."

"Yeah, after our brouhaha in Hawaii, I sang, *"Rambling rose/ rambling rose/why I want you/heaven knows...."*"

Lacy clapped her hands. "I sang to you after our second brouhaha in Hawaii. She tilted her head and sang a verse, *"The only thing different, the only thing new, I've got your picture, she's got you...."*"

Luke looked down. "You got me there."

She reached out.

"Luke, this is just like the old days when we met at that little porch off the church. Remember, with evergreens all around? I sang, *'When I fall in love, it will be forever, or I'll never fall in love....'* You always teased me for, *'little things mean a lot.'*"

Luke patted her shoulder. "That was back when you were sweet and innocent."

"I still am," she declared. "How would you know different? You disappeared from my life. I sang, '*You were the next of kin to the wayward wind . . .*'"

"Yeah, right. *You* were the one always traveling. I never saw you summers."

"Okay, last song and then we say good-bye. Remember, Luke, when we were dancing back at Springfield Prep, and you sang something from the Four Lads?" She walked to him. "Come outside and I'll sing it to you."

Luke took her hand, and they held onto each other under a pair of Oklahoma oaks, with a little light shining, but mostly shadows, warm and comforting. Lacy reached up and sang into Luke's neck. "*When other nights and other days, may find us gone our separate ways . . .*"

"I know," said Luke, squeezing her. "'We will have these moments to remember.'"

She took a deep breath. Holding Luke in her arms, she kissed him passionately, longingly. He remembered the two kisses so long ago and so far apart. This kiss was so magical and unexpected, so poured into the present moment, so passionate. He forgot about all the Polynesian kisses and wiped them off his golden memory wall. There was nothing like this kiss, and the one after it, and the one after that...

Lacy put fifteen years of loneliness and passion into her kisses. "I've waited forever for this!" she whispered to him.

"Me, too," he whispered back. "You are not going anywhere." And they held each other and kissed each other for the rest of the night. Toward midnight, Lacy stepped back and her hand drifted across her blouse. She took his fingers and helped him unfasten her two top buttons.

"I'm not leaving," he said, stepping forward.

Lacy murmured, "You never saw this before, did you?"

Luke said, "But before we were just kids." His lips moved down and kissed Lacy in places he had never kissed before. His hands came around and cupped her breasts so tenderly.

"I knew there was something missing before," Lacy said. "I didn't give you much to remember me by."

"I never would have left if you had kissed me like that."

Lacy leaned up and kissed him one more time. "When you come up to the river of no return, you will never be able to leave me again. Just try it. I dare you."

And then she was gone.

How did she know? Luke thought. He didn't sleep one wink that night. His imagination flickered with Northern lights, or some form of aurora borealis. Lacy's kiss carried all the South Pacific passion in it, and more, because of their lifetime of secret and not-so-secret love, featuring decades, not years, of attraction.

Luke dearly wished Lacy had made love to him, not just that night, but other nights long ago. All he had were memories of far-away beach loves and passion-practice. And there was no doubt both he and she had all those opportunities through their young adult years. *He wondered about her. Thirty years old. I would never want somebody so puritanical that they never made love. Not even Lacy.*

Luke remembered being untouched and love unexplored until the playful Polynesian sweet and guiltless approach to sex caught up with him. Their cultural gods made love themselves, and sex flowed in the same warm currents as eating, sleeping, singing, and swimming. In the back sea villages where he had stayed, love and sex were available in the middle of the night, even if it was in the very same fale where everybody slept.

When everybody was asleep, life was fun in the darkness or the deepness, no areas off limits, all sweet, the slow and rhythmic waves of the ocean, always moving, always comforting, always approaching, then the sweet crack and crash of the waves on the beach, followed by their slow retreat off the sweet sands, only to return again. It was similar to spinner dolphins playing in the far-off waves, casual, happy, no overtones of puritanical reactions, just riding waves and celebrating life. Natural sexuality lived in the breezes and the fragrances gently surrounding the islands, squeezed and surrounded by the warm caresses of ocean.

But after seeing how the airmen, the soldiers, and the sailors treated the women on the islands, or in California, or in Oklahoma, he wanted to wait and to go no further until he was married.

Luke could wait and couldn't wait at the same time, until he and Lacy finally enjoyed pure sweet Polynesian lovemaking. He had mellowed and matured with his heart and soul intact. He knew sex would be innocent and playful with Lacy once they got married. And he was keenly aware that in the many years he and Lacy were apart, she would have experienced the same type of initiation with care and integrity intact, with her self-differentiation in place, just as his was.

51

The huge KC-135 tanker, developed from the revolutionary 1950s Boeing 707 design, flew out of Tinker AFB with Luke aboard. His friends made sure of it. Chance and Dakota sat next to him in the back section, ribbed with no window and nobody else to talk to, as though trapped in the belly of a whale. *So this is what Jonah endured.* But it wouldn't be long before he was spewed out onto the shores of the river. And then he would follow the leadings of God. He would no longer avoid his calling, just like Jonah. He knew it was time to make a decision and settle things with Lacy and their long on-again, off-again romance. He needed to find out once and for all.

There was other catching up to do. It had been years since he ran the Middle Fork of the Salmon River. There was a reason for its name. Years ago, for a lark, he, Chance, Dakota, and Chris decided to take up the training for whitewater rafting guides. He, Chance, and Dakota had gone separate ways after two months of training in the most dangerous season, springtime, when the rivers run higher and harder, always. Chris had stayed on, hoping to work his way up. Become a co-owner some day.

Luke pulled out the *River Rafting Guide's Manual*. He dropped into a small, strapped place for cargo, and studied every page and diagram. While reading, his mind flew back to Lacy. He couldn't stop thinking about their rocky whitewater trail of love. Despite their distances apart, she had always been with him and in him. She was, in Air Force lingo, an ACM, additional crew member on whatever flight he took or worked on.

But now, he'd just seen her in person! He touched her. He kissed her at Will Rogers Airport. She cried for him when she walked past the gate. *How did I ever get so lucky? Could it be?*

Before he knew it, the wheels touched down at Mountain Home Air Force Base, where his good friend Clark Diesel was stationed as pilot. In addition to his other duties, Clark flew Blackhawk helicopters in the National Guard Search and Rescue Team. He was married and had a real mountain home next to the National Forest. He picked up the Tinker threesome and they went out to dinner on the way home. By the time they got home, Clark's wife and two kids were already asleep.

Arising at 0500, they returned to the base. Clark and his crew whisked Luke, Chance, and Dakota from Mountain Home up to Ketchum and then to Sawtooth City. But along the way they were called on a mission. Clark got permission to land on a plateau. Luke, Chance, and Dakota climbed up the mountain with Clark's medic and rescued one adult and one teenage rock climber whose rope had failed on Galena Summit. The teenager, a short, athletic kid named Laurence, had dropped a steep fourteen feet onto a rock ledge, landing hard on his right hip. He was sure he broke a bone; so was his father. He writhed in terrible pain, which did nothing to lessen the embarrassment he felt over being rescued. His father, tall and lean with bushy hair and a big mustache, was equally agitated. Mr. Sayers felt responsible for the incident. Straight rock-climbing takes much more training than trail hiking.

Luke called Clark on the radio and waved him to come up higher. Clark landed in a small clearing on the mountainside. Luke, the pilot, Jim, and a crew member medic hiked down with Laurence in a stretcher and lifted him onto the Blackhawk. The National Guard medic was first concerned about the lumbar discs as a matter of practice, but then focused on the painful hip injury. He checked Laurence's vitals, injected a painkiller into his hip, and then with Luke's help carefully placed him on a horizontal rope hammock.

Once they transported Laurence and his father to the emergency pad on the roof of the hospital in Sawtooth City and got them into the emergency room, they climbed back to the roof and took off. After a half-hour flight Clark had to land, let the three out, and return to base. As Clark climbed aboard the Blackhawk, its blades slowly whirling with Jim at the controls, Luke called out, "Thanks for the hop, Clark. We owe you big time."

Clark waved and disappeared inside the helicopter. He took the controls and the Blackhawk rose twenty feet, dipped its nose, and roared away. Luke, Chance, and Dakota did not want to wait for the shuttle. They ran down the road toward Stanley, so happy to be alone in the wilderness again. Nobody lurked in these woods with an AK-47 or a grenade launcher! They looked around as they ran effortlessly, marveling at the beauty of the Sawtooth Wilderness, thinking how perfectly the name matched the landscape.

All of a sudden, the Echo River whitewater shuttle bus zoomed past on the other side of the road, honking and then braking sharply. The driver pulled a violent U-turn behind Luke, far beyond what busses were built to do. Chris Wallop was at the wheel, just as Luke expected. The bus began to go past. Chris applied the brakes and screeched to a halt five feet away. Chris leaned out of the driver's window and shouted, "Hey, Luke, just like old times—you, Dakota, Chance, and me up on the Middle Fork." His smile dropped into a frown. "Hey, what do you have against driving cars? Just like your enlisted years, always hitch-hiking."

"Why drive when you can run?"

"Great to see you, Luke!" Chris jumped out of the driver's side and rushed over. He was a strong solid man with disheveled blond hair, blue eyes, quick speech, and pleasant Germanic features, Chris always reminded Luke of somebody he had seen in the movies. Not a lead actor, but an action-oriented sidekick. He gave Luke a bear hug and moved down the line to Chance and Dakota.

Luke danced on the road, and yelled, "What a miracle this is!"

"What are you talking about?" Chris asked. "You survived all those missions you flew in Vietnam. You are the miracle. How did you get time off to come all the way up here?"

"I extended six months so I could fly the Snake, what we call the Cobra. When you do that, they give you thirty days' leave. Is that cool, or what?"

"You're crazy, man, going back over there, when you could be here at home. You could be a river-runner. Nobody shooting at you."

"You've never seen the Cobra, man. It's a fighting machine, and I have a fighting chance to survive the missions. So many Hueys have been shot down, you wouldn't believe it. They are so wide and so big, and can carry fourteen heavily armed troops along with a crew of four. Such easy targets. The Cobra is super small and thin and fast. We are too fast and too little as a target. There's only the aircraft commander and the pilot, crew of two."

Chris looked at him closely. "Luke, you look skinnier. Older, a few wrinkles."

"Thanks a lot, buddy," Luke said. "You try eating rice three times a day, and see how you look."

Chris looked at Chance and Dakota. "I haven't seen either of you for years. You both look great to me. You haven't aged a bit."

"Are those sunglasses prescription?" Luke asked.

"Hell no! You think I'm going to do whitewater rafting and worry about my glasses falling off?" Chris replied.

"No, I meant your eyesight with Chance and Dakota."

Luke reached out and shook Chris's hand. "Thanks for fitting me into the crew. I don't know about Chance or Dakota, but I think I can handle assistant boatman. I have a lot to review about the Middle Fork. Did you bring a map? Can you guys bring me up to speed?"

"Of course we brought maps," Chris said. "We know how you are, man. You wouldn't take a trip to heaven unless they showed you the map first."

They laughed and Luke nudged Chris. "I sure got tired of seeing the map to hell. The Viet Cong sent me invitations all the time—by lead messengers."

"I hope you sent them all to hell, map or no map," Chance said.

Luke kicked the dirt on the shoulder of the road. "I wish I could have! What choice did I have, flying Huey slicks? The Viet Cong got to shoot first. If I'm carrying wounded out, or inserting fresh combat troops in, I can't pay attention to those bastards."

He raised his arms. "That's why I am flying Cobras. Attack and destroy. No freight hauler. No troop insertions. No search-and-rescue. As General Patton said, 'Don't die for your country! Let those poor bastards die for their country.'"

Luke walked toward the bus door. "That's why I'm a Snake Driver. My main job is to send them all to hell. Pure and simple."

After Chance opened the passenger door, Luke jumped onto the bus, with Dakota and Chance right behind. Before Chris started the engine, he spread out the Middle Fork map across the broad dashboard. Luke leaned over and studied the map. "I like this AO. Give me the mission run, man. Anything looks better than the Mekong Delta."

"What's an AO?"

"Area of Operations."

Chris warned him. "Don't let first appearances fool you, Luke. Check this out. You only ran this baby maybe four times and that was a long time ago. We're putting you on the company list but not responsible for the passengers. You're a sweeper, and you'll be running the river on your own. The sweeper floats last in the flotilla. You carry the rescue gear, the safety gear, and the first aid."

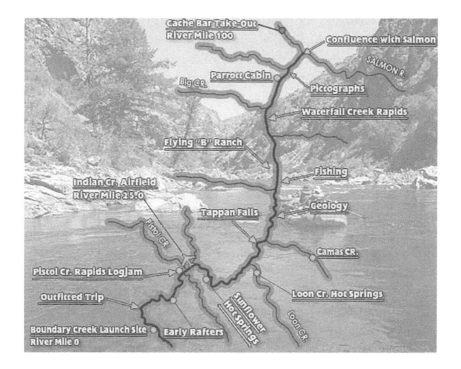

Top of Form

Chance chimed in, focused on the map. "Okay, so down here at the bottom at River Mile 0 is our Boundary Creek Launch Site," he said, using his finger as a pointer. "This is where we outfitters put in at around six thousand feet. The river is narrow and fast. We are propelled downstream toward the northwest, with three minor changes in direction. Then the river turns on itself, almost a right angle, and heads east. During the turn, we have three more changes of direction before the river takes a northeast heading. There's a hairpin turn, and then *Bam!* Pistol Creek Rapids and Logjam."

"Remember when we had to dynamite that logjam on the Pistol Creek Rapids?" Dakota asked. "We couldn't go anywhere. We had to break loose a few key logs, pull them out, chip away at it."

"Yep, we jammed dynamite into that one big log to bust it up. That helped," Chance said.

363

Chris had the most experience. He pointed back at the map. "See Indian Creek Airfield, where some people fly in? It's a half-hour flight to the put-in at River Mile 25. Very scenic."

"I know that's where Lacy's family and friends will put in." Luke stopped studying the map long enough to glance at Chance and Dakota. "So our put-in at Boundary Creek gives me a day's practice, yes? What about you, Chance? How do you get up to speed? You're down on the Duck Valley Indian Reservation, right on our Idaho border. What about you, Dakota? You're down riding mustangs on the Indian Reservation in Nevada. You don't even know what water is, let alone whitewater."

Chance smiled. "Tiara gives me time off twice a year to come up here and work. I love this river. I worked my way up to being a lead guide to spell Chris. He needs time off." He paused. "By the way, I'm lead guide on this trip. You're out of the question, Luke. You will be too distracted with Lacy. I saw how the two of you, at Tinker, caught up after five years. The pot is boiling."

Dakota broke in. "I get up here just as often as Chance. "So tell me, rookie. What rafting techniques will you use when we put in at Boundary Creek?"

Luke gave him the old rehearsal they used during training: "Avoid obstacles, spin off rocks, do the high side on the raft so we don't flip, punch through the holes in the river, and catch the eddies so we can break free."

Chris looked over approvingly. "It's all coming back. Good going, buddy! By the way, you had a long day. Are you hungry? Want to stop?"

Luke thought about Lacy and shook his head. "I'm ready to ride to the river." He settled back in the seat. Chris whipped the bus into gear. The old crate roared down Sawtooth Valley on the road to Stanley. They flew by Fourth of July Creek before Luke had time to locate it on the map.

"Hey, Chance, go ahead. Quiz me on the basics!" Luke's voice grew stronger with excitement as the trip began to play out in his mind. "Whitewater rafting and flying helicopters have a lot in common. Success with both comes with intense training. Failure can occur any time."

As if in approval, Chris sounded his gentle, long, easy laugh. "Yep, yep, yep. We'll get you back in the groove. Riding a raft isn't everything. You have to know the natural history of the wilderness area, the wildlife. You have to know the pace of our trips. You have to be good with the preparation of our meals."

Luke groaned. "That will be the toughest part."

Chris said, "No, not for you, Luke. The toughest part is to play the part of the fun, sensitive, gregarious, and entertaining river guide, without giving yourself away. You're a little intense. By the way, have you kept up with any fitness training while flying in 'Nam?"

Luke shook his head, suddenly a bit worried. "Just haven't had the time. 'Seems as if all I'm doing is flying."

Chris looked out the window. "Yikes. We need to describe you as a guide with superior strength, endurance, athleticism, and energy. The physical qualities of being a river guide are hard and demanding."

"Don't worry," Luke said. "For Lacy, I can climb up to super-man level. Just give me a few days."

Chance laughed short and hard. "That's all we've got, a few days." He cocked his head. "Do you remember boat types and lengths?"

Luke sighed. "Of course. The paddleboat is fourteen to fifteen feet long, with the lead guide in it. Most people like that boat. It can take eight to ten passengers. The oar boat is sixteen to eighteen feet long, and takes only three or four passengers. The sweep is the largest on the river, twenty-two feet long, with no guests—until now."

Chance laughed. "You think you can get Lacy on your sweep? You're dreaming."

Luke ignored him. "Finally, for the adventurous guests, there is the single or double-seated kayak. They range between eight to ten feet long, and the new rubber-made ones are just becoming available. I hope Lacy doesn't think she's ready for the kayak."

Chance nodded. "After Lacy's and your reconciliation, why is Russ still coming? From what Lacy said, Russ won't man up to the kayak, not with his fear of water and roughing it. Most guests alternate between the paddle boat, the oar boat, and the kayaks."

"Who knows? Russ has been a star at whatever he tries. He might get used to the river."

It was getting dark. Chance lapsed into silence.

Fatigue swept over Luke, along with concern, very little of it heightened by his tiredness. He didn't know the Middle Fork like he did the Rogue. Now, he was making himself responsible for precious people on this upcoming trip, one most precious of all. *What in the world am I thinking?*

They bumped, grumbled, lurched, and swayed their way out to Boundary Creek, traveling from dirt road to the entrance to wilderness in pitch dark.

When the four arrived at camp, there were seven hired-out river runners, not six.

When they arrived at the campfire, first Chance introduced Luke to the river runners. Then all four of the old friends—Chris, Luke, Chance, and Dakota did a victory dance, Indian style, around the campfire. Shouting and whooping, they didn't care what anybody else thought. At last, they were all together. And all were ready for adventure.

52

Although it was late, now they were all set for supper. The fire still blazed. They feasted on grilled steak, cowboy beans, and camp coffee over the golden embers of split oak as they talked about the next day. Chance would work with Luke and Dakota on the sweep as they went down the first section of the Middle Fork, and Kent and Ernie would take the oars boat, so Ernie could receive more training. The other four would bring out the paddleboat.

As they were talking, Luke looked across the fire at Jackson, Victor, Jerry, and Ben, all of them bundled up. Jackson fidgeted as if sitting didn't come easily to him; his Creole upbringing In New Orleans made him always ready for action.

Victor was tall and rangy, with long brown hair and rimless granny glasses—which had become the rage in America and Britain since John Lennon started wearing them—as if he were studying life up close. Jerry's chiseled nose and high cheekbones gave away his American Indian heritage, especially with his long black hair. Ben was stocky and muscular with black hair and riveting eyes that burned beneath bushy brows.

With the day's warmth sucked from the thin air, Luke was glad to have a campfire. "Four of you are going to take the place of eight paddlers? You guys will be pretty busy, hmm?"

Ben laughed. "I'm looking forward to it, building upper body strength. I've been practicing by lifting logs, moving rafts, whatever I can."

Victor smiled. "Ben's sitting up front. Otherwise, the raft will tip over backwards."

"Thanks buddy," Ben said, thoroughly enjoying the good-natured laughter spreading around the campfire. "I'll remember that when you fall out at Velvet Falls. It's got your name on it. Hey, Luke, did you bring your fishing pole? There's great fishing on the second section."

"No, didn't have time. I picked up some barbless hooks, though, and Chance said he'd buy me a fishing license. Did you?"

Chance nodded.

A smile spread across Luke's face. "If you have a pole, Ben, I'd like to have a chance to catch and throw back a few beauties."

"Tomorrow morning at breakfast, let me tell you about all the fish we see every day on the Middle Fork," Ben said. "The water is so clear, we can't even count how many fish we see in an hour, let alone a day."

"I can't wait." Luke got up to find a place to cast his sleeping bag for the night. "Thanks for the great food, guys."

"Tomorrow, it's your turn to cook," Jason said.

Chance walked over to the fire with his sleeping bag over his shoulder. "Oh yeah, Luke, I forgot to tell you. You're the cook tomorrow."

Luke couldn't resist. "You'll be sorry . . . Just kidding!"

"Good night," they all said.

Luke found a place underneath a dense Douglas fir, away from the campfire so he could see the stars. When he sank into his sleeping bag, a few feet from the river, the stress of flying nonstop in Vietnam caught up to him. It seemed like the first time he had taken a break alone since he'd last slept in the pilot's bunker at Cu Chi. He thought he could sleep for twenty-four hours.

The stars drifted across the sky for Luke. Lacy's face appeared on the moon, smiling, expanding. The Corona Borealis constellation sparkled and winked. The stars within it formed a perfect outline for Lacy's face.

Right below the constellation, Lacy seemed to fill the night with her presence, a statue shimmering in the night air. His eyes felt like twin projectors, tiny points of light sending out a magnified image across a film screen for the universe to behold. She stood erect, her shoulders thrown back and set strong. Her glossy black hair floated far down in waves behind and in front of her. Beneath the shoulder straps of her shimmering negligee floated the promise of curves, hills, and valleys.

She held her head with poise and self-assurance, forehead tilted slightly toward him. She parted her hair on the right side and brushed it over to the left. Her ears were small and well suited to the diamond-studded silver earrings dangling in the moonlight. Her eyebrows curved beautifully above her striking deep-set gray eyes, perfect for the night's sky and smoldering with golden currents. The size and intensity of her eyes captivated him. There was no way she could be ignored or her presence diminished. Her nose was straight, strong, and slender, carved out of Michelangelo's finest marble quarry. Every element of her beauty made it clear she was a force with which to be reckoned. She was beauty in action, not beauty waiting to be rescued or ravished.

Her lips were perfectly formed around a mouth slightly wider than one might expect, but suited exquisitely for the flash of her white teeth groomed for the most beautiful smile in the universe. So kissable. When her lips parted, Luke recognized the female equivalent of the famous Jay Gatsby smile: *I am affirmed by the powers of the universe and I know everything is possible. There are no limits on what I can do when she is with me.*

Her voice sounded clear, musical, like a one-voice symphony created to charm the universe with its laughter and singing. Her voice penetrated into his soul and echoed far out into the universe. Her songs of romance and longing cast a spell on those lucky enough to hear her. She sang solo. Mere walls could not stifle her beat, her rhythm, her message. And her laughter rolled like one happy wave after another. It traveled into the Three Brothers Shoals in Samoa and then rippled off softly onto the beach, where it flowed into all the conch shells and grooved into their memories.

Lacy. She soared and floated and shimmered above him. As morning approached, she distilled herself into a tiny wisp of incense and floated back down into his heart as if she was the genie and he was the sea-green bottle in which she lived.

Morning arrived at quarter past five. Chance appeared above Luke—where was Lacy? Gone like the darkness dissipating upon dawn's advance?

A dream. Only a dream.

Damn. Luke shook himself and looked again, lifting slowly onto one elbow. Chance's face was not what he wanted to see right now, but Chance erased some of Luke's disappointment by handing him a hot cup of coffee. He sat on a log five feet away. "I even remembered the spoonful of honey," he said. "I know who you were dreaming about. Sorry to disappoint you."

"Hey, thanks for the coffee, buddy. I could use it. Do you guys always get up in the middle of the night?"

"This first section, just like the last section, has steep vertical walls. It's daylight out there. It takes much longer for the sun's rays to hit us here. At the end of the day, we'll be soaking in hot springs, and you won't even remember the cold dark morning."

Twenty minutes later, he'd packed his toothbrush, washed his face in the cold, clear water, and tucked his gear in a large waterproof bag. Luke sat in front of the morning campfire cross-legged, studying the put-in location. Around them were giant rugged peaks, rock canyon walls, fragrant fir and pine forests, all deep green, all alpine.

Chance strode over. "Luke, you have so little time to apply what you studied on the way up here. You've got to absorb two weeks of river guide training in one day—and that day is today. But don't worry. We'll get back in time. Who knows? Maybe this is your opportunity to go back to 'Nam all spoken for."

"Always the romantic," Luke murmured, unconvinced.

"Dakota and I got lucky with Quanah and Tiara," Chance said. "It's your turn."

"Chance, think about the Middle Fork. What's the first big threat?"

"Velvet Falls. It misleads. People think it appears smooth and easy, which it does. But then, watch out! Many a rafter has tasted water they had no desire to drink."

"Okay, what else about the first section of river?"

"Countless minor rapids after Velvet Falls demand attention. If you misjudge one, the next one will smack you, and then, before you know it, the next. They come so fast.

Chris said, "Hmmm. Marble Rapids, Grouse, The Tappans . . . can't forget the Tappans."

"Right," Chance said. "But you have to prepare for Impassable Canyon, Luke. That's where Lacy will be in the most danger. The river is so tight. It looks like there is no room downriver for the rafts to float. Give me some names, man."

Luke leaned over. "We've got the Redside, the Porcupine, the Cliffside, the Weber, one right after the other."

The others nodded and agreed. Chris said, "Next comes the Ouzel—maybe the largest rapid on the river. We have to talk about that one. And then what?"

Luke looked down. "The House Rock, the Hancock, and the Devil's Tooth in very quick succession. I'm flat-out worried about losing it on the Rubber and then getting taken out with that one-two-three punch."

"I'm glad you feel that way. We need to prepare for that. The last two days on the river are the most demanding. Everybody thinks by then, 'Oh, I can handle it all. I've been through all the Middle Fork can throw at me in four days . . .'" Chance's voice trailed off, leaving only a disbelieving grimace on his face. He shook his head.

Luke wondered what possessed him to think of this as a good way to win back Lacy. What a way to spend his precious R&R before heading back to 'Nam? Hiring on as a professional river guide for a hundred miles of the most wild and untamed river in the West, with Lacy's life possibly at stake?

He sighed. "Call me crazy, Chance. Just like now, I'm too used to sitting. A hundred miles of whitewater. Man, oh, man, I need to touch some kryptonite—with all I have ahead of me."

"Once you grab the oars and get on the river, the kryptonite will come back to you. Whitewater rapids are kryptonite for us river specialists."

"If anybody can get me up to speed, you're the man. I had one day to learn how to survive on the Mekong Delta when I first arrived in 'Nam."

53

Chris arrived. "Let's get started!" He leaned forward, concentrating. "The Middle Fork begins small and fast, and the canyon walls are close. You can feel an almost intimate presence. Today we run fewer river miles. When we pick up the rafters at Indian Creek, we get into a daily routine: breakfast around eight, pack up, load rafts, and hit the river at about ten. We do three hours of rafting, and then we hit a beach for lunch. After an hour, we run for a couple more hours, and then set up camp."

Luke nodded, the tin cup of coffee warming his hands. "We're talking three distinct sections and three distinct canyons as well, on the same river." Though spoken as a statement, it was really a question.

"Yep, yep, yep. Campsite activities change with the canyons, too. There's no place to hike around here. Too steep. But the second section has trails and views."

Ben arrived, toting a smile and a green ice chest. "Luke, you have a choice. I've got cutthroat trout and rainbow trout, six of each. I threw about ten back."

"You're the expert. But I'll start out with something new, the cutthroat trout. Thanks for breakfast!"

"I caught them. You cook them."

"Fair enough. But give me a hand with skinning and filleting, will you?"

"Of course! That's part of the fisherman's job," Ben said.

Ten minutes later, they dug into pan-fried trout, cowboy beans, and bacon to go with fresh pots of camp coffee, and hot potatoes roasted in the coals before Luke fished them out.

Chance knew what kind of day it was going to be. "Take the potatoes to go. We don't have time for hot coals during lunch."

Luke couldn't wait. He grabbed his potato. "I haven't had coal-fired potatoes since our college days, Chance. My snack to go has got up and went."

Victor looked over. "Luke, you ate more than Chance. That's a first."

As Chance laughed, Ben looked up. "Luke, how do you like these cutthroats?" He paused between bites. "Did you know the Middle Fork is a native hatchery? It's never been stocked with man-made hatches."

"You can taste that native wildness. There's a little extra bite to it, a richer flavor. This is the best pan-fried trout I've had."

"Did Chance ever tell you how many kinds of fish you can spot?"

"Not all of them."

"You've got your Dolly Varden, your cutthroat trout, your rainbow trout, your steelhead, and you've got the Chinook salmon. One third of all Chinook spawn up here."

"How would you know that?" Jason asked.

"My dad worked in Fish and Game all his life out here in Montana and Wyoming," Ben said. "He ended up as a supervisor at Yellowstone."

"You were lucky," Victor said. "You grew up out in the wild. I came from the Phoenix area, where they have three rivers and fifteen dry washes."

Chris walked over, his eyes focused. "Okay, guys, let's clean up, pack up, and hit the river. Some of us have a lot to learn today." He slapped Luke on the shoulder. "Today, you are a river-force captain, not an Air Force captain."

"I left the Air Force, remember?" Luke reminded him. "I'm in the Army now."

Chance hooked up the bus to the long trailer stacked with the three boats. With Luke's help, he backed the trailer down to the rushing water. They slid the paddleboat, the oar boat, and the sweep into the river's edge, tying each firmly to separate pine trees along the bank. Chance pulled out the bus and trailer and pointed it toward home so the two drivers could haul the bus and trailer back to Stanley.

Kent and Ernie entered the oar boat, Chris and Luke jumped into the sweep, and the other four hopped into the paddleboat. Kent and Ben untied their ropes. One by one, the smaller rafts rushed away in the current, their crews yelling and *hoo-rawing* the day, paddles flashing in midair.

"Before we go, I want to give you a quick overview," Chris said.

To keep the smile on his face, Luke started talking. "I studied your entire booklet, and when you give instructions, I will demonstrate your catch phrase, 'River Listening.'"

His eyes widened. "You know what that means?"

"Yes, or as you would say, 'Yep.' I attend so closely to what you say, without judgment or criticism, that I can repeat back in my own words what you said."

Nobody could smile more quickly than Chris, and he didn't let Luke down. His eyes and teeth gleamed. "I will give you total details on this first section. All the countless little rapids can do you in just as well as the big rapids if you aren't careful. But once we pick up Lacy and her family, you will be distracted. While we're alone, I want to give you a thumbnail sketch of what's coming after Lacy. Let's look at the map."

"Good idea. You go, Chris."

Luke held onto the huge sweep, getting a feel for it. Then he sat back and listened.

"Once we get you into the groove, you'll be on your own," Chris explained. "You carry the rescue gear, and the first aid supplies. With your combat diving experience, if one of the rafts behind us flips, you'll be able to take immediate action. We can't row back upstream. That's why it's called the River of No Return. I'm supposed to go first to set up camp. After today, I'm not going to be able to be with you much."

He leaned forward, with a slight frown of concentration. "Here's my first worry for ya. At Indian Creek, where we pick up the two families, the Middle Fork suddenly takes a sharp turn. It plunges southeast toward Sunflower Hot Springs."

Luke glanced at the little creases on Chris's usually smooth forehead and listened carefully.

"A few hundred yards further, the river takes a sharp hairpin turn toward the northeast. There are many small changes in direction, and then we hit Loon Creek Hot Springs. We stop and relax and soak with another overnighter, to prepare ourselves for Tappan Falls, where the river takes another sharp turn."

He pointed at the map. "We pass Camas Creek coming in on the right and proceed in a northerly direction. All along here, we stop to do our geology shows. We stop and overnight at about River Mile 50. Further down the river, there's great fishing, and we take a little time to catch a few trout and salmon, and then throw them back. See the Flying B Ranch up on the left side? We stay overnight on the little beaches past there."

"So far, so good," Luke said.

Chris jumped in front of Luke, his arms upraised. "So repeat everything I just told you!"

Luke closed his eyes to concentrate and repeated the directions in his own words, as quickly as he could.

Chris grinned. "By Jove, I think you've got it." He pointed at Luke for emphasis. "The last two days are the most demanding. Impassable Canyon earns its name. Big intense rapids, one right after the other."

Luke interrupted. "Red Side, Webber, Cliffside, Ouzel, Hancock, Devil's Tooth, and House Rock, all before we float into the main Salmon."

"Yep, yep, yep. You've got it, man." He pointed. "Look over here. Waterfall Creek Rapids, then Big Creek rushes into us on the left side, and we proceed to the northeast. We hit River Mile 75. We stop near the Parrot cabin, right on the river. The next day, we'll see the Sheepeater Indian pictographs on the canyon walls on the right, just before we hit the confluence with the Main Salmon River."

Luke held up his hand. "I'm going to have to find a way to capture those Sheepeater pictographs."

Chris pointed one last time. "See this? When we hit the Main Salmon, we're jerked into a hard left turn, heading northwest. At Cache Bar takeout, we end our river rafting at River Mile 100. It's the wildest, most exciting hundred miles you will ever travel, I guarantee it!"

Chris stood up, reached forward, and untied the sweep. They jumped out to push off, and their sweep lumbered out into the middle fork of the Salmon like a killer whale on a daredevil waterslide. The Salmon was so deceptive in its narrowness that it seemed like a creek.

Luke recalled the uncommon frown Chris displayed a few minutes earlier when he told about his first worry, and realized the Middle Fork below the Indian Creek put-in was not his primary concern. Chris flashed his usual brilliant smile, as if he knew what Luke was thinking. "You steer, and for today, I'll be the navigator. We're on our way."

From an aerial view, the Middle Fork snakes through crusty canyon walls, its pristine and primordial green force tumbling through scattered stands of pines. Dusty dry mountainsides muscle in to crush down and dam up the Middle Fork's audacity as it flexes its gradient muscle, but to no avail. The river gathered allies here and there as it coursed downward for a rendezvous with the main Salmon River.

The Middle Fork takes no offense at the granite obstacles that tumble into its riverbed day and night, fair weather or foul. Along an extended front, the Fork refuses to accept defeat from larger and denser forces. It exercises an awesome power of flexibility as it flows around, through, under, over, and between the grey sedimentary and volcanic assassins that fill its bed and banks, crouching in a thousand battle stances. Between the rocky battlegrounds and volcanic battlefields, the Middle Fork rested in pools calm and serene, its brow unwrinkled, its purity sustained.

To the west lies the Salmon River suture zone, protecting river runners from the depths of Hells Canyon separating Idaho and Oregon. This zone traces an imaginary line between the little Idaho towns of McCall and Riggins, where the Pacific Ocean plates became subducted and where the western boundary of the North American sialic crust lies. It used to be part of the Continental Divide. The Middle Fork flows from the Sawtooth Range, through the Salmon River Range, and up to the Bitterroot Range.

Luke tried to chart his course between the whitewater swirls, whirlpools, souse holes, reversals and waterfalls, and the deep green eddy cushions and eddy fences. He looked ahead when he could. Victor and Chance headed up the small flotilla in the lead boat with all the supplies, rowing from the center in a sitting position. Ben manned the steering oar in the stern of the paddle boat, with four paddlers sitting in front of him. Chris stood tall and rode high in the front of Luke's sweep, arms uplifted in assurance and celebration of the day.

Luke shot a quick look back from his stern oar rig in the sweep boat, watching their Boundary Creek put-in disappear around a bend in the river. The sweep was such a strange-looking raft, as though two rafts were piled on top of each other, then covered with heavy black rubber sheeting around the bow, stern, and sides to blunt the damage levied by rocks and canyon sides. The stern rig oar was eighteen feet long, thrust through a rough rectangular opening and with a blade angled at the throat, looking more like a rudder.

54

There was no way to man the sweep sitting down. Luke stood on the poop deck platform, suddenly the tallest guide on the river. Nobody expected the sweep to look pretty as it navigated the wild river with its one-man crew. Luke did his best to stay in the middle of the current as they bumped and shucked their way down the white water. He set another oar rig in the front of the sweep, allowing him to steer from the bow to respond to any immediate obstacles.

Elkhorn Creek rushed in from the left and Luke had to avoid a house rock looming three feet above the rapids. He sweated past Soldier Creek and caught a glimpse of Walkers Peak on the left. This enabled him to keep his bearings, just in time to avoid Rapid River Creek from slamming into the sweep on the right and pushing it into a back eddy, which could trap him.

Chris watched closely, speaking only if he thought Luke was about to screw up. While Luke was grateful for the buddy system, he didn't want to let Chris down or disappoint him.

Velvet Falls Rapids approached fast. Chris warned Luke how many rafters had misjudged its strength by its seemingly harmless appearance. Luke steered to the middle of the channel, riding down the tongue, and headed for the clear chute between obstructions. The current was steeper and faster than the surrounding water. Downriver and around a bend, he watched the boil line, where upwelling water misled many rafters. Some of the surface current pulled upriver, while the undercurrent pushed the other way. Sweat beaded on his forehead.

Chris turned Luke's way and smiled. "Whoa, you're putting too much into this. Let up a bit, or you won't have the muscle you need for serious rapids like Pistol Creek."

"Okay." Luke grunted and leaned back on the huge oar, trying to catch his breath and regain his spirit. Running whitewater rapids had nothing to do with miles and hours. Its progress was measured in meters and minutes. The Middle Fork of the Salmon took Luke's measure, fifty challenging feet at a time, not the other way around. Every minute seemed like an hour while riding the rapids, his muscles straining, back twisting, legs balancing.

Soon, his body felt like it had just finished a half-marathon. On a hilly course. It seemed like afternoon. It was still midmorning.

"We're five miles past Velvet Creek Rapids!" Chris yelled.

Luke jumped at the news and barely scraped past a boulder fan from incoming Horn Creek on the left side. The sloping fan-shaped mass of boulders deposited by the tributary constricted the river and caused large rapids. Chris vaulted over to lend a hand.

More continuous rapids rolled underneath the sweep. Luke shifted his view constantly from upriver to downriver, from the front to the rear of his raft, watching for shifting bars and backrollers that formed beneath ledges. Many times, he came up to rocks and off-drops, only to hear Chris yell, "Do the Boof!"

Luke "boofed" the best he could, sliding over the surfaces so his raft landed level, the bottom down and boat on the surface. He learned the hard way not to land nose down and either dive deep or flip. That was the first slip he had years ago when he began to learn rafting techniques. Chance and Chris ragged on him every time they passed the same spot of the river.

A minute later, Chris taught Luke how to cartwheel. He had to. They were heading toward a big rock disaster in midstream. Luke didn't know what to do. Chris yelled, "Spin the raft just before we hit! We will rotate the raft off the rock."

Luke made the wild maneuver he didn't think he could do and they spun around.

Chris yelled, "See what you did? We didn't go into the rock. We went around the rock! Good going, man!"

A few seconds later, Chris waved his arms to get Luke's attention. "We're almost halfway to Indian Creek. We heading in for a lunch break. You need to rest a bit before you hit the next four rapids, because after them we hit Pistol Creek."

"What?" Luke bit his lip to stop groaning. Chris pointed, and Luke headed for a calm pool with a little beach on the side. Chris jumped out, tied them down, and rummaged in one of the dry bags underneath the poop deck. Luke jumped off the sweep and stretched out beneath a lodge pole pine next to a Douglas fir and Ponderosa grove. He tore off his tennis shoes and soaked in the sun. The rest of the crew lounged on a beach close by. Luke had no strength to walk over and visit.

Chris held up two box lunches and a six-pack of cold soda. "Up on the Montana Rez, the Indians call this Cherry Soda, 'Red Pop.' You'll love it."

They ate lunch while he gave Luke the rundown on the next section of nature's torture chambers. A half hour later, they started moving. Luke took time getting to his feet. "How about a six-pack to go?" Luke asked. His body felt like it should be sundown, but the sun soared high in the sky.

"Here come the rapids!" Chris yelled.

Luke felt like he was back in heavy artillery school at Fort Sill. With a wild yell he challenged Artillery Rapids, slinging out a slew of cowboy yee-haws and yodels as he rocketed past the River Pack Bridge Rapids. From one moment to another, he learned the difference between a chute and a channel. Chance warned him about the confluence of two rivers when they would experience the abrupt drop. He avoided plunging over any drop where the water fell freely. He learned the ferry maneuver, moving the raft laterally across a current. Chris also schooled him on gates, the short passages between two obstacles, before he zipped through Mortar Creek Rapids. He saw hanging tributaries, streams entering the Middle Fork through waterfalls, on the wall of the main canyon. Then he took one deep breath after another as he navigated through the incoming Cannon Creek Rapids.

Under these conditions, heightened awareness took on a different meaning than it had in Vietnam, but no less vital. Every cell of his being moved with the raft. He made the shift toward a vivid, energized way of seeing and experiencing the Middle Fork, which infused him with acceptance and appreciation. He felt like he was living in the middle of a predictable miracle.

Nothing in Sixth Weather Squadron, flying the Huey, or speeding past the enemy in his Cobra prepared him for this pell-mell rush down a wild river. Nothing in army combat diving prepared him for the tornadic torrents of water. Swimming a mile in the surf off Coronado Island in California did nothing to prepare him for the Middle Fork. Luke was glad Chris could not hear his heart pounding or his lungs straining to capture more fresh air.

"Get ready for the last biggee on day one—Pistol Creek Rapids," Chris yelled. "Ben calls it Russian Roulette. You don't know which chamber is going to get you."

Sufficiently forewarned, Luke began running the famous Pistol Creek Rapids with heightened awareness and a quick prayer. It didn't matter.

"Stay away from the inside!"

They accelerated into a lower S curve, Chris's warning swallowed up by the swirling waters. Luke jammed the oar to guard against a house boulder on his near left. He headed toward the three huge rocks looming in midstream but remained in the middle of the S curve. He cranked the oar blade madly to the right for forty feet and then madly to the left, so he could ultimately sail parallel to the homicidal granite obstructions. He steered for the outside, as if he wanted to kill himself on those huge raft-killers, but at the last minute, the main current caught the raft and sharply swept him to the left. Feeling like he might pass out, he shot past the Pistol Creek rocks to his right.

Chris gave Luke thumbs up. He had said before that most greenhorns hugged the inside of the Middle Fork, sure that they would get past the three rocks in that manner, only to find the inside course sending them straight into the maw of the granitic trio.

"You did it, Luke! You came through the first run! You pulled perfect on Pistol Creek. You've just about done your first whitewater marathon as a professional rafter!"

"What do you mean marathon?" Had Chris lost his grip? Luke stared at him, the skin stretching on his frowning face.

"You've got twenty miles of whitewater behind you and under your belt. Another five miles or so and you'll just about have your marathon by the time we beach at Indian Creek."

Luke leaned on the big oar, took his eye off the river, aimed the sweep down the center of a stretch of the Middle Fork pockmarked with whitewater, and looked over at Chris. "And I thought hop-scotching a Huey through a jungle canopy into enemy territory every day was a challenge," he yelled, his voice and chin raised.

He should have known better. Just after he said that, Chris yelled, "Luke, man the bow oar! That whirlpool is going to drag us right into that sleeper rock!"

Luke scrambled up to the bow and dug in the oar, then cranked it to port side. The river roared in his ears as the sweep rushed toward the big hole. Instead of dropping nose first into the deep hole and flipping the monster raft upside down—which could have crushed Chris—Luke swung its rear end around and caught the lip of the whirlpool on its outer edge. Their forward momentum saved them as they caromed past the gaping hole. It transfixed him as he hovered for a moment above it. The whirlpool center looked like the mouth of a monster racing from the blackest depths. All the surrounding whitewater waves were tentacles of huge, hungry squids, reaching out to pull them into their mouths.

The rear end of the sweep whirled around and yanked Luke into death's watery grasp. He lost his balance and fell overboard. Even dropping like a rock in his Huey, with the engine killed in autorotation, was nothing compared to dropping into the mouth of this aqueous monster.

With lightning quickness, Chris clutched the side of the raft, reached down and hauled Luke aboard before he disappeared underwater.

"You got your baptism," he announced. "No full-water immersion. We never know when that whirlpool might kick in. You okay?"

"I'm good. I don't know about baptism, but I feel saved. Thanks, buddy."

Luke stood up, wiping water out of his hair and eyes. Chris slapped him on the back. "Let's turn this baby around."

They proceeded backward down the river. During a lull in the whitewater, they swapped oars and Luke returned to the back of the sweep, trying to regain his "Stone Cold" nickname from army combat diving.

When the memory of how he gained that nickname flashed through his mind, Luke reasserted his calm warrior stance. Chris moved back to the middle of the raft. After a moment, he pointed at Luke and began to laugh. "I got you! I got you! You just about killed us, but I got you!"

"What are you talking about?"

He howled in glee. "I got the combat pilot to let his guard down!"

Chastened, Luke shielded his eyes from the sun and peered upriver, determined to never be caught off guard again. "What did you have on me, a bet that I'd flip the raft?"

"Oh, yeah!" he grinned. "Chance bet me twenty bucks you'd flip the sweep on the first day. I stood up for you and bet you would not."

"I am glad you won the bet. You sure did your part."

"Chance said to me, 'Chris, you can't make it easy on him. Don't *you* be the vigilant one. That's his job. You have got to get his guard down. I'll bet you another twenty you can't get his guard down. He's coming off combat missions.'"

Luke shook his head. "I can't believe it. You had to prove Chance wrong, so you set me up?"

Chris shrugged good-naturedly. "You know how I am with money. I couldn't let Chance win either of those bets."

"It's not enough to master the whitewater. On top of that, Chance had you betting against me! My own diving buddy. I think he got you on that one."

Chris laughed. "I wouldn't put it past him. Business comes first. He doesn't want friendship to get in the way of safety. You are the one you have to prove yourself to. He wants your learning curve to go skyward. Sometimes, the best way to learn is through mistakes."

Luke shook his head. "It's always good to know who's on my side."

A few minutes later, his renewed vigilance paid off. Chris was studying the Douglas fir along the surrounding canyon walls, trying to spot wildlife. Luke saw the lump of blue water ahead to the right, flowing over a submerged log.

"Hey, Chris, come over here!" He gently aimed the sweep toward the log and then moved up the deck toward the left side, pointing toward the water. "Look at the size of that steelhead!"

Luke leaned back and grabbed the oar for stability. Chris hustled over to the left side of the raft and leaned over to look, just as the right side struck the submerged log with a huge thump. The sweep tipped violently and Chris catapulted into the Middle Fork, arms and legs flailing as he desperately tried to stay on the sweep.

"I got you! I got you!" Luke howled. He brought the sweep around in time to catch Chris who was treading water madly.

"Man overboard!" Luke announced as he dropped Chris a rope. Chris rolled over the side and climbed aboard, wet, cold, and smiling ruefully. "I should have known you'd do that."

"That's the military mind," Luke said. "Don't get mad. Get even."

A minute later he pointed. "Is that Indian Creek beach coming up on the left?"

Chris yelled, "Hell, yeah!"

As he steered ahead, Luke said, "What's the rest of the crew going to think about the rookie and the Chief River Guide being all wet?"

Chris roared with laughter. "I'll figure something out. Tomorrow, we'll be rafting down the river and you'll want to look good for Lacy. Just when you think you've got her impressed with your skills, wham-o! You'll fall overboard like a rookie. And I will get Lacy to fish you out!"

Chris laughed so hard that his clothes shook, hastening their drying in the arid canyon air. They sailed to Indian Creek beach, where the other two boats were already onshore.

The rest of the whitewater crew watched them. A hundred yards of sandy beach welcomed the raft, and calm surface blue water replaced the murderous deep green water of the Middle Fork canyons. Gentle swells of lowlands, grasses, and groves of lodge pole pines signaled relief from the claustrophobic canyon walls. Indian Creek was a flood plain of a river valley. The openness made it a natural place for an adjacent airstrip.

Chris pointed. "Bring the sweep over there."

Luke jumped out to pull the raft. When he neared the shore, Ben, Victor, Chance, and the others helped to drag the monster raft out of the water. Victor nodded. "You guys made good time." He gestured toward Luke. "Chris, you have any problems with the rookie?"

Chris shook his head. "We're here on time, aren't we? No damage to the raft. No problems."

Ben shook Luke's hand. "Good going, Luke. I've got a mess of fish ready to fry."

Chris walked over to check all the equipment. Chance and Luke went into separate tents, changed clothes, and came out to relax and wait for the plane. Before they knew it, a Salmon Air twin-engine flew low overhead, buzzing the camp, waggling its wings. Chance nudged Luke. "There's hotshot Melvin, still flying like he's in Vietnam. He was an FAC."

Luke stared at the plane. "He went from Forward Air Control to bush pilot? I hope he's not on his ninth life. You know those guys have a very short lifespan."

"No worries about Melvin. Let's hope the De'Luca and Wilder families haven't gotten airsick."

Luke had an ominous thought, *What if they get seasick on the whitewater? That will take all the fun out of the adventure. To say nothing of campfire romance.*

Luke walked over to Chris. "How much time have we got before they get here?"

"Fifteen or twenty minutes. They'll be expecting a good dinner. You have got to show your hand at cooking on the river too, Luke."

"Why me?" Luke groaned. "If airsickness doesn't get them, I hope my cooking will not get them either."

55

United Flight 787 from Chicago to Boise brought the De'Luca and Wilder families together in closer proximity than usual. In row six, Mr. De'Luca sat across the aisle on the left, while his best friend Amos Wilder sat on the right side. Russ Wilder and Lacy's brother, Brent, sat behind Mr. Wilder and Lacy sat behind her father with Laurie Wilder. Neither Mrs. De'Luca nor Mrs. Wilder would ever go on such an excursion.

Lacy glanced around, musing how she and Russ seated across the aisle could share ideas. After her return and reconciliation with Luke and the Sixth Weather Reunion, any interaction with Russ proved awkward. Wade and Amos could discuss business, Russ and Brent could share their anticipation of the rafting trip. Laurie and Lacy had been close friends forever.

At times, Lacy reverted back to her role in her youth—she wanted everyone to have fun and enjoy each other's company. About an hour before landing she brought out a handful of journals with a brochure tucked into each one celebrating the newly opened Middle Fork of the Salmon River. She got up and handed them out to each member. "Every night, if we survive the day on the river, we can keep a journal on our adventures. It will be hard to take photos pitching around on those rafts."

Lacy opened her journal and found quotes she had copied years ago when she was determined to find her voice. American history and American freedom and emancipation of all kinds were her favorites. She loved Thomas Paine's writing and his role in American history. Abigail Adams was her first heroine, the woman who spoke out on gender issues a hundred fifty years before the country began grappling with them. The first quote came from Paine. The next five quotes she had copied were from Abigail Adams. The final quote was Lacy's, back when she protested the very war in which Luke was fighting.

"Youth is the seed time of good habits, as well in nations as in individuals."
—Thomas Paine, *Common Sense* (1776)

"I long to hear that you have declared an independency. And in the new code of laws, which I suppose it will be necessary for you to make, I desire you would remember the ladies, and be more generous and favorable to them than your ancestors."
—Abigail Adams to John Adams, 1774

"Do not put such unlimited power into the hands of husbands. Remember all men would be tyrants if they could. If particular care and attention is not paid to the ladies we are determined to foment a rebellion, and will not hold ourselves bound by any laws in which we have no voice, or representation."
—Abigail Adams, letter to John Adams, March 31, 1776

"If we mean to have heroes, statesmen, and philosophers, we should have learned well-educated women. If much depends as is allowed upon the early education of youth and the first principles, which

are instilled take the deepest root, great benefit must arise from literary accomplishments in women."
—Abigail Adams (1744–1818),
letter to John Adams, August 14, 1776

"I will never consent to have our sex considered an inferior point of light. Let each planet shine in its own orbit. God and nature designed it so—if man is Lord, woman is Lordess—that is what I contend for."
—Abigail Adams (1744–1818), letter to
Eliza Peabody, her sister, July 19, 1779

"The Boy is a Freeman as much as any of the young Men, and merely because his Face is Black, is he to be denied instruction? I have not thought it any disgrace to myself to take him into my parlor and teach him both to read and write."
—Abigail Adams (1744–1818), letter
to John Adams, February 13, 1797

"The Vietnam War: I am simply amazed at America's inability to question its leadership. Americans have been so cowed by the specter of enemies abroad, so terrified of the boogeyman lurking in the shadows of the world that they blindly accept whatever the current administration decides is best. The wisdom or foolishness of its policies is irrelevant. No one has yet been willing to challenge them, as they should."
—Lacy De'Luca, Vietnam War Protest,
Streets of Chicago, Summer 1968

* * * * * * * * * * * * * *

The contents of Lacy's journal' shocked her. Surely Luke must be part of the problem Abigail wrote about. *What will Luke think? He must know I am his worst critic.* She thought about the two families converging on him. Luke had not seen any of these family members for years. Maybe decades. What would he think when he saw them? Her father and Mr. Wilder would not believe he was a registered assistant boatman. They knew nothing of his Special Forces medal, his DFC, and his Silver Star. They didn't know about his unique Leadership Degree from the University of Arizona.

She thought about the similarities of the families. Both Chicagoland families included four children. Dad and Mom (from the De'Luca family) had Kate, Courtney, Lacy, and Brent. Only Dad, Brent, and Lacy would ride the river. Amos Wilder and Beth (from the Wilder family) had four children as well: Clint, Russell, Adam, and Laurie. Only Mr. Wilder, Russ, and Laurie would whitewater. She looked in front where her father sat. *What would Luke's relationship be like with Dad? I hope they put the past behind them. It sounded like Luke had, from what he said at the Weather Squadron.*

This will be a decisive trip, she thought, *in many ways.* She looked at her dad, studying him. De'Luca stood just less than six feet tall. Even when he traveled out to the wilderness for adventure, he always dressed in his latest suit and tie, a habit from his early days as a clothing store owner. His dark hair remained impeccably combed, with shorter length on the sides and short sideburns, although she still liked to see him in the mornings with his hair akimbo. He had a striking forehead with a curly front wave. His blue-grey eyes shone clearly beneath the arch of his eyebrows. His cheekbones were a trifle high, like hers, and his nose was straight and just the right size. She always thought of French and Italian nobility when she looked at Dad. He had the Italian flair for fashion.

Out of the corner of her eye, she secretly studied Russ Wilder, who loomed large in the row seat across the aisle from her. He avidly read books about feeding millions of starving people in underprivileged countries. He cared about the poor and the deprived just as she did. Russ stood six foot two, tall for his age even by the time he turned fourteen. With dark brown hair, mature manners, a high forehead along with an immense vocabulary and a huge smile, he was successful in business, astute with men, and had great charisma with women. Lacy wondered why he wasn't married and why he hung around her in such a non-committal way.

She had known him since he was seven. Lacy knew Russ had a quick, inquiring mind, and easily passed for an adult when he entered his freshman year of high school. Quick with his hands, at age sixteen he could operate heavy machinery for his father's construction company—even a hundred-forty-ton DP crane—and he owned his first plane before he was twenty-five. His mature outlook and hard work was rewarded with great entry-level jobs in his father's businesses.

Later, when awarded a scholarship in a work/study program in foreign affairs at Northwestern University, he finished college ahead of time and began work for his uncle, a colonel who had a top management job in a CIA unit. She knew subsequently he had learned three new languages and had since traveled extensively. *Uh-oh*, she thought. *Never home. What kind of life is that?* He got bored easily with women. He also expected a woman to be like his mother, always home, always there.

Wait a minute! I spent two years on my own in Jamaica! My parents do not see how different Russ and I are.

Lacy felt better when she reviewed the checklist. She had everything she needed. Two sets of clothing—one for the river and one for camp. Her swimsuit would be the first layer, covered by quick-drying shorts; also both tennis shoes and sandals, wool socks, long-sleeved shirts, fleece sweater or jacket for the cool nights and steep canyons where sunshine arrived late and left early. She'd also need a hat, bike gloves for paddling, baseball cap with visor, protector, rain jacket and pants, and hiking boots for day hikes.

Then her mind drifted. As an assistant boatman, Luke would be the only person in the sweep, though it carried rescue equipment and safety equipment. *And*, she thought with a happy grin, *his special guest*. Instead of proceeding ahead of the other boats, he would follow behind them, so he could learn from the more experienced river guides. But she knew his combat diving experience could save any person flipped off the raft.

The seatbelt sign flashed. Lacy smiled. In twenty minutes, she'd be in the same state as Luke—for the second time in a week after not seeing him for five years!

56

All six De'Luca and Wilder family members filed off the flight and walked through the airport, headed for the Salmon Air counter, where the small plane would transport them to the Indian Creek airfield. Lacy's dad handed her the itinerary. After they boarded the ten-passenger aircraft, she scanned through the coming days of Chisholm and Wolfe Whitewater Adventure:

> 25 Mile Middle Fork Marker:
> Past Boundary Creek. Indian Creek Airfield and
>   Put-In:
> Chisholm Whitewater crew coming from
>   Boundary Creek, 0 Mile Marker.
> De'Luca Family and Wilder Family arrive @ 6 pm
>
> 37 Mile Marker:
> Loon Creek Hot Springs
> Past Marble Rapid, Grouse Rapid, Tappan Falls
>   Rapid, Camas Creek
> Geology Views
> Fishing
>
> 60 Mile Marker near Flying B Ranch
> Soldier Cr., Wilson Creek, Big Creek
> Into Impassable Canyon

Into Redside Rapid, Porcupine Rapid, Cliffside
Rapid, Weber Rapid

Lacy sat by the window of the little plane, read the itinerary, and daydreamed about each day's events and activities. She marveled at the mountainous landscape unfolding below her as she nibbled on her box lunch, trying to ward off feelings of excitement. But soon a lack of sleep and a warm afternoon enfolded her. A nap caught her in a weak moment, and it wasn't until the changed pitch of the twin-engine transport caught her attention that she opened her eyes to a campground on the river below.

The plane tilted left and then right. Lacy realized the pilot was signaling the whitewater crew below. She peeked out the little port-hole and saw a familiar figure standing near the campfire waving.

Luke!

The shuttle ride seemed more like a magic carpet to Lacy. She couldn't feel any of the bumps and ruts along the dirt road. Before she could take a deep breath, the little bus pulled into the Indian Creek put-in campground's parking space. The driver welcomed them at the bottom of the steps, reaching forward to take Lacy's arm with one hand and her luggage with the other. After everybody got off the bus, Mr. De'Luca, Mr. Wilder, Russ, Brent, and Laurie made a beeline for the guest tents.

Not Lacy. She wasn't even the first in line. She dawdled at the end, pulled out a handkerchief, and pretended that she needed to blow her nose and wipe the dust off her forehead.

Looking demurely down at the ground, a moment later she saw a pair of familiar tennis shoes appear magically in front of her. All the air rushed out of her lungs when she lifted her head and slowly took in the whole view of Luke. Only three feet away, he stood smiling the biggest smile, with a warm, smoky campfire smell radiating off his shoulders.

He stepped forward. "Lacy, you're here. You really came!" He paused to take her in. "I've waited my whole life to relive the moments we had as kids." He leaned forward and swept her into his arms, kissing her without even thinking about it. Then he recovered with a start and stepped back, looking over toward her father and Russ Wilder, even though their backs were turned away from him.

"Don't worry, Luke." Lacy smiled. "You and I will have time to catch up over the campfires. I am so excited we are both here. It's just like you used to say, "*We* are meant to *be*. She stepped forward and hugged Luke as if she'd never let him go. "Oooooo, I love this," she murmured. "It is meant to be."

Luke looked over toward the tents. "Do they even know I am here?"

She rocked back on her heels. "No-o-o—not yet, but they will soon enough."

"Are you ready for dinner?"

"Give me a few minutes. I'll see you at the campfire."

Luke served Lacy dinner from the grill, fresh salmon, baked potatoes with butter, chives, and sour cream in tinfoil, fresh green beans from a garden in Stanley, rich red Merlot from the Columbia Crest winery, and blueberry cobbler. Ben and Victor tossed up a full garden salad. Everybody was happy. After dinner, the rafting party set chairs around the campfire, made introductions, and told related stories both wildly funny and wildly dangerous.

Wade and Amos managed to live through the news that Luke was a member of Wolfe Whitewater. Chris was meticulous as he introduced the Wolfe team. "Chance, Luke, and I all learned whitewater rafting together a long time ago, when we were just out of high school. Chance has been able to come up twice a year and has become one of my best lead guides. He will be the lead guide on this trip."

When he came to Luke, he said, "Luke LaCrosse and I went through army combat diver training program together when we were in ROTC down in Arizona. Now he's an Army captain, a command helicopter pilot, and he's using his R and R from combat flying in the Mekong Delta to help us out as an assistant boatman."

Russ Wilder congratulated Luke. "I will tell you about my combat duty some day, Luke. I have a feeling you and I should be friends."

"Thanks, Russ," Luke managed. "I've never been on the same side of the table with you."

"I'm sorry about that, Luke," Russ said softly. "I'm just a great friend of the family. Of course, I think Lacy's the greatest thing to hit Chicago since the Bears. But if Lacy has found somebody she loses sleep over, then God bless you both. I'd be happy for you."

Luke nearly fell into the campfire. What a great guy! So it was all just a misunderstanding. All the years of hurt and hard feelings flew up in the sky along with the campfire smoke. It wasn't Russ's doing. Relieved, he sat next to the campfire. Hmmmm. *So I guess Lacy was badly hurt and angry that I hadn't trusted her. After all our history, and all the way she had come to see me in Hawaii.*

After Russ and Luke sat down beside each other, both fathers came over and thanked Luke for his service. Both of them commended him for becoming an officer and a pilot. They accepted his role on the rafting trip but then leaned in to ask, "Then who will take care of us fishermen?"

"You'll ride in the oar boat with Victor or Ben," Luke said. "There may be a few calm pools between the rapids."

"Thank you for taking time off to help your friend, Luke. He speaks very highly of you. We all feel safer knowing you and he both have combat diving experience."

"You are welcome," Luke managed to say. He was relieved and happy beyond belief.

"Okay, everyone, sit down," Chance called out. "It's time that Ben led us in some songs."

With his old camp guitar, Ben took requests from the audience. Most of the songs were Western, all new to the De'Luca family. Toward the end, because Luke loved the Sons of the Pioneers, Ben helped them sing all through "Cool Water," "Home on the Range," and "Happy Trails to You." The rest of the night flowed as smoothly as the wine. Luke stayed up to wash dishes and watch the campfire. Everybody else fell asleep. Chance had given a short safety talk before dinner and promised a longer one after breakfast on the following day.

A half hour after everybody was asleep, Lacy left her sleeping brother Brent, slipped out of her tent, and walked over to the campfire. She and Luke shared a soft late-night chat, talking about life as if there were yesterday and no tomorrow.

They moved closer, sitting cross-legged firmly side by side, and the moon stood still. Luke's body language mimicked Lacy's. Her eye contact reflected the fire's flames, warm and constant. Lacy's pupils were large and her lips were parting. They held hands as if they could never let the other one go, disappear, or fade away. That had happened at least once too often. They had no awareness of anybody else in the camp. Soon they didn't reflect the campfire, they were the campfire. The soft darkness surrounded them and held them together. Praise and compliments and nodded affirmations were visible and literally sensible to any curious black bear watching at river's edge.

The moon waxed and waned until the stars emerged, galaxies within the lost-lovers' gaze. Luke folded Lacy in his arms and kissed her again and again until she kissed back, murmuring with each kiss. And then the talking was all kissing. Even the deep, savoring breaths between their long kisses were magic. Luke's combat awareness disappeared. For the first time in months, he relaxed.

The stars began to fade, and then vanish into the cloak of daylight. Luke disengaged himself carefully and pulled Lacy to her feet. "We've got to get some sleep, honey, or tomorrow the guys will laugh when I flip over."

"What about me?" Lacy said, kissing him one more time. "I'm going to ride with you and keep your mind on important things, not just the rafting."

Luke awoke to the smell of coffee brewing and bacon sizzling. At 7:30 a.m., Lacy made his day. She appeared with the other early birds and took a chair in the camp semi-circle. Ben and Luke sprang into action, getting Lacy, Russ, and Brent little trays with steaming cups of coffee, freshly squeezed orange juice and slices of cantaloupe and watermelon. Lacy's smile warmed up the whole canyon. "Whoever thought I'd see the day," she said.

Luke laughed. "I think snow leopards can change their spots, too, so let's never say never, Lacy."

Chris stood by as Chance, Victor, Dakota, and the other guides stepped up to put on a full breakfast by 8:00 a.m. Some stood back to back at the grills and campfires, while others stood at the tall table to serve their dozen guests as each filed by with his or her own tray. Chance performed double duty by serving them as well. If any trays were still empty by the time they reached Chance, he announced, "For all those who want to eat light, we have fruit, yogurt, and cereal. The little milk containers are in the cooler beneath the table here."

57

After breakfast, while the rest of the team packed the gear and stowed it on the rafts and sweep, Chance began his safety talk to the guests, who were seated in a semi-circle. Everybody was dressed in river running clothes: bathing suits underneath, tan and khaki shorts, mostly short sleeve shirts—some plain, others wildly colorful—and tennis shoes.

There were twelve river runners, including an attractive couple from South America, Mitch and Gaynelle Mayer, who brought their British accents and a nine-year-old. There was also Krista, an attractive teacher in her thirties who ran a Montessori school in Northern California. A father and son duo, Gregory and Jonathan, came from North Carolina. Gregory had been given the adventure as a seventieth birthday gift.

Chance wasted no time. Although he had introduced the team the previous night, he made a more formal introduction of the other six river guides along with Luke, who stood behind him.

Chance beckoned to Kent and Ernie. "Let me start. Here's Kent and Ernie, Mr. Deep and Mr. Shallow."

Everybody laughed. Chance continued as if he hadn't cracked a joke. "Kent is the tall guy with sandy hair and the quick sense of humor who works well in deep water. Ernie is the short guy with blond hair and glasses who works well in shallow water. They will take turns on the oar boats."

Everybody clapped as Kent and Ernie bowed facetiously.

Chance beckoned to the other river runners. "Here's Victor, Jerry, Ben, Dakota, and Luke. They will take turns on the paddle rafts and two of them are trained on the sweep. Dakota and Luke, my buddies from Sixth Weather Squadron, will take turns on manning the big sweep. Luke, our assistant boatman, with the help of Chris, brought the big sweep down from Boundary Creek put-in yesterday."

Everybody laughed. "Jerry, here, don't his high cheekbones and long black braids give away his Native American bloodline? He says the Cherokee Nation ran rapids in what is now the Carolinas and Georgia before Columbus arrived. With him as the paddle captain, you will be either paddling or in 'the position'—your oar handle held high and forward at arm's length, to plunge the blades down as deep as you can.

"Ben is our worm-and-stick fisherman, who can catch fish faster than a fly fisherman. He's quick, always busy, good with a guitar and singing around the campfire. Don't think he's from below the border, though. He's proud of his Basque heritage from the high mountains of Spain and knows a thing or two about fishing. Let's hear it for our paddle-raft men!"

Everybody applauded, and then the four stepped back behind Chance. He led the guests through a quiz on definitions of the various classes of whitewater rapids. "Okay, somebody give me a definition of a Class I whitewater."

Brent De'Luca raised his hand and hollered, "Slow flow, no rapids, no fun, and good for sun-soaking, little kids, and grandparents." Everybody laughed.

Chance responded, "Right. Now, does the Middle Fork of the Salmon River have any Class I whitewater?"

Jason raised his hand. "No, sir! We didn't come to raft on Class I."

Chance smiled and nodded. "Right again. A hundred miles and a hundred rapids! Wolfe Whitewater river guides don't mess with Class I here. How about Class II whitewater and what is it good for?"

Krista raised her hand and waited to be recognized. Chance nodded. "Class II whitewater is mostly slow, some splashes of whitewater but good for swimming," she said.

"Good answer. Give that teacher an apple. Who is ready to run on the Class III whitewater? How would you describe it?"

Lacy raised her hand. Her answer floated past Luke on the morning breeze. "Class III gets exciting, there's moderate whitewater but less chance of spills."

"Nice job. You must have done your homework. Do I have anybody rooting for Class IV whitewater and what makes it different?"

To the surprise of Russ and his father, Amos, Laurie raised her hand and waved it wildly. "I love challenges! Sign me up! Class IV rapids are for people like me, adventurers. You get heavy whitewater, boulder gardens, some good drops, and above average soakings!"

Chance smiled but held up his hand. "Your courage is commendable. After you have proven yourself, Laurie, we will give you the opportunity to try Class IV rapids. But you will need a helmet and then show us the correct technical skills first."

Amos raised his hand. "Chance, most of us are trying this for the first time. Please tell us how we can get our skills up to speed quickly. I read that last winter, the snows gave the Snake and Salmon River basins over 110 percent runoff for this summer."

Chance grinned with delight. "That's right. That's why we are experiencing spring runoff all the way through August. Helmets are a must. But only experienced paddlers and hardcore adventurers get the chance to run these. We actually have a swimming and fitness test that rafters have to pass first."

Wade raised his hand. "We're all here to have fun and enjoy the adventure. Let's just keep it that way. Call me Wade, not Mr. De'Luca."

Chance laughed. "You're right, Wade. We don't start off with the big ones anyway. Today we go past a couple creeks and smaller rapids and then go through a little challenge, Marble Creek Rapids." Everybody smiled. "Under no circumstances do we want to broach—or turn the raft sideways to the current. In heavy water, that spells certain upset. Every raft has a rope bag. Any rafter who goes overboard becomes a swimmer." He drew everyone in a circle around him. "I am going to give you our boat descriptions one more time.

Partly so you will remember which boat you are on, and partly to use if you ever want to change from one boat to another.

"First, the paddle boat: anybody like plenty of exercise? This boat is about fourteen or fifteen feet long, powered by strokes of six or eight members of the paddle crew. Depending on the danger of the river, one and maybe two of the paddlers will be our own river-runners. The river guide sits in the stern and gives paddle commands. Sometimes we have a youngster to call out the count from the front.

"Second: the oar boat with paddles. This boat is sixteen to eighteen feet long, carries gear and supplies and from one to four guests who are just along for the ride, and four paddlers. The river guide sits in the stern with two huge oars and at least four paddlers sit in the front. His assistant will spell him. Depending on the danger, two paddlers may be one of our crew.

"Third: the oar boat. This boat carries gear and supplies, even a kayak, and from one to four guests. The river guide sits in the middle, and does all the work with two huge oars going out each side. No paddles. One assistant.

"Fourth: the kayak. This one-person craft or the two-person craft is just eight to ten feet long. This 'rubber ducky' is available only to those with prior experience. We bring one of each to give you a demonstration. You have to wear helmets and at time wetsuits. Kayaking is not allowed for guests until well below Boundary Creek, and past Indian Creek. This is the ultimate vessel for the active river runner. You have the whole trip to learn how to kayak. Just watch Chris.

"If you are a swimmer, always go downriver feet first on your back, using the backstroke. Whoever is closest to the rope bag, throw the rope to the swimmer. Grab and hold onto it. Before you know it, we'll have you hauled safely aboard your raft."

"Each raft captain will answer any question you have."

Chance and Chris loaded everybody into the various boats.

The paddle boat came first, captained by Chance and spelled by Victor. Krista and Brent on the right, Laurie and Jason on the left, while Ernie and Jerry sat on either side for a total of six paddlers. Lacy wanted to paddle in the front.

Then the oar boat with paddles followed. This was captained by Ben and spelled by Kent. The four paddlers were Mitch, Gaynelle, Greg, and Jonathan, ten people in all.

The oar boat, or sweep, came along third and was manned by Luke with two huge oars, spelled by Dakota. No paddlers but room for up to four guests. The sweep carried a pair of kayaks for the daring and qualified guests, and it served as the cleanup boat, picking up anybody who got flipped out of the first two rafts.

Chris took the kayak anywhere he was needed, from first boat to fourth. He knew Chance could handle the trip as lead guide, but Chris was mobile. He was the ace in the hole. He could scoot across the rapids and help any of the three rafts.

They were all on their way. Luke couldn't believe he went along with the two dads' request that Russ and Lacy ride with them. Wade and Amos rode the oar raft with Russ and Lacy, captained by Victor and assisted by Ernie; Mitch, Gaynelle, Greg, and Jonathan rode the oar raft with paddles, captained by Ben, assisted by Kent; Krista, Brent, Laurie, and Jason rode a paddle boat captained by Chance, assisted by Jerry. Luke brought up the rear on the sweep.

They pushed off from the Indian Creek put-in. Once they reached shallow water, Chance called all four crafts together. Jerry jumped out and held all four ropes.

Chance looked around at the rafters. "There are a few terms I want you to know before we start. The first is Bow Jumper. Today, that's Jerry. He gets off the raft, pulls it to shore and holds that raft. Every time we put in to shore, you'll see how important this job is. How many of you have rowed a boat sitting backwards?"

Most raised their hands. Chance nodded and smiled. "Good! We need two more bow jumpers. "Remember, both the oar captain and paddle boat captain have got to see where they are going. They row forward. The second term is River Signals. We always use river signals to point in the direction we want someone to go. We never use signals to point to where we don't want you to go. A very important term to remember. Your safety may depend on it.

"Any questions? Okay, let's go!"

Jerry jumped back on board. They retrieved their ropes, then paddled, oared, and swept their way through the flat water. Soon, they shot through the first rapid—three sets of whitewater, a big rock on the left, rocks in the middle, and water cascading down the center. Luke didn't have time to check the other three crafts. The chute he entered was twice as fast as the water to the left of the rapid. To the right was flat water. All of a sudden, the midstream dropped five feet straight down and the sweep flew through three mini-waterfalls.

They reached calm water for a small stretch. Upstream, Luke saw Victor and Ernie's paddle boat out in front, followed by Ben and Kent's oar raft. The whitewater tipped the rafts left and then hard right. The second raft slid and then flipped high in the air over the tilted rocks. Chance and Jerry appeared immediately with the paddle boat to flip the oar raft right side up. Ben and Kent climbed back into the oar raft, Ben with his oar firmly gripped so he would not injure any swimmers.

Gaynelle had flown out first. Greg, Mitch and Jonathan tried wildly to recover, but they splashed into the waves right behind the first two. Gaynelle flinched and looked wildly around, calling out in a wavering voice. Greg flapped his hands in a panic and his head went under the water. Jonathan clenched his teeth and swatted at the foaming river. Mitch was determined. He had prepared for obstacles and strategized how to overcome them. When he hit the water, he immediately began to swim toward Victor and Ernie who back-paddled the lead Oar raft toward those in the water. Mitch was first in the lead raft, followed by Gaynelle, who needed the most help.

Greg and Jonathan were all smiles when they climbed aboard. They had gone from paralyzing fear back to life again.

On the sweep, Luke and Dakota picked up Lacy first, because she was closest, then Wade, Amos, and Russ. Luke paddled between the rafts to provide a temporary mobile dock for the guest transfer. They all tied together, got shipshape, and set off again.

"Next stop is Loon Creek Hot Springs," Chance shouted. "Remember, if whitewater rafting was easy, anybody could do it. Today you got your baptism. Total immersion! And you bounced right back—onto your boat. Now you are real river-runners." Everybody cheered. "We do the flip just so you will all enjoy the soak."

They navigated down the easy Loon Creek tributary on the right and pulled in at Loon Creek Hot Springs. They all soaked in the long concrete basin built by the side of the Middle Fork. The forty-foot-long, four-foot-wide trough was constructed of wood and set up against a gentle riverbank of rocks and grasses, surrounded by heavy undergrowth above and below the tub. It was easy to fit everybody into the tub. And everybody needed the break and the comfort. Luke and Lacy found a way to relax together without being too obvious. Afterward, the river crew served lunch and everybody relaxed in the shade. Lacy came over and got her wish: she wanted to ride with Luke and Dakota on the sweep. She thought it safer.

"We went through twelve rapids in twelve miles." Chance pointed up on the canyon walls. "Look at the bighorn ram."

The ram stood on a ledge far above, visible against the sky with a sturdy tan body and white rump, his huge horns erupting from his head. The horns curved into a nearly complete circle behind his head to emerge at points just below and behind his eyes. Luke saw it as nature's way—survival of the fittest—protecting the ram's neck and eyes from the cougar's customary leap from above.

Rafters pulled out cameras to take photos, oohing and aahing. Then they jumped back into their rafts.

Chance yelled, "Okay, people, we go through Grouse Rapid and then Tappan Falls is coming up. Get ready!"

Luke felt safe in the big old sweep. It didn't seem to tip, but he had to keep it in the middle of the current. They navigated through Grouse Rapid. The oar boat, with its rafters yelling, cart-wheeled around a huge rock. Luke could see Victor using the double-oar turn, pulling on one oar while pushing on the other.

Chance yelled back, "Luke, heavy water coming! Fast current, large waves from holes and boulders! Watch out for the turbulence!"

Luke looked downstream with horror. There was nothing but whitewater.

They approached the Marble Canyon rapid. Steep canyon walls confronted them, with a huge fissure running diagonally down to the river. Just at that moment, the Paddle Boat hit a standing wave caused by obstacles on the river bottom and it rocked to the left. Screams and paddle flashes ensued.

"The front paddlers thought that standing wave would propel them forward, not slap them backward!" Chance yelled back from the second boat.

"Brace yourself so you won't fall forward."

Just as Luke stood tall, Victor's paddle boat shot over the main falls and down a steep, ten-foot drop. Water poured in from both sides of the Middle Fork. The raft went up and then plunged down, its bow dipping far beneath the water. All six rafters disappeared in foam. The front of the raft rose and flipped on top of all the rafters.

Luke waggled his stern oar as fast as he could to arrive on the scene.

This time, Ben's oar boat was full of saviors, not swimmers. They back-paddled and picked up all six lead rafters. Chance rushed madly after the lead raft, caught up with it, grabbed the handy trailing rope, and flipped the raft right side up. Luke loomed up between the two manned rafts and again provided a temporary dock for the transfer of the six guests back into the lead oar raft. Mr. Wilder moved across Luke's sweep like a shadow.

Russ's face looked ashen. He looked over at his dad, then at Mr. De'Luca, then at Luke. "Thanks, Luke."

"That's my job," Luke yelled. Lacy nodded. "This time I got to watch from the sweep."

Russ followed his dad back onto the oar boat.

Luke took Lacy by the hand and re-settled her safely in the middle of the sweep, with dry towels and clean clothes from the dry bags he was carrying.

When they passed Camas Creek, Chance gave the signal and they pulled over for the first overnight on the Middle Fork.

"We have thirty-seven miles behind us, folks!" Chance yelled to everyone. "That's twelve more miles than the Wolfe Whitewater Guides ran on the first day from Boundary Creek."

Everybody within earshot clapped and yelled. Luke was so happy to have Lacy aboard. He couldn't believe that two of the four rafts had already tipped and flipped, and that twelve of the twenty people had suffered swift immersions. *Nobody hurt. Nobody missing. Thank God. But they still had to get through the rough Class IV rapids ahead.*

Luke shook his head. *Am I ready for the Middle Fork? How did any of the passengers think they were ready for the Middle Fork? We must stay only in the present moment. Fear of the future will spoil the gift of the present.* The good news—his learning curve turned vertical. He had the big rudder and two oars. He could not maneuver the craft much, to express some independence from the current's flow. He had to become the Middle Fork, feel its rhythm, get in tune with it, and go with the flow.

58

After flipping a couple of rafts, the camp on Camas Creek was a bit subdued, although Ben sang and enticed people to perform skits after dinner. Evening crept in quickly, along with clouds that obscured sunset. Luke escaped dinner duty and enjoyed the meal with Lacy, although he had to help clean up later.

"Tomorrow, you will see us do some fun cliff jumping at Funston," Chance announced. "Let's get a good night's sleep and roll out a bit earlier tomorrow morning."

Nobody objected. Lacy and Luke spent the extra time laughing and playing down by the river. Luke had a miner's flashlight and they explored the area around them. When they said goodnight this time, they hugged and kissed longer. Luke knew she loved being with him. But there was no doubt in her mind that she saw herself as a paddler. She wanted that ride with Chance and Luke wanted her to get that ride.

Morning broke. Lacy and Luke met again at the early-bird breakfast for fifteen minutes of closeness before the day cranked up. Chance called Luke over to the serving table, and he pitched in.

After breakfast, Chance pulled him aside. "What else can we plan? Do you think everybody is relaxed and not fearful of flipping?"

"It's all good. If we can stop near the calm pools coming up, Amos and Wade will be happy to fish with Ben," Luke said. "Everybody else will enjoy the cliff jumping at Funston. Oh, and

Lacy wants to get on your paddle boat. Will you teach her to be a front paddler? She would love that."

"Sure, Luke, I will even start her out up front. Her brother Brent is a natural. I'll get him up there as well."

They packed their equipment and put in. Middle Fork Canyon took Luke's breath away with its beauty, the cliff walls climbing into the sky, and the water so clear and blue-green that it sparkled in the sunshine. When they reached Funston, the river was wide, deep, and beautiful. Everybody wanted to be the bow jumper so before Chance knew it the rafts were beached.

He pointed up a little side canyon. "Mr. De'Luca, Mr. Wilder, take your fishing gear. See those pools of deep water? You will get lucky. If you need any help, call on Ben."

Half of the rafters found a rock or cliff from which to jump. The others sipped drinks and watched. Brent and Chance shocked everybody by doing backward somersaults into the Middle Fork. Lacy stood twenty feet up, wearing her turquoise bathing suit for the first time. Every man gazed with held breath, especially Luke. When she jumped, she held onto her bathing suit as she hit the water. The men wished they were swimming underwater, yesterday's tips and spills forgotten.

An hour or two after resuming their run, they stopped at Sheepeater Hot Springs to relax while Jerry shared a history lesson on the Sheepeater Indians. They hiked and climbed, and Victor discussed the geologic story of the area. They were impressed that the Middle Fork had cut right through the Salmon River Mountain Range.

Right above Flying B Ranch, they found quiet pools and enjoyed some good fly-fishing. Amos and Wade caught steelhead and Dolly Varden trout, and Wade actually caught a sizable salmon. Ben filleted them, stowed them away on ice, and promised everybody a great fish fry.

Everybody kept notching their belts with key landmarks reached and passed. They had floated by Mormon Ranch, Brush Creek, and above the whitewater of Haystack Rapid with smiles and nothing but beautiful scenery.

Chance found the Stillwater clear pool thirty inches deep on a backwater tributary, off the main river. Luke and Chance surprised the guests with set tables right in the middle of the pool, with a great lunch spread. Everybody stood around the tables eating chips and hummus, cold cut sandwiches with fresh lettuce, pickles, and mayonnaise, along with lemonade, iced tea, and fresh peanut butter cookies. After lunch Luke and Lacy sneaked away and found a fourteen-foot waterfall in the far curve of the pool behind a small ridge.

They played in the pool below the falls like a couple of kids, wrestling and splashing, reliving the fun of their teenage romance. Luke could not believe Lacy in a bathing suit. She reminded him of his past natural crushes in the South Pacific, Polynesian girls from Samoa and Tahiti, women who sang and danced, who were not the least self-conscious, and who all had long black hair and striking figures. In America, women with naturally black hair are much rarer than brunettes or even blondes, he thought, and Lacy's was every bit as striking as Dakota's Native American goddess, Quanah, or Chance's own Samoan goddess, Talia.

"How have you kept your youthful figure? I remember when you were eighteen! You don't look a tad different." He spoke after taking ten too many looks at her curves and beautiful legs.

Lacy rushed over and pulled him under the waterfall, clinging to him so that they both went under the water.

When they came to the surface, breathless, she still managed to kiss him passionately, water dripping off their hair and running around their merged mouths. "I'm stronger than I was back then," she said. "I enjoy running, and in the cold Chicago winters, our family membership in a gym made all the difference. My brother and I both hung out there, many a day."

"Luke, where are you?" they heard Chance calling.

"Whoops. We better get back," Luke said. "Let's put our shirts on, so we look like rafters, not swimmers."

They kissed again and held hands lovingly until they came around the bend.

"We didn't eat much lunch," Lacy murmured.

"Who needs it?" Luke was happier than he had ever been.

Minutes later, they all climbed aboard and headed out for the main stream. They bounced through Jack Creek Rapids and then Rattlesnake Rapids. Chance still had Lacy paddling up front. She looked backward at Luke when she could. And he could see her all the time. Life was good.

Chance could tell Lacy was getting the hang of it. She gave him little updates on their passage. She asked questions about what they would do in one situation after another. She was learning the whitewater rafting lingo and knowledge. They bumped underneath the Waterfall Creek Bridge, managed all the reversals and souse holes and plenty of excitement with the Waterfall Creek Rapid, and pulled up to Big Creek for their second overnighter. Big Creek was such a misnomer; the map showed eight tributaries feeding it before its final confluence with the Middle Fork.

"We are at mile fifty-five," Chance shouted. "Eighteen miles is enough for today. Tomorrow we enter Impassable Canyon. But tonight, happy hour, all those mouth-watering cheeses we brought just for the occasion, and the best wine of the region. Everybody off the rafts and onto the beach! Crew, unpack the overnight gear. Day one is done, and day two—hats off to you!"

Everybody cheered. It was a perfect day to regain all cheer and good spirits. The spills of the first day were forgotten.

Lacy and Luke weren't the only ones who drank more wine than usual. Ben cooked up all the fish Wade and Amos had caught, making those two the day's heroes. Everyone sat in their camp chairs in a close circle, striking up conversation and playing some of the games Chance and Ben offered up. Soon, everybody dragged their weary bodies to bed, their bellies warm. Krista and Greg were hitting it off really well, too. After his dad got to sleep, Greg and Krista could be found somewhere near the camp kissing.

Determined to outdo that couple, Lacy and Luke stole away and found a cave above the rushing river. In front of it they built a little campfire just for themselves. They kissed and held each other a long time, soaking in togetherness, not the whitewater of the Middle Fork of the Salmon River. It was just natural, like in Polynesia. Then they sat together at the mouth of the cave, Lacy in front of Luke, his arms around her. The roar of the river diminished, and sounds of the night floated up to their ears—crickets chirping, an owl hooting, fish jumping in the pool.

"We used to go to the same church together when we were kids," Luke said quietly. "Do you still go? Have your beliefs changed?"

Lacy turned her head. "No. I don't still go, but I still believe in God, the Bible, and you."

"Mine are the same. The older I get, the less I know. I hold myself to climbing a higher mountain of spiritual challenges. I pray more than I did before, but I'm finally learning to pray for others. Mindfulness conquers selfishness. I think flying into danger helps clarify vision."

He paused and tender feelings replaced thought and reflection. "My life is nothing compared to our soldiers being ambushed, killed, and wounded in the unforgiving jungles when our leaders back home don't think we can win and don't want to quit."

"This is 'a you' I never knew," Lacy murmured.

She turned around. "Luke, what in the world kept us apart so long?"

"Will you go first, honey? I can't right now."

Lacy let out a long breath. "Well, I've thought about it some, trying to figure out where my responsibility lay. I can't speak for you. Well, I was my daddy's little girl. I could do no wrong. And I always got what I wanted. But you didn't fit into that. And after I realized I needed to speak for myself instead of letting Daddy speak for me, I started to see where we went awry." She stopped, surprised at herself. "And you, Luke?"

"Your dad didn't think I was right for you. I let his and my brouhaha at my graduation stop me for a long time. I felt as if you took his side rather than mine. So it was foolish pride that kept us apart."

He sighed. "Believe it or not, years later I realized he was right. I needed to make something magnificent out of myself for you. So in Hawaii, when I said I needed time, I meant that. I needed to grow so much more."

Luke slowly rose and stood tall above Lacy and above the camp-fire. His face in the golden firelight was etched in her mind. He smiled and stretched his arm out toward the river. "Since we parted years ago when you were in college, I dreamed about coming to our river of no return, to the top of my bucket list of adventures, to capture your heart."

He turned around. "I wanted to become a unique and distinguished leader with that college degree and the rank of an officer. I was willing to face death to become a combat diver, and I drove myself to become a man in the top two percent of the military. Now as a combat helicopter pilot and army officer on the way up, no man is my superior, except in rank."

Lacy gleamed and radiantly smiled. "I love your talk," she said.

He cast his eyes up to recall something. And he smiled. "I want to share my favorite battle, the Spartans' last stand in 480 B.C. The Battle of Thermopylae raged on a narrow mountain pass. King Leonidas of Sparta marched with an army of 7,000 against the King Xerxes' Persian army numbering over a million men according to Herodotus, but estimated by modern historians at 100,000. On that mountain pass King Leonidas had only three hundred men left, but he fought the Persians to the death."

Lacy smiled warmly and said, "I know that battle. Maybe everybody does."

"I'm coming to the best part," Luke said. "The part few people know. There were two Spartans who survived. When taken to King Xerxes, and told they could have whatever they wanted if they worshipped him as their king, they said, 'We bow down before no man.'"

"I love that," Lacy said. "My father finally got the message. I finally learned the importance of being my own person."

"That saying changed a little bit for me. Now it's, 'I bow to no man.'"

"Even better," Lacy said.

Luke wrapped it up. "Whoever and whatever it is that society respects in a man elevates me and my family to the same level as any upper-class family born with unlimited money and unearned status. I bow to no man."

He relaxed, "I needed to get right in my own eyes as well as your father's eyes. That's why I wrote you from Vietnam. In my mind, I had earned the right to see you, connect back with you, and court you. I had no idea if you were available. By the end of this trip, I had prayed that you, your dad, and I were all on the same page, that we could coexist with at least respect and admiration if not love."

"You and I are on the same page now, honey," Lacy said, looking up at him. She jumped up and wrapped herself around him, bare skin against bare skin, and her mouth warm and hungry. They kissed forever.

When they sat down again next to each other, Lacy said, "By the way, where did you learn to kiss like that?"

"Honey, you can't spend time in the South Pacific, in Polynesia, without learning about happy times."

"I know what that means," she said.

Luke swallowed and had to think fast. "No, no," he protested, "I didn't mean *that* definition. I remember where you and I left off. We were rookies back then."

They got up, laughing, and walked back to the camp.

She turned around and kissed Luke one more time.

"See you tomorrow, honey," he whispered. Back at his tent he got out a favorite photo and wrote a prayer beneath it.

> *I know you love me, Lord, because you never say*
> *there is no hope for me.*
> *You work kindly with me, and you love and disci-*
> *   pline me*
> *in such a way*
> *That it is hard to understand the depth of your con-*
> *   cern for me.*
> *I know you love me, Lord, because you never forsake*
> *   me,*
> *Even though many of my friends and associates do.*
> *You love me, Lord, even though I am far from*
> *   perfect.*

When I am deeply aware of my failings, I remember that
I have value, because I came from you and belong to you.

59

The next day arrived too soon. After a hearty breakfast, the rafters packed up and took off, with one thing on their minds: Impassable Canyon. Lacy was back on the sweep with Luke. The name "Impassable" took their breaths away. It loomed ahead, and it didn't take long to get there.

Luke looked to his left. Huge, grey volcanic rocks extended from the earth's core, standing like bleachers for the home team, covered with a thin film of shiny green moss, covering water that bubbled up and boiled furiously. A plunging gradient caused unstable water to erupt everywhere but in the downstream direction. A hundred feet downstream, the Salmon jagged abruptly right, its deeper waters reflecting a stunning blue-green depth.

Coming into Redside Rapid, the middle current dropped fourteen feet in a chute only four feet wide. It was no place for the broad-beamed sweep. Luke worked his mid-boat oars furiously and banged his way through the wider channel, almost flying off the deck when the sweep smacked straight into a midstream boulder before it reached the bottom of the channel. Dense undergrowth and heavy stands of pine confirmed they were floating beneath the forested slopes of the Salmon River Mountain Range. Luke reached over, ducked Lacy's head down below branches hanging above the river, and jumped back to his oars.

As they swept around a bend, Luke looked back to catch the steep mountain range behind them, the river crystal clear and green, sparkling in the sun. Meanwhile up ahead beyond Porcupine Rapid, Chance scouted ahead and found a place alongside the river where he could provide direction for the steep drop, boulder garden, and abrupt curve to the left. All were in the same narrow chute that ran steeper and faster than the surrounding waters.

One by one, they dropped into the chute—Victor and Chance on the paddle boat, then Ben and Jerry on the oar boat, trailed by Luke on the sweep. Luke had been on roller coasters before, but nothing prepared him for this watery version. He lost what felt like a quart of perspiration doing everything he could to escape from being trapped or wrapped around a boulder. Chris brought up the rear in the kayak, cheering Luke on. Once out of the chute, Chris mad-paddled past all three rafts.

Up ahead, the Middle Fork didn't look wide enough to carry the rafts. For a moment, Luke longed for the easy circle of canvas camp chairs, where everybody relaxed and sipped wine, and he walked over to the table every so often and feasted on its trays of freshly cut veggies, side plates of tasty round crackers and delicious sliced cheeses. Behind the table were big red and white five-gallon coolers full of tea, lemonade, or cold water. And beyond them Luke imagined eight tents pitched along the riverbank.

Reality struck him like a shot to the jaw as he navigated through deep green pools surrounded by steep canyon walls, striped with black and white granite. Far ahead Chance double-oared the paddle boat around a corner, yelling count to the paddlers. "Paddle! Paddle! Paddle!"

Dakota and Jerry had it easier with both oars and paddles. Currents flowed upstream and downstream next to each other. Luke oared out of the upstream path and looked ahead to see steeply tilted canyon walls closing down on him. A huge green mountainside loomed five hundred feet up in front of him. It looked like he was going to disappear down a rabbit hole. For a minute he lost his cool, close to yelling out his fear.

Instead of the rabbit hole the river slammed him to the right and he made the impossible turn with a terrible tilt, sure he was going to flip the sweep. *Flip the sweep! Nobody does that!* Just as Lacy, frozen in fear, anxiously looked up at him, the river opened up again and Luke stood tall. The sweep rushed headlong toward Weber Rapid, passed intervals of five large rock outcroppings, and narrowly avoided each rock protruding four to eight feet above the swirling current. Luke studied the currents, sweat pouring off his forehead, trying to stay in the best channel. He heaved a sigh of relief after the sweep swooshed between the third and fourth rock outcroppings. Still in the middle of the rapids but below the worst of them, he glanced behind. He saw something like a huge speedboat wake behind him. The ferocity of the river and constricting canyon walls caused the waves to violently careen into each other. His sweep raised a long tongue of water, a following wake, two feet higher than the rest of the river.

Ahead of him at the bottom of the rapids, Chance found a small cove. He yelled and signaled to the others. "Break time! Come in! Come in!"

The paddle boat struck for shore as the oar boat pulled in. A minute later, Luke arrived, shivering and cold. Chance ran over to secure the sweep, but Lacy beat him to it. She jumped out, edged the sweep up, and tied it off.

After they all pulled in, tied up, and hiked up a little creek, they walked single file on a trail above the creek until they reached a tall golden rock above a deep green pool. Daring each other, the crew jumped off, one after the other, maybe a twelve-foot jump. Then five of the adventurers jumped, each hesitating before taking the big step.

Lacy and Luke walked past the golden rock above and the green pool below, hand in hand. They looked at each other.

"I have something for you to take back to Vietnam," Lacy said, handing him a hastily written poem. "But it's for the rest of your life."

"Thank you, darling," Luke said, giving her his poem. "This is just for you to read until you are on the runway and I am landing on it."

They read them in the full moonlight and made as much love as they could. The moon waned in the sky before they stopped kissing and caressing and touching. "I know all your hills and valleys better than my own," Luke said, kissing her neck, her shoulders.

"I have more hills and valleys than you do. You will have to wait on some of them," Lacy said.

"Wait! I am a straight A student. What about Advanced Placement?"

"Ha-Ha-Ha! You will have to wait your turn, just like everybody else." Lacy couldn't help laughing.

"That is not easy! What do you mean, everybody else?"

"Everybody else who wants to make whoopee before trading rings," she laughed. "Someday when we are not going in opposite directions, you might get lucky."

"When we get together we will both be lucky," Luke reminded her.

"Until you finish your deployment, every day apart will be like a month," Lacy said.

"It better not be for a year. Then it will be like a century," Luke said.

"I am so glad we don't exaggerate," Lacy said, elbowing him gently.

They absolutely could not get enough of each other. But they were clear on what they were taught. Touch only. They both knew all things would change after they settled down in one place.

"So what is it, Luke?"

They walked back to camp as Luke thought for a minute. "We are engaged to be engaged," he said.

Lacy hugged his arm. "Everybody can live with that."

They returned to the golden rock and the deep green pool. Everybody was hanging out below on the sides of the pool. Lacy and Luke walked right up to the cliff and jumped off. Both yelled loud enough to change the course of the river, and smiled at each other. When they splashed into the water and went down, Luke, heavier, plunged to the bottom. No stranger to water, he dove up and kissed Lacy. She opened her mouth in shock. Luke dragged her to the surface, coughing and spluttering.

Chance yelled, "Luke, can't you take better care of her? We're not supposed to help them drown!"

Everybody howled. Luke was embarrassed. But Lacy took a deep breath, coughed, and called back. "It wasn't his fault!" The group ran back to the rafts and jumped on, refreshed and glad the dangerous whitewater rumbled on behind them and not with them.

They lunched near the Parrot Cabin and studied the colorful Sheepeater Indian pictographs inscribed on the canyon wall. Luke caught a photo of the pictographs for Chance and then looked up above the canyon wall. There, looking over her shoulder at them stood a beautiful doe, her ears upright, big brown eyes, a few bushes obscuring her tan buckskin, and a black tail hanging over her white rump. Luke squeezed Lacy and they melted into the moment. "She reminds me of you," Luke murmured. "See that cute rump?"

"You are not getting lucky yet," Lacy slapped him on the butt.

Before they returned to their rafts, Chance gave Luke his scouting report. He knew this whole trip was a challenge for Luke. He had told him in detail about Impassable Canyon, but not about anything else. And he worried. Luke had to know what was coming.

The huge gauntlet began with Ouzel Rapid, then Houseboat Rapid, followed closely by Cliffside Rapid and Devil's Tooth. Lacy rushed up. "I want to be on the paddle boat again. Do you mind, Luke? And Chance, will you let me paddle up front again?"

Chance said, "What about Russ?

"This is the only challenge I've seen him unable to meet," Lacy said. "He, my dad, and his dad are hanging out as passengers, and sometimes hanging over the sides. We never should have let the three of them come."

Luke responded instantly. "The river guides will take extra care of them. Don't worry. So far we have done that."

He remembered Lacy's request. "Absolutely get on the paddle boat. You are paddling with the best—Chance!" Luke was glad Lacy wanted adventure. Now that she had the strength of their at-long-last-love, she would take more chances.

Everybody jumped onto their rafts, and they swept down the Salmon River. Chris took the lead in the kayak. While rushing down Houserock Rapid, Luke saw ominous signs. Huge trees had uprooted and slid down the mountainside in a recent windstorm. Seven or eight trees sprawled into the rapids like scattered pixie sticks. Any of them could cause injury, or worse, if a raft collided with them. Luke already knew heavy hydraulic gaps were coming, with reversals and powerful current differentials, where big water, massive waves, and violent currents were the obstacles, instead of the customary rock obstacles.

His focus changed. He knew Chance's paddle raft faced immediate danger. The paddlers flashed into view above the spray—Lacy and Brent the bow paddlers, Krista and Russ the middle paddlers, Laurie and Jerry the rear paddlers, and Chance in the stern with the steering oar. Thank God Jason was riding with his parents in the oar boat.

The current swung upward and shot back on itself. This treacherous meeting of currents could drown the most skilled swimmers while swamping, trapping, or flipping rafts. Steep waves curled heavily onto their own upstream faces. Near Luke, backrollers and side-curlers rumbled next to holes and almost into one big souse hole, right below an underwater obstruction—probably a boulder. Water poured from upstream, downstream, and both sides. The paddle boat dipped down, lost to view.

It popped up again—the bow going airborne, and then taking the stern with it, catapulting all seven rafters into the air. Chance was the last to go airborne as he clutched an oar. Luke could see Chance held the blade behind him and over his head, careful not to hit the rafters. Somehow, he knew Chance would give the oar to one rafter to hold onto and probably save the rafter from serious harm.

In a matter of seconds, the alert captains swung around on the oar boat, Victor and Ben double-oaring, then madly rowing upstream to find and take on the swimmers. Luckily, the empty raft was sucked down into the hole, and the water shooting back upstream flipped it right side up. *What a miracle.* Chance tied the flip line across the raft's bottom and around his waist, so he could right the boat. He was able to pull himself over to the raft and climb back aboard. At the same time, Jerry stayed on top of the foam, swam over to the raft and climbed aboard.

In an eye blink, all three rafts threw out lines, dug deep, tied together, and stayed in place, making a catch harbor for Luke. Chance and Victor saw Luke on the sweep coming in hard and fast, like a Navy jet on an aircraft carrier. They hooked his lines and held him tight. All three rafts had bow and stern lines, and Chris came up to direct the emergency. They readied the painter—a line or rope twenty feet long attached to the bow of the paddle rafts and the stern of the oar rafts with metal D-shaped rings. These ropes were the difference between life-saving and life-ending. Nobody could battle the force of a whitewater rapid, stay on the surface, and be guided back to the raft without them.

There were five precious rafters missing. Jerry jumped on board the sweep, Kent climbed into the paddle raft. Chance and Luke swung into Army combat diving action. They donned the special goggles and fins they had brought and tore off their life jackets. They had to go deep. Each had two small bottles of oxygen to strap on their belts, aviation-life-support-equipment brought in on the search-and-rescue plane Luke took to get to Stanley. As a pilot in 'Nam, he strapped both on his vest for flying over water. Each bottle had a breathing mouthpiece with a built-in regulator. Luke and Chance both had combat diving headlights looped around their necks for accessibility.

60

The swimmers were nowhere to be seen, below the surface. Chance and Luke grabbed good lines and ropes. The other guides stood ready with rope bags and life jackets to throw to them. Luke and Chance scanned the upwelling waves and guessed where the swimmers could be. The big water meant fast currents, large waves, and huge back-wash, immense volume, extreme violence. In addition, new branches and tree limbs appeared beneath the surface.

Chance pointed. "Strainers!" There were caves on each side of the river under the banks where the swimmers could be sucked up and drowned. It was the word guides didn't want to hear on the river. It would not be an easy rescue.

Luke and Chance looked at each other and gave the signal. They knew which battle drill to use. Every second counted. They had reviewed every conceivable situation. They took the standard operating procedure for this incident. Chance took one end of the stern rope and tied it to a tree limb under the surface on the right side of the channel. Luke swam laterally downstream with the rope and tied it diagonally around a safe boulder above water on the left side. Then he swam back underwater and looked for ledges and tree limbs in the channels on the left.

After Chance secured the line, he would look under for ledges and limbs in the channels on the right. The swimmers were trapped somewhere underneath the surface. Luke knew the only way they could rescue all five was to pull them out of the holes and get them all on that one rope. If they couldn't hold the rope, they'd snap them onto the rope with their life jacket D-rings, with two guides on hand to snap them off after the rescue. Chance signaled two guides to swim out to the center of the river holding onto the rope so they could snap the drowning swimmers onto the rope if need be. The other guides gave thumbs up.

Luke and Chance donned their ultra-bright headlamps and snapped them on tight. They checked all their gear on their belts. Oxygen tanks, knives, survival gear, extra oxygen hoses. After gulping three deep breaths, Chance dove right while Luke headed left. As he held one end of the rope and madly thrashed left, Luke saw a shelf with rushing water and deep crevices where the water poured through much faster. There were two channels veering left to check on his way back. He spotted an underwater ledge and two tree limbs trapped beneath it.

He broke through to the river's bank, found a secure boulder, and swiftly tied his rope around that rock, praying for time and good fortune. He inhaled deeply, jumped back in, prepared for a long dive, and pulled himself upstream hand-over-hand, just beneath the surface. Lacy's smile consumed his mind and heart, but he needed to focus on all of the swimmers in the river. He blinked his eyes against the raging current, a collage of faces—Lacy, Laurie, Brent, Russ, Mr. Wilder and Mr. De'Luca, imprinted on his brain.

He dove well below the underwater ledge, knowing the rushing current could push the swimmers beneath a ledge and then pin them, as if a diabolical suction device operated from the river bottom. He spotted white thrashing arms and long brown hair floating upward. Both swimmers were panicking, neither capable of analyzing or assessing the situation.

Was it Lacy? Laurie? Luke drew face to face with Laurie, then Brent. He took the oxygen bottle, clamped off Laurie's nose, put the mouthpiece between her lips, and prayed for a response. Her eyes flew open as bubbles covered the mouthpiece. Safe! Luke then gave the other oxygen bottle to Brent before pulling Laurie from under the ledge. He brought her to the surface, clipped her on the line, and raised his arm to Ben and Victor to come get her.

Luke dove back down to the ledge where Brent sucked on the oxygen tank and he hustled him to the surface and clipped him on the rope. Ben and Victor were approaching quickly. As he looked downstream for Lacy, Luke spotted Chance and Krista snapping Russ onto the flip line. A quick glance saw Mr. De'Luca getting clipped on the rope. Dakota held onto the line, and Kent and Ernie moved over to pick them up. Ben and Victor went back to the rafts to find Mr. Wilder.

Taking another desperate breath and snapping the oxygen bottle back on his belt, Luke submerged, focusing entirely on finding Lacy. She was a good swimmer, thank God. He guessed her to be further down-river, but there were reversal currents that swirled back upstream as well. He found a reversal current to carry him down to the bottom, over to the side, and back upstream. He crisscrossed his side of the channels darting back and forth as he had been trained. He looked everywhere, praying for divine guidance or vision. He couldn't see any other nooks, crevices or ledges. There was nowhere else to look.

Suddenly, a large colorful salmon darted in front of Luke. He followed the fish with his bright headlight into a dark dead-end cave below the riverbed that looked as if it had only one entrance. Wrong! The salmon swam into the wall. What? *Should I turn around?* At the last second, his ghostly river guide caught an upwelling current and shot straight up above him. *I am going crazy!* All he could see were the sides of a tunnel. The rushing current had nowhere to go but up. *I have no choice.* He found himself in a narrow shaft, propelled by the volcanic surge of the river and followed it, desperate for air. The salmon broke free and disappeared.

Luke trailed the salmon's thrashing tail until they both exploded out of the water one after the other. Luke heard the salmon flipping around frantically, just as he gasped for air, nearly passing out. When he came back to his senses, he double-clicked his headlamp to make sure it was working. He looked around, dazed. He was on a ledge in the cave above the river's water level. The water had receded back down the shaft. The salmon had gone back with it. For a moment that was all he focused on. *The salmon saved my life.*

He heard a moan. *But salmon don't moan. I must be hallucinating.* He banged the water out of his ears. He heard another moan, this time behind him in the darkness. He rolled over onto all fours and saw Lacy. He grabbed the hook on his belt for the underwater lantern to see more clearly.

He saw an inert body. *It was Lacy! Lacy!* Luke crawled to her. "Lacy! Lacy! Lacy! Are you okay?"

No response. He put his finger on her neck. A pulse! He tried again just to make sure. It was so faint, and he was trembling and gasping. But she was alive! He tilted her head back to give her a chance to breathe. He leaned down ever so carefully. There was just a tiny hint of breath. "Airway clear," he panted, pushing aside fear for the one he loved. Luke knew he would trade his life for hers. He knew he would never let her leave again.

Training from combat diving and whitewater rafting procedures came to his rescue. "Breathing. 'Rescue breaths!'" His right palm on her forehead, and his left palm on her chin, he tilted her head back and lifted her chin forward. He pinched her nostrils shut and sealed his lips onto hers. He gave two rescue breaths and watched to see her chest rise. He repeated the procedure five times more, watching her chest and leaning down to feel any breath from her mouth.

Nothing.

The life-saving acrostic came to him. "A, B, C. Airways. Breath. Compression!" He placed the heel of his left hand in the center of her chest between the nipples and immediately placed the heel of his right hand over his left hand and interlocked the fingers. He added thirty chest compressions for a minute after two rescue breaths. He knew he had to push down two inches with each compression, but kept praying, "Please God, I don't want to break her ribs!"

Still nothing. He could hardly breathe, but she had to have two more rescue breaths. When he finished that, he started compression sixty times a minute. Then two rescue breaths.

Still nothing.

He could not do more than sixty times a minute, praying for her, talking to her during the compressions. "Come on, Lacy, come on, Lacy, come back to me, come back to me!"

Two more rescue breaths. She heard him! He felt her chest rising slowly. He tilted his ear to her lips and felt the coming of a regular breath. Luke quickly rolled Lacy on her side. Water gushed out of her mouth, once, twice, and once more. Within a few more seconds Lacy's eyes flew open. Her body convulsed and quivered. She stared at the wall, bewildered. Her chest shuddered. Breath after breath came gasping out as if she could never get enough air. She shrank into the fetal position, still lying on her side.

Tears flowed out of Luke's eyes as he sat back on his knees. He cried, great muffled sobs filling the cave. He couldn't help it. "Thank you, God! Thank you, God! Thank you, God!" His whole body shuddered from exhaustion and relief. "Lacy! Lacy! You're back! You're back!"

Lacy turned over on her back and looked up. Luke supported her as she lifted her head up. "What's the matter? Why are you crying?"

"You're alive. You're alive!" Luke said, his voice barely more than a whisper.

"Where are we? What happened?" She choked out.

"You flipped out of the raft. You went underwater. You lost consciousness. I thought you were gone!"

She just stared up at him. He leaned down and said firmly, "Don't talk, Lacy, just breathe. We are in a cave above the river, but we are under the river bank. We are under the river."

She slowly shook her head in disbelief and asked again, "What happened?"

Luke kept his patience. "Your raft overturned. You were swept underwater and ended up in this air hole. You are alive! Thank God! You are alive."

Lacy held onto Luke, gripping him tightly. "What do you mean we're in a cave?"

"We're in an above-water cave. But we're underground. Thank God this is an air pocket. We have air in here. And thanks to this lantern, we have light. I've got one oxygen tank. Are you okay? Any broken bones?"

"Please, help me up, Luke."

He stood up, a little weak on his feet. When Lacy rolled up to her feet, she said, "No, no, no broken bones. I'm fine, Luke. But look at my neck. It stings."

Luke bent over. "You have a gash on it, right here. I already put pressure on it and it stopped bleeding. But I can't tie a tourniquet."

Lacy turned around and hugged Luke. "You found me! You found me!" She wouldn't let him go.

"Rest easy," he said, "and then we'll get out of here just the way I came in. Thanks to that beautiful salmon—she led me right to you."

"What salmon?"

Luke looked around. "I know there was a salmon. I will never forget what she looked like in my headlamp. She was swimming right in front of me. She was full grown, she was fast, and she had beautiful markings. When we get out of here, I will draw a picture of her. I will show you a photo just like her. She was so beautiful. And she led me to you."

Lacy's eyes widened. "That is so wonderful! That is so wonderful!"

He took her over and pointed. "She led me underneath the water, and then underneath the river bank. See that hole! No wider than five feet! And then up into this cave no wider than this!"

He turned around and shined the light on the walls. "Look! Not even fifteen feet of space and filled with air too! What are the chances of that?"

The sassy Middle Fork of the Salmon had lifted Lacy off her raft, spun her around in its tornadic currents, and swept her into a hidden cave, as though it were an underground tornado shelter. It saved her life. Led by a kind of pilot fish, Luke had found her bruised, bleeding, and unconscious, and brought her back to precious life and perfect safety.

They took deep breaths from the oxygen tank, and Luke eased himself down halfway headfirst into the rising water. Lacy leaned down and got in the tunnel with Luke headfirst. He nodded to her, grabbed her from behind, and dove down through the tunnel. When they dropped back into the river Luke held her close and swam powerfully with his right arm, kicking hard with his feet. Lacy was able to join him in his efforts. When they bobbed up out of the water into the surface current, Luke waved his arm and yelled out to Chance. The rope they had strung was there! Luke and Lacy grabbed onto it and a minute later Chance and Dakota had them in tow and got them out of the river and onto the bank.

61

Lacy was safe and not alone. Luke pulled out Brent and Laurie, Chance pulled out Russ and Mr. De'Luca. Victor had saved Mr. Wilder almost immediately after the flip. All the rest of the rafters were tired, exhausted, but exhilarated that nobody was lost. Then they resumed the whitewater adventure as if redemption were an everyday event. For the rest of the trip, everybody felt like family. Lacy and Luke were inseparable.

As they all sipped celebratory wine around the campfire one night, Russ said, "Instead of the other degrees awarded me, I should have earned a Divinity Degree. I could have married Lacy and Luke any time in the last few days. They already act like a happily married couple."

Everybody around the campfire clapped and cheered. Luke and Lacy blushed, even in the firelight.

"Don't get ahead of me," Luke called out. "I popped the cork. I didn't pop the question."

"He's not going to get away without doing that," Lacy said loudly, her chin held high.

Mr. De'Luca surprised everyone. "My wife and I will be there and do our part when it comes."

Luke said, "Thank you, Mr. De'Luca. I like *the when*, and not *the if!*" Lacy and Luke jumped up as Mr. De'Luca came over to hug them both.

Everybody loved the dinner that night and spent lots of time enjoying it and loving life. The menu was equal to any restaurant. Grilled trout basted with butter and lemon, roasted potatoes in tinfoil in the coals of the campfire, fresh green beans from nearby farms, camp coffee, and mounds of delicious apple crisp from a Dutch oven. After the camp dinner, everyone returned to their tents except for Luke and Lacy. They remained at the campfire.

She sat in his lap. "Luke, you saved me. You saved me. I love you. I am so fortunate."

Luke couldn't resist. "When a person's life is saved, she belongs to the savior. That's a native rule all over the world. That's why I did it. And now I own you. At last."

They both laughed.

"Yes, you do. And you outrank me, you with your chest-full of medals."

Lacy sat up straight. "Hey, wait a minute! I just realized something. As a pilot you saved so many soldiers in Vietnam. That was your job. And you don't own them. And you saved some lives as a combat diver. And you don't own them. It's what soldiers do. Ha! So you don't own me, either!"

"Well, you can't blame me for trying."

"Luke, didn't you feel a little like my dad owned me?"

"I used to. But that's what fathers do."

Lacy carefully asked, "So what do you think of my father now?"

She ignored one of Luke's deepest grudges, also one of her deepest regrets—her father's lack of respect for Luke, based on her father's perceived disparity between where he thought Luke would end up and where he wanted Lucy to end up.

Luke looked into the warm red coals, thinking about what she said. *Lacy's dad managed his own chain of Marshall-Field type department stores in and around the Chicago metropolitan area. He had a similar chain of stores around San Francisco as well. Mr. De'Luca had lunch with Mayor Daley on a regular basis. He even starred in his own Chicagoland TV commercials. His handsome, distinguished looks, which reminded Luke of an Italian opera singer, certainly helped. During the holidays, he actually sang requests with a beautiful baritone voice that could climb the ladder into a low tenor. Luke's father had achieved an astounding success through singing, but it was more of a means to an end. With Lacy's father, it was a lifetime thing, part of his culture. The men envied him and the women adored him.*

Luke squeezed Lacy's hand. "I have no quarrel with him now. I used to take it personally. But maybe looking at death and realizing who is fighting for our freedom, and who is making money off this war, I learned so much about class disparity. You and I had many things in common, and I always imagined that we were growing on parallel paths, no matter where we were or who we were with. Now I realize how out of touch I was. We live in two different worlds. Like I'm the warrior and you are a member of the upper class royalty. You exist in a social stratum far above me. I was such a naïve innocent. When we were kids in puppy love, I never knew the distance between us, our families. Even in high school, I thought we could make it."

"Of course we can make it, Luke. Here we are."

He paused, picked up a stick, and stirred the fire. "Maybe we still can." As he stirred, he murmured, "It's your turn to bring me up to date."

Lacy stood up and stretched her arms into the deep, cool Idaho night. She looked down at the campfire, mesmerized for a few moments by the fiery coals. Cool night, hot fire, Luke. "When you left me in Hawaii after our brouhaha and went back to the Nevada Test Site, I was so hurt. I didn't care if you were in danger or not."

Lacy leaned back. "I went back to school full time and graduated with honors and all that jazz. I moved up in Dad's company, working on acquiring new companies, buying out our competition, real hard-ball stuff."

Something caught her mind, and a warm smile erased her pensive stare. "At least I don't have to worry about you wanting in. The last thing you'd do is business management. And the first thing you'd reject is some position where you have to answer to my father."

Luke stared at the river, unwilling to be part of that thought.

"Now wait, Luke, don't dwell on that comment."

She looked up, shielded her eyes from the campfire, and searched the sky for stars. "You won't believe what I did. I can hardly believe it myself. I got tired of marching to the family drumbeat of one more business acquisition, one more Rolls Royce, one more mansion on the Gold Coast above Chicago, one more bank account. I dropped everything my dad wanted and joined the Peace Corps for over a year. Worse than that, I went to Jamaica, where there was no white superiority and miles and miles of black majority. I needed my own space and more adventure. Chicago has its limits, you know. I learned that from you. I had to get out." She shook her head.

She definitely got Luke's attention. "What was that like? You, in Jamaica? How did you survive down there living on peanuts?"

"That didn't matter. Helping people find a life mattered. The natives loved the program I developed to help them get an education and enter the job market. We even had students get jobs in Florida, Texas, and Mexico City. My specialty was an Upward Bound program in the Peace Corps for girls and women. I had good connections from my father's business, of course, and from the university. We helped females advance into the job market more than anybody ever had. It really mattered, because there's nothing much more for females to do in Jamaica than to get married and have children. And they never had just a few children, Luke, quivers and quivers of children, by men who have no education or initiative or real purpose in life."

"Lacy, for fun compare your lifestyle down there with your lifestyle back home."

"Compared to Chicago, it was like traveling backwards. I went from driving my own red Camaro convertible or being driven by a chauffeur. From taking yellow taxis anywhere in Chicago during the week, I went to being a passenger in a big, slow, dirty, open-air bus full of people, lots of babies, and farm animals. Jamaica. What a trip. It once took me twenty-four hours to go sixty-three miles. I could have run it quicker."

"I want to hear more about that. Why?"

"The bus driver had a girlfriend on the routes I took, and he would stop for dinner at her house. Everybody on the bus waited an hour and a half for him to finish. I wanted to jump into the driver's seat myself. But in the Peace Corps, you can't pull rank. You have no rank. You are there to teach, nurture, inspire, and build confidence and programs. You work with whatever system they have. I was like you in the Army, off on a foreign deployment, living in tents, and unable to go anywhere on my own time."

Luke laughed. "We do have more in common."

"I had a whole new appreciation for the Army. I had time to think about a lot of things down in Jamaica. I had time to grow up, Luke. I learned to lead others. I used my education to reach out to others, instead of just using my teenage puppy personality and jumping up for people who paid attention to me, as if I needed to please them."

Luke sat up straight. "We both learned so much with our new perspectives. Thank God we got away from home."

"Oh, yes. The Peace Corps was good for me. I grew up, walked my own walk, and threw out my old perspectives. I came home, found an apartment on my own, not at home, overlooking Lake Michigan. I went back to work in my father's company and developed more programs for the poor people in Chicago as well. So many black youths in the Chicago area had the same disadvantages as the Jamaicans. After a year the mayor of Chicago established an award for our Personnel Upward Bound Program."

She made a face. "I went from being Daddy's Little Girl to supposedly being one of Chicago's most influential women of the year. The one element that seemed to stop my personal growth actually turned out to be the one element that enabled me to grow the most."

Luke turned to her. "What was it?"

"You," Lacy said, leaning forward and kissing him. Her voice dropped to a near whisper. "I had to discover my own life and stand on my own. I had to see you from Emerson's perspective, not my father's. Remember? It went something like this. 'True friends, true soul partners, can live fulfilled apart in the universe, just by knowing the other exists?'"

Her next question gave him pause. "So how did you discover the truth about life and the truth about us?"

Luke exhaled and started slowly. "To begin with, after my R&R, I told my CO if he would keep me in the Cobra attack helicopter squadron, I would extend for six months or even longer. I want to even the score for all the Hueys that were shot down, and all the pilots that have been killed. How could our government have allowed that? The Hueys were like a flock of geese flying over an artillery embankment. And I want to move up in rank so I can have influence in the decision-making process."

Lacy realized the danger Luke faced every day with no fear and no sense of self. She looked down at the coals for a minute and then made a decision. She took his hands and looked him in the eyes. "I've always loved you, Luke. For fifteen years of solitude and soul confinement, I've loved you. It was like living in a state prison down in Joliet. We had three years together out of all that time."

Tears rolled down her cheeks, something Luke had never seen. "Upper class and middle class don't mean a thing, Luke. What your dad does and what my dad does is not important."

She began crying. "How could we be so right as teens and youths, and be so wrong as adults?"

Luke knelt down in front of her and pulled her so sweetly into his arms, kissing away her tears, kissing her softly and gently, soothing away her sadness until she stopped crying. "We're here right now, Lacy."

When the embers stopped glowing, Luke took her into his lap, his arms wrapped around her, happy to wait for her to fall asleep.

Lacy softly moaned and held Luke tight. She knew intimacy approached. She thought back on her life. *When Luke and I were growing up, I was committed to sex after marriage. Did I save myself for Luke? Not completely. How could I when everything pointed to us not having a future? Sooner or later, everybody who is not a nun is going to experience what love or passion can lead to. But after a while we get to decide what to continue and what not to continue. I am glad I wanted to wait for something more. I am glad I am still saving the best for Luke. Nothing in the past will blemish me, cast doubt on me, or challenge my independence.*

Lacy had always liked money—a lot. She was raised with it, and she liked the finer things in life. Her mother took her shopping early and often. Lacy had the finest wardrobe. Earlier, this created status problems with Luke, culminating in the rift in Hawaii over Russ's wealth and social standing compared to Luke's. Lacy realized she had found herself with a crush on Russ in Hawaii, partly because of the great family pressure over the past five years to marry him. But also because he represented the status quo of the wealthy and privileged class into which she was born. He had his own yacht, his private plane, his contacts with important people everywhere. And her family loved him.

When Luke found out about it, he was steamed and overly jealous. But he had no room to talk, nothing to stand on. What could he offer Lacy?

Then she found her inner self and dated several different guys, never ending the relationship but finding away to stay independent, balancing her time between businesses and trying to find "the right guy" because her personality suggested it. She had so many disappointments that made her look at Luke again.

It wasn't just Chance's idea to get her to come to the Sixth Weather Reunion near Tinker Air Force Base outside of Oklahoma City. As Lacy grew older, she saw richness of heart and not the wallet as the most important asset, and that shift led to the reunion in Oklahoma City.

When she finally drifted off, she knew Luke and she had their whole life in front of them. Everything else had been a prelude.

62

Lacy and Luke had gotten out of the cave, had really gotten to know each other, finished the trip, and Luke had gone back to Vietnam. Letters had gone back and forth at least twice a week. At times there were no letters because of Luke's locations. There were injuries, secret missions, and places from which Luke could not write. Lacy was anxious to see Luke and know for herself. What she did at work came second nature to her, but her nights never ended.

Finally, Lacy stood in the middle of Tornado Alley. March growled around her, the jet stream howling overhead out of Canada at two hundred knots, dipping and diving its way across the United States—an illegal alien of the most monstrous variety. A sharp spring gust slapped goose bumps on her legs. She patiently waited on the tarmac, looking down the long runway at Fort Leonard Wood, Missouri. Luke was on his way home from the second half of his Vietnam deployment, in an Army transport full of both officers and soldiers, some of whom were gravely wounded and slated for an immediate ride to the big base hospital.

She remembered being more than wounded herself, and close to death in that little cave on The River of No Return. Led by a beautiful salmon, Luke had found her bruised, bleeding, and unconscious, and he brought her back to precious life and perfect safety.

Lacy's inner sight left the realm of her memory cells, and she focused again on the tarmac. For the umpteenth time, she looked back down the runway. *Now it's just Luke and me—all our goings and comings, our exits and entries, our touching downs and lifting ups as though our lives are a series of seasonal weather events. Lacy brushed away tears. Please God, no more trials! Give me my ticket to heaven—life with Luke right here on earth.*

She picked up the sound of the approaching Army transport. Far down the runway, but coming toward her, the plane's wheels sailed over the runway and touched down. She savored the wheels-down moment. Lacy's heart squeezed tighter and tighter with every concrete section of runway as the plane taxied to a stop, its propellers free-spinning soundlessly.

Ten hospital attendants followed the two runway personnel as the privates pushed the big stairway up to the plane's left fuselage, and stood at the bottom, waiting for the steward inside to crank the door open. When he did, the attendants ran up the stairs. In less than two minutes, five wounded soldiers were ferried off aboard stretchers. Five ambulances raced from the tarmac before anyone else disembarked. Seven soldiers on crutches came down next, making their way carefully and manfully down the stairs, and heading toward a beaten up, well-traveled brown Army bus. And then twice that number walked down the stairs with no help. Nobody appeared at the top.

Where was Luke? Was he whole? Healthy?

Lacy closed her eyes and prayed. When she opened them, Luke waved wildly from the top of the stairs. She stretched out her arm, and then watched in horror as Luke labored down the stairs, holding onto the railing.

His left leg…What's wrong with his left leg?

She ran to meet him near the bottom of the stairs. He walked gingerly toward her, trying to hide his limp, his left leg stiffening. Lacy's brain raced through grave, dark possibilities: *Is he wearing a prosthetic? Will he be able to run and whitewater raft again? Will we be able to finally live the life we've longed to live?*

Luke held his arms wide. Lacy flew into them, unable to contain herself. "O Luke, you're home! You're home! We're together at last."

She covered his face with kisses, then stopped, face in his neck, afraid to look into his eyes, afraid of what he might say. "Honey, are you okay? What happened to your leg?"

Luke leaned down and kissed her until she couldn't breathe. 'I am perfectly fine. I am home—wherever you are, honey."

He took her by the shoulders and held her at arm's length. He grinned sheepishly. "Don't worry about my leg, honey. I sprained my knee is all, trying to help a paraplegic—a wounded pilot, my wing-man, Eddie—get on board the plane. He refused the stretcher and he refused the crutches. He insisted on coming home with me. We took a tumble and he fell on me. When we landed it took me a little longer to walk down that aisle. I didn't want anybody to see me."

He took a deep breath and looked around. "Next week, I'll be good as new. And the week after that, look out." He wiggled his eyebrows.

He took off his heavy outer coat, leaned down, and swept her up. He brought her back inside his arms and kissed her, Polynesian style, two hearts squeezed close, his heart beating faster and faster. And her heart—he could feel each heartbeat—thudding against him. He could feel her warm breasts pushing into him, her hips seeking his, her mouth all his.

"Wait one minute,' he said. And then Luke reached down to turn on a little recorder in his front pocket. Etta James began singing her trademark song, 'At Last.'

"I love this song," he said, "and finally it's mine to sing." And he sang to her. He whirled her away from a few other people out there on the tarmac. "Let's dance," he said, singing along with Etta. Lacy was the princess at the royal ball. Etta's song sang it all...for Luke and Lacy...so many years...so many hopes...so many disappoint-ments...so many hurdles. And now so much love to overcome the lonely memories.

He finished by holding Lacy tight and singing in her ear. 'At last! It's you and I in heaven...And you are mine at last.'" When she began crying, he kissed her tears away....one drop at a time...just as she had done to him in Hawaii.

"Oh," Luke said, "when we get to the military baggage claims area, I have something special for you. I worked on it for a lifetime. Remember the famous duffle bag you ran into at O'Hare Airport?"

He had a wide grin. If he could have, he'd have whooped in excitement.

Lacy looked up with her face beaming and her heart racing. *After all these years, could it be?*

No matter how hard he tried, Luke could not contain his grin.

They held hands as they walked inside the Army hanger. There was Luke's duffle bag stacked up against the wall. He forgot about his leg, pulled Lacy over with him and reached down to grab his duffle bag.

Lacy exclaimed, "No, Luke!" He looked over at her.

"Don't you remember that I kicked your butt in soccer before we fell in love?" Lacy said. "I'm just as strong as you. It's about time we did everything together. You take one strap and I'll take the other. We lug it out to the car together."

Luke looked at her as if she was a stranger.

Lacy picked up her half of the duffle bag. "Come on, I can't wait to see your something special."

Luke gave her an amused smile. "I was in the military too long."

Lacy reached over and smacked him on the butt. "What am I going to do with you?"

"I have some ideas."

They got to the car and both hauled the duffle bag over and up and onto the rear seat.

When he got Lacy settled in the front seat, she reached up to pull him down and kiss him, lipstick everywhere. "Wait!" he said and gently closed her door, looked down into the rear view mirror, and wiped the kisses off.

Lacy laughed as Luke went to the rear door, leaned down, opened his duffle bag and pulled out a beautifully wrapped gift, thin, and light. The wrapping paper was thick and covered with a maze of small roses. He stepped over to the driver's side, sat down in the driver's seat, and closed the door, shivering in the cold.

He took a deep breath, clouding up the windshield, and handed the gift to Lacy. She unwrapped it, fingers trembling and heart racing, not wanting her imagination to get the best of her.

She tore off the last of the wrapping, turned the light, thin gift over and looked at it for a long time. Then she kissed the photo, holding it tightly against her heart. Luke wondered if she already knew. Finally, Lacy held the gift up in front of them with her right hand. The ceiling light shone down; the photo and the prayer were framed underneath a special pane of glass. When Lacy again saw the photo of Luke's hand holding the most luscious cluster of grapes she had ever seen, she moved closer to him, her lips parted, her pupils soft and shining large.

She leaned forward a little bit and with her left hand she skimmed her fingertips along his jaw line. "It's so beautiful, it's so beautiful," she kept saying. "Read it to me, Luke, read it to me."

Lacy sat close and held onto him as if she'd never let him go. And he read it to her, slowly, gently, and lovingly.

> *Lord, I know You love me,*
> *Because you send us*
> *The most magnificent promise:*
> *"Blessed are all who fear the Lord,*
> *Who walk in his ways.*
> *You will eat the fruit of your labor.*
> *Blessings and prosperity will be yours.*
> *Your wife will be like a fruitful vine within your*
>   *home;*
> *Your children like olive shoots around the table."*

When he finished, Lacy was crying as she asked Luke, "Is this a marriage proposal?"

"No, honey, it's a promise," he said. "Stand by. I'm going to come around to your door and ask you to step out."

Before she knew it he had gone around to her side and opened the door.

Lacy got out and stood beside the car, her heart beating fast.

Luke reached into his coat pocket, pulled out a little box, and held it up to Lacy. And then he gingerly got down on his knees. "I can't do one knee, honey. But I am happy I can kneel at all."

She broke into tears, feeling both the pain of his injury, and the joy of what was coming next. *At last, indeed!* She almost reached down to hug him and pull him up.

He couldn't resist. "I bow to no man, Lacy, but I bow to you." There were tears in his eyes too.

When he spread apart the velvet setting, with a sharp intake of breath, Lacy saw two sparkling diamonds inlaid within a classic setting of two hands folded around each other. She was overwhelmed.

"I've seen that design in Paris," she said. "I never thought I'd see it on my finger."

He picked up the ring by its double gold bands and held its diamonds up to her. "This is my marriage proposal," Luke said. "I love you, Lacy, and I always have. Will you marry me?"

"Yes! Yes! Yes!" Lacy pulled Luke up and completely enveloped him. Five minutes later when she stopped kissing him, she said, "When can we get married? Where can we get married, Luke? We waited long enough!"

"The third time is the charm!" Luke said excitedly. "I have reservations for an engagement party next weekend! We can plan our wedding out there."

She couldn't help gasping. "Hawaii?"

His voice went up another decibel. "Yes!"

She danced around him. "Oh, Luke, I am so happy!"

* * * * * * * * * * * * *

63

AFTERWORD

Upon his return home to the Duck Valley Indian Reservation, Chance Chisholm had been anxious to tell Tiara the good news about his best friend Luke. Chance sat her down in front of their fireplace. "What a change! Luke and Lacy went from estrangement and separation in Hawaii to reconciliation on 'The River of No Return,' of all places! When he gets back from Vietnam, they will finally go public, I just know it! I was so happy to see them welded together at the reunion and on the river of no return. Finally he will pop the question."

Tiara settled down onto their favorite rug. "So Lacy De'Luca will become Lacy LaCrosse? Hmmm. Luke LaCrosse and Lacy LaCrosse. The sounds all go together, like poetry.

"But before that happens, tell me how Luke, Dakota, and you all got together?"

Tiara Nu'u'uli was taught to celebrate her Polynesian life in the South Pacific. She had little exposure to men in the military. Her family had always warned her to stay away from them. Like Luke, Chance didn't stay in the Air Force. He and Tiara had fallen in love in Samoa, gone to New Zealand for teacher training, and returned to Samoa to teach. It wasn't long before Chance and Tiara had teaching positions in Duck Valley because they had the skills of working with children of different cultures, languages, and races. Chance knew that soon Luke would live close by.

Chance said, "I first shared a double bunk with Luke in basic training," Chance said. "From there on we were best friends and sidekicks all through our enlistment. We had a ton of adventures in Sixth Weather Squadron. They used to call us weather warriors, or fellow airman, but nothing says it like sidekick. Sidekick is more than friendship under adversity. Proverbs 27:17 says it best, "As iron sharpens iron, so one person sharpens another.""

Chance said, "Here's what I'm hoping. When Luke completes his deployment in Vietnam, he already has an advance notice of a choice assignment at the Nevada Test Site. We both were stationed there. He will be able to move up the ranks and become a ranking officer at NTS and another secret base outside Las Vegas. And they have secret test flights out of Area 51 for our newest fighters or reconnaissance aircraft. Luke and I saw the test flights of the SR-71 prototype when we were there. I love that plane. Their motto: 'Life begins at 80,000 feet.' Luke will be on tap for something like that as well."

"What will Lacy do?"

Chance replied, "Because of her success in the Chicago area, Lacy has an invitation for a top management position in the Upward Bound program for Native Americans in Las Vegas, Nevada, and surrounding counties. When the right time comes, she can act on it, accept it or not."

Tiara said, "What about Dakota?"

Chance grinned. "Dakota Duval and I were fast friends before we joined the Air Force. I came from a farm outside Crystal Lake, over thirty miles north of Glenview where Luke grew up. And Dakota came from the South Side of Chicago, over sixty miles away from me. See the map? Isn't that remarkable?"

"Wait," Tiara said. "Tell me how you came from Crystal Lake? In Illinois? Your last name is Chisholm and your family grew corn in Oklahoma."

Chance paused. "You know my family has Carolina Cherokee heritage. We had names I couldn't even spell. We got dragged into

Oklahoma on the Trail of Tears. A hundred years later our farms in Muskogee County were top corn producers. Thanks especially to the Cherokee and Choctaw nations from hundreds of years ago; corn is the great Native American gift to American settlers."

"I remember that," Tiara said. "But Chisholm?"

Chance said. "Okay, corn and cattle go together, prosper together. You can't have one without the other. So we intermarried with a few Chisholms from next door, who blazed trails and raised cattle. Then we had terrible drought in the 1930's and again in the 1950's. After a big fight, my grandfather and his brother left the clan in Oklahoma and moved to Illinois. The soil is rich, the rains never stopped, and they prospered. I love it up there. But nobody knows we are Cherokee."

Tiara lifted her head. "Didn't you tell me that Dakota thought he was black his whole life and then found he had Shoshone blood, maybe from right here in Duck Valley?"

"Yes, Chance said. "Maybe that's why we were like brothers and didn't know it."

"So tell me how you met?"

"You'll hear more about it in the second book. Dakota and I met at Comiskey Park, home of the Chicago White Sox. Both my uncle and his father were total White Sox fans in a city and suburbs where everybody loved the Chicago Cubs."

Tiara said, "The Cubs and the White Sox? In Samoa and Rarotonga, even in Tahiti, we gave our teams warrior names. How can people cheer for bear cubs? Or white sox?"

Chance laughed out loud. "That's what everybody says! But even we who grew up far away on a farm loved those teams. They were like family, not a team and not a name. Hey, the Chicago Bears! That's a great team and a great name."

He went on. "The Cubs were located at Wrigley Field in the northern suburbs. It was safe; everybody went there. They didn't care if the Cubs never won. But the South Side of Chicago! You had to be brave to go there. You would be like a white pimple on a black man's face there at Comiskey Park. And nobody likes pimples!"

They both laughed. And Chance said, "But guess what? Once at a night game, my Uncle Arnie and I sat right in front of Dakota and his dad. We didn't know each other, didn't talk to each other. Dakota and his dad were not given to speaking with whites from God-knows-where. My uncle and I were in middle rows behind and to the right of first base, a dangerous place for foul balls.

"I always took a baseball glove, hoping to catch a major league baseball. That night in the third inning a foul ball came screaming right at me. I jumped up and caught it. The man behind me said, 'You just saved me from a trip to the hospital! That was coming right at my face!'

"And from then on we sat together, the Chisholms and the Duvals. Dakota and I would call to find a game where we could meet. We loved it. Boys love baseball games and hotdogs, cotton candy, and popcorn. The adults love the cold beer and the Wisconsin brats."

Tiara spoke up. "You made me thirsty. Will you get us a beer?"

Chance jumped up, "I am getting us a couple cold beers right now. You want any munchies?"

"Popcorn. I never had popcorn growing up. I never knew why."

"I grew up with corn fields all around me," Chance said from the kitchen. "Samoa does not grow corn."

He returned with his hands full. "Here's a beer for you in your favorite glass and a bowl of fresh popcorn for us. I know you don't like drinking out of a bottle, and you never did. But I'm used to it. They didn't have glasses or mugs for beer out on the islands."

"Honey, I never did like drinking beer, period, until I married you. Bad guys coming into port got off their navy ship in Pongo-Pongo harbor or Apia harbor, and always drank beer out of bottles— one bottle after another. Who are the uncivilized? The poor native Polynesians? I think not."

He sat down. "Okay, where was I? Oh yeah, right along with Luke and Dakota, I served in Tornado Alley, Samoa, Christmas Island, Johnston Island, Hawaii, and points west. You know about Luke and Lacy now."

"Chance, tell me about Dakota."

"Down in Samoa, you knew all about this. Dakota wanted to marry Moana, your dear friend, and follow his dream of settling down as a teacher in Tutuila. He knew from his childhood in Chicago that education was important. He saw so many friends drop out and give up. He wanted to inspire little children to learn in their own unique ways. Moana wanted Dakota to come home to her every evening. She was eager to help him grade papers and prepare lessons for the following day. Little children were drawn to them both. They even thought of adopting a few children right away rather than waiting for one of their own. In Samoa adoption requires no paperwork."

Chance's voice rose. "But that football player-turned-missionary, Tom, tricked us all. He brought the force of religion on Moana and coerced her into marrying him. Her family and her whole church wanted this. It seemed so perfect. So Tom and Moana got married, right out from under Dakota. We were all hurting and alone with him at the end. Moana left him high and dry at Three Brothers Shoals on Tutuila. What else could possibly go wrong?"

He jumped to his feet. "But, I have good news! We will catch up with him on his new adventure in Nevada. Dakota was sent to the Nevada Test Site when he got back to Hawaii. Sure, he grieved over Moana until he met an Indian named Quanah Autumn. I can only tell you about some of the adventures they had! She came from a family of mustangers. She had Paiute, Shoshone, and Hispanic blood in her family. She was tough, drove pickup trucks and broke mustangs. She and Dakota ran from radioactive clouds, they saved mustangs, and they chased cowboy pirates. They rode the trails searching for Quanah's father and his favorite mustang, Nightwind. And much more."

He lifted up his bottle to toast Dakota and in his enthusiasm mistakenly drained it all. He winced, caught his breath, and said, "Let's not get ahead of ourselves, honey. That whole second story is coming next."

"What about us, Chance?" Tiara sat up and clinked her full glass against Chance's empty beer bottle. "When will you tell the story about us?"

Chance stood up again. "Well, we definitely had our challenges. And there will be lots to talk about."

He paused a minute. "Oh, that's our third story. It comes right after Dakota's."

Tiara was disappointed. "Why can't we be the second story?"

Chance said, "We haven't had time to look inside ourselves, to arrange our experiences into a story. It all happened so fast. I've been trying to keep up with my sidekicks, Luke, and Dakota. But, honey, we're saving the best for last."

Tiara brightened up. "Okay. And I can help you with our story."

Chance nodded, took a deep breath, and summarized. "So we follow three stories, not counting the girls. We have three families."

He raised his eyebrows and cocked his head with a deprecatory smile, "We have 'three young lions who lacked and suffered hunger.'" We have three highly trained servicemen or soldiers. We have three sidekicks who worked everywhere on dangerous projects together. We have three wild lifetime adventurers, and three wild lifetime romancers."

He wriggled his eyebrows like his dad's favorite comedian, Groucho Marx. "Maybe we have four romances. Or maybe five."

He felt sticky beer splash all over him. "Now what did you go and do that for?"

"I'm sorry I spilled my beer on you," Tiara said. "Three romances are enough."

* * * * * * * * * * * * *

Appendices

FAMILIAR SIXTH WEATHER SQUADRON (MOBILE) MEMBERS INCLUDING THOSE WHO SERVED @ 1960—1964

John Addesa 56-60, Tony Arno 60-68, John Baker, Albert Bardusch, Col Claude Barrow, Thomas Beauchamp, Larry Beaver 61-62, James Benedict 60-65, Wilbur Biggs 70-73, Carl Bishop 61-68, Roger Black 62-76, Doc Blanchard, Robert (Bongo) Bongiovanni, Pete Brightwell 59-63, Kenneth Brown 66-77, Buck Bucklin, Robert Chapman, Jack Cheatham 62-65, Col Norman Clark, Herbert Casey, Brian Connolly 62-64, Carle (Hammer) Clark, Richard Dakin, Thomas Davis, Cesar Contreras, Shirley Eldringhof 62-70, Jim Eldringhof, David England, William Callicutt, Ernie Fisher, Roy Frieburger 58-64, Robert Epps 61-69, Don Fry, Don Garbutt, Stephen Gladish 60-63, John (Tom) Grace, Gerry Guay, David Griffith 62-64, Pat Grona 58-63, Donald Hall, Paul Harding, Jay Hartz, Ed Herman 60-63, Charles Hewitt, Gene Hayes, Frank Hollingsworth, Jerry Hunt, Clifford Jones 51-58, 60-63, Richard Kamp 62-70, Joseph Kerwin, Bill King, Harry Kohler, Tony Landa, John Lassiter, Bud Leinbach, Ted Lungwitz, Alfred Mayo, Gordon McCann, Barbara McCann, Roy McKissak, Tadd Kowalzyk 62-67, Clarence (Chuck) Miller, CMSgt Chuck Morris, Col Elwin Mosely, Donald Nissan, Marty Piel, Jake Powell, Neil Prete, Col Bernard Pusin, Elmo Reddick, Dusty Rhodes, Robert Ridenour, Art Rowland, Ed Skowron, John Schumacher, John Taiclet, John Tasertano, Ted

Tooley, David Weiner, Jerry Williams, James (Tex) Winder, Bill King, Fred LaPierre, Johnnie Mac Larson, Ronald Manning 60-65, 67-68, John Lassiter, Charles Lee, Harold Maille, Steve Heinrichs, Jerry Hunt, William Leinbach, Chuck Morris, Thomas Rivers, Ralph Robb, Michael Seaver, Joseph Stewart, Delford Tooley, Melvin Turnbow 60-63, Edward Vanderwall, Dave Weiner, Jack Wilson, Tex Winder, Ernie Workman, Jerry Yeager, Jim Young, Ken Zinke; SMSgt John Schumacher, Phil Downey, Jim Fraser, Hal Henderson, Tony Landa, Bill Stricker, Joe Lake, Doug Wilson, SMSgt Thompson, SMSgt Ken Benson. Leonard Allen, Ken Austin, Kenneth Barker, Chuck Betzold, Robert Bodner, Ed Brown, Stanley Campbell, David Carmichael, Ben Lee Carr, Herbert Casey, Brinan Connolly, Fred Cummings, Hazel Dawson, Robert Demchak, Tom Dorgan, Steve Doty, Karl Doughty, David Douglas, Phillip Downey, Ken Dropco, Robert Duvall, Mike Fazio, Larry Flohaug, Douglass Freese, Donald Gerth, John Grant, Don Hassenbein, Mike Heatherton, Douglas Hesbol, Caryl Hll, Thomas Jensen, Bill Kneller, Harold Maille, Jr., Keith Marchese, Richard Jensen, Donald Jones, Lorrain Jones, Nancy Jones, Wesley Keiffer, Thomas Kinney, Paul Laman, Charles Lee, Smokey Lentz, Michael Longo, Len Matthews, Jim McGregor, David Morell, Robert Orshoski, James O'Sullivan, Carl Phipps, AnielloPrete, Daniel Rea, Elmo Riddick, Angela Reid, Tom Rivers, Candi Rivers, Ken Robinson, Joe Scannell, Miguel Sena, Ed Skowron, Ruth Tasetano, Lathan Vamado, Irv Watson, John Webb, Lee Webb, Mike Whiteman, Jan Whiteman, Edwin Whitley, Adele Williams.

Times of service were not available for all personnel.

Helicopter Patches

Assault Helicopters First Air Cavalry Division Vietnam